# BEFORE WE COLLIDE

Also by Kate Dylan

*Mindwalker*
*Mindbreaker*

*Until We Shatter*

# BEFORE
# WE
# COLLIDE

## KATE DYLAN

HODDERSCAPE

First published in Great Britain in 2025 by Hodderscape
An imprint of Hodder & Stoughton Limited
An Hachette UK company

The authorised representative in the EEA is Hachette Ireland,
8 Castlecourt Centre, Dublin 15, D15 XTP3, Ireland (email: info@hbgi.ie)

1

A CIP catalogue record for this title is available from the British Library

Hardback ISBN 978 1 399 72878 2
Trade Paperback ISBN 978 1 399 72879 9
ebook ISBN 978 1 399 72880 5

Typeset in Baskerville MT Std by Manipal Technologies Limited

Printed and bound in Great Britain by Clays Ltd, Elcograf S.p.A.

Hodder & Stoughton policy is to use papers that are natural, renewable
and recyclable products and made from wood grown in sustainable forests.
The logging and manufacturing processes are expected to conform
to the environmental regulations of the country of origin.

Hodder & Stoughton Limited
Carmelite House
50 Victoria Embankment
London EC4Y 0DZ

www.hodderscape.co.uk

*This one is for both my family family and my writing family.*
*I couldn't do this without you.*

# THE SEVEN SHADES OF MAGIC

## Red
to control——compulsion spells and glamours

## Orange
to strengthen——spells that fortify, affect, weaken, build, and break

## Yellow
to alter——the ability to change composition, state, or meaning

## Green
to heal——medicinal spells and spells that affect the body

## Blue
to hasten——the acceleration of processes to great speeds

## Indigo
to foresee——the ability to predict the future

## Violet
to know——learning spells and spells that impart knowledge

# EZZO

I've drunk too much. Way—*way*—too much, and I'm not in a place where it's safe to do that. I'm not even sure where I am, to be honest; I was already half a bottle in when I got here. To this strange new bar, in a strange new city, full of strange new customs but all the same hate and lies. All the same nightmares. Because no matter how far I go—or how much I drink—I can't escape the sound of her scream and the hell of her shatter. The taste of my grief.

So, I order another. And another. And another after that, relishing the burn of the whiskey. The oblivion. The relief. A liquid escape from reality that only ends once the barkeep grows tired of my misery and insists that I leave.

*Fine. Then I'll leave.* I stumble out of his musty, overpriced tavern, the harsh tendrils of morning throwing the unfamiliar streets into sharp relief. Magnolia brick instead of the pallid gray I'm used to; terracotta roofs instead of sun-kissed slate; paved stone roads instead of uneven cobbles.

Sarotuza.

The farthest city away from the one I left behind.

From the memories I abandoned there.

The buried shards of emerald glass.

I don't know why I thought it would feel different to any of the other cities I've travelled through this past year—if the drink can't numb the pain, what was a change of scenery going to do?—and anyone who says that time is the answer clearly doesn't understand the question.

*Why did she have to die?*

Or better yet, *why couldn't it have been me?*

*It should have been me.* The thought is bitter, and sour, and vile. I was the one the spell was aimed at, after all. The spare wheel who had already fulfilled his purpose. But death doesn't take those who deserve it the most. If it did, it would have come for them, not her. The ones responsible.

*How you doing, Ez?* The scry around my neck warms with a question of its own, as though sensing my despair. Novi always did have a knack for knowing when I'm at my lowest.

*Alive.* I clasp the crystal in my hand and reply with the same one-word missive I send her every day. Never more, never less. And the only reason I still respond at all is because as a Hue, I know what it's like to worry about those you love. To lose sleep wondering whether they were caught by a Council tracker, killed by a Church enforcer, or shattered by the Gray.

There are oh-so-many ways to die when your very existence is illegal.

*And yet, not a single one has deigned to come and claim me.*

I stagger through the streets towards the inn where I'm staying, garnering dirty looks from the bleary-eyed merchants making ready to start their day. They shake their heads and mutter disapprovingly at my disheveled state—a judgement I've grown all too familiar with since I stopped counting my drinks. Just as I've grown all too familiar with the sinking feeling that comes with having lost my key. Again. A problem since the door to the inn is kept locked until the sixth bell and I'm not carrying my picks.

I have no way of getting inside.

Or at least, no normal way.

But if there's one upside to being a Hue, it's the ability to shed my physicality and walk through walls. Not in the real world, of course—here, I'm as physical as the ground beneath my feet; I have to marshal my energy and phase into the Gray.

Even in my drunken state, the magic comes as easily as breathing. In the space between blinks, color turns to ash and light turns to charcoal, a rainbow of grays that undulates like water bleeding through black ink, draping the streets in a smokey veil. Once I'm safely ensconced in the shadow realm, I become invisible to the typics. Incorporeal. Able to wisp straight through the inn door, and up the stairs, and into my room, where I then phase back in perfect time to collapse on the bed instead of falling right through it.

Maybe if I still cared about my life, I wouldn't have done my phasing in plain sight, where anyone could see me.

Maybe if I hadn't drunk so much, I'd have thought to check the coast for Shades before succumbing to the threat of dreams.

But I don't.

And I did.

And Eve is still gone, and she's dead, and I want to be.

So I don't bother running when the Council's trackers burst through my door and rouse the entire inn. I don't bother fighting when they haul me up from the mattress or protesting my innocence when they hurl the term half breed at me in between jeers.

I just let them cart me off to my execution.

And, if I'm being honest, my capture comes as a relief.

# CHAPTER 1

# RAYA

Certain futures can be trusted no matter how incompetent the seer. The sun will always come up in the morning, the shadows will always welcome a Shade home; everything else is up for . . . interpretation. The key word there being *interpretation*—given that the future doesn't much like to be known. Glimpsed, yes. Altered, maybe. But never *known* with an infallible degree of certainty. Not even to an Indigo Shade. And especially not to me.

Raya Wryvern. The seer who can never get the answer right.

*Never mind the answer—I can't even ask the right questions.*

Which is how I find myself here, in a storage cupboard at the forgotten end of the Academy, covered in sweat, and cobwebs, and a fine sheen of rage.

Akari did it again.

She tricked me.

Veiled her intentions so that I'd interpret her future wrong.

*Damn it. Damn it. Damn it.* I bang a fist against the shelves, filling the air with an angry wafting of dust. The future that Professor Lyons asked me to predict wasn't even that complicated—all I had to do was discern where in the castle Akari would hide her flag. And while his instructions to her were to try and confuse my vision, this close to guild selections, I'm supposed to know how to account for those lies. I shouldn't still be failing the most basic of tasks—not to mention failing to live up to my potential.

Of all the Indigo Shades at the Academy, my power is the strongest; I proved that much years ago.

I see more futures than anyone else.

With more clarity than anyone else.

Across more questions than anyone else.

Good stock, they call it. The product of a long and esteemed line of Indigos who upheld the sanctity of their magic by refusing to marry across blood color, with none that ever dallied with a different color of Shade, or—Gods forbid—stooped low enough to bed a typic.

But power and pedigree can only take you so far when they're not supported by natural instinct or skill, and while the fates may be inclined to answer my questions, there's nothing they hate more than being asked the same question twice. That's why it's imperative to ask the *right* questions. In the right order. At the right time.

It's the difference between asking: can *I* win this fight, and: can *we* win this fight. A subtle change in phrasing that might lead to two completely disparate visions, so you have to be sure before you reach for the magic and whisper the words in your mind. Commit to a direction.

Which is where I struggle.

I've simply never been that good at choosing my words in a way the future considers *right*. A problem since getting it wrong means getting the wrong vision, chasing after a future that's unlikely to come to pass.

*Ending up in a fucking store cupboard.*

And to think, the Council is convinced that Green Shades have it hardest, when in reality, healing must be a cakewalk compared to this. What I'd give for a guaranteed, replicable result that works one hundred percent of the time. To not have to constantly guess at how best to cajole the future. Not offend it into growing teeth.

I make my way back to class slowly, grudgingly, steeling myself for the rebuke that is sure to come. Around me, the Gray ripples like an ocean of obsidian night, the shadows curling through the air like vapor, dulling the world of its tint. A monochromatic rainbow, Akari calls it, and we're the lone specks of color penetrating the haze. Safe from the typics in this realm they cannot reach.

Safe from the dangerous elements in our own ranks, too, since it's impossible to phase in or out of this building—the Academy is unique in that regard. Where the rest of the Gray exists as a perfect overlay of the physical realm, the Academy has no direct counterpart to speak of. We are a pocket among the shadows. A castle made entirely of magic that exists in the absence of place, accessible only by portal, though when it's plotted on a map, it sits at the very heart of Sarotuza. The city of sun, stone, and sea. Famed for its beauty—and its distinctive palette of reds, golds, and teals. A vista I used to miss when I first came to live in the shadows, though it's amazing how fast you adjust to living in a world stripped of color. Better that than living in a world steeped in iron and fear, where the Church is doing its twisted utmost to outlaw your kind. Cleanse the continent of magic.

"So where did Raya go wrong?" By the time I make my way back to the seeing tower, Professor Lyons has already predicted my failure, the disappointed scowl of his deep-set features setting a flame to my cheeks.

"She wasn't specific enough in her question," Akari is quick to say. Outside the classroom, she's on my side. Always. Inside it, she's a pit viper biting at my heels. Just as I need her to be. Because if she doesn't do it, then someone else will. And because she knows as well as I do that if I don't prove I can direct my visions—definitively, without constantly seeing the wrong thing—then come graduation, I'll be hauled in front of the Council to have my magic bound. That's the price of not learning to control my power when they've given me chance, after chance, after chance to hone my skills. Too many chances, some would say, on account of who my parents are. If not for the position they hold as co-heads of the seers' guild, the decision to bind my color would have been made six months ago, when I failed to pass my initial trials. Instead, I was allowed to continue on to guild training.

*The future demands a relationship as well as aptitude,* my mother had said. *A Shade with her degree of power deserves more time to establish that rapport with the fates.*

So they gave me more time.

Which makes it all the worse when I fumble my assignments in such an obvious way.

"That's right, she wasn't specific enough in her question," Professor Lyons repeats. "What did you ask, Raya?" He turns to appraise me, the judgement in his expression pinching his broad face sharp.

"To see which door Akari opened before dropping the flag," I mumble, staring at my feet instead of the sea of eyes scrutinizing my mistake. Not just other Indigos, but Shades from the other six specializations, as well. In the year leading up to guild selections, we're all taught together, so that we can learn to better understand each other's gifts, facilitate the other shades of magic and help minimize their weaknesses. So instead of keeping my embarrassingly flawed logic to myself, I have to share it with an entire rainbow of classmates, steep in their judgement and hear them mutter insults under their breath. *Fate-touched* has become a particular favorite, an Indigo who's lost the ability to talk to the fates.

"The idea was that she could think of a hundred different rooms in which to place the flag, but she'd have had to physically open the door to the one she left it in." I try to ignore their sniggers, to ignore the fact that the whole Academy believes that I'm destined for nothing but disgrace.

A bound Shade is a pariah.

As useless as a typic but with the added stain of shame—the kind that would irrevocably tarnish the Wryvern legacy. My parents are barely coping with the humiliation of an inept daughter; a powerless one would send their last nerve up in flames. If the Council casts me out, they'll quickly follow suit and disown me. Hells, they wouldn't even need persuasion.

"And what should Raya have asked?" Professor Lyons poses the question to the other Indigos in the class.

"Which door Akari closed once she *relinquished possession* of the flag." The answer comes from Anders brown-noser Prince, a self-righteous annoyance of a Shade who has none of my raw power, but an insufferable amount of skill.

"Very good, Mister Prince." Professor Lyons rewards his star student with a nod. "And why is that the correct framing?"

"Because *dropped the flag* isn't specific enough; it allows for the possibility that the flag was picked up again as a means of muddying the future. Whereas *relinquished possession* implies a finality of intent. Less likely to be misinterpreted." It seems so obvious once Anders explains his reasoning. Then again, that's always been my problem: I'm no good at thinking around the mud, particularly when I'm casting on the spot or under pressure.

"That's right," Professor Lyons says, turning to address us all. "Remember, the best way to see the future isn't to look forward, but to work back, account for as many eventualities as possible so that your questions elicit the path least likely to change. That's why you must choose them with care." The afternoon bell rings loud with his assertion, marking the end of the day's classes.

"You need to stop rushing, Ray," Akari says as we speed towards the dorms. When we're in the Gray, we don't have to walk, we can shimmer, shed our physicality and wisp through both shadow and wall. Within reason, of course; we're not allowed to wisp into rooms uninvited or circumvent a closed door, not in the Academy and certainly not when we're out in the wider world. No shimmering into places we're not supposed to be; that's the Council's official stance on exploiting our ability to transcend the bounds of the flesh, their way of keeping the typics from losing their minds entirely, declaring us too big of a threat.

"Did you hear what I said?" Akari bristles at my lack of reply. "You're so busy trying to prove that you can read the future as fast as that twit Anders, you're not thinking through your questions properly."

"I'm not going to have time to *think through my questions* during trials," I remind her. That was the exact reason I failed to pass the last round. By taking too long, being too indecisive, not trusting myself to simply know how to construct the right questions to ask.

"Well, not thinking them through isn't doing you much good, so maybe you could try slowing down?" she says, raising a perfectly arched brow. Akari has always been what you'd call striking, even before she grew into her confidence and her willowy height. Her eyes are long and angular, her skin a pale ochre in tone, and her hair black, bobbed, and sharply cut, a perfect complement to the razor-edge of her cheekbones and the way her lips purse when she's mad. Especially at me.

"Can we please stop pretending that it'll make a difference?" I snap, too keyed up to keep my frustration from biting. It's one thing for me to cling to a dying hope—this is my life we're talking about, my magic that's going to end up bound—but quite another for Akari to indulge that delusion. Six months ago, maybe; I still needed her optimism back then, her help training. Whereas now, it's starting to verge on condescending. We both know that I'm running out of time to make good on my pedigree. Perhaps I should just quit dreaming already and make peace with that fact.

"I'm not *pretending* anything." Akari's voice hardens in pitch. "Trust me, if I thought you had no chance of making it, I'd have told you that to your face—if only so that you'd quit whining." She softens the jibe with a wink and a smile. "Seriously, Ray, this story only ends with you losing your magic if you let it. It's not about being the best or the strongest, you just have to do enough to skirt by," she says, unlocking the door to our room. "So, spend this last month proving you know how to direct a few basic questions and the seers' guild won't be able to keep you out. Then you can take a job somewhere far, far away from them. Far away from your parents, too, since they're hardly helping with your state of mind."

On that, at least, Akari's right. Once I'm in the guild, I won't have to spend my life in a seeing tower like my parents, seeking complex futures for the Council to consider and discount. I could travel the world as a ship's weathervane, become a gambler's aide or a gambling hall's safekeeper, advise banking houses on how to best preserve their coin and their wealth. Hells, I could simply sell glimpses of the future to anyone who can pay. There are plenty of ways for an Indigo to make a living—just as long as they prove that they can accurately predict.

Which is the one thing I'm yet to master.

And while I appreciate Akari's belief in my ability to learn the theory, I've been grappling with my power for years now, and the result never changes, no matter how hard I try or how long I let my questions steep. I'm just not built for this brand of seeing. The only thing that's likely to help me is if there were an entirely new method of—

*Wait. No.* The thought that strikes me is like a bucket of water tossed into a cold wind. Not a new method of seeing, an old one. A practice long since abandoned on account of the damage it can wreak.

"What if it's not about directing my questions," I say, sounding the idea out. "What if I could show them the value of my power a different way?"

"Is there a different way to see the future?" Akari drops down to her bed, shrugging out of her academic robes. Black with the symbol for strength embroidered at the collar and sleeves, to signify her Orange color. "Other than asking questions, I mean?"

"There's a different way to ask questions," I say, shedding the itchiness of mine.

A way that requires more power but less skill.

"You had better not be talking about what I think you're talking about." Akari catches my meaning right away.

Open questions instead of the specific ones I've been taught to wield.

The one type of question that's forbidden.

"It could work," I say, ignoring the risk. "If I can figure out how to harness the resulting vision."

"You are not figuring out *anything*." In the space of a heartbeat, she's shimmered over to my side of the room, so that we're standing nose to chin and eye to anger, barely an inch of space left between us. "Getting expelled isn't going to solve your problems."

"I'll only get expelled if they find out," I tell her, refusing to flinch.

"Which they *will* when no other question you ask yields a vision," she hits me with the obvious objection, the reason every Indigo child is warned against asking an open question from the moment they're old enough to cast the spell.

Because an open question isn't just a *wrong* question—it's not merely too broad or too vague to pinpoint a path in a meaningful way—it's a question that encompasses so many possibilities that it serves to antagonize the fates. And while they will, generally, still deign to answer them, they may also decide that every subsequent question would now count as a repeat, and shut you out for weeks, or months, or years. There have even been cases of Indigo Shades losing their ability to cast for good, staying fate-touched forever.

"Come on, Kiri, the risk of that happening is so small." I hold my ground, stubborn. That is how our magic used to be practiced for centuries before the guild started refining it to a skill. It's said that in the old days, the most powerful seers didn't even need to worry about repeat questions, they could just trust that the future would always steer their path away from the cliffs. But since that kind of magic is impossible to sell and even harder to replicate, year by year, question by question, the guild set to streamlining the technique.

They turned a nebulous art into a teachable science.

I'm just no good at wielding my power in the way that they picked.

"Ray, swear to me you won't do this," Akari says, clamping her hands around my shoulders. "Swear it right now, or for your own good, I'm telling."

She'd never tell.

She'd yell at me until one of us dropped dead of exhaustion, but she'd never tell—we've known each other too long for that, practically lived in each other's pockets since the day the Academy assigned us a shared room when we were six. Back then, we didn't have so many classes in common, nor did we have any idea that I'd prove to be an awful seer while she grew into the most accomplished Orange in our year. We stuck together because my famous name coupled with her useful magic meant that neither of us ever got teased when we were kids. Then as we got older, the bond we'd forged began to transcend the politics of power and the vast mismatch in our gifts. And never, in all those years of breaking into the kitchens after dark, cheating on our homework, and covering for each other's trysts, has Akari ever threatened to tell. The only reason she's threatening to do that now is because she knows it'll knock some sense into me.

It *should* knock some sense into me.

When I first realized that I was in danger of losing my color, it *would* have.

But now we're a month shy of guild selections and I'm staring down the barrel of a problem I can't fix. An open question *could* save my future. If I can control such a difficult feat of magic, the guild would have no choice but to acknowledge my value. And if I can't, well . . . the worst that'll happen is I stop having visions altogether—which is exactly what will happen if I fail my trials again.

I can either endanger my magic now or let the Council bind it later.

At least this way, I stand a tiny chance of averting my fate.

I'd be jeopardizing my future on my own terms.

"I'm obviously not going to do it, Kiri." I squirm out of her grip, and since I don't yet know if I'd actually have the guts to follow through on this gambit, it doesn't feel like a lie. Though, in reality, the idea is less a blossoming bud than it is a weed that's taken root inside my head. Growing, spreading, propagating, sprouting a whole field of wants, and what-ifs, and a hunger to do away with sense. Because the truth is, using my power the way the Academy teaches has never worked for me, and if there's anyone strong enough to corral the fates without consequence, then it should be the daughter of the two most celebrated Indigos to ever grace the guild.

So maybe I won't be jeopardizing my future so much as forcing it back into its natural place. Maybe the only way to get the future I want is to stop playing by the rules and take a risk.

# CHAPTER 2

# RAYA

But it's not a risk I can take in front of Akari. When the future grants me a vision, I fall into a state of trance. My head snaps back, my eyes blink white, my lips shape a silent recounting of what I see. It's not a subtle flare of magic; it's a very obvious tell. And since I've never asked an open question before, I've no way of knowing if the effects will be as fleeting as a regular vision or if I'd be sucked into a prolonged bout of seeing. Asking it in front of Akari is a non-starter.

Which is a problem given that we're basically attached at the hip. We share the same dorm, the same schedule, the same friends, and now that I've raised the possibility of destroying my future, she'd get suspicious if I were to suddenly break with routine.

So, I bide my time.

I accompany her to the library for our afternoon study session, then down to the dining hall for a bowl of mediocre stew, followed by a game of cards in the common room and a couple of ginger ales. It's only come the ninth bell that I finally manage to steal away clean. Though instead of heading to the washrooms to scrub off the day, I snake a path towards the seeing tower, the one place in the Academy where no one will bat an eye if they notice me asking the future for help. Where, at this time of night, I'm all but guaranteed to be alone.

Or not, as the case might be.

"How was your bath, Ray?" Akari's voice greets me the second I push open the door. She cuts a menacing figure, leaned up against the window with her arms crossed and her features draped in shadow, silhouetted like a vengeful ghost among the swirling gray. She must have shimmered here the moment I made my excuses and left her side, beat me to the crime. That's the other problem with having a friend who knows you inside and out—they can always tell when you're up to something.

*And when they'll need reinforcements.* As I step into the room proper, I realize who else Akari's drafted in for this task.

"What is *she* doing here?" I scowl at her arrogant mistake of an ex. Slender, tall, with deep bronze skin and a cascade of dark curls that falls to her waist, Saleen is the kind of beautiful that turns heads, so I've always understood what drew Akari to her—just not what kept them together for three full years when that beauty is very much skin deep. Saleen is self-absorbed, self-aggrandizing, and selfish. But by far, the worst thing about her is that she thinks she knows better than everyone else, that she's somehow morally superior for finding fault with the Council at every turn. I've lost count of the number of times I had to pick up the pieces after she decided to start some need-less fight about a condemned Shade or some new law she didn't like, or get into a screaming match about Akari's ambitions to become a tracker when she graduates.

*You're better than that, Ari. You could be so much more than a mindless soldier.* Saleen's always been infuriatingly judgemental for someone whose parents have been trackers for over thirty years. Though the only thing that matters right now is that she's also a Red.

Control magic.

The ability to glamour and compel.

Bend others to her will.

"*She* is here to help save you from yourself," Akari says, dropping her voice low. Even if the two of them weren't fresh off the heels of a very public break-up, she'd still know better than to tell anyone what I'm planning, and Saleen doesn't need all the gory details to stop me casting an illicit spell. Unlike premonition, compulsion is far less specific, and Saleen is one of the Academy's most promising Reds. Or at least, she would be, if she weren't so intent on wasting her potential. You can add that to the list of things that annoy me about Saleen: she has all the skill and aptitude I'm missing but none of the drive or will.

"She is *not* compelling me," I hiss, though there'd be little I could do to stop her if she did. That's what makes Red magic so terrifying: there's no shielding yourself from it, you can only fight the effects once you're in their grip, and even then, it's damn near impossible. My only saving grace is that not even a vindictive viper like Saleen would go so far as to do it without permission. To a typic, sure—for enough coin, certain types of compulsion are freely available to purchase. But not to another Shade. Never to another Shade. If she does that, she won't just be expelled from the Academy, she'd be hauled in front of the Council she so reviles, forced to either bind her magic or turn rogue and live on the run. And there's no way she'd risk that just to do her ex-girlfriend a favor. Not even Saleen is that reckless.

"Then I'll take the three silvers I was promised and be on my way," she says, idly picking at her nails. "Whatever spat you two have going is your business."

*By my colors.* "You're paying her to do this?" I fix Akari my most dangerous look.

"No, I'm paying her to *forget* she did this. And if you aren't planning to do anything stupid, then why does it matter how I spend my coin?"

It matters because she doesn't have the coin to spend, so the last thing I want is for her to spend it on me. On my bad idea. Akari doesn't come from a wealthy family like I do; she lost her parents when she was young, wound up in one of the Council's care homes. Everything she has she makes by siphoning her magic into pre-made charms and selling them in the city, and that's not exactly a legal endeavor at our age, so money is always tight. But since I recognize the stubborn set of her shoulders and the way her eyes are blazing with an angry flame, I doubt there's anything I could say, in this moment, to change her mind. And while I know that she'd never force a compulsion spell on me, I also know that she won't be letting me out of her sight again without it, not now that she's confirmed that I do, in fact, mean to cast the open question. Which only leaves me with one option: let Saleen do her worst. That way, Akari won't realize just how desperate I am.

Desperate enough to remember that she's not the only one with a useful ex.

"Fine. Let's just get this over with," I grit through my teeth, steeling myself for the suffocating weight of the spell. This won't be the first time a Red messes with my mind; this past year, I've trained with enough of them to grow painfully familiar with the sensation. The helpless loss of control. But at the end of each class, those spells were promptly lifted, whereas this one will be built to last. To stifle my ability.

"You will not do . . . whatever stupid thing Akari doesn't want you to do." Saleen complies with a lazy flick of her wrist. Hardly the most elegant of phrasing, but compulsion feeds on brute force rather than clever wording, and she's always enjoyed inflicting her will on others, so the power drips effortlessly off her tongue. I don't just hear the magic in her command, I *feel* it, like a chain of iron coiling tight around my intent, smothering the impulse. Between one moment and the next, the very idea of an open question becomes as heavy as the ocean, an unyielding pressure that's pressing harder, and harder, and hard. Even just thinking around it in the abstract quickens my pulse as though I've run the castle from tower to jail.

"You sure that's going to hold?" Akari glowers at Saleen's lack of effort, as though she's suddenly remembered how irritating her ex's worst qualities can get.

"Have I ever cast a spell that didn't?" Saleen holds her hand out for Akari to grace with silver. "The compulsion should be good for about a week—after that, either find some more coin or tell your Indigo to find some sense," she says. Then before I can think up a suitably scathing reply, she shimmers out the door.

"I can't believe she charged you as much as a typic." I mutter a belated curse at her back.

"Oh please, you absolutely *can* believe it." Akari rolls her eyes, folding down to sit among the cushions lining the tower floor. "And you owe me three silvers, by the way, for keeping you out of trouble."

"I will give you three silvers—but you'll have to think of a different reason for why, because I am not paying for the pleasure of being compelled." I stretch out beside her. "And just for the record, I would have never gone through with it."

"Yes, you would have," Akari says.

Because yes, I would have.

Because we both know how fast the threat of binding has been tightening around my neck.

And because as much as Akari has been trying to hide her worry, I've noticed her smile slip a little bit further every time I fail. She claims our friendship would survive the loss of my magic, but that's a very big promise for any Shade to make, never mind a would-be tracker. Come graduation, she'll be joining the Council's elite band of soldiers, a guild filled with their strongest and brightest while I join the ranks of their worst.

Bound, disowned, dishonored and disgraced.

Unable to so much as phase into the Gray, let alone cast or wisp or shimmer.

And while Akari loves me enough to keep her promise, I love her enough to offer her a clean break. Not burden her with my presence.

"Which is supremely stupid since all you need to do is pass your trials," she continues, pulling her legs flush with her chest. "Forget what anyone else thinks, forget who your parents are, and just . . . focus on that."

*That's easy for you to say.* I don't lend voice to that less-than-fair remark. Akari's magic has always come so naturally to her, as steady as her nerve and as effortless as breathing. She's never had to work to wrestle it into submission, or watch her classmates flourish while she struggled to complete basic tests. The only futures I've ever been able to see with any certainty are too small to matter, like where I might find a book in the archives or a friend in the city, how long a bout of sickness will linger or what the cooks are making for lunch. Questions that only reveal an imminent, already decided path.

That won't be enough to get me through my trials.

For that, I'll have to accurately predict a more sprawling future—and Professor Lyons isn't likely to accept anything short of perfection from the biggest disappointment in class.

Neither will my parents.

They risked their reputation by forcing him to give me another chance.

They need me to make good on the skill they promised.

Which is why I can't just let Akari compel this urge away.

If my life is to take an unwanted turn, then the very least I can do is make an effort to steer the ship. And if I steer it right into the rocks, well . . . I'll drown knowing that decision belonged to me.

*

Come the midnight bell, I'm still intent on asking the open question, regardless of the risk.

So, I wait for Akari to fall asleep.

Then I wait to confirm that she's not faking.

Then I wait another hour just to be sure that this time, she won't intercede.

*You can yell at me tomorrow,* I mouth a silent apology before shimmering, ignoring the decree that prohibits us from wisping through closed doors when we please. What's one more broken rule when I'm about to break the cardinal? And besides, at the Academy—where the typics can't perform their displeasure or lend voice to their fear—we tend to skirt this particular rule more than most. Back before Killen and I broke up, I was wisping out of my room and into his three nights a week.

*You really shouldn't be bothering him with this.* The guilt is a snake coiling knots between my ribs. Before we got together, Killen and I had been good friends for years. He was the first boy I ever liked. The first boy I ever kissed. Along with several other firsts we gave each other, until I had to go and add first broken heart to the list. My choice, not his. And all of my attempts to keep things amicable have been firmly rebuffed since.

Killen asked me to stay away from him and I should respect that.

I should find a different Shade to help me lift the spell inflicted by Saleen.

I should and I should and I should.

But I don't.

My physicality melts away, the air turning to power as I harness the most primal part of my magic. When we shimmer, we move like light and disappear like the darkness, transcending the color in our blood, and our specializations, and our guilds. We become part of the Gray, one with the shadows in a way that's difficult to describe but easy to maintain. The one facet of my power that's never given me any trouble.

I make no sound as I speed through corridor and wall, leave no trace in the ether other than a fine rippling of wind, all but invisible unless some eagle-eyed Shade were to make a point of looking. Unlikely at this early hour. I learned that much back when I was sneaking off to meet Killen for a different kind of end. That's how I know the shortest route through the castle and that his roommate, a fellow Indigo called Damian, sleeps like the dead.

That's how I know exactly how to get Killen's help.

Despite the fact that he hates me.

His room is exactly the same as the last time I saw it: messy, but only on his side, the wall above his bed covered in dozens of the shadow-dulled pictures he likes to take—a strange sort of hobby for a Blue. Killen's magic affords him the power to accelerate, to make processes happen at a greater speed. Perhaps that's why he's always been more interested in freezing them in time, capturing the moment with a pre-spelled charm. Studies of life at the Academy, mostly, but he also used to love taking pictures of me, and those used to command pride of place above his headboard—until the day he left them in a flaming pile at my feet, which he then proceeded to accelerate to ash.

I can only hope that his anger has abated since then.

That six months will have blunted the hurt.

"Killen," I whisper, placing a firm hand over his mouth. "Killen, *wake up.*"

He jerks upright in the bed, his green eyes widening to perfect circles, the shock in them quickly giving way to confusion as he catches sight of me through the rippling dark.

"What the hells, Raya?" he hisses, batting me away. "What are you—? Did you *wisp* in here?" His sandy hair is mussed with sleep and sticking up at odd angles, his skin as flush and sun-kissed as I remember, warmth radiating from him like an indoor sun. Killen always did run hot.

"Would it have really been better if I'd knocked?" I ask, keeping my voice low.

"When people knock, I can ignore them." Killen raises the sheet between us like a shield, distracting from his lack of shirt. "And you don't get to wisp in here anymore, remember? You lost that right when you called things off."

*For absolutely no reason,* is what Killen is too disconcerted to add— though the vision that showed him cheating on me with another girl would suggest otherwise.

*Since when do you believe everything the future shows you?* he'd spat when I confronted him about his prophesied betrayal. *You're wrong about your visions all the time, Raya, why are you so desperate to believe this one? Gods, why would you even ask the future if I was going to cheat?*

Unlike me, Killen always knew how to ask the right questions.

Even when the answers would have only caused him more pain.

Because the truth is, I didn't ask the future if he would cheat, I asked it if the two of us had a future, and that's what it showed me in reply. Not the blurry kind of vision that's open to interpretation— this offering was crystal fucking clear, awash with both sights and feelings. I'd tasted no shame in it, no hesitation, no guilt. What Killen felt when he kissed the blond-haired girl with the roaming hands was love, and lust, and absolute need. Which would have been the worst part if not for the fact that all *I* felt was relief.

That's why I was so keen to believe it.

Because the thing about the future is that once you see it, you can change it, and if you change it, was it ever the future at all? Except for the fact it was. An inevitability, but at the same time, not an excuse to do nothing, and this vision was all the excuse I needed to call us quits.

"Look, I get that I'm the last person you want to see right now, but I need a spell." I skip us past the pleasantries and get straight to the point.

"You need a spell," he repeats, staring at me as though possessed. "In the middle of the night. From your ex."

"From a *Blue*," I correct. And as much as I'd rather not tell Killen this next part, he can't rid me of Saleen's compulsion if he doesn't know it exists. "I lost a bet and found myself at the wrong end of a Red." Though I do massage the truth just a little, since he doesn't need to know the *whys* that led to me being compelled.

"And you want the magic accelerated off?"

"I don't like not being in control of my own mind."

"Funny, because I don't like doing favors for my ex-girlfriend."

I had a feeling he might say that.

That's why I came prepared.

"It's not a favor if you're getting something in return," I say, tossing him a hefty purse.

"Pass." A flash of embarrassment colors his cheeks, the heat glowing stark against the smokey shadows. "Go pay some other Blue."

"Don't be an idiot. I know you need it." The words escape before I can stop them, twisting his hard-cut features into an angry mask, his embarrassment turning to offence.

"I don't *want* your money, Raya," he grits, stubborn as ever. Killen never did like talking about money, or more precisely, talking about his family's lack of money compared to the wealth of mine. It used to drive me nuts when we were still together, because coin—or a lack thereof—does not a good Shade make. Hells, Killen is a far better Shade than I've ever been. Smart, meticulous, thorough, a natural hand at channeling his gift. Which is why I didn't just go to some other Blue; I came to the one I could trust to do the job well.

"Fine, but I'm going to leave it here whether you help me or not, so you can either have it for no reason, or for a spell. Your choice," I say, knowing full well that he's less likely to accept a gift than a trade, choose charity over favor. And for a long moment, I see the need to argue in his eyes, to tell me not to bother leaving the purse because he'll only find a way to give it back. But the truth of the matter is, he does need it. He's needed it ever since his father left and his mother grew too depressed to leave the house. Killen can't afford to let this much coin slip through his fingers. No matter how much getting it from me might sting.

"Whatever." He finally relents with a sigh, sending a sharp ache shooting through my ribs. I don't like hurting Killen. I never liked hurting Killen—that's why I stayed with him so long in the first place.

Because I did love him.

I loved his kind heart, and his crooked smile, and his unending capacity for compassion and grace.

I just didn't love him the same way he loved me.

"Anything I should know about the spell I'm accelerating?" Killen asks, snapping me out of my regret.

"Just that it's a compulsion spell with about a week's worth of juice left." I steal a quick glance at Damian, to ensure that we're not being overheard.

"Relax, he'd sleep through an invasion."

"Right, yeah. I remember." It's a stupid—*stupid*—thing to say, and it hangs awkwardly between us, like the memory of a life unmade. I remember a lot of things about this room, and this bed, and all those nights we spent pretending Damian didn't exist. I remember running my fingers through Killen's hair and along his sun-kissed shoulders, stealing kisses between classes and getting sucked into conversations that stretched on for hours on end. I remember that it wasn't all bad, actually. That even the wrong guy feels right, sometimes. But most importantly, I remember that if it were up to Killen, we'd still be together—which is why I shouldn't make things worse by giving that admission air.

Unlike with Saleen, I don't have to brace myself for Killen's spell. A Blue's power is the most curious of magics in that you can only feel it working if it's used to accelerate a physical process within the body, otherwise, it's all about watching the desired result unveil. With just a flick of his hand, Killen could turn a light drizzle into a rainstorm, bake a loaf of bread the second it touches the oven, speed up the task of reading a book or filling a well. *He could even kill with it.* I shudder as his eyes close in concentration, as he places two fingers at each of my temples and orders the color in his blood to wake. If he felt like breaking the law, Killen could command my heart to beat right through my chest or force my blood to circulate so fast it wore a hole through my veins. He could quite literally age me to death between heartbeats.

"Okay—that's you sorted."

But of course, Killen doesn't do any of those things, and he pulls away before the static charge building between us grows thick enough to spark a blaze. "I designed the spell to affect any and all Red magic, so your mind should be fully yours again."

"Thanks." I silently probe for any hint of Saleen's compulsion, testing to ensure the validity of Killen's claim.

*An open question . . . I want to ask an open question . . .*

True to his word, the thought garners no resistance, my reckless endeavor freed of its magical cage.

*Now you just have to go through with it.* I do Killen the courtesy of not lingering where I'm not wanted, though once I'm safely out in the hallway, the choice he made possible fills my stomach with lead. Do I shimmer back to my room and forget about this terrible idea, or head towards the seeing tower and cast the biggest risk an Indigo can take?

*All you need to do is pass your trials. Just . . . focus on that.* Akari's voice sets a guilty flame to my bones. It was no small thing for her to turn to Saleen for help, no victimless effort. For while my split from Killen was welcome, her breakup with Saleen was a lesson in devastation, a pain made worse for the fact that Saleen wasted no time before very publicly making her way through a pretty parade of girls. If I do this now—if I risk my future—I'd be spitting in the face of the kindness Akari did me, at great personal cost.

*Go back to bed, Raya.* I slow my shimmer as I reach the corridor's decisive turn. *Forget about the open question and go back to bed.*

But I don't go back to bed.

And I can't forget about the open question because it feels like the only hope I have left, the only way to prove that I deserve to keep my magic.

So instead, I set my shoulders and shimmer off towards the seeing tower, making the decision with my gut instead of my head. Desperate times call for desperate measures and this one will either ruin my prospects or improve them no end. The only way to know for sure is to sink down to the cushions, reach for the color in my blood, and lace it around the four forbidden words that I should never ever think with magical intent.

*What is my future?*

# CHAPTER 3

# RAYA

When the future comes, it doesn't come with instructions. It comes with smells, and tastes, and flickers. With feelings, and certainties, and betrayals. Colors. It comes in sparkling glistens of sapphire, a rich, vibrant blue that's as endless as the sky and as deep as the ocean, as beautiful as the gem for which it was named. But then a bell vibrates through the vision and the blues fade to reveal a cascade of radiant gold, orange, and red, a bronze glow flickering at their edges.

Come morning, those colors will change everything.

*He* will change everything.

Through the swirling haze of magic, I glimpse the boy who will ruin my life.

Dark brown hair, coppery brown skin, warm brown eyes—dead with indifference. And though the future shows me nothing of what will draw me to him in such an absolute way, I know instantly, in my heart, that I will love him. That I will be recklessly and irrevocably in love with him.

But that he is pain.

That inside him, there is nothing but pain and grief and despair, so much so that it burns its way through my skin.

This boy is going to break me.

And it won't matter because all around us, all I see is death.

Our death. The death of our magics. The death of the Gray.

My death.

Which is impossible since an Indigo cannot see their own passing; that's the most fundamental truth of the future: it cannot predict its own end.

And yet, I see the moment the color in my veins withers. The moment his does, too, since we meet our deaths together. We all meet our deaths together, Shade, Hue, rogue, and Gray. Not with a whisper, but with a poisonous swell, on a scale so unimaginable it rips day from night and light from shadow. My mind from the vision. Leaving nothing behind but the sour stench of fear and the lingering touch of danger, a question the future poses to me instead.

*What in the name of all three Gods was that?*

# CHAPTER 4

# EZZO

Death doesn't come as fast as I'd hoped—or as fast as it should. When the trackers came for Mom, they didn't bother hauling her back to their prison; the punishment was as immediate as it was absolute. For she had committed the cardinal sin of falling in love with a typic—of giving birth to his child, to me—and for that, there could be no forgiveness. No mercy. Because four hundred years ago, a man told a lie to further his agenda and condemned countless generations of Hues to death. He was afraid of us. Afraid of how varied our gifts could become. How unpredictable. And so, he persuaded the world that we were a threat to the shadows and purged the continent of our kind.

Four hundred years later, that lie has become our judge, jury, and executioner, and no one cares to question the faulty logic because the truth doesn't benefit their side.

So, we die.

And we die.

And we die.

If not as children, then the first time we slip up as adults—though my lapse in judgement wasn't so much a slip as it was a fall, head first, into a death sentence. Such is the fate of a Hue who gets so drunk he phases in public and gets himself caught.

*But doesn't see it coming.* The thought is a grotesque joke among the pain, just another case of history repeating. As a Sapphire, my gift allows me to sense the presence of other Shades, trace the colored trails they leave in the shadows. It's not a direct translation of my mother's power—diluted magic doesn't manifest in entirely linear ways—but since she was an Indigo—a seer—I was born with a sideward twist on that ability. So if I had been paying attention, I would have noticed the Council's trackers converging on the inn, waiting for me to phase into the Gray so they'd have all the evidence they need to strike. Hells, they might well have been watching me for hours. Days even. Just as their predecessors had watched my parents in the run up to their attack. I wasn't paying enough attention that day, either. Maybe if I had been, I could've stopped the killing, done more than just flee through the cloying pools of blood.

A lifetime ago, I learned the true cost of not paying attention.

But lately, I've been ignoring that lesson, begging the future to drag me into the black.

To reunite me with Eve.

*The future sure is taking a while.* I hit the concrete with blinding force, my breath rasping out sharp and shallow. I think it's punishing me for eluding the Council's justice until now, living so embarrassingly long on borrowed time. Maybe that's why my captors seem more preoccupied with my age than my execution: twenty-one name days is simply too much life for a Hue, and they're desperate to learn *how* I've managed to evade their clutches. Or at least, that's been the main focus of their beatings. The reason there's a grimy floor pressed beneath my ribcage and a stern boot crushing my lower back. A man with bruised knuckles pummeling me bloody.

"Who was your scry bonded to?" he asks again, forcing me to my knees by the hair. And fuck, it hurts—the physical part of me is acutely aware of just how loud every inch of me is screaming. But after three full days of questioning, the pain feels oddly removed, as though they're just layering pain on pain on pain now, and even before they began their interrogation, I was already itching to shed this mortal cage of flesh, sinew, and bone. I'm merely waiting for this game to grow tired.

"What scry?" I spit red across my jailer's shoes. That's the one thing I did right when the trackers came for me. I may not have had the good sense to try and escape them, but I did manage to rip the chain from around my neck and destroy the crystal. They can do their very worst to me all day long, but I'll be damned if I let them have Novi. This past year, she's been the only thing that's kept me from giving up entirely, and the scrys we use to communicate could have led them straight to her door. So when the trackers kicked in mine at the inn, my first instinct was to send a single word down the bonded connection—*caught*—and then crush the magic underfoot.

Let them spend the rest of my life wondering who received that message.

Let that mystery haunt them relentlessly after I'm gone.

*And Gods, just let them end it already.* The wish is a balm to the violence their Shade continues to impose. Yesterday, it was a Blue they sent to question me. To speed my heart, and shorten my breath, and spell me to the brink of unconsciousness then back from the edge. The day before that, they'd sent an Orange and a Green. One to snap my bones and the other to heal them, make me whole again so that they could do it over. And though I half expected today's interrogation to be carried out by a Red, magically compelling truth is an unreliable endeavor at the best of times and the Council has clearly deemed that avenue too gentle a sport. They don't want to break me with a bloodless ask and answer; the pain is the point. So instead, they sent another Orange. A hulking brute of a Shade with hate in his eyes and malice for teeth, who seems content with inflicting today's injuries with his fists and seasons his efforts with the same pointless set of questions as the Shades who came before. *Who is helping you? How did you survive all these years? Are there any other half breeds in the city?*

"If you don't talk, they'll kill you," he says between blows, his words laden with warning.

"They're going to kill me anyway." My voice rasps around the cell, reminding him of that foregone conclusion. I can't stop it, he can't stop it, and there's no need to play pretend. We both know where my story is headed.

"Tell us who helped you and we'll delay your execution." The Orange changes tack, his threat blunting to a softer drawl. "Get you healed up. A decent meal. Nice bed to sleep on."

"Yeah . . . neither of us wants that." I grunt as he lands another kick to my stomach, rending my breath brittle. Because I know, for a fact, that he doesn't—*he* can barely stand to look at me without cringing in disgust, convinced as he is that I'm a blight on the Gray, a plague that needs eradicating. And while this certainly wouldn't have been the death I'd have picked for myself, there are worse ways for a Hue to go.

Being betrayed is worse.

Having your heart stopped by a Green spell is worse.

Getting shattered by the Gray is worse.

And I allowed every one of those things to happen to Eve.

So no, I don't want a healing, or a decent meal, or a nice bed to sleep on. I don't deserve them. And if I'm being honest, I've been choosing death since the moment the shadows shattered my heart alongside Eve's, dying in slow motion. I didn't want to stay in Isitar and grieve with Novi; I didn't want to rebuild our lives or try to heal together; and I sure as shit didn't want to be anywhere near Cemmy and her duplicitous Gold. What I wanted then—and now—is for this misery to end sooner rather than later. And if at all possible, with fewer broken bones.

By the time the Orange grows sick of asking his questions, I'm in no shape to answer them. He leaves me bruised, bloodied, and beaten, lying face down on the floor with the air screaming through my lungs like a curse.

"Fucking half breeds," he grumbles as the cell slams shut behind him, not bothering to drop his voice before issuing one last command to the Shade guarding my door. "Have this one ready to move in the morning, the execution's set for the ninth bell."

Tomorrow, death will finally come for me.

# CHAPTER 5

# RAYA

I snap out of the future with a vengeance, the ghost of my vision burning hot behind my eyes. The seeing tower comes back into focus in a furious rush of fear, and shock, and sapphire, my heart pounding my ribs bloody as the future's muddled revelation echoes mercilessly through my mind.

*No, no, no, no.* Reality hits and it hits me hard, unleashing an avalanche of regret that tastes of acid and bile. A few minutes ago, I was so certain of this course of action, so sure that it was the only way to prove my worth and pass my trials, show Professor Lyons that I can make use of my magic. Whereas now . . .

*No, this can't be right.* I run both hands through my hair, twisting the auburn strands so tight they threaten to snap. Asking an open question was supposed to give me invaluable insight, not this useless mix of love and impossibility.

A boy and my own death.

A future I don't care about and another I shouldn't be able to see.

*Maybe I asked the question wrong?* As I shimmer back towards the dorms, that thought works to calm the roaring swell of panic. Maybe my inability to ask the right questions has finally done me a kindness. Maybe this scrambled missive is just the future's way of telling me to stop messing with forbidden power.

*Maybe, hopefully, please.* I spend the rest of the night cursing my rash decision, trying to make sense of the mess of colors, feelings, and sights. Could all the death I saw be a metaphor of some kind? Or a riddle? Or a test? What if open questions don't elicit the kind of visions I've been taught to interpret? What if they require a whole different set of skills I don't possess?

*Gods, Raya, how could you be so stupid.* It suddenly occurs to me just how little I know about the spell I so recklessly cast. We've always been prohibited from asking open questions, so Professor Lyons never took the time to explain what the resulting visions would look like; the discussion begins with *don't do it* and ends with *because most Indigos aren't powerful enough to weather them unscathed.*

But I'm not most Indigos—everyone made that plenty clear from the moment I set foot in the castle. They made me believe that I *was* powerful enough to do this, and if nothing else, I was certainly desperate enough to try.

*Well then*, try, *Ray.* It's Akari's voice that spurs me to act. That's what she'd say if I confessed to this blunder, and she'd be absolutely right. I may have made this decision recklessly, but it would be more reckless to not even give the magic a chance. What I lack in this moment isn't power, it's knowledge. I need to learn how to decipher the madness instead of dismissing it out of hand.

*The archives.* In an instant, I've lurched out of bed and set to dressing. If there are answers to be found, that's where they'll be.

"Is there a reason you're banging around at the ass crack of dawn?" Akari grumbles, blinking up at me with bleary eyes.

"Not a good one. Go back to sleep."

"You go back to sleep." She tosses a pillow at my head. "Class doesn't start for hours."

"Yeah, well, you were right—I need to focus on my questions." I feed her a half-truth in lieu of a lie. "I want to sneak in some reading."

"Then sneak quieter next time." Her face disappears beneath the covers. "And don't sneak too hard."

"I wouldn't dream of it." I slip out of the room before she wakes enough to notice the guilt in my voice and the crime in my expression, the devil on my shoulder whispering, *fate-touched, fate-touched.* Akari went to great lengths to stop me wrecking my future, only for

me to go to even greater lengths to cast a spell I don't fully understand. When she finds out what I did, she's going to read me for riot,
and I don't need the future's help to know that she *will* find out. The
least I can do is make sense of my vision before that happens—that
way, maybe it'll feel like less of a betrayal.

The Academy archives command their very own wing in the castle, three whole floors filled with a veritable oasis of books, papers,
scrolls, ledgers, and guides. These shadowed halls contain everything
there is to know about magic—new, old, outdated, and banned. The
real question now is: where do I start looking?

*In which book will I find the answers I need?* My first instinct is to reach
for the power in my blood, ask the future.

*Except you can't.* In place of the vision I expect, my mind meets only
silence, as though my color has drained itself dull.

*We don't ask open questions because it's impossible to predict which subsequent
questions the future will consider a repeat.* I've lost track of how many times
Professor Lyons has issued us that warning, spelling out the risk so
clearly the words rang like crystal. *An open question jeopardizes our relationship with the fates. It's too big of a risk for too small of a reward—that's
why the practice is forbidden.*

The full weight of what I've done turns my mouth bitter. A part of
me had hoped that he was overplaying the danger, steering us away
from the old technique in favor of the new method the Council likes.
I didn't truly believe that I'd be one of the unlucky few who lose the
ability to ask *everything*. The big stuff, yes, obviously, but not these
minor, inconsequential asks.

*Too late to worry about that now* . . . I shimmer towards the stacks
that house the Indigo collection, trying not to let the panic eat right
through my skin. The fates have ignored some of my questions
before; it's not terribly common, but sometimes, no matter how hard
or how perfectly you ask, a vision simply won't appear—usually
when the answer encompasses too many unmade choices. That's yet
another reason why open questions are considered bad form for an
accomplished seer: they can only show you the broader strokes, they
don't shed light on the finer details. And though the question I just

asked *should* lead to an outcome that is solid and clear, the silence doesn't necessarily mean that I've lost the ability to cast for good. The future could just be trying to teach me a lesson.

*Consider that lesson well and truly learned.* I start scanning the shelves for any book that might prove promising. An archivist could direct my search more effectively, but it's too early in the day for one to be on duty, and they all know me by name and color, so if I do ask for help, they'll wonder why I'm not using my regular tricks. That, plus the fact that I'm sniffing around a forbidden magic, would almost certainly arouse suspicion, and that's one risk more than I'm willing to take. So instead, I guess, plucking out the titles that seem most likely to fit. *A Variable Magic . . . Harnessing the Future . . . On Premonition . . .* By the time I settle on a book to start with, there's a hefty stack of literature gathered at my feet.

*The Evolution of Indigo Techniques Through the Ages.* As I crack open the lengthy tome, I once again instinctively reach for my magic, imploring the future to take pity and narrow down my search. *On what page will I find the information I'm looking for?*

The nothing I receive back is even frostier the second time.

One ignored question I could rationalize away as a fluke, but two? In the space of a few minutes? That feels more like a sign. And it's not pointing in a great direction.

*The old-fashioned way it is.* I start flipping through the musty pages. It's almost funny, really. I've spent so long being told that I'm bad at using my power, I never fully realized how dependent I've grown on the future for the little things. The mundane, day-to-day questions that don't impress Professor Lyons but help me get through the week.

*Nothing more mundane than having to search a book cover to cover for an answer that isn't there . . .* It takes me a full bell to discount the first lot of books I gathered, then another to round up a new set of options and make the barest hint of a find.

*A Future Worth Seeing: An Indigo's Guide to Preserving Their Relationship with the Fates, by Eldrick Fernay.* The spine on this behemoth is thick with dust and worn through with age, the vellum inside curling at the edges. Doesn't get much use, clearly. Then again, why would it? For generations now, the only rule that mattered for *preserving our relationship with the fates* was to avoid asking open questions altogether. Reading up on the whys wasn't time well spent.

> An open question is a question so vast it forces the fates to reveal the threads of destiny.

The relevant chapter opens exactly as I expect.

> But owing to their distinct distaste for repeat premonitions, the fates are then—

*Yes, yes, I know this already.* I click my tongue and flip ahead, skimming over the parts I've long since committed to memory.

> The future may continue to withhold answers for days, months, or years . . . Some Shades lose the ability to see indefinitely . . . Once cast, there is no way to reverse the spell.

*No way to reverse the spell.* The words practically leap off the page, sending my stomach to my knees. That means I can't walk it back or beg the future's forgiveness. I have no choice but to work with the vision I received.

*So then, please, tell me how to do that.* The minutes speed by as I search Fernay's treaties for any such tips. There are pages that list, with unerring diligence, all the constructions of phrase the future may deem 'open', others that detail first-hand accounts from those Shades the fates chose to punish, as well as whole essays on the Council's choice to start phasing out the technique. It took them years to come to that decision, it seems, and the seers' guild only agreed to forbid the practice after it lost half its number to something Fernay calls 'the event'.

*Would it have really killed him to say a little more?* I curse the shocking lack of specifics. If the man could spend a dozen pages waxing lyrical about the political unrest that followed the loss of those Shades' power, why not spare a paragraph or two for the reason that so many suddenly found themselves on the outs with fate when they'd been asking open questions just fine until then.

*A curiosity for a different time.* Chapter by chapter, I tear through the rest of his ramblings, praying to all three Gods that Fernay dedicated at least a few words to dealing with the effects of the questions themselves, how to interpret this type of vision. And finally—colors help me, *finally*—after a tediously long search, I manage to spot the heading I need.

## Fate-Touched Magic

Indigos who choose to break with the Council's modern stance on casting are referred to as fate-touched on account that they have deliberately entered into a turbulent relationship with the fates.

There are a myriad reasons for why a Shade might elect to do that, the most compelling of which being that it grants them access to the wider range of visions the open method allows. These include the ability to see fated paths as well as simple futures, where fated paths is taken to mean a future that is impervious to change or decision-led collapse.

The churn in my gut blunts an inch. Clearly, the term *fate-touched* used to have slightly less disparaging connotations or else Fernay wouldn't be speaking of it in such a detached, measured way. *Fated paths as well as simple futures* also suggests that I may still regain my ability to see normally, and *wider range of visions* implies that there could actually be some benefit to testing the future's patience.

*Now, if only Fernay would tell me what those visions are or how to read them . . .* I grumble at his inability to stay on subject. At the way he, once again, skips the instructions in favor of chasing some non-related thread.

A curiosity of fate-touched visions is that they can be projected from mind to mind.

Right. Because having broken the rules, the first thing I'd want to do is go and show other people that I broke them.

**They can also remind you of significant moments from your past.**

Wonderful. Another entirely useless skill. Fernay sure does love those. So much so that he spends the next few paragraphs listing examples for why an Indigo might wish to be transported back.

*Of all the pointless, irrelevant things to care abou—*

"Erm . . . what are you doing?" Killen's voice snaps me out of Fernay's ramblings, startling the book from my hands.

"What—? *Nothing*, I—I'm just studying." I hurry to slam the incriminating tome shut, though there's no hiding the vast pile of texts still gathered around me, their very telling titles and the fact that none of them are recent enough to have been assigned.

"Since when do you study before class?" After last night's encounter, Killen's tone is less than polite, his eyes cold with suspicion.

"Since I can't afford to fail my trials again." I feed him the same half-truth I fed Akari, the blood in my cheeks flaming to life. Where money is Killen's sore spot, my lack of ability is mine—and he knows that because we were still together when I failed my trials the first time around. When the threat of a binding sent me crying into his arms.

*I didn't fall in love with your magic, Raya. Bound or not bound, it won't change how I feel about you.* He'd said it so sweetly—so earnestly—and all it did was squirm my insides. Because had our roles been reversed, I *would* have cared if he'd lost his power. I would have cared and it would have ruined us because I just didn't love him enough. And it was that realization that prompted me to ask the future for a reason to break his heart.

"Why are *you* here so early, anyway?" I'm quick to steer his attention back to safer ground.

"I work here," he says, cheeks reddening to match mine. "Three mornings a week. For a few months now."

"Oh." It feels like I should have known that. Like I should have done a better job checking up on him after we split.

"You're just lucky I'm the only one on duty today." Killen shrugs, crouching down to attack the mess of books I left on the ground. "The other archivists don't much like it when you ransack the shelves."

"No, please, you don't have to do that—" I try to beat him to the pile. Too late.

I see the exact moment he gets it, the strange assortment of puzzle pieces pulling together in his mind.

Me, wisping into his room, out of the blue, in the middle of the night.

Asking him to rid me of an unwanted compulsion spell.

Stealing into the archives to read about forbidden magic.

"Raya, please tell me you didn't do what I think you did," he says, face paling to powder.

"Gods, of course I didn't." Even to my own ears, it sounds like a lie. And not a very good one.

"By my colors, are you *insane?*" he hisses. "What were you thinking?"

I wasn't thinking—not really. I was trying to save myself the shame of having my magic bound.

"Look, this isn't your problem, okay? I'm handling it."

"*Handling it?*" The disbelief deepens his voice to a growl. "You asked an open question, Raya, that's not something you can just *handle.* Lyons is going to find out!"

"Not if neither of us tells him!"

It's only the sudden scream of the class bell that spares me the ferocity of Killen's next reply.

Except.

Wait.

The pitch of the sound is too loud and shrill, the sequence too drawn out and rigid.

That's not the class bell at all—it's the Council bell, a call to assemble that's only ever invoked when there's a crime to be tried.

The trackers have captured an illegal Shade.

# CHAPTER 6

# RAYA

When the Council bell rings, we don't ignore it. Trials are a rare occurrence at the best of times, and there's not a Shade at the Academy who doesn't thrill at the idea of witnessing one in real life.

Up until a few months ago, the Council used to carry out their justice in the physical realm, in the gilded chamber they command at the very heart of Sarotuza, where both Shade and typic could hear testimony on the crime. *An exercise in appeasement*, my father called it, designed to remind the city that we police our own kind. *The typics enjoy watching us punished. It helps keep their fear at bay and the Church from lashing out.*

But that was before a fanatical cleric broke with the sacraments and made a play for power. The Divine Meridian is his self-proclaimed title, the one true voice of the Gods. An entirely absurd assertion, but thanks to his budding cult of adoring zealots, the streets have grown more hostile of late, more laden with iron. For while the Church is only ever a spark away from declaring war against those with color, the Meridians don't just want to banish us—or even kill us—they want to *bleed* us. Because for some unfathomable reason, they believe their messiah's claims that it'll immune them to our power. Yet another absurd assertion, seeing how it's been proven, time and time again, that possessing our blood achieves nothing. Neither does injecting it, bathing in it, baking it into bread, or drinking it like wine.

But alas, you cannot reason with madness, and so, after the Divine Meridian killed his third Shade, the decision was made to start conducting trials at the Academy, so as not to present him with an opportunity to target us en masse.

"We are not done talking about this, Raya," Killen seethes, speeding after me as I make to leave the archives.

"Yes, actually, we are." I duck clear of his grasp. "So either go tell Lyons, or don't tell him. Either way, I'm going to watch the trial."

"Is that what you think I care about? *Telling Lyons?*" The hurt in his voice is a stone to the gut. "You know what, fuck you, Raya, you always do this," he hisses. "Every time you think you're failing, you make the most appalling decision you can."

"That is *not* what I do," I say, though the accusation fits like a glove.

"It's what you did with us." He plants himself in front of me. "You had a bad setback so you went looking for an excuse to end things in case the Academy kicked you out."

"You need to drop this, Killen." I wish I could shimmer past him. But he can shimmer, too, and he's faster than I am, and I don't want to have this particular argument on the run.

"No, not this time. Not until you admit I'm right."

"Killen—"

"Gods, just admit it, Raya. Don't you think you owe me that?"

"I ended things because I didn't love you!" The truth explodes out of me in a vicious rush, harsh and angry. *And cruel.* For six months, I repeated the same lie ad nauseum, just to avoid the hurt now blowing his pupils wide. So much worse than when I accused him of cheating. But what can I say—when Killen's right, he's right: I do make bad decisions when I'm cornered. It just so happens that breaking up with him wasn't one of them.

"No, wait, Killen, I'm sorry, I didn't mean that." I immediately long to take it back. "Killen, please, *wait—*"

But he doesn't, and I can't say I blame him.

The last thing he needs from me right now is more lies.

With the Council's summons ringing a stern command through the castle, the corridors are a mess of excitement and eager eyes, all rushing towards the court chamber to jostle for the best view of the proceedings.

"What the hells happened to you?" Akari asks as I join her up by the balustrade, smack bang at the center of the gallery, directly opposite the dock where the accused is going to stand. "You look like you're about to cry."

"No, I'm—I'll tell you later."

"Okay . . ."

Around us, the chamber yawns as deep as it is wide, the vaulted ceilings stretching up towards oblivion, turbid and black. Behind the dock, the judges' bench hangs equally thick with shadow, a row of high-backed chairs spaced evenly against its side.

Seven chairs, seven judges.

One to represent each shade of magic.

"Are you sure you don't want to talk about it now?" Akari presses, placing a gentle hand to my arm. "Because we can."

"No, really, it's fine." I force a smile from my grimace. "Any idea who they've caught? Is it a rogue we've heard of?"

"Is there a rogue you haven't heard of?" Her lips quirk with the jibe.

"Very funny," I say, though I suppose I have been a little more obsessed with the trackers' news blasts of late, the lists they keep of Shades who've broken with the Council. Shades who—like me—were in danger of having their magic bound and so they ran before that could happen. Or Shades that flouted the decree against procreating with a typic. Or Shades that simply didn't like being told what they could do with their color, or having to sacrifice a percentage of their earnings in tithe. These past few years, the spate of Shades turning rogue has grown from a slow trickle to a flood, with more than ever choosing to turn their backs on the Council. Going rogue allows their magic to get stronger. Wilder. And while exile is the nightmare scenario for me, for others, it's a tempting proposition, especially now that there are two religious factions vying for power in Sarotuza—one of which is, quite literally, hunting us for blood.

"So, rumor is, it's not actually a rogue at all—it's a *Hue*." Akari laces the word with scandal.

"Wait—a *Hue?*" My voice rises an octave. "Like, a real one?"

There hasn't been a Hue on trial in Sarotuza in over a decade. They usually put up too much of a fight to reach the court chamber, choosing to die in the struggle rather than be taken alive. Probably because they don't see the point of trying to plead their innocence; since their kind is illegal, there is only one verdict the Council can hand down. If the trackers truly have caught a Hue, then this trial isn't a trial at all; it's an execution.

"Yes, a real one—look, here it comes." Akari points to the door at the rear of the chamber, where a solemn procession is beginning to arrive. Three trackers up front—as announced by the sickle pins fixed to their collars—then behind them, the Hue, his head held low and his wrists bound in irons, limping ahead of the seven elders who'll be passing judgement on his crimes.

*I guess he did put up a fight.* I cringe at the broken sight of him. Between the split lip, the angry bruises, and the blackened swell to his eyes, all I can really make out is the coppery brown of his skin and the blood caking his hair and hands, the sharp wince of his breaths as he's shoved to his knees in the dock and chained to the marble, facing the gallery.

"Gods, it's unnerving, isn't it? How much they look like us?" Akari's whisper is one of a hundred fascinated murmurs rippling through the crowd. At least half of the Academy has turned up for the occasion, mostly from the older classes, though there are a few younger faces peppered throughout the hall, as well. Hells, I even spot Saleen's sullen superiority lurking in the corner—despite her disparaging opinions on the Council. I guess no Shade can resist the lure of a good spectacle, no matter how hard they pretend otherwise.

"Yeah. Unnerving." My gut twists in reply. I've never seen a Hue in the flesh before, let alone at this short a distance or in such damning circumstances. And though I've always known that outwardly, they're indistinguishable from a typic, I never stopped to consider how that would also make them indistinguishable from us.

Apart from the eyes, of course. A full-blooded Shade wears their magic in their eyes. A spiked rim around the iris for those of us who heed the Council's call for civility, burned black to the edge for those who choose to walk the lawless path. Whereas in a Hue, the magic is imperceptible—though I can't confirm that much for myself seeing how this one is keeping his gaze fixed too firmly on the ground. That's what makes these illegal half breeds so difficult to capture: we can't see their color—and we all bleed red when you cut us, Shades, Hues, and typics alike. The only way to identify a Hue is to catch them in the act of phasing, an inevitability that often happens in childhood, when the shadows start calling to them in the dark. I'm actually amazed that this Hue has lasted as long as he did. If I had to guess, I'd say he's pushing twenty, maybe even twenty-one.

"What do you think his gift is?" I ask, examining him with interest. Hues don't share in our specializations; their colors are a dilution of magic, and thus, more varied and abstract. Some of their gifts are trivial, while others are downright terrifying in their might. The only truth that's universal to every Hue is that they can't survive the Gray for long. The shadows revile the typical tint of their blood. Seek to expel it. Without a complicated spell called an In-Between, the Gray would rush in and shatter this Hue like glass. Which is yet another reason why these proceedings were originally held in the physical realm, where the accused weren't in danger of spontaneously hastening their own demise. Though now that the court has been relegated to the Academy, it does beg the question of how, beat up as he is, this Hue is sustaining such a taxing spell? Or why he's even bothering to sustain it—to keep himself alive—when he already knows the outcome of his trial?

"No idea, but I think we're about to find out," Akari says as a charged silence settles across the crowd, the presiding judge—Councilman Lars Denata, head of the trackers' guild—having called the room to order. The councilman is a stern man of almost sixty, his ashy hair salted through with silver, his sun-worn skin toughened to a pale and leathery hide. Like the rest of the judges, he wears a heavy robe that's embroidered to announce his color—Orange, like Akari—as signified by the hammer symbol that graces his cuffs. A formidable man both inside the court and out of it. I should know: growing up, my parents had him over for dinner all the time.

"We have convened here today to rule on the most egregious of crimes: the birth of a half breed." His voice booms loud across the chamber, stern and menacing. Though for his part, the Hue doesn't so much as flinch. He doesn't look up. He doesn't fidget. He barely even seems to hear him.

"In direct contravention to the Council's decree, an Indigo Shade, now deceased, deigned to mate with a typic, resulting in a Sapphire Hue whom she did not surrender."

*A Sapphire?* The words rip through my chest like a pack of starving mutts.

A Sapphire. This Hue is a Sapphire.

The same color as my vision.

"The violation of this decree is not only illegal, it also presents a clear and ongoing threat to our kind. It allows for offspring that endanger the Gray by draining it of its magic, thereby jeopardizing the shadows and our way of life."

This time, I swear I see the Hue snigger, though that doesn't make a lick of sense given that he's about to die.

"You will all do well to remember what you witnessed here today," Denata continues, turning his attention to the sea of acolytes hanging off his every syllable. "For it is a needless tragedy and an unnecessary burden on the members of this tribunal, who have no choice but to call for the Sapphire's immediate execution. Does the condemned wish to address the court before his sentence is carried out?"

Alongside the shock of the Hue's color comes a shock at the speed of it all—how in the space of a minute, he went from accused, to condemned, to being offered his last rite. And while I absolutely understand the need for this law, I can't help but find the lack of ceremony unsettling. This half didn't choose to be born any more than the rest of us choose our parents, and even a justified killing feels as though it should warrant a little more pomp and judicial pride. I mean, hells, I've had reprimands from Professor Lyons that lasted longer than this trial.

*Say something.* I find myself urging the Sapphire to speak on his own behalf. To beg, or scream, or grumble, to rail against what he must believe to be gravely unjust.

But he doesn't.

He merely sets his jaw and lifts his head in defiance, as though he's long since made peace with this outcome. As though some part of him yearns for it.

"Very well. This court will now administer the punishment. Please fetch the executioner," the councilman says, sending for the Green who will end the Hue's life. That's when the Sapphire finally grants himself a moment of unadulterated spite, allowing his eyes to rake across the gallery and condemn the rest of us. That's when, for the briefest of seconds, they bore straight into mine.

*No.*

His gaze is a bolt of lightning to a meadow of dry brush.

For while his face may be bruised beyond recognition, there is absolutely no mistaking that burnished shade of brown.

*No, no, no, no.*

It can't be him.

It can't be the boy from my vision.

Even the future wouldn't be so cruel as to imply that I'm destined to fall in love with a half.

*It's not him because it can't be.* I try to reason away the horror. Brown eyes are hardly uncommon, after all, and the rest of him is too beat up to identify with any kind of certainty. But most of all, it can't be him because he'll be dead in a matter of minutes. Already, his executioner is circling him like a shark, keenly awaiting the councilman's command to unleash her magic. A command which suddenly can't come soon enough.

"Gods, just do it already," I mutter, gripping the balustrade so hard the wood groans beneath my fingers.

"Easy, Ray." Akari places her hand over mine, though I can tell by the set of her jaw that she's also feeling a little untethered. Neither of us has ever witnessed an execution, and no amount of schooling can prepare you for watching someone die.

Not even when it's necessary.

*It's unnerving, isn't it? How much they look like us?*

It's even more unnerving how resigned this Hue is to meeting the black.

How he seems to be rooting for it.

*Then why doesn't he just shatter?* I lean forward for a closer look at him, trying to decipher the serenity in his smile. All he'd have to do is drop the In-Between and then the shadows would grant him his wish, rush in and smash him like a fragile vase. He could end his life on his own terms, right here, right now. But for whatever reason, the Sapphire remains still and silent and alive, and as the Green raises her hand in preparation, I'm ashamed to admit that I'm the one who falters in anticipation of his demise. Thanks to last night's vision, I've already seen more death than I care to count; I don't need to watch a flash of magic stop this Hue's heart. I just need it to happen.

*Come on, come on, come on.* His death will prove, definitively, that my premonition was a lie, just another nonsense answer to a question I shouldn't have been asking.

So when he drags in a breath, I hold mine.

And when the spell builds to its crescendo, I close my eyes, as if out of respect.

Maybe that's why I miss the exact moment chaos erupts, when a different spell altogether incapacitates the trackers and sends his executioner flying back.

*What in the—?*

"Ray, get down!" Akari jerks me to the floor as a dense and heavy fog descends across the crowd, mingling with the shadows to turn air to smoke and day to night. The haze is everywhere. It's everything I see, everything I feel, everything I touch. A perfect blinding.

*Too perfect.*

I'm suddenly struck by just how uniform the darkness has become. How it's lacking in form and texture. How there's no caustic smell to the smoke and no irritants stinging my eyes.

*Is this a glamour?* I blink until the illusion begins to crack.

Breaking free of a Red's compulsion might be close to impossible, but their glamours grow brittle the second you recognize them for what they are. Whoever wanted this Hue spared has somehow trapped the entire chamber inside this magical cloud of black, distracted us from the real threat.

*But . . . why?*

Why would some rogue Shade want to save the Sapphire so badly they infiltrated the Academy? The most impenetrable building in Sarotuza? Better yet, how is it that I was able to shake off their glamour when no one else has?

*Killen.* The answer hits me all at once. Just a few hours ago, he'd used his color to rid me of *any and all Red*, and that spell won't dissipate for a few more hours still—if not days. He's the reason that, through the crush of panicked bodies, I'm able to spot the rogue Shade approaching the Hue. Though—inexplicably—he seems no happier to see her than I am.

From my place in the gallery, I can't make out the angry words they're trading, but after a brief and terse exchange, the rogue starts fussing with the Sapphire's chains, then when his cuffs snap open a minute later, they both flee towards the back of the court.

*You should follow them.* The idea whispers through my mind, bold and tempting. If I can stop these two illegal Shades from leaving, then maybe the Council will finally look past my inability to predict. Maybe this is how I buy myself a second reprieve.

"It's a glamour, Kiri! The smoke isn't real!" I say as I spring to my feet and take off after them. To my surprise, both the Hue and the rogue are running from the chamber instead of shimmering—which makes sense for him; he lacks the power to speed through the shadows, but why *she's* not shimmering them to safety is anybody's guess.

As is why he wisps right through the wall but she takes the time to open the door.

*Colors help me, is she trying to get caught?* For a long moment, I'm too stunned to give chase. What kind of rogue doesn't shed their physicality when it matters? How did such incompetence even manage to break into the Academy in the first place? Or incapacitate this entire hall?

*Those are excellent questions for later.* I, on the other hand, do shimmer, closing the space between us in a few fractured blinks.

"Hey you—stop! Stop right—"

"*Don't.*"

The command jerks me to a halt a mere inch from the rogue Shade's side, close enough that—if my arms were still working—I could reach out and grab her by the cowl. Close enough to see her eyes.

*But that's—it's not possible.* The breath catches in my lungs, the magic silencing my startled questions. Her irises aren't burned black to the edge the way a rogue's should be, and there's no spiked rim, either, so she's also not a Council Shade.

This girl is another Hue.

As is the guy that just wisped through the wall and spelled me immobile. *Using a Red's magic.* I can still see the ghost of it flaming in his eyes.

"She's cleared the way for us—let's go," he says, prompting the girl away.

*I did no such thing.* I want to yell at him, to make it perfectly clear that I would never work with him or his illegal friends. But his compulsion extends to my tongue, it seems, and before they both hurry after the Sapphire, he adds an additional caveat to his command.

"You will not tell anyone what you saw here," he orders. And by the time my limbs unfreeze and Killen's spell accelerates his will off me, the three of them are long gone.

# CHAPTER 7

# EZZO

It's amazing how fast your luck can change, how in the space of a heartbeat, a clear sky can darken with a vicious storm. A second can mean the difference between life and death, happiness and misery, an execution or a reprieve.

Oblivion or an escape.

After three days of beatings in a lightless cell, I was aching to face the first and under no illusion of attempting the latter. Because what would have even been the point? All year, I'd been skirting the fire, courting the trackers' attention in the hopes that they'd do their jobs well, end it for me. And besides, with my wrists chained to the dock and a whole gallery of Shades staring back at me hungrily, it would have been pointless to try. There was no getting out of that court chamber. I was going to die, today, at the Council's hand, for a made-up crime that shouldn't exist, and if that was to be my fate then the last thing I intended to do was show them fear.

So when they concluded my sham of a trial in less than a minute, I didn't protest. And when they asked for my parting words, I didn't give them the satisfaction of hearing my voice break. Instead, I'd picked a random Shade in the crowd—a pretty girl with hazel eyes, auburn hair, and a fine constellation of freckles dusting her ivory skin—and glared at her until she looked away, startled, as though my condemnation was the true injustice. It was supposed to be my final act of rebellion, a way to leave a lasting impression while the static charge of magic was building to a murder in Green.

Just like the one that took Eve.

It seemed fitting that I would meet the same death as she did.

Romantic almost.

A relief.

But then, between one breath and the next, every Shade in that chamber was screaming and the three guards flanking me were suddenly blasted back into the brick.

It should have been impossible.

It *was* impossible.

Until I spotted Cemmy weaving through the panic and then I knew exactly how my luck had turned. Because where Cemmy goes, Chase follows, and with Chase comes enough stolen magic to incapacitate an entire court.

*Novi sent us.*

I should have realized she'd find a way to save me from all the way across the world.

I should have never scried her my warning.

But I did, so now I'm sitting on a grimy floor, in an abandoned house at the forgotten end of Sarotuza, laying low until the three of us can escape the city without getting caught.

"Here—this should help with the swelling." Cemmy hands me a cool strip of cloth.

"Fuck off." I'm quick to bat her away. It's been one year, four months, and seventeen days since I was last forced to share air with this self-serving liar of a Bronze; one year, four months, and eighteen days since she led us all into the ambush that shattered Eve. And while I should be grateful for the rescue, I would have sooner died than seen her or Chase again, nor did I need to see them looking more content together than either of them ever did alone.

"Ez, come on, I'm trying to help," she says, shuffling back to lean against the wall. She's still every bit as pale and sharp as I remember, her blond hair hanging straight past her shoulders, her blue eyes as piercing as they are cold.

"I don't want your help, Cemmy. So please, just go." I do my resolute best to ignore her, staring at the moldy ceiling, the boarded-up windows, the splintered cracks in the plaster, anywhere except her worry until, with a heavy sigh and a *suit yourself*, she disappears through the door.

*Good.* I wince as I sit up straighter, dabbing the cloth to the worst of the throb. I don't want her to think that all is forgiven. Because a life saved doesn't somehow erase the one she cost—and that's all I can see when I look at her: the absence of Eve. How needless that loss was. How preventable. How it might never have happened if Cemmy had put her faith in us instead of the Gold.

"I told you he won't talk to me." I hear her say from the corridor, then a long moment later, her more dangerous half stalks into the room.

"I'm not interested in talking," I grit the words through a clenched jaw.

"I'm not here to talk; I'm here to heal," he says, dropping into a crouch.

"Well, I don't want that, either."

"Then by all means, you're welcome to stop me."

Before I can even think to try, he's placed both hands to my side and engaged his power, pressing hard enough to prove a point.

*Point made.* I suck a harsh breath through my teeth. In my current state, we both know I'm too weak to fight him; even without the magic, he's got a good couple of inches on me and no broken ribs. Though the moment his healing spell touches my skin, I lose the will to pretend I don't want it. After four days of constant pain, the dulling of it is overwhelming, a heady release that makes me forget how Chase's stolen color is won. The hurt he has to inflict to get it.

"Do I want to know where you found all this Green?" I ask as he turns his attention to the bruises marking my face. The metallic sheen of his magic extends to other parts of him, as well. Golden hair, silver eyes, a bronze tan to his skin, chiseled features that even Eve acknowledged were pretty. A beautiful trap.

"From the same place you've been frequenting all year," he says, a note of judgement creeping into his voice. "A tavern."

"Kind of a risk, don't you think? Courting Shades so publicly?"

"It's always a risk." Sweat beads at his temples, the feat he's performing exacting a heavy toll. "But the trackers aren't looking for a Gold right now and when we run, we need you to be able to keep up, so I did what I had to. We'll leave just as soon as the search for you quiets."

"You and Cemmy shouldn't bother waiting, I'm fine on my own."

"Yeah, you look like you've really got it together." With another burst of magic, he eases the painful swelling around my eyes. "Why didn't you see the trackers coming?"

The question irks me to no end. Back in Isitar, I used to scour the Gray for trails all the time. I made it my duty to keep our palette safe from the Council. But then *he* turned that very power against me, used it to force another Hue into his master's genocidal plan. So if he's wondering why I've lost the zeal for watching the shadows, then he can consider himself Exhibit One.

"Who says I didn't?"

"Colors help me, have you even been checking?" He sees straight through the lie. "Or were you actually trying to get yourself caught?"

"You know what, I prefer my healings without the lecture, thank you very much," I snap. Novi can talk to me like this. Cemmy, too, at a push, since we were friends for years before she blew that trust apart. But this Gold has known me for all of five minutes and he used every single one of them to ruin my life. It was the Shade *he* led to Isitar who cast the spell that stopped Eve's heart and robbed her of magic, allowing the vengeful shadows to rush in and shatter her like glass, and it was the lies *he* told that kept us from putting that Shade down in the first place. Chase hasn't earned the right to berate me for anything—let alone for endangering the shell of a person his treachery left behind.

"How did you even find me, anyway?" I ask, seething. "Have the two of you been stalking me this entire time?"

"No, we were in Heresse, actually." Chase takes the bait without biting. "But then Novi scried to tell us you were in trouble, and we decided it was worth the trip to try and get you out—though we didn't know if you'd still be alive when we got here or if we'd be able to track you down. You got really fucking lucky."

I don't feel lucky.

The three days I spent getting beaten by a rainbow of Shades didn't feel lucky.

And neither does the life I have ahead of me now.

"I hope you don't think this makes us even," I say when Chase finally exhausts his supply of Green and pulls away, his energy drained and his breath rasping.

"We'll never be even," he agrees, and Gods, even his contrition has me itching to rip his throat out. Chase knows he did wrong and he's taking responsibility, to the point where railing at him feels like a petty waste of time. A waste of anger. Because, deep down, I know that at the root of his lies was a good reason, a sister he loves just as much as I loved Eve. But knowing and forgiving are two different things and they don't always go hand in hand. Sometimes, when you break things, it makes them stronger, more resilient. Sometimes broken things stay broken.

Which is why I can't stay here.

With him.

With her.

With the memory of the happiness they took from me even as they forged their own.

I have to leave. Right now. Before the need to hurt them back rears up and swallows me whole.

"Ez, please—you can't go out there; the city's crawling with track-ers." Cemmy chases after me as I make to flee the house. She hasn't changed at all, if I'm honest. Still stubborn enough to try and sway me, still reckless enough to break into a Council stronghold despite the devastating odds.

Still familiar enough to implore me with *Ez*.

"Gods, when is that not true?" But I don't want to be swayed, and I don't want to be chased after, and the more she tries to prove she cares, the more the pressure of these past few days—of this past year—threatens to come bursting out. "We're Hues, Cemmy, there will always be trackers after us, no matter where we go or how low we lie. We exist, they hunt us, we escape, they do it over, until one day, we simply run out of time. That's the story." And it's not the kind you can change by holing up in some house.

"Fine. You want to leave? Leave. Drink yourself into another prison, I can't stop you. Just take this with you." She presses a brand-new scry crystal into my hand.

"I don't need a babysitter, Cemmy."

"And I have no intention of becoming one," she clips, crossing her arms. "But I promised Novi we'd look out for you, so at least do *her* the favor of wearing it. That way, when something happens—"

I don't miss the fact that she says *when* not *if*.

"—we'll know what to tell her. You can give her that much, can't you?" The look she fixes me could sublimate stone. "I mean it, Ez. You want to punish me? Go right ahead, we both know I deserve it. But don't punish Novi, okay? She's done nothing to earn it."

The words wrap a hand around my heart and squeeze, pumping shame into my blood. I've known Novi since I was ten years old, more than half my life. She was the first Hue Eve and I found when we started searching Isitar for others, and the pin that kept our family together every time the world threatened to pull us apart. Cemmy's right—she hasn't earned my silence, and if something were to happen to me, I'd want her to learn the truth so that she could grieve and move on.

"Fine, I'll wear the scry." I relent, slipping the chain over my head then tucking it beneath my shirt. "Happy?"

"Be safe, Ez," is all she says in reply.

Then, true to her word, Cemmy steps aside and lets me go.

# CHAPTER 8

# RAYA

The Sapphire's escape is all the Academy can talk about for hours. A Hue has never evaded the Council's justice quite so publicly before, and to have done it in a flurry of Red magic—from right under the nose of three trackers and the elder in charge of their guild, no less—the whole castle is up in arms.

As the only Shade to have witnessed the truth of what transpired in the court chamber, I spent a full bell telling the trackers what I saw, another bell ducking compliments for breaking free of the glamour so quickly, and another one after that trying to sidestep the question of *how*, because admitting that I bribed my ex so that I could live down to my reputation and become fate-touched wasn't really an option.

Though it is still a problem.

And not the kind I'll be able to hide come tomorrow's class.

Just this morning, the future made a resolute point of denying me answers, after only offering me a single vision that was as impossible as it was insulting and abstract. Nothing in the books I searched shed light on anything it showed me. Nothing explained how I could have seen my own death, or why the future would bother harping on about some romance—and a super fucking illegal one, at that.

A Shade and a Hue.

Together.

In love.

The very thought is enough to shudder me senseless. That's not a future I would ever allow to happen—regardless of whether it was fated or not. *Or impervious to change.* Fernay can take his assertion and shove it somewhere crass. Professor Lyons has also taught us about this type of path before, but he held that they're *averse* to change, not impervious, and I'm more inclined to believe him than some centuries-dead scribe. Averse just means I'll have to try harder, and that's if I even accept that anything in that vision has a basis in fact.

*Which it doesn't.*

"Raya—are you listening to me?" Akari tosses a pencil at my head, snapping me back to the present.

"Yeah, I—what?" I try to shake the guilt from my expression. I've not yet told her about the open question or the preposterous premonition that came after. I meant to, I really did, but the moment I returned to our room, she demanded to hear the same story I'd told the trackers, then she demanded that I accompany her to the archives so that we could study up on Hues, and then it just . . . didn't feel like the right time anymore. We'd veered too hard towards a different subject.

"I said: are you sure all three of them were halves?" she repeats, glancing up from the book in her hands. "It was pretty chaotic in there, could you have maybe . . . gotten it wrong?"

"I saw their eyes, Kiri—and they were as close to me as you are now. No spiked rim, not burned black. Then when the third one compelled me, his irises definitely flashed."

"Okay, well, then that makes the girl a . . . Bronze and him a . . . Gold," Akari says, turning my insides to ice.

A Bronze, a Sapphire, and a Gold wielding Red magic in an Orange-convened trial.

That's every single color from my vision.

"Erm . . . and how exactly did you decide that?" My foot taps a nervous staccato against the table. Of all the visions in the world, this can't be the first one I actually get right. It just can't be.

"By looking at this list of known Hues and their gifts." Akari spins the book around. "According to this, only a Bronze can interact with their surroundings in the Gray, so no other half breed could have unlocked the chains—and it would explain why you saw her open the door instead of wisping through it. Her physicality wouldn't allow for wisping. Then, since you're certain the second one didn't use a pre-spelled charm to compel you—"

"He didn't," I say, adamant. If he had, then not only would I have found some spent crystals in his wake, but his eyes wouldn't have flashed Red with the casting.

"Then he must have been using live magic, so his gift has to be stealing power, and that equals a Gold." She taps the relevant paragraph.

"But that—" *Doesn't make any sense, does it?* "Can a Gold even steal enough magic to glamour an entire chamber of full-bloods?" A feat that, on a good day, would be a struggle for a seasoned Shade.

"Who the hell knows." Akari shrugs, pointing to another Hue on the list. "This says that a Sapphire can sense the presence of other Shades, so how did this one get himself caught in the first place? And this part claims that only an Emerald can cast a stable In-Between— the rest are supposed to be pretty terrible at it—which also doesn't fit with what you saw."

No, it doesn't. All three of them made it look easy, like the spell was an afterthought, not a strain.

"So basically, nothing about this is adding up?" I sigh, my nails raking deep trails along my scalp.

"Not even a little. But you do know what it means, right?" The enthusiasm in Akari's voice is at direct odds to the defeat in mine.

*It means I'm no closer to disproving my vision.*

*It means our guesswork has failed to set us on the right track.*

*It means I should really tell Akari the whole truth already.*

"That . . . the Academy's not as impenetrable as we all thought?" I say instead.

"Well, yes, that too." Akari snaps the book shut and leans hungrily across the table. "But it also means that there are three Hues in Sarotuza right now."

I instantly catch up to her meaning.

"Don't tell me you're getting ideas."

"Don't tell me you're not, Ray. This is like . . . the mother of all opportunities. A month away from guild selections and there are three prizes running around the city? Imagine how grateful the Council would be if we were to round them up? I bet they'd let us skip trials altogether. Hells, they'll probably even give us a reward."

It's a nice fantasy—and not unlike the one that drove me to chase after the Hues in the court chamber. A way to knock my future onto a brighter path.

*Or you could make things worse*, the more cautious part of me is screaming. *Play right into the future's hands.*

*Except that's not how it works.* I remind myself of the same truth I'm constantly telling others. You can't stop the future from happening by burying your head in the sand; you have to do something—*change* something—or else you're deliberately leaving your fate to chance, and I refuse to sit around and do nothing when there's even the slightest possibility that this Sapphire and I might wind up falling in love. I should not, cannot, and *will not* let that happen.

"Getting out of the castle won't be easy," I say, starting with the obvious obstacle to this plan. "The portals have been on lockdown since the escape and I doubt we're the only ones who'll think to ask for an exception." Because if Akari had this idea, then every other ambitious Shade in the Academy is likely having the same one, and the last thing the trackers are going to want is a bunch of acolytes interfering with their hunt. And even if none of that were true, we'd still need to come up with a good reason for why we should be allowed to leave the castle. Ever since the Divine Meridian started bleeding Shades, the portal keepers have been strictly controlling our comings and goings, and that leash has only grown tighter as his number of victims climbed into the double digits. For the same reason it *should* have been impossible for two Hues to get into the Academy, it's going to be impossible for us to get out.

"No . . . but we have something the rest of them don't," Akari says, waggling her brows.

"Which is?"

"Your *faaamousss* parents." She stretches the word like gum. "I'm sure they're just *dying* to congratulate their daughter for breaking through that glamour so fast, seeing what no one else did."

"Argh, I promise you they're not." The prospect is downright nauseating. The only kind of *seeing* my parents have ever wanted me to do is the kind that takes place in a tower. So while they may be glad to hear that I did something right for once, their interest in my triumph will dissipate the second they realize my power wasn't involved.

"I mean, I know that—and you know that—but the portal keeper doesn't." Akari's smug to the point of giddy. "If we say you've been summoned, he'll believe us."

Yes, he probably would. That's the upside to having powerful parents: you get away with bending the rules. The downside is that if I tell the portal keeper that I'm off to visit my parents, then I would actually have to go visit my parents, or else the lie would get back to them in the end. It always does.

"We'll be in and out, Ray," Akari promises, as if reading my mind. "You'll show your face, give them the highlights, then I'll step in, make some excuse, and we'll be on our way. Simple."

I guess it would be simple.

Unpleasant, maybe—depending on my parents' mood—but simple.

*And you could ask them about the* other *part of your vision.* A more pressing agenda suddenly takes root. I've been so consumed by the path that leads to a Hue, I'd all but forgotten about the one that leads to my death—to every Shades' death. If there's anyone who could shed light on that impossibility, it'll be the two most decorated Indigos the seers' guild has ever trained. That alone makes this a trip worth taking.

Once the decision is made, Akari and I don't linger. Our chances of beating the trackers to the Hues are slim to non-existent as it is, and they only grow slighter with each minute we delay, so we quickly pack away the books we've been studying and speed off to put this escape plan to the test.

"Erm . . . Ray . . . is there something you'd like to tell me?" We're almost to the portal hall when Akari spots the problem waiting for us outside the door, the Blue Shade tracing our approach with narrowed eyes.

Oh, fuck. Killen. Every part of me sinks, the memory of our fight searing through my veins like acid. I can still see the hurt I inflicted in the lines of his face, hear the echo of my words thunder between us. *I ended things because I didn't love you.* He didn't deserve to learn that truth quite so callously—or at all, if I'm honest; he was better off not knowing it. That way, he could keep laying the blame for our split at my feet.

"I don't know why he's here," I say, though I do have my suspicions. Killen always was good at seeing the big picture, and if there's anyone who would benefit from a reward for the Hues' capture, it's him. He probably spotted this opportunity long before we did. Which makes the real question: why is he loitering out here?

"Give us a minute, okay?" I tell Akari. Then I stride over to Killen and drag him out of earshot by the sleeve before he can betray my secrets.

"You haven't told her yet, have you?" He instantly puzzles out my intent. "About the open question?"

"No, I haven't—and would you please keep it down?" I hiss, shoving him back into an empty classroom.

"Sure, I'll keep it down." He shrugs as I pull the door shut behind us. "*If* you take me with you."

"Take you with us?" I gape at him. "You don't even know where we're going!"

"Oh please, we both know you're going after the Hues. By way of your parents, I'm guessing, since they're not letting acolytes out of the castle for anything else." The bitter edge to his voice suggests that he's already tried his own luck and failed, stuck around in the hopes that we'd fare better.

"You're right, we *are* going to see my parents—but that's it," I say, because what's one more lie when I'm about to spin another ten.

"Come on, Raya, you owe me." This time, Killen's words are less a taunt than they are a plea. "My spell's the whole reason you were able to see through the glamour so quickly, wasn't it? All I'm asking is for you to return the favor."

Which he wouldn't do unless he was truly desperate. Killen needs to chase this reward just as much as I need to impress the Council, and that's a reality that should sway me. It should blunt my irritation and erode the selfish urge to go after the Hues alone. But the truth is, I don't see how I could explain his presence to Akari, and the portal keeper is more likely to bend the rules for two Shades instead of three. Especially if he's already turned one of them away.

"It wasn't a favor, remember? You were handsomely paid." So I play the villain, and for the second time in the space of a few hours, I watch my words blow Killen's pupils wide open and rob him of breath. Hurting him really is the one thing I'm spectacularly good at. "Now, if you don't mind, we're *just* going to visit my parents. We'll barely be gone a couple of bells."

"Fine, be that way." His jaw hardens, the storm in his expression clouding over as if to say: *if that's how you want to play it, I can be vindictive, as well.* "But if you aren't back exactly when you're supposed to be, I'll be telling Professor Lyons everything I know. Akari, too, since you're too much of a coward to tell her yourself." The threat lingers long after he's shimmered out of the classroom.

Everything he knows is enough to get me expelled from the Academy.

It's enough to get my magic bound early and ensure that I'll never see the future again.

*So go fix it.* Instead of indulging the panic, I shake off the guilt and rid my face of the dread.

If Akari and I come back with three Hues in tow, nothing Killen can say will matter.

If we do the impossible, my magic will remain safe.

CHAPTER 9

# RAYA

When you spend your every waking hour in the Gray, you forget how beautiful the world looks in color. The shadows don't just dull the rainbow of its vibrance, they charge the air, change the texture of breathing. And while the absence of pure magic can blunt the edge of our gifts, there's a crispness to the physical realm that makes the two planes of existence hard to compare. The Gray is comfort, and power, and safety, whereas leaving the shadows feels like jumping into a kaleidoscope of vivid flowers, swimming in a lake of mottled ink.

The portal deposits us at the Academy interchange, an imposing junction house that's lavishly gilded and adorned. Where the typics have to mine their splendor, Yellow Shades can charm it into being, turn flint to marble and mica to gold, chalk to onyx and shingles to precious stones.

*If only they could charm away the iron.* The moment Akari and I leave the grounds, I begin to taste the metal in the air. A faint annoyance at first, like an irritating tickle, but the weight of it slowly builds in sharpness as we snake our way through the streets, growing increasingly suffocating in its might.

The Council's bane, we call it.

The one natural element that can sap our magic of strength.

In small quantities, the effects are more irksome than they are dangerous, but when it's laced into every roof tile, flagstone, and wall, it can kill a Shade dead. Spend too long around too much of it, and we don't just lose our ability to cast, we lose our ability to phase. Which is a problem since phasing into the Gray is the only way to replenish our magic once it's been stripped.

"Gods, the Church is getting brazen," Akari says as the swell of nausea reaches her, as well, the sick, unsettling feeling that starts in the blood and churns our stomachs raw. "They must really be encroaching on Council territory for it to hit this hard so quickly."

*Much quicker than it used to,* I can't help but think as we carve a path towards the color district, the sole place in Sarotuza where we can still go to escape the hate. In other cities, the divide between Council and Church runs far neater, a west versus east divide, for instance, or fully segregated rings. But Sarotuza is a stubborn mistress and the faithless here have been fighting the spread of religious reform tooth and nail. They won't give up their homes—or their access to magic—just because the clergy say so. They like the convenience a Shade can offer them, the way that spells, charms, and talismans do a better job at accomplishing a task both fast and well. Because why would they pore over tedious texts when that knowledge can be easily imparted by a Violet? Or spend months tending to their orchards when a Blue can accelerate them to fruition in days? A Green can cure their cancer instead of treat it, a Red can enhance their appearance with a glamour, and with a sprinkle of Orange, their houses will withstand a storm instead of flooding come the summer rains. They have no intention of forsaking those luxuries for the Gods, nor do they intend to let the Church drive all the charm houses into a single borough. The result is a city that's constantly threatening to erupt with violence. A hazard for both typic and Shade.

"So now that we're safely out of the castle, are we going to talk about what happened back there?" Akari asks in way of distraction, fixing me a pointed look.

"You mean with Killen?" I know damn well she means with Killen. And Akari knows I know it, too.

"Yes, Raya, I mean with Killen." She jabs an elbow to my side. "That boy has been a ghost for six months and now he's suddenly waiting for you outside the portal hall? That doesn't feel random."

That's because it wasn't.

"So . . . I may have . . . run into him this morning at the archives," I hedge, not yet sure how much of this story I'm ready to recount. "And we may have gotten into a fight."

"About . . ."

"The real reason we broke up."

"Oh, Ray, you didn't." Her face fills with a mix of disappointment and understanding, like she's both mad at me for doing it, but worried about me at the same time.

"I didn't mean to," I say, sheepish. "But he was pressing my buttons and it just sort of slipped out."

"So that's why you looked so upset in the court chamber," she mutters, filling in the rest of the blanks. "I'm guessing he took it badly?"

"Can you really blame him?"

"No, I suppose I can't. But maybe it's for the best." Akari rallies, turning her wince into a shrug. "Maybe now he'll finally stop hoping you'll forget about that vision, and move on."

"Maybe." I'm grateful that she leaves it at that. "Are *you* finally ready to move on?" I nudge the limelight in her direction, prodding at the Saleen-shaped wound she ripped open on my behalf.

"Yes. No. I don't know." Akari tenses, the admission escaping her in a nervous rush. "I thought I was, but then, last night, she was right there, and we were talking a little before you came in, and it almost felt like we were . . . us again. Like maybe this whole 'happy and over it' thing she's been doing is just an act. But then I went to try and talk to her after the trial and she was as cold as if last night never happened. She wouldn't even let me in the door, Ray, told me to go away because she was tired. So now, I don't know what to think anymore, except that there's something going on with her—has been for months. I just can't figure out *what*."

This time, the nausea in my gut tastes more like a guilty conscience than the iron lining the streets. I've known for a while how unhappy Akari has been since the break-up, especially as—unlike Killen—she never got a reason for why Saleen was calling it quits. Not even a fake one. They were simply together until, one day, Saleen decided they weren't. By way of a note, no less, a cowardly *I'm sorry but I can't do this.* And now I've not only gone and forced her right back into those helpless feelings, I went and asked that open question, as well, inflicted this hurt for nothing.

"Akari, I—" *Have to come clean. Right now.* "There's—"

"Hey, check this out." But Akari's attention has already drifted towards less painful ground, her brow furrowing as she considers the wealth of flyers that have been tacked, haphazardly, to the street-lamps. "These are new." She studies the worn scraps of paper. There are dozens of them, each scrawled with a name, an age, a date, and the word *missing* in increasingly large text.

"They're all children." The churn in my stomach turns to dread. "Seems an awful lot, don't you think? To have disappeared so close together?" Over the past few months, it looks like, though the flyers seem to have multiplied significantly in the past few weeks.

"Yeah," Akari says with a shudder. "It really is."

"Is it strange that we haven't heard about a problem this widespread?"

"It's strange that we haven't been *blamed* for it." Her voice hardens. Because—yes, that's exactly the type of lie the Church would tell, and if not them, then the Meridians. Ever since their "divine" leader rose to power, the pitch of the hate in Sarotuza has changed. The lies used to be simple: magic is a sin, we are a plague, the Gray is unnatural . . . the same tired rhetoric that's been regurgitated for hundreds of years. Whereas now, we have a false prophet telling a very different story and placing a price on our heads. Which the Church was fine with, at first, back when the Divine Meridian was little more than a disgruntled cleric. But the second he started threatening their power, the clergy took a firmer stance—and they're not above denigrating us as a means to unseat him.

The Meridian takes Shades so, in return, we take children? That's an accusation that would incite some pious rage. It's only a matter of time before the Church adopts it.

"Come on, let's just shimmer to the house." Akari takes my arm and blinks us into the Gray. "The sooner we get your parents out of the way, the sooner we can start tracking."

"Why don't you start now?" The shadows immediately relieve the burn of the iron, lending me the strength to say, "I can go on my own."

"Are you sure?" She has the grace not to look too excited. "Because I'll come if you need me, I know your parents can be a little—"

Dismissive? Judgemental? Cruel? Cold enough to make me question whether it's a daughter they wanted, or a continuation of the Wryvern name?

"I'll be fine, honest." Sometimes, it's actually easier to weather the chill alone.

"Well, in that case, maybe I'll sneak in a spot of trading before we track." Akari flashes me her teeth. "Come find me when you're done?"

"Yeah. But be careful, okay?" I add, not just because there's still a Shade-hunting zealot on the loose, but because, strictly speaking, she's not allowed to do that out here. At the Academy, our professors turn a blind eye to our extracurricular trading since spelling charms is a great way for us to hone our skills. But in the real world, the trade in magics is closely monitored, and the Council doesn't much like it when a Shade conspires to rob them of their cut.

"Don't worry, I promise to pick a nice, crowded, *faithless* dive." Akari winks. Then before I can remember that I broke my magic, she shimmers off in search of some willing typics to pitch.

*Damn it.* I curse at the air. I didn't think to ask *where* she'd be trading and she didn't think to tell me because she's so used to me relying on the future for such basic, easy-to-discern paths. By the time I'm done with my parents, Akari will have already chosen a tavern, which would have made tracking her there a pinch—even for a thoroughly inept Indigo. Unless, of course, that Indigo decided to become fate-touched.

*A problem for later.* Since there's no changing the past, I continue on towards the color district, hugging the shadows until I reach the gate to my parents' manor, where I can phase back into the physical realm without fear. There's no iron here, no Gods or typics. Just two decorated seers and a legacy I can't hope to succeed.

The path leading up to the house is a snake of flowers, with indigo roses, oleanders, and tulips artfully arranged to form a sea of eyes, in nod to the symbol that represents our color. And though the house itself is Sarotuza's usual mix of warm brick, arched windows, and terracotta tiles, it's bigger than most of the neighboring manors by quite some margin, with three domineering stories that sprawl proudly across the grounds, a stern tower reaching skyward at either end.

Seeing towers.

So that my parents can always consult the future at will.

"Miss Wryvern, are the guild masters expecting you?" Their seneschal—a surly Blue with graying hair and a dour frown—meets me at the door, her voice laced with a note of irritated surprise.

"Not exactly, no. Could you please fetch them for me?"

"They are currently entertaining a guest in your mother's study," she clips with a huff. "They are not to be disturbed."

"Then I'll wait outside until they're done." I sweep past before she can argue. And since I'm also a Wryvern, she technically works for me as much as she does them. She has no choice but to let me.

A flurry of muffled voices greets me as I scale the stairs to the tower, slowly growing louder in volume and clearer in pitch.

"How were they able to breach the castle?" My mother's questions have always been blunt, but they're a gentle touch compared to my father's manner.

"Are we interrogating the portal keepers?" he demands. "There must be a traitor in their midst."

"We are." It's Councilman Denata's voice that booms through the door in reply, freezing me in place. "And rest assured, any such sympathizers will be swiftly caught and dealt with. What I wish to know is how we didn't see this coming." By *we* he very clearly means *them*.

"The future isn't a book to be read, Lars," my mother reminds him. "Our seers seek answers based on the concerns brought to them by the other guilds, and the trackers had not made us aware of this possibility."

"Well, consider yourselves aware of it now," Denata barks, livid. "The brazenness with which those half breeds made a mockery of the court cannot be allowed to stand. Have your seers start searching futures immediately."

"Of course." My father's tone turns placating. "Though I'd be remiss not to warn you that half breeds can be difficult to divine— it's the diluted blood, we think—so this may take some time."

"Then you'd better get started, Bastian. I want those abominations rounded up fast."

"I'll go instruct the guild right now. Let me walk you out, Councilman."

A moment later, the door to the study swings open and both men depart the tower with urgent strides, so engrossed in their mutterings that they don't even notice me lurking in the antechamber.

"Mother?" I wait until they're gone before poking my head inside. Perhaps it's for the best that my father is otherwise preoccupied. He's not an easy man to talk to on a good day, and since the moment I *brought shame on this family* by failing my initial trials, they've all been pretty bad. I'll have more luck teasing the truths I need from my mother; I just have to be careful in how I go about phrasing my asks. If she finds out I fate-touched my magic, the only thing I'll be getting is kicked out.

"Raya? What a surprise." Her face puckers in question. "I was under the illusion that the public portals were still shut." The word *public* curdles like sour milk on her tongue. She and my father actually have their own private portals right here at the house, for when they need to conduct business in the castle. But I've never been allowed to use them; I haven't yet *earned* that privilege.

"Erm, yeah, they are, but they made an exception so that I could come and tell you in person what happened at the trial," I say, shuffling into the room proper. My mother keeps her study decorated in the customary Indigo style, with dark painted walls and a mountain of lavish cushions piled neatly atop the rug, only a small desk and two chairs in way of actual furniture. Sitting on the ground—or in a gloomy tower, for that matter—isn't actually a requisite for seeing the future, but the practice stems back to a time when the elders believed it was, a respectful nod to tradition.

"Oh, yes, Lars mentioned that you performed admirably during the crisis."

It's amazing how even the smallest hint of praise from her is like a warm cockle to the heart.

"If only you would apply yourself to your magic in the same way."

And how quickly her barbs can deflate me. We're barely even past the pleasantries, and already she's managed to express her disappointment at having me for a child, at getting stuck with a daughter who can't corral the future. Unlike other Shade pairings, she and my father didn't have to wonder which of their colors I'd inherit; since they're both Indigos, there was only ever one possible outcome for the color flowing through my blood. I, like every other Wryvern before me, was born to speak to the fates. Yet somehow, I wound up speaking a different language.

"I actually do have a question for you about my magic," I say, and it deflates me even more to see her ears perk and her interest spark. I've never had that much in common with my mother. She's dark of hair where mine's reddish, tanned where I'm pale and freckled, and pinched everywhere my features sweeten to a heart. In looks, I'm actually the spitting image of my father. In everything else, I'm the black sheep in a pen full of prize bucks.

*Just get this over with.*

"I wanted to ask if—? Can a—are there any circumstances in which an Indigo might see their own death?" I wince as the words finally sputter their way out, all too prepared for the force of the reaction they might receive.

"Good Gods, Raya, has the Academy truly taught you nothing?" My mother's voice instantly grows sharp. "An Indigo cannot see their own death. You've known that since you were five."

Yes, I have.

But then I asked an open question and the future showed me something it can't.

"So, there are no exceptions?" I ask. "Like . . . ever?"

"The future doesn't make exceptions." She dismisses the idea out of hand. "The future is simply the future."

It's an axiom Professor Lyons has fed us hundreds of times, another fundamental truth of seeing. Except the future does make exceptions, doesn't it? Or else why would some Shades lose the ability to cast altogether when others simply find themselves sidelined for a short while?

"Not even if an Indigo is fate-touched?" So I keep right on pressing, though I'm well aware that I'm flying dangerously close to the sun.

"Colors help me, are they still forcing you to learn that nonsense?" Luckily, my mother thinks I'm incompetent, not reckless, so it doesn't occur to her that I might have risked what little ability I had.

"No, I was just . . . doing some reading around constructions and that term kept cropping up."

"Then you should already know that our methods have evolved beyond such rudimentary forms of premonition," she clips.

"I know, but it used to be quite common, right? Indigos would choose to do it?"

"Some—yes, but it was a very different time. Back then, the guild wasn't responsible for helping the Council with the day-to-day minutiae. Their seers worked in much broader strokes and their efforts weren't as crucial to keeping us safe, so they could afford to risk some of their number. All of which is irrelevant, because being fate-touched changed the way those Shades saw, not the laws of seeing, and the future *cannot* predict its own end. The closest it could come is by predicting the end of the means by which we see it."

"The means by which we see it?" It takes me a minute to decipher the precise turn of her phrase. "Are you saying it could show us the death of all magic?"

"Oh, don't sound so surprised, Raya." She sighs as if the Academy truly has taught me nothing. "Our magics are subject to the whims of fortune just like everything else. They're not beyond fail."

"But I—" *I don't understand.* "Our colors live in the blood. If they were to fail, wouldn't that mean we'd—"

"Die," my mother confirms, as mundanely as she would the weather. "A Shade cannot exist without magic."

*Which is exactly what I saw.* A violent shiver races down my back.

The death of our magics.

A loophole in the fabric of fate.

"Has anyone ever . . . seen that before?" My voice roughens as it shakes.

"There has been one documented case, I believe." Where others would be perturbed by this macabre line of questioning, my mother merely looks pleased that I've finally taken an interest in my gift. "Around four hundred years ago. Though that future was promptly averted."

Right. Of course. Or else we wouldn't be here.

"So, you're not . . . worried about it happening again?"

"I do not busy myself with the futures I don't see, Raya—and neither should you." Her patience finally dissipates. "Our methods are better now, more detailed and precise. If there was something to see, we would have seen it."

Except they didn't see it—I did. Which makes the obvious question: why?

*Perhaps because they're no longer asking the right way?* I think back to Fernay's cryptic ramblings. What if the "event" he referenced was this near-death of magic? What if that's what prompted so many of the guild's number to endanger their relationship with the fates? Because it was the only way to glimpse the coming catastrophe? What if, in our search for a safer method of seeing, we've accidentally created a blind spot that's put us all at risk?

Or worse yet, what if I'm seeing the same unreliable nonsense as ever?

What if I asked the question wrong and misinterpreted the answer?

What if, as usual, I'm the problem?

*Akari will know what to do here.* The moment I escape my mother's tower, I resolve to tell her the truth—to actually get the words out.

*Where will I need to go?* Consulting the future is such a force of habit that for the third time since morning, I reach for my magic before I remember that it won't work.

*Son of a—oh.* The vision that assaults me lands as swiftly as a summer storm, as though the future has deigned to grant me a reprieve.

**The Golden Stag Tavern.** The sign is crystal clear in my mind, not abstract, as is the street it's on and the part of the city it's in. Not one of Akari's usual trading spots—and far beyond the safety of the color district—but at a shimmer, I can reach it by the next bell. And when I do, I'm going to confess to everything. Killen's spell, the open question, my deadly premonition . . . all of it, in the hopes that together, we can figure out if what I'm seeing in my head is likely to come true—and if there's a way to stop it.

# CHAPTER 10

# RAYA

One thing I've always admired about Akari is that she walks through life without fear. To the point that, sometimes, she walks right up to the line. But since she didn't grow up in a wealthy family like I did, I can't judge her for doing whatever it takes to survive. Akari trades her magic because she has to, because outside the Academy, life costs money, and because the world didn't leave her with much of a choice. And for the most part, she does it responsibly. She wouldn't sell a spell that wasn't legal, for instance, despite the inflated prices some of the more nefarious offerings can draw. The weakening tonics, the bone dissolvers, the property breakers and destructive blasts . . . there are plenty of forbidden Orange spells that Akari would never mess with—let alone entrust to a typic. And while she'll cast the occasional bespoke spell for enough silver, she mostly deals in pre-made talismans and charms, specific acts of magic encased in a crystal that her buyers can activate at will.

Need to do some heavy lifting? An endurance charm can keep you going all day. Want to stop a piece of furniture from collapsing? Use a support charm to help it stay stable and carry more weight. Simple, harmless bits of magic that are cheap enough for any well-to-do typic to buy—and more importantly, untraceable once they leave Akari's hand. She always brings a small stash with her when she visits the physical realm.

*Though she doesn't usually do her selling here . . .* The Golden Stag isn't just a seedy dump, it's a seedy dump on the very worst street a Shade can visit. Iron ore mixed into the flagstones, iron bars on the windows, iron spokes on either side of the door. I have to hug the shadows just to reach it, and even once I'm safely inside, the lingering taste of metal is oppressive. It's not quite as hostile as the Church-owned taverns that bar us from entering altogether—nor has the owner invested in iron furnishings or ferrite-rimmed mugs—but it is the kind to make it plenty clear that Shades are not welcome to drink here. The kind where—if I had my own stash of pre-spelled talismans—I'd be using a Red to glamour away the spiked rim in my eyes, maybe even add some flecks of gold to better blend in with the faithful. The gilded pigment they imbibe is apparent in almost every one of these patrons, a mark of piety they wear in addition to the muted palette of clothes, their way of signaling to the world their hate of blood color.

*What the hells was Akari thinking, coming here?* I keep my hood up and my head down as I weave through the restless crowd. This is the exact opposite of a nice, faithless dive—though it is packed to the rafters, rich with mirth and song and just the faintest hint of violence, like an ember that's about to ignite. A crime waiting to happen to a typic, never mind a Shade, and it's only once I reach the shadowy enclave at the back that I realize my mistake, the reason I've not been able to find Akari.

Unbelievable.

I curse as I spot the disheveled figure hunched over the table by the wall.

It's always easier to see why the question I asked was wrong than to ask the right one in the first place, and once again, I gave the future an excuse to steer me off course.

*Where will I need to go?*

Now that I've broken my magic, I shouldn't have assumed that my tried-and-tested tricks would work the same way they did before. I can no longer rely on the fates to behave in a predictable fashion. Instead of sending me to Akari, they sent me directly into the path of a condemned boy.

Unlike this morning, there's no question it's him—no blood, no bruises, no swelling to disguise the sharp cut of his cheekbones and the chiseled line of his jaw. No wince to his movements when he downs the liquid in his glass then motions to the barmaid to bring him a couple more. He's been healed since he escaped the Academy. Which either means that he was bold enough to solicit a Green himself, or brazen enough to send his Gold in search of one when every tracker in the city is out hunting Hues. Hardly a discreet choice to be making, in any case. I think I'm starting to see how he got himself caught.

*Then go catch him.* I will my feet forward. This is exactly what Akari and I came out here to do, and while I never truly believed we'd manage it—I knew from the moment Akari floated the idea that an afternoon trading was likely her actual goal—the fates have now conspired to bring the Hue within my reach.

*You can do this, Raya.* It's not the prospect of dooming him that has me hesitating, it's the passive nature of my gift. I'm not a fighter. I can't subdue him or compel him or even torture him like an Orange, a Red, or a Blue. The color running through my veins only allows me to see the future, and right at this moment, I can't see a single reason for why he'd let me drag him back to the court.

*Do it anyway.* I set my shoulders and steel my resolve. It doesn't matter that my stomach is clenched sick with the iron or that this Hue has several inches on me, a whole lot of lean muscle, and an entire tavern he could sway to his cause. He's already experienced the cost of resisting a tracker, and if he's here, drinking in plain sight—*alone*—then I'd venture he's still plenty shaken after his close encounter with the law. I don't need an active power to catch him, I just need to convince him that surrender is the painless way to go. That coming peacefully will make his inevitable end more bearable.

*He'll only believe it if you do.* I affect an air of confidence as I slip into the seat across from him, making ready to unleash the threat that'll persuade him to go. But before I can so much as get a word in—or make clear who I am or what I'm here for—he looks up from his glass to say, "You're not very discreet for a tracker," and put me straight on the back foot.

"Erm . . . well . . . you're not very clever for a Hue." I try not to sound as unnerved as I suddenly feel. It's one thing to think that I have him cornered, quite another to learn that he allowed that noose to tighten around his throat.

"Eh, with so many of you on the way, running seemed kind of pointless." He shrugs, leaning back in his chair. "Though maybe I would have if I'd realized they were sending in the rookie first."

"Who says I'm a rookie?"

"The robes you were wearing this morning." His tone sharpens to a knife. "I remember you from the gallery at my trial. You looked away right before the good part."

I hate that he noticed.

I hate that he remembered me.

I hate that he's somehow leading this conversation.

"Don't worry, I'm sure you'll do better next time. But if you don't mind, I'd like to finish my drink before we go."

"I'm sorry, you'd like to—? What?" His request stammers me silent.

"Finish my drink," the Hue says, slower this time, as though speaking to a child. "This place may not look like much, but the whiskey isn't bad."

"I still don't—" *I don't understand.* "You want to finish your drink and then you're going to . . . come with me? Just like that?"

"Would you prefer it if I didn't?"

"No, I—" Would prefer it if something about this conversation added up. "Okay, well then . . . fine—but make it quick," I tell him, trying to take back control. Inexplicable or not, his refusal to fight does simplify things for me, even if it is making me wonder when the other shoe will drop.

"Don't worry, the Gray will survive my existence until the cavalry gets here," he mutters, swirling the amber liquid around his glass. "Gods, you Shades are all the same, aren't you? So fucking married to your lie you can't even imagine the truth anymore. Maybe we should have just let it all end last year." He downs the rest of his whiskey in one. "Maybe the shadows deserve to die."

The words turn my blood cold.

I see a vision about the shadows dying and less than a day later, the condemned Hue from that very vision is muttering about the death of the Gray? That can't be a coincidence. And neither can the fact that he keeps implying that there are more of me on the way.

*Oh . . . shit.* I could slap myself for not catching it before. This Hue is a Sapphire; his gift allows him to sense the presence of other Shades—I remember that much from the list Akari and I were studying. That must be how he knew I was coming, and how he saw the Council's actual contingent of trackers on the hunt for his head, assumed we were all part of the same unit.

Except I'm not part of the same unit, and the moment they arrive, I'm going to lose my chance to question him further.

*Unless you both escape before they get here.* The voice in my mind is growing downright obscene. Because helping him escape is a ludicrous idea, isn't it? It goes against everything I've been taught to believe. He's a Hue, a half breed, an unnatural perversion of good magic, and his capture—his *death*—is exactly what's supposed to happen.

It's the law.

And that law was designed to ensure the safety of every other Shade.

But my vision could also affect the safety of every other Shade, and if nothing else, I need to understand how all these disparate pieces are connected, uncover the bigger picture the future wants me to prevent.

*You'll get him out, learn what he knows, then hand him in.* Crazy as that might sound, I can't see another answer—at least not without confessing to the open question that led me here, which would destroy my credibility, what little is left of my reputation, and any chance I have of passing my trials. The second the trackers hear that truth, they'll dismiss the darkness I saw as nonsense, just a silly girl misinterpreting a power she doesn't understand. In order to fix the mess I'm in, I need to offer them something concrete. I need to prove that I can still control the magic in my blood. Do something useful with it for a change.

*A little help would be nice.* I close my eyes and reach for that magic now, begging the future—no, commanding it—to quit holding its grudge. If it does, in fact, have a reason for sending me to the Hue, then it should see the value in helping me spring him from the tavern. And if it doesn't, well . . . that would be an answer, too.

*How will I get him out of here?* My hands fist at my sides. *Show me, damn it—show me how I'll get him out!*

The future's reply comes so fast and solid, it almost knocks me off my seat, an entirely different type of vision to any I've ever experienced. It's like watching a play act out scene by scene and action by action, complete with a script, stage directions, and the show master whispering instructions in my mind.

**Say it.**

"If you still care about your friends, you'll do exactly as I tell you." I spring to my feet and deliver my first line, just as the vision bid me.

"I don't know what you're talking about." The Hue's head immediately snaps up, the self-pity in his voice hardening. "I'm here alone." He's either a terrible liar, or too drunk to sell the part.

"So, if I were to tell the trackers that there's also a Bronze and a Gold in Sarotuza, that wouldn't bother you?" I ask, continuing down the script. "If I were to point them to Isitar, you wouldn't want to warn Novi or Lyria?"

Whoever those girls are, they're clearly important, because all at once, there's fear in the Hue's eyes, real and potent.

"There is no *them*, understand?" He rises to meet me glare for glare. "You want me, you can have me. But *just* me."

The future sure did call this one right; he doesn't care about his life half as much as he does theirs.

"I'm not interested in your friends," I say, stealing a glance at the door. "But if you don't follow me right now, the trackers will get you, and then they'll get them. So, are you coming or not?"

"Lead the way." His surrender is clear and quiet. And though he only resisted me for a few seconds, the converging threat of trackers must have used that time well.

*Crap, that's them.* A chorus of angry jeers ripples through the crowd, yells of "get out" and "your kind isn't welcome here" filling the tavern.

"Hood up and get behind me," I bark, quickly lifting my own. Then when the Hue plants himself a whole universe too far away, I grab hold of his arm and add, "Closer. We're going to have to move as one." The sudden sense of him is an unnerving weight at my back, the warmth of his skin a searing branding iron. It feels wrong to be standing so close to a Hue—to be touching him, helping him. To be the reason he'll get to keep breathing.

**Take five steps into the main room.** The future's next instruction is as detailed as the last. Fernay's book did say that being fate-touched would allow for a wider range of visions, but I never dreamed that the fates would suddenly provide me with such specific, real-time aid, especially with my magic behaving so erratically. And while every fiber of my being is begging me to move in the opposite direction—*away* from the trackers instead of *towards* them—the certainty of the vision isn't up for debate. For the first time in my life, I don't doubt that I'm interpreting it correctly.

"This way," I whisper, heeding the command.

"Are you insane?" The Hue, on the other hand, is lacking that faith in fate. "They'll see us!"

"Not if you do as you're told—now, duck." I pull him down beneath the nearest table a split second before a group of trackers sweeps past, their cloaks rippling with an invisible wind.

"Search every corner of the building. No one leaves until we find it." The leader—a Red, as announced by the ruby sickle pinned to his lapel—sends his team fanning out in all directions, despite the mounting levels of hate, the cacophony of wishful threats that only stop a lick short of actual violence. Trackers aren't allowed to unleash their magic on the typics unprovoked, nor are they allowed to damage their property or hurt their livelihoods. In return, the typics have to let them complete their work, which they do because it benefits both sides. But that doesn't mean they have to like it, and there's no law against them voicing their disgust.

*Hold your position.*

As two Blues and a Yellow stride towards us, I put a hand to the Hue's shoulder, urgently mouthing the words: *stay still.*

"But they're coming this way!" he argues, wild with the need to run. Seems his sense of self-preservation has finally kicked in.

"I don't care—we don't move until I say so."

Until the *future* says so.

*And that'll be any minute now . . .* Sweat beads at my temples, my own faith in this escape plan beginning to crack. This brand of divination is as new to me as it is untested, so who's to say how long I can actually sustain it, or how much help the future is willing to provide?

*Don't you dare abandon us now, damn it. Show me the next step.* Those trackers are still headed straight in our direction and in a matter of seconds, there will no longer be a way out. Not for him or for me.

"I really think you should reconsider that deci—" A frenzied yell swallows the rest of the Hue's protest, belonging to one of the more intoxicated typics, who barrels into the trackers and tackles them to the grimy floor.

**Under the table to the right.** The future seizes the opportunity and so do I, bidding the Hue to stay low as we scramble out of their path.

"They're going to tear them apart." It's hard to know if he means the typics or the Shades, but right at this moment, I can't spare the time to look, not while the next set of instructions is flashing behind my eyes.

"Up—now." I jerk us forward, taking three long strides towards the bar then a sideward lunge to hug the wall, where we stay for a nerve-wracking beat—long enough for the remaining trackers to storm past in their rush to assist their friends—before bending low to avoid the business end of an Orange spell. Between the yelling, and the fighting, and the magic now shooting through the air, there's no way to predict where the trackers will turn their attention next—it's only the future's ability to see what we can't that guides us through the cracks in their periphery, choreographing an elusive dance that beggars belief. After it helps us narrowly avoid capture for the seventh time, even the Hue quits muttering curses under his breath. He's now following me through the tavern without question.

Truth be told, when push comes to shove, it's my hesitation that sinks us, my unwillingness to blindly obey the whims of fate. We're almost to the door when they show me one final maneuver, of the Hue and I pressed together, glued in a sickening, lip-locked embrace.

They want me to kiss him.

Right here in front of everyone so that the trackers will dismiss us as two idiot kids with no restraint. And though I feel no want in the action—no lust or attraction—the thought of touching him like that still freezes me in place. If the future thinks I'm destined to fall in love with this Hue, then the very last thing I should be doing is kissing him, for any reason, good, bad, essential, or else. I will not encourage this atrocious idea.

*Show me a different way!* Even as I push back against the vision, I fear in my gut that it won't work, that I was too slow making a decision and now the window for our escape has closed.

"You there—*stop*."

I hear the exact moment the trackers spot their Sapphire, taste the power in the Red command that compels the two of us stock still. My body seizes up from under me, every bone, muscle, and tendon stiffening like rock. By virtue of my proximity to the Hue, I've been marked as an accomplice, and the moment the trackers catch sight of my face—of my eyes—they're going to ask a wealth of questions for which I'll have no response.

*Shit. Shit. Shit.* As much as I could probably talk my way out of trouble, the Hue could easily talk me back into it, and while my word should hold more weight than his does, his truths would still raise too many eyebrows for me to leave this tavern unscathed. The trackers will want to know what I'm doing here, for one thing, why I took it upon myself to interfere in a sanctioned manhunt and almost cost them their prey. And while Killen's acceleration is already gnawing at the edge of the compulsion, there'd be nowhere for me to run even if I were to break free of the spell. For every tracker in the tavern, there'll be three more waiting in the Gray. Phasing isn't an option.

*Please, I'm sorry for not listening, but you have to help us*, I beg the future, though with a dozen trackers circling, I'm not sure what—if anything—I expect it to say.

*Certainly not that.* The phrase it whispers in reply makes absolutely no sense. Not to me, at least, but apparently it will to my Sapphire friend.

**Tell him.**

That instruction is much easier said than done while I'm still immobilized by this Red.

*Then get un-immobilized.* I grit my teeth and focus my energy on fighting the spell, throwing every ounce of strength I have into cracking the magic. *Come on, come on, come on.* I think of shattered glass, brittle wood, broken shells and fragile cobwebs, ignoring how, behind me, the air ripples with the trackers' closing steps. *This compulsion is weak, unstable, it cannot silence me or control what I do.* And right now, I don't need to do all that much, anyway, just turn my head, inch by inch, until I'm able to catch the Hue's eye and repeat the futility the future wants me to say, to watch his pupils blow wide when he hears it.

"We'll die like the stars."

The words ring loud between us, insistent and unexplained.

And then the world explodes.

# CHAPTER 11

# EZZO

I wasn't trying to get myself caught again. I mean, I knew it was a possibility when I stormed away from Cemmy and Chase, but it wasn't actually my intent. The only thing I wanted in that moment was to find a tavern where I could drown myself in a bottle of sharp mistakes—and I *was* careful about it. More careful than I've been all year.

I picked a place in a street lined with iron, since the metal only bothers me when it's used as a shackle, and because it reduced the likelihood of stumbling across another Shade. I found a dark corner to disappear into, so that no one would pay attention to my misery or my face. And every so often—when I was sure I wasn't being watched—I blinked into the Gray for a heartbeat to search the shadows for trails.

The coast was clear the first time I checked it.

And the second time.

And the third.

But with every drink, my head was growing fuzzier, and when I finally remembered to check it for a fourth time, it was already too late. I counted at least twenty trackers converging on me from all directions, a single Indigo sent ahead to keep me distracted and trapped in place. The girl from the court chamber with the hazel eyes and the weak stomach. An odd choice, I'll admit, but with so many others shimmering through the Gray towards me, I didn't see a way out, no matter what kind of scouting party they sent.

What I didn't expect was for the Indigo to try and escape the Golden Stag with me.

Or to say the one thing I never thought I'd hear again.

"We'll die like the stars."

The words are a spear to the heart, a ghost whispering from beyond the grave.

It was my mother who first taught me that phrase, the same day she taught me all the fanciful ways a Hue might meet their maker—shattered by the Gray, executed by the Council, put to death by the Church. Such are the options when your very existence is illegal, on both sides of the magical divide.

But my mother was an Indigo and when I was six years old, she told me that she'd seen my future and that wasn't to be my fate. *You and me, we're going to die like the stars*, she'd said. At the end of a long life, in a blaze of glory that would streak across the heavens, beautiful and proud.

And nonsense, of course.

My mother didn't die like the stars, she died like a rogue Shade, not in a blaze of glory but in a pool of blood, hunted down like a dog for the crime of loving a typic and having his child. And Gods, I was so mad at her for that—for allowing me to hope for better.

*We deserve to hope for better.* It was only once Eve came into my life that I was able to take those words and shape them into something new. She'd lost her family, too; her father, her mother, all three of her siblings, her whole family butchered when she was only ten. She barely even spoke when I first found her. She didn't smile for months. Didn't trust for years.

But together, we found a way to heal.

And to love.

And while the horrors of our past were never truly gone, we chose not to let them dictate our future.

Eve became my future, and *we'll die like the stars* became the words we'd whisper to each other when we were afraid, a fragile promise we never shared with the others. It was ours alone. Private.

Or at least it was until this Shade said them.

How she broke through the compulsion to do that, I don't know, but she did, and coming from her, the words felt more like a warning, not unlike the one currently emanating from my scry.

*Get ready to run.*

Cemmy never did learn when to take no for an answer, and if her Gold has a specialty, it's using the magic he steals to get his way, so I shouldn't be surprised that once again, those two have chosen to meddle.

*Meddling is the future's way of showing you something,* Mom used to tell me, back before she slipped into the past tense. *When you feel its hand guiding you, listen to what it's trying to say.*

It doesn't take an Indigo to decipher what Cemmy is trying to say. But with the Red's compulsion still spelling every part of me frozen, I can't send a message back to describe the full extent of my predicament, or alert her to just how many trackers she and Chase will be facing if they do come bursting in unprepared, how they'll only be condemning themselves to the same prison. All I can do is rail against the magic keeping me helpless, try to break free of its clutches before the three of us wind up dead.

Too late.

With a crash and a hail of debris, the wall to the tavern bursts apart, showering the Golden Stag's occupants in a biting rain.

*Go, now.*

Thanks to the sharp shards of iron the explosion unleashed, the Red's oppressive hold on me has fractured, releasing my body from its magical cage. And though I know I should listen to the urgency beating against my chest—the voice screaming that my best chance is to go, now, without sparing a thought for the Indigo girl who threw Eve's promise at me like a threat—I can't shake the feeling that she'd said those words for a reason.

*We'll die like the stars.*

It was the future who told her to say them—of that, I'm certain; I recognized the state of vision she kept falling into while trying to orchestrate our escape. Which makes the real question: why was she trying to help me escape in the first place? Why is the girl from my execution suddenly working to change my fate? What could an Indigo possibly want with a Hue so badly she'd risk acting against her own Council?

*Some truly excellent questions for later.* I snap-make the decision. Or hells, maybe the drink does it for me, but I turn back and pull her out from beneath the wreckage.

"You can stay with them or come with me." I offer her a hand and a choice. "It's up to you."

And for a split second, she hesitates, a mix of shock and suspicion warring in her eyes. She's looking for the catch, the lie, the hidden agenda, as if stunned to discover that she's suddenly the one in need of help instead of the one lending it—and that a Hue is willing to help a Shade at all. But for whatever reason, she seems as eager to avoid the trackers as I am, and that makes us briefly aligned.

"Let's go." The second she takes my hand, we're running. Past the mess of startled typics and upturned tables, out through the hole Chase rent in the tavern, and away from the symphony of dazed surprise and outraged yells. With a whole armada of Shades on our tail, phasing into the Gray isn't an option, so we're forced to run through the streets instead, following the clipped instructions Cemmy's sending down my scry.

*Take a left then two rights; there's a market you can use for cover.* And enough iron on the way to get us there unseen—if the Indigo can get that far. Which is a problem I failed to consider when I lost my mind to this whim. The second we emerge into the maze of metal, she doubles over, as though hooked around the waist by an invisible snare.

"We can't avoid the iron until we lose the Shades, so you need to suck it up," I say, dragging her forward.

"It's not that easy, half breed." She spits venom between shallow breaths. "That stuff is poison."

"Well, then you're free to phase away whenever you'd like; I can't exactly stop you." Nor would I mourn her loss or try to convince her to stay. If she wants to put an end to this reckless alliance, then quite frankly, that's a win for me. I won't have to deal with the fallout.

"Where are you taking us, anyway?" the Indigo asks, biting back the pain.

"Somewhere there's a lot of people," I say, since from the shadows, the trackers can't see us so much as they can see our echoes, ghostly flickers that are indistinguishable from one another in the Gray. Two echoes fleeing a tavern together are a pinch to follow; they're a pair of fireflies leaving behind them a glowing trail. But once we mix in with a crowd, the task will grow much harder; the trackers will have no choice but to blink back into the physical realm and search us out in the flesh—which I very much doubt they're going to do in a market this laden with hate.

*Shit, it's a Church market.* Cemmy chose our escape route well. Not only is the entry arch cast from iron, but thick spikes of the metal line the narrow walkways and sit between wares. There are ferrite amulets on the tables, iron charms hanging from the awnings and strung around the merchants' necks, enough that the second I force her into their midst, the Indigo groans and loses her feet—and her stomach.

"We just have to get to the other end," I say, tightening my grip on her hand. While it does seem cruel to subject her to such agony, turning back now would mean the end of us, and I won't force her to stop running when she can call uncle on the suffering at any stage. She's *choosing* not to phase away from the pain. And as long as she retains that ability, that decision should be hers to make.

We weave through the stands as fast as the color in her veins allows, praying that the typics won't notice the blood that's started crying down her face. Back when Mom was still alive, we didn't live in such a hateful city, so I never saw the damage iron could inflict on a Shade first-hand. Not to this extent, anyhow—nor would I ever expect any Shade to let it get this bad. Yet here she is, still stumbling after me.

*What the hells are you running from that you'd rather endure this?* Just this morning, this girl was wearing Academy robes and attending executions with her classmates, so unless she suddenly decided to turn rogue in the last eight hours, she has no reason to fear the Council, nothing to be gained by helping me evade their clutches or fleeing them herself. Then again, if she wasn't part of the hunting effort, then she had no reason to be in that tavern, either. Absolutely nothing about this Indigo makes sense.

"What in the name of all three Gods, Ez?"

Though I guess you could say that about me, as well.

"You were supposed to lose the trackers, not bring one with you!" The second we reach the alley where the others are waiting, both Cemmy and Chase erupt with rage.

"She's not a tracker," I'm quick to say—at the exact same moment the Indigo mutters, "I'm not a tracker."

"But she is from the Academy." Chase recognizes her every bit as fast as I did. "She's the one who broke through the glamour and ran after us."

*She is?* That piece of information doesn't quite seem to fit. "I thought you said you took care of that Shade?" Though it would explain how she knew that I escaped with a Gold and a Bronze. Just not . . . anything else.

"I did take care of it." Chase prickles. "I compelled her to keep her mouth shut."

Yeah, well, the trackers compelled her to stay put, and that also didn't stick.

"You shouldn't be compelling anyone," the Indigo snaps, as if to remind us that she can hear. "Stealing magic is illegal."

"Everything we do is illegal." Chase bites in reply. Then to me he says, "You better have a damn good reason for this."

Reason, yes. Good one . . . not exactly. Because how am I supposed to admit that I put their lives at risk over a few words that reminded me of Eve, or that I have no idea why those words possessed me to bring the Indigo along, other than they just did, that leaving her there felt like the wrong decision. *I don't know* isn't going to cut it as an answer here, so instead of offering them a good reason, I settle for a viable excuse.

"She's an Indigo and her power might come in useful," I say, lacing the lie with conviction.

Because when you're on the run, the future makes for a good ally.

# CHAPTER 12

# RAYA

For the longest time, I didn't see the point in seeing the future. Sure, my parents were renowned for it—built their wealth on it, even, and their reputations—but to me, the rules had always felt too rigid, the questions too particular, and I couldn't understand why anyone would want to spend their days searching out answers that might still change.

*The change is the point, Raya,* my mother had said, every time until I stopped asking. *If you can't change the future, then there's no point in being able to see it, and there's no point in being able to see it if you don't mean to enact change.* It took me years to get my head around that idea, to accept that the choice to see is in itself a change to the paths we tread. It's destiny and free will all at once, a snake that's eating its own tail— and it can steer you in any which direction. Towards the right path, yes, but sometimes, towards the wrong one, as well.

*So incredibly wrong.* My mouth tastes of copper and the rest of me feels like lead, my head throbbing as though it's been struck by lightning. Pieces of the day assault me in broken fragments: my open question, the fight with Killen, an execution stayed with stolen magic and a vision that led to a Hue and an iron hell.

*But at least the nausea's gone . . .* I don't remember exactly when I lost consciousness, but I'm fairly certain that I was still out in the street, in the physical realm, in the company of three illegal half breeds who were brazenly discussing my fate. My potential usefulness. Whereas now, the world has dulled to a colorless haze, a caress of shadows swirling gentle circles around me.

The Gray.

I'm back in the Gray.

Where my power can replenish and the pain will eventually abate.

*But where in the Gray?* My relief is brittle and short-lived. Because the room I'm in is entirely unfamiliar, and when I try to move, a shooting pain in my wrist keeps me firmly anchored in place.

*Oh, crap—and this cuff's iron.* I force in a breath to quell the panic. In the shadows, the metal won't sicken me or sap my strength, but as long as it's encircling skin, it will keep me tethered here, both to the Gray and to the pipe it's attached to. A pipe in an abandoned house, by the looks of things, so run-down that even the shadows can't disguise the wealth of grime and decay. Soot-burned brick, moldy plaster, a termite-bitten floor, derelict to the point of condemned.

*And yet this pipe is rock solid.* No matter how hard I try to wrench it off the wall, the cracks in the mortar won't give, even despite their crumbling texture.

"It's been reinforced with magic," a voice says from the doorway. His voice—the Hue; I recognize the deep tenor and the bitter edge, though it's no longer laced with the fuzzy slur of drink. He's sobered up since we escaped the tavern, which means that I've been out cold for an hour or two, at least. Maybe longer. Since all the windows in this room are boarded up, it's impossible to tell.

"You do realize this won't hold me forever," I bluff, staring daggers as he folds down to sit opposite me, legs crossed with his elbows resting on his knees. An Orange could spell this cuff open with a snap of their fingers, a Yellow could turn the pipe to spaghetti, while a Blue could cause it to rust so fast it simply withered away. For a Shade with an active power, this tedious ring of metal barely presents a challenge, let alone a threat. And this Sapphire doesn't know I'm a—

"You're an Indigo." He meets my lie with the truth and a pointed glare. "Your power is passive. It can't affect the cuff."

Damn it. My stomach gives a painful lurch. He knows what I am. That he's got me well and truly trapped here.

"Did you figure that out with your gift?" I ask, refusing to betray fear.

"I didn't need to use my gift." He shrugs dismissively. "I know what talking to the future looks like."

Right, of course, because he's a Sapphire and Sapphires are a dilution of Indigo magic. One of this Hue's parents was a seer.

"So then, you know that it's an imprecise art," I say, trying to minimize my appeal. "Keeping me here won't help you. *I* won't help you."

"Then why did you help me before?" he asks, straight in with the one question that requires an answer too damning to admit.

"I wasn't helping you; I was helping me." Though it does present an opportunity to twist this conversation to my benefit, get a few answers from him.

"By betraying your own trackers?"

"No—" That was merely a side effect of this idiocy, not the aim. "By getting to the bottom of a future they can't predict."

"Which is?"

"The death of the Gray," I say the words calmly, clearly, studying his expression to see how bluntly they hit.

"Then I'm sorry to be the bearer, but you're a little late to the party." The Sapphire doesn't even flinch. "We dealt with the threat to the Gray over a year ago—no thanks to you Shades. Where were you when the shadows were being drained of their power, huh?" There's suddenly a crack to his voice that's widening with pain. "Where were the trackers when we actually needed them? Where was the Council or the seers' guild? Why didn't you step in to prevent that future then?"

*Because I wasn't there.*

*Because I hadn't seen it yet.*

*Because I don't have the faintest clue what you're raving on about.*

"You're wrong." I fight the urge to call him a few other things, as well. "The threat to the Gray isn't gone—I only saw it this morning."

"Well, then you're clearly not a great seer, because unlike you, I was there when we stopped the Amber, and I know for a fact that she doesn't need stopping again."

It takes everything I have not to reel as though he'd slapped me, not to let on just how close to home his insult landed—regardless of how offhandedly it was said. As to what another Hue has to do with anything, I have no idea, but at least he's starting to offer up some solid details.

"I also saw my own death," I tell him, testing to see how far his knowledge of my power extends.

"Yeah, that's not possible," he mutters, climbing back to his feet. "That's the one thing an Indigo can't see."

Good, so he is familiar with the basics, maybe now I can push the advantage my way.

"I used to think that, too, but it turns out there's a loophole to that rule and the future *can* show us our deaths—just as long as they're caused by the death of all magic. That's why you have to let me go, so that I can stop it," I say, rattling my cuff. "Please, I promise I won't tell anyone where you are. If I was going to turn you in, I would have done it back at the Golden Stag."

For a long moment, the Hue remains silent, his head cocking to the side as he considers me with interest, his eyes narrowed but his attention piqued.

*I'm not dangerous.* I make a nervous show of biting my lip and wringing my fingers, of hunching my shoulders to appear as small and unassuming as I can get. He may not have told me much about this . . . *threat* he claims to have averted, but in the space of a few minutes, he's told me enough that I could do the rest of the legwork myself, figure out if I'm dealing with the same thing. I no longer need to keep him from the trackers, and by now, the shadows have replenished my color enough that, if he did remove the cuff, I could shimmer out of here before he could even think to give chase. Hells, I could probably catch him off-guard and shimmer him along with me, end this disastrous hunt by delivering the Council its Sapphire. All I need is for him to fall for the pretense and undo the—

"Why did you say 'we'll die like the stars'," he asks instead, snapping me out of the fantasy.

"Erm . . ." My first instinct is to lie, though not for any reason other than I don't want to give this Hue more truths than he's already learned. But of all the questions he could have asked me, this one seems like the most innocuous. He already knows that I'm an Indigo, so what difference would answering it really make?

"Because the future told me to," I say, like it isn't ridiculous. "Why? What does it mean?"

"That's none of your business." The Hue instantly frosts over, his face darkening with a deep contempt. Far too strong a reaction to such a nothing answer, if you ask me, to the point that the tension in his jaw doesn't just speak of irk, it screams of anger, as though I've gone and robbed him of something precious. As though he was desperately hoping for me to say something else.

"You were right—this was a mistake." He turns to tell the faceless shadow hovering outside the door, "She's all yours, do with her what you will."

My whole body tenses at his sudden change in demeanor, shrinking back against the wall as his golden friend comes striding in. Where the Sapphire is striking in a quiet, understated way, the Gold can only be described as ostentatious. Blond, tanned, obnoxiously pretty, with brushed silver eyes and features that look as though they're carved from marble.

"They're going to come for me, you know," I say as he stalks towards me, my wrist fighting the iron shackle anew. "Your compulsion didn't work; I was able to tell them everything—about you and the Bronze. They're going to come."

"I hope they do." His voice is sharper than the Sapphire's. Colder. Dangerous in pitch. "See, us *half breeds*, we're not like you full-bloods; we don't just kill everything we're scared of."

*That is not what we do,* I want to yell at him, to correct this absurd assertion that the Council's law stems from fear. We purge the world of Hues because of the threat they pose to the Gray; that's it, that's all there is to it. And yes, that's distasteful, and violent, and I imagine— to their eyes—entirely unfair. But such is the cost of keeping the shadows safe from ruin and I'll be damned if I let this Hue shame us for prioritizing the greater good over a few biological mistakes. Though as the Gold drops into a languid crouch before me, all that actually escapes my mouth is an absurd assertion of my own.

"I'm not afraid of you."

"That's funny—" He leans in closer. Close enough for me to feel the malice radiating off each syllable. "Because you look quite afraid to me."

*She's all yours, do with her what you will.*

There's only one thing a Gold could want from an Indigo, and it's the very last thing I'd ever want to give.

"Please—there's no point in taking my magic, I swear; it won't work for you—it doesn't even work for me!" I scramble to catch the Sapphire's eye, to implore him to call off his power-hungry friend and show some mercy.

For all the good it does me.

What little warmth he'd exhibited before is gone now, and I may as well be speaking a different language given how absolutely he ignores my plea, how he simply stands there, frozen, and drops his eyes to his feet.

*Who's the coward now?* My vindictive triumph is a fleeting, feeble thing. Because I can't force him to watch the crime he's permitting, and shackled as I am to the pipe, there's nothing I can do to stop the Gold from wrapping his hands around the exposed skin at my wrists, no amount of struggle that would sway his mind or break his grip.

"This'll hurt less if you hold still," he tells me, reaching for his gift.

"No, please, don't do this—you don't have to do this, *please*."

But he does do it.

And the second his magic hooks its talons into mine, my protest turns into a scream.

It's in that moment—as the pain consumes me—that I realize my vision was nothing but a vicious lie, a cruel misdirect, a cosmic trick. Because there's no way I could ever fall in love with anyone who would condone such brutality.

I will never forgive the Sapphire for this.

# CHAPTER 13

# EZZO

I thought I had the stomach to watch. I thought I wanted to see Chase strip the Indigo of her superiority. I thought I wanted her punished for weaponizing Eve's words.

*The future told me to.* She'd said it so simply—so flippantly—that it downright filled me with rage. Because how dare she turn that phrase against me? How dare the future use my most private memory as a bargaining chip to be traded and played? Handing her to Chase felt like justice in that moment, and I wanted to stay while it was carried out as a way to even the scales, pay her back for my execution.

But though I've known, for a while now, the true violence of a Gold's gift, I've only ever learned of its effects in the abstract, never been close enough to witness them for myself, hear what that pain sounds like.

*It sounds like a mistake.* The Indigo's screams are a tempest, piercing and wrong.

The look on her face is worse.

Her cheeks are wet, her eyes bloodshot, her skin as pallid as a drift of snow, every delicate feature twisted into a pleading mask of anguish.

*We were always going to need her magic.* I try to rationalize the guilt away. Since the trackers know they're hunting a palette of three Hues, her ability to see the future could mean the difference between capture and escape. This isn't about Eve, it's about survival. Necessity not retribution.

*You keep telling yourself that.* Just because something's true doesn't make it right—or easier to bear.

"Come on—it's better if you leave him to it." With a gentle hand, Cemmy leads me into the corridor, pulling the door shut behind us as a means of muffling the sound of pain.

But there is no muffling sound in the Gray; the shadows carry it like a feather on the wind.

"Is that how you stomach it?" I ask. "You just leave him to it?"

"We do what we have to, Ez. That's always been true."

Maybe. But it sure grew more violent when Chase entered the fray. And there's always a reason to ask him to steal us more magic; we always need another advantage to help outrun our parents' sins. Today, the Indigo just happens to be paying the price for them.

Gods, *the Indigo,* it suddenly occurs to me that I didn't even ask her name.

*Good luck getting it now.* I flinch as, beyond the wall, her torment rises in pitch. The extraction won't kill her—unlike Hues, full-bloods have enough magic to survive the drain, and so long as Chase doesn't take too much, her power will regenerate—but right at this moment, she's probably wishing for death. Or at least, she's probably wishing that we'd never met, or that she'd handed me over to the trackers while she still had the chance.

*I wasn't helping you; I was helping me. Getting to the bottom of a future they can't predict.*

I didn't get the sense that she was lying when she said that, but it does raise the question of: why does an acolyte believe that she saw something no one else did? That no one else *could?* I mean, if the future truly has seen its own end—if it wants to prevent it—then why would it send that vision to one girl instead of an entire guild?

*That's her problem, not yours.* I shake the sea of whys from my head. The only thing I need to do is help the others flee Sarotuza so that we can go our separate ways, live to see another city.

An eternity seems to pass before the Indigo's screams begin to abate, the torture stretching endlessly, until at long last, Chase emerges, looking not one bit ashamed. He's spent his whole life learning to live with the cost of his power; he's beyond feeling pity for a crying Shade.

*You should be beyond it, too.* I swallow down the bile and will the nausea to go away. The last Shade I was forced to work with was a monster, and this one was all too happy to corral me with threats. They're the bad guys. Always have been. So why should we feel guilty for surviving in whatever way we can? The trackers hunt, we evade them, they catch us, we die an agonizing death in a cell—or in a court chamber—and no matter how small we make ourselves, how quiet, the Council's soldiers still come knocking in the end. They keep pushing metal to its breaking point then acting all surprised when it breaks.

"I don't suppose you have any tips for using her magic properly?" Chase asks, drawing me out of my malaise.

"Tips? Why?" I blink at him. "You've cast seeing spells before." Wasn't that the whole point of doing this in the first place? Of inflicting such a mountain of pain?

"Yeah, and they're always a bit temperamental," he says, brow furrowing to a deep vee. "But I guess I'm mostly wondering why she seemed so adamant that it wouldn't work for me—that it isn't even working for her?"

"You were about to take her magic, Chase." I shrug, since as far as mysteries go, this one basically solves itself. "Maybe she thought that would stop you."

"Maybe." He doesn't look or sound convinced. "It's more the way that she said it, like she was . . . I don't know, confessing to something she didn't want to admit. Something real."

Except it can't be real because I *saw* her using it. As we were working to escape the tavern, she was communing with the future every step of the way—and in a pretty intense fashion, falling in and out of the trance more readily than my mother ever did.

"Well, you've taken it now, so you may as well try to use it," I say, unwilling to let all that ill-gotten color go to waste. "Just remember that premonition is question-based. The more specific your phrasing, the more reliable the vision."

"So, if I ask where the trackers are heading, will it show us which parts of the city to avoid?"

"It should—in theory." Though in practice, who the hell knows what answer we might get. Mom always said the future was intractable.

"Then let's test the theory." Chase closes his eyes, his face clouding with concentration as he reaches for the Indigo's magic and begins to wrestle with the fates.

A few long seconds go by.

A few more.

A minute.

And then—right as I start to wonder if maybe the Indigo wasn't lying, after all, if maybe her magic really is broken and we just tortured her for no reason—the future descends on him with a vengeance.

Chase's head jerks back, his spine arching, his skin paling white as the cliffs. A strangled howl of fear escapes him, wild with hurt, and shock, and broken pieces of destiny so violent they send him crashing to his knees, his hands flying up to cup his temples.

"Chase?" Cemmy barrels up the stairs to meet his panic. "What the hells happened, Ez? What did you do?"

"I didn't *do* anything," I say as she drops to his side. "He was trying to use the Indigo's power and then he suddenly just . . . freaked out." And not in a way I've ever seen before. My mother's visions were calm, temperate things. Noticeable, yes, but never vicious. Never punishing enough to cause her pain.

"Chase." Cemmy puts a gentle hand to his cheek. "Chase, can you hear me?"

With a sharp exhale, he snaps out of the future, the storm in his eyes clearing, the bloom of Indigo around his irises dulling violet until it fades.

"Hey—*hey*, look at me," Cemmy urges, softly coaxing him back to speech. "What is it? What did you see?"

"The Gray," he breathes, low and frantic. "I saw it dying, I—I saw the magic dying." His fingers instantly close around the scry at his neck, the one bonded to Magdalena, his Amber sister who recently came within an inch of causing that very thing herself.

"Mags, is she——?"

"She's fine." The tension in his body instantly deflates. "She says she's safe and hidden. Whatever this is, it isn't her."

"Could it still . . . *be* her, though?" Cemmy aims that question at me. "I mean, if it's the future he's seeing, then doesn't that mean it hasn't . . . happened yet?"

"Technically, yes, but the timeline doesn't fit," I tell her, thinking back to Mom's stories about the fates. "If Magdalena's safe today, then it would take months before the shadows started feeling the effects of her gift." Or at least, that's how long it took her to destabilize them last year, when the Church triggered her power and locked her in an iron cell. "The future doesn't usually reveal itself quite so far in advance. There would be too many unmade decisions standing in the way."

"Then maybe it's a different Amber." Cemmy grasps at the next straw. "That dilution might be rare, but these things are random, right? We could have fluked into another one by sheer chance?"

"Well, if we did, they're not in Sarotuza," I say, crossing my arms. "I'd have noticed an Amber."

"Are you sure about that, Ez?" Her reply is as condescending as it is blunt. "Because you've not exactly been paying attention lately."

"Yes, I'm sure." I bristle, but I make a show of blinking into my magic nonetheless, checking for any trails I might have overlooked. My gift isn't limitless, but it does allow me to sense Shades from dozens of miles away, to track even the barest hint of them through the shadows. I only missed Magdalena's trail back in Isitar because it never occurred to me to search the reformed side of the city—let alone an impenetrable fortress controlled by the Church. Today, I'm not making that same mistake, and a systematically thorough search later, I'm a hundred percent confident when I declare, "Sarotuza is Amber free."

"Okay, so they're somewhere else, then." Cemmy's frustration is glib. "If the Gray's dying again, what other explanation could there be?"

"No—whatever's happening, it's happening here." This time, Chase is the one to argue. "I can't explain it, but I could . . . *feel* that we're in the right place. The vision, it was . . . chaotic, fractured— more like flashes of truth than an actual scene. But the future wants us involved, I just know it. And this is where it wants us to be."

"Well, that's too bad because we're not staying," Cemmy says, as though that decision isn't up for debate. "We have to leave as soon as possible. The entire city's looking for Ez."

"Looking for us, actually." I break the news to her with a sigh. "Turns out, the Indigo has a knack for resisting compulsion; she told the trackers about you two, as well."

"Gods, of course she did." Cemmy drags a breath through her teeth. "Then you know what, fine, since she's so intent on sticking her nose where it doesn't belong, she can also tell us what this damn vision is supposed to mean." It's always act now, think later with Cemmy, run straight at the problem until you slam into trouble head first.

"No—let me do it." I reach out to stop her, unwilling to let that temper make a bad situation worse. "When I was in there before, she mentioned something about the death of the Gray, I just didn't believe her. Maybe I can get her to say more."

*Or maybe she'll tell you to pick a hell and go rot in it.*

Given what I allowed Chase to do, I wouldn't blame her for cursing me right out of that room. Right out of the shadows, too, if I'm honest; that's what I'd be wishing on her if our roles were reversed. But for whatever reason, the future chose to weave our paths together and lead us to this point.

It chose to meddle.

And meddling is its way of showing us something.

# CHAPTER 14

# RAYA

If I ever doubted that Hues deserved the hand fate dealt them, I don't anymore. I always knew that their kind was dangerous, that their gifts were unpredictable and their blood was a poison to our world. But with so few left, I've never really *seen* it. Never *felt* it. Never imagined that I'd find myself at their mercy.

*What mercy?* If not for the fear and the anger, I'd have probably succumbed to the Gold's torture and slumped into unconsciousness against the wall, let oblivion take me. But I refuse to give him that satisfaction. I refuse to give him my total surrender after everything else he took.

*This'll hurt less if you hold still.*

Gods, what a fucking joke. Even now, my skin still burns with his magic, my whole body trembling like a leaf in autumn, the ache from the iron replaced by a pain that penetrates to the bone. There's bile on my tongue, sweat in my hair, salt on my cheeks from when I begged him to stop.

And I did beg.

And beg.

And then I cried, screamed, and begged some more, without sparing a thought for how pathetic it made me look. Because his gift didn't just feel like suffering, it felt like dying. Like having my very essence ripped apart by feral dogs.

*This won't kill you*, he kept telling me, though when I finally get free of this pipe, I very much intend to kill him. It would be no less than he deserves—no less than *all* of them deserve. For a few blissful moments, that fantasy stokes the rage in my soul. I picture my hand slipping out of the cuff and wrapping around the Gold's throat; I picture the look on his face when he realizes that I'm not as weak as he and his half-breed friends first thought; I picture handing them over to the trackers and watching a Green stop their hearts in front of a triumphant court. But then a shadow wisps through the door to my prison and despite myself, I recoil, flattening against the wall in an effort to disappear entirely.

"I'm not going to hurt you." The Sapphire quickly retreats to the far side of the room, as if to prove that he means to keep that promise.

"Like you'd even have the stomach for it," I spit, reaching for a few of his very own choice words. "I saw how you looked away right before the good part." Hells, I saw the way his Bronze had to lead him out before he puked. "Don't worry, half breed, I'm sure you'll do better next time."

"Ezzo." He barely flinches as he sits. "My name is Ezzo."

"Good for you." I make it plenty clear that I won't be sharing mine in return. If these Hues are so willing to hurt me now, then I can't imagine what they'd do if they found out who their prisoner truly is. How important her parents are. I've absolutely zero doubt they'd try to use me as leverage. "Are you going to let me go?"

"We're not going to kill you, if that's what you're asking. Killing is what your kind do." It's practically the same line his Gold fed me right before he violated my will. *We're not like you full-bloods; we don't just kill everything we're scared of.*

"I just experienced first-hand what your kind do, *Ezzo*." I glare at him until he blinks. "Or does torture not count in your opinion? Are you perfectly okay with hurting Shades so long as it suits your needs?"

"Not as okay as your Council is with it." The shame in his voice turns to grit. "Do you know what it's like to have your bones broken by an Orange, or to have a Green heal you over and over so that they can keep pulling you apart limb from limb? Because I do," he says, absently clawing at his ribs. "I also know what it's like to be starved for days and beaten for hours. So please, tell me all about how *your* kind doesn't play with its food."

The memory of him in the court chamber—bruised black, swollen, and bleeding—assaults me unbidden, every bit as uncomfortable now as it felt when they were leading him in.

"It was the trackers' job to—"

"*Find* me." Ezzo doesn't allow that flimsy excuse to pass my lips. "Their job was to find me and get me in front of the Council. The pain they inflicted was a choice."

"Well, then . . . they must have had—"

"A good reason?" he asks, cutting me off again. "Because I didn't run, or put up a fight, or try to escape."

It's getting harder and harder to contradict him.

"Then, I don't know . . . you must have—"

"Right. *I* must have." He rolls his eyes, bitter. "The problem couldn't have possibly been on your side."

"My side does what's necessary to protect the Gray because *your* side is draining the shadows." I don't know why I'm even bothering to debate him on this when that's what it comes down to in the end: the pursuit of the lesser evil.

"My side is a handful of Hues who barely make it to adolescence— hasn't it ever occurred to you that we're in no position to be draining anything?"

The assertion is a little rich coming from the Hue who just had his golden friend drain me.

"That's only because we've kept your numbers in check!" I grind the truth to a sharp point. "Before the purges were instituted, your kind almost collapsed the Gray! A few bad apples don't change that."

"How about twelve bad apples, then?" Ezzo's expression hardens, his fingers drumming an agitated concerto against his knees.

"Is that number supposed to mean something to me?"

"Not particularly, no. It's just the number of trackers they sent to kill my parents." His admission catches me entirely off-guard. "I was only nine at the time and the village we lived in served as a night-port between two cities, so when I saw that many trails converge, I assumed it was a trading party, not a raid. Because why would the Council send twelve trackers to apprehend one Indigo and her typic husband? That wouldn't make any sense."

And yet, I'm suddenly sure he's about to tell me that's exactly what they did.

"So that morning, when Mom sent me to pick berries from a nearby field, I didn't understand what she was doing," Ezzo continues, his voice clouding with grief. "I didn't realize that she and Dad had chosen not to run, not to fight, because it meant saving me, changing *my* future. But I can tell you this much: the mess your trackers left of them . . . that wasn't justice, it was glee. They enjoyed it."

Despite the pain still coursing through my body, it's impossible not to feel a pang of pity.

"Look, I know it may not seem fair, but they did break the law," I say, softer than he deserves.

"Ah, well, I guess that explains why the trackers had to break so many of their bones, then." His face fills with disgust, his eyes darkening to midnight. "Though I do wonder what the justification was for cutting off their ring fingers and tossing their wedding bands in the hearth. Is that part of the training?" He doesn't give me a chance to reply. "Better yet, do you think there's a reason they had to stab a typic and passive Shade so many times their blood ended up on the ceiling, or do you want to tell me again how those *few bad apples* are the exception to the rule?"

My stomach twists, and clenches, and bucks. If he's telling the truth, then what those Shades did to his parents is inexcusable. The trackers are supposed to deal in quick deaths, not torture. In punishment, not cruelty. In order as mandated by a trial.

*Snap out of it, Raya, he's a Hue; they lie.* Hells, if he thought it might save him from execution, he'd probably say anything to solicit my sympathies. Invent any atrocity.

"Tell me what you know about the death of the Gray." His change of subject is as unexpected as it is abrupt.

*Oh . . . so that's why he's here.* I should have realized he'd have an agenda, something he was hoping to learn from this conversation before it veered wildly off track.

"The Gold tried to use my magic, didn't he?" That must be what all that urgent yelling was about, why Ezzo didn't believe my claim before but is considering it now.

"Yes, he did—and that Gold is Chase, by the way. The girl is Cemmy." He makes a point of sharing their names, as if to remind me that they're more than just illegal colors. "But the future wouldn't answer his question. Instead, it sent him an abstract vision of the shadows dying. I take it that's what you saw, too? What you were trying to say earlier?"

"Wouldn't you like to know." Now that I've deduced what he's really after, he'll be getting nothing from me but snide remarks.

"What did you mean when you told Chase your magic doesn't work?" Ezzo tries again, subtly changing tack.

"You should get your hearing checked, half breed. My magic works fine."

"See, I don't think it does." His head shakes as he calls my bluff. "My mother was an Indigo, remember? And she never had a vision like that. She never used them the way you did in the tavern, either, so . . . fluidly. So seamlessly on the fly."

"Maybe she wasn't as good as I am."

A muscle in his jaw twitches, the nerve I hit sharpening the hate in his eyes.

"No, if it was a matter of skill, you wouldn't be sneaking around behind the trackers' backs. If you're seeing something they can't, my guess is it's because you've done something you shouldn't. What I can't figure out is *why*?"

*Gods, of course he can't.* What could this Hue possibly know about following the rules or having to prove his power? The best he can hope for, on a good day, is not getting caught, and sooner or later, his luck is going to run out—probably sooner, given how much he likes to drink. And since he's already embarrassed the Council so thoroughly, when they do finally catch him, I doubt they'll risk another trial.

The moment the trackers find Ezzo, they'll kill him.

Put an end to our mutually fated path.

*So anything I share should be safe* . . . Perhaps I've been playing this all wrong. If Ezzo won't live long enough to betray my secrets, then maybe instead of fighting him, I should be feeding his curiosity, using his thirst for answers to satisfy mine.

"Because I was failing, okay?" I drop my head to the wall and lace my voice with resentment, feigning a break in will. "I'm no good at communicating with the future the right way and they were going to bind my magic if I didn't turn things around, so I asked a question that's forbidden and now my visions are all messed up. Happy?"

"It's a start," he says, softening an inch. "Do you believe they're real? These messed-up visions?"

"The ones I had in the tavern were—and before you ask, I don't know why they were so specific when this one is so abstract. No one's talked to the future like this in hundreds of years; I'm still trying to work it all out." Though his Gold did just go and prove that fate-touched magic remains fate-touched even when it's running through another's blood, so I suppose I do know that now.

"Is that why you came looking for me at the Golden Stag?" Ezzo asks. "Because the vision showed you that we were somehow involved?"

"Yes." I cringe at his poor choice of phrasing, adopting the truth he wants to hear in place of my true goal: claiming credit for his arrest. "It seemed like the best way to prove that I could still be a seer. That I haven't broken my magic for good."

"Yeah, I wouldn't put too much stock in the Council's idea of *broken*." This time, the edge to his words is directed at them instead of me. "They have a nasty habit of changing the rules when they feel like it."

"Which means what, exactly?" If he's going to make accusations, the least he can do is spell them clear.

"It means they *lie*. Especially about magic."

"That's ridiculous," I say—because it is. Because why would the Council lie about magic when they want us to use it? When they make their money off it? When it keeps us safe?

"Is it?" Ezzo raises an eyebrow. "Just think about it for a minute—think about everything they've ever told you about illegal half breeds like me. Aren't you wondering how I'm sitting in front of you right now? Here? In the Gray?" He motions to the veil of shadows swirling around us. "Aren't you wondering how I haven't shattered yet?"

I have been wondering that, yes. Not since he chained me to this pipe—I've had more important things on my mind—but it did occur to me when the trackers first led him into the court chamber; I did wonder how he was able to maintain such a difficult spell despite being so beat-up.

"Are you saying you *don't* need to cast an In-Between to survive here?" My disbelief drips with surprise. Because—hells, even the Council couldn't maintain a conspiracy that contrived.

"No, I'm saying I've been casting one this whole time, so easily you didn't notice." He emphasizes that second part, the part that breaks with established fact. "It's a myth that the Gray seeks to expel Hues, a lie the Council started telling when they decided to purge our kind. They knew that they could never fully eradicate us—Shades have been bedding typics since the beginning of time—so instead, they made it harder for us to survive, spent decades rewriting our history, spreading misinformation, and burning records until ta-da"—he snaps his fingers—"we were all suddenly learning a faulty version of the In-Between spell."

"I'm sorry—burning records and tampering with spells?" I have to pick my jaw off the ground. "You do realize how utterly insane you sound?" And how utterly impossible that would be. For what he's claiming to hold true, the Council would have had to mess with every scroll, book, and ledger from here to Isitar, corrupt the sanctity of every archive.

"More insane than banning a way of seeing the future?" Ezzo's questions are growing increasingly sharp. "More insane than you seeing something the entire seers' guild missed the second you decided to break bad?"

"Yes, that's—" The objection dies on my tongue, my mother's words bubbling up to contradict it.

*There has been one documented case. Around four hundred years ago.*

Right around the time the Council started purging Hues from the continent.

*That can't be a coincidence.* As much as I hate to admit it, the timeline he's alluding to fits, and it would explain how a similar catastrophe could have gone unnoticed by the guild last year.

"I'm not saying I believe you," I hedge, considering my words with care. "But even if I did, your Gold—*Chase*—already has my magic, and the future showed him the exact same vision it showed me." Give or take a few of the more sordid details. "There's nothing else I can tell you."

"You can tell me your name." The interest in Ezzo's voice is sincere. And though I'd much rather tell him to go to hell, I might be better off giving him a reason to see me as more than just a petulant Shade. Maybe then, he'll feel like he's won something and let me go.

"Raya." I offer him my first name only, not the Wryvern legacy. "My name is Raya."

"Well, okay then, Raya." For a long moment, it feels as though my gamble might pay. Ezzo doesn't smile, exactly, but he also doesn't look mad anymore; he looks like the boy from my vision, the one with the warm eyes and the heartbreakingly lovely face. The one who could still choose to grant my freedom.

But then—right as his shoulders set into a decision—the door to the room crashes open and the Bronze called Cemmy comes bursting inside.

"The trackers are raiding this sector. We have to go, now," she says, lurching Ezzo to his feet. "They can deal with the Shade."

*No, no, no, no.* I rail against the iron keeping me captive. "Please, you can't let them find me here." Not this far from the Academy and helplessly bound in chains. There'll be no explaining that to my parents, or to the class masters, or to the guilds. My future will officially be ruined.

"Please, Ezzo, you have to let me go." I'm not above begging him like I begged his friend. "Let me go and I'll forget everything that's happened. Chase can even compel me to forget."

"Right, because that worked so well the first time," Cemmy mutters, urging Ezzo away. Then when he turns to hesitate in the doorway, she steps around him to say, "Ez, come on. You can't possibly be—"

Instead of cutting her off with his words, he does it with his hands, shaping a series of signs I don't have the language to read.

Though, evidently, she does.

And I don't need to read sign to interpret the tenor of her answering rage.

"Colors help me, I hope you know what you're doing." After a brief but terse exchange, she whips towards me, fishing out a key from her pocket and a knife from the belt at her hip.

"No—*please*—"

"Relax, it's to stop you from shimmering, so I suggest you hold very fucking still." She presses the tip of the blade to my chin, hard enough that I can't even draw breath without the metal biting.

"Ready?" she asks as Ezzo joins us by the pipe, the question meant solely for him.

"Ready."

What happens next is a sleight of hand so deft I don't even realize it's happened until the deed is complete.

*You have got to be kidding me.* I fight the urge to scream as I finally understand the switch the two of them had conceived. Because instead of letting me go, the Bronze has gone and tethered me to a wholly different prison.

She's gone and cuffed me to Ezzo.

# CHAPTER 15

# RAYA

"Have you lost your mind?" I glance between Ezzo and the iron cuff, cursing our new-found proximity. "I already told you everything I know!"

"You told me everything you wanted me to hear, there's a difference," he says, dismissing the Bronze with a quick exchanging of signs. "Now, are we staying to meet your tracker friends, or shall we run while we still can?"

This Sapphire is clearly more perceptive than I first thought.

"I'll do you one better." Without a word of warning, I shed my physicality and shimmer us out of the house, praying that the sudden burst of speed will destabilize his In-Between, shatter my problem to pieces.

"Disappointed I'm still here?" Ezzo asks when I jerk us to a halt at the top of the street.

Way, *way* more perceptive.

And far more adept.

"You know, I could just shimmer us straight to the Council and say that I was the one who caught you."

"Right, because I'm sure they'd believe you *willingly* cuffed yourself to a Hue with iron."

"I'll tell them that's how dedicated I am."

"Then I'll tell them to ask why you don't have the key."

"And I'll say it got lost in the struggle. Not that it would even matter since they'll believe my story, not yours."

"Maybe." He shrugs, entirely unperturbed. "Or maybe they'd never look at you the same again. Especially once I describe, in painstaking detail, how you used the future to help me escape the tavern. I bet they'd love to learn all about your messed-up visions."

"Fuck you, Ezzo." I hate that he's right and that he damn well knows it. I hate that if we're caught together like this, the trackers *will* take the time to ask questions and then everything I'd tell them he'd contradict. I hate that I'm stuck and I'm stuck and I'm stuck with him. "If I ask the future where to hide, will you believe the answer?"

"Will you actually get an answer?" His lip curls with the jibe. "Or will it just show you the same thing it did Chase?"

My Gods, this Hue is annoying.

"Let's find out," I grit, though deep in my gut, I already suspect I will. There's been a pattern to my visions since I became fate-touched, a trend to what questions the fates choose to ignore and what truths they choose to reveal—and he's at the very heart of it. As long as we're cuffed together, I'm confident they'll allow me to see.

*Where will we not be found by the trackers?*

The moment I engage my magic, I'm rewarded with the vision we need.

"We're going east," I say, though why the future's sending us deep into Meridian territory is beyond me.

*Perhaps the trackers won't think to look there.* The Gray blurs to ash and twilight as I shimmer us through the streets, the shadows taking on a crueler, heavier feel as we enter the world of fanatic reform. Here, it's not just the stench of iron that marks the buildings as hostile, it's the sigil that's been inked in blood on every door where his followers live. The sacred star, the Meridian calls it, an intricately pronged sun that appears to shine with a light from within.

The seal of a prophet.

Or at least, a man who claims divinity.

"What is this place?" Ezzo appraises our destination with open interest and wary feet.

"An old halfway house," I tell him, wisping our way in. "The Meridians used to meet in vagrant spaces before their numbers grew large enough to commandeer their own church."

"I'm sorry—the Meridians?"

"You've really not been paying attention, huh?" I'm kind of amazed at just how oblivious he is, how he managed to drink right past the biggest crisis in Sarotuza. "They're a fringe religious group that broke with the sacraments—though I guess they're not actually that fringe anymore; they've gained a lot more power over the past few years and tons of new followers. There are thousands of them now, I think. Maybe more."

"And the Church isn't trying to shut them down?" Ezzo asks, studying their brazen symbol.

"It's trying, but their leader is popular and he's doing the one thing the Church can't while it's still bound by the accords."

"What's that?"

"Killing Shades for sport." I don't miss the flash of satisfaction that flames in Ezzo's eyes.

"Sucks to be hunted, doesn't it?"

Nor do I bother dignifying his self-serving reply. "So, what's your plan here, exactly?" I give the cuffs connecting us an angry tug. "Follow me around the city forever?"

"Not forever, no, just until I figure you out," he says, smug as sunshine.

*So forever, then.* My teeth grind themselves brittle as we make our way through the house. "Shouldn't you be more worried about your friends?" I drag him down to sit among the remnants of a ruined couch. "Or do you not care what happens to them?"

"They're safer without me." Where I sink into the tattered cushions, Ezzo sinks right to the floor, unable to control his physicality.

"Doesn't that get annoying?" I had quite forgotten about the limitations of his hue.

"I've never known any different." He offers me another shrug. "In the Gray, I wisp; it's just what I do."

"So then, how's the cuff staying on?" I ask, rattling our wrists.

"They really don't teach you much about us, do they?" Ezzo fixes me a pointed look. "Iron is one of the few exceptions, but only when it takes the form of something like a cuff or a cage—something that surrounds me without break—then it stops me phasing the same way it does you. Beyond that, it's a pretty small list. I can interact with other Shades, my clothes, the ground . . . the same things you still inter-act with when you shimmer. Oh, and anything endowed with magic, so charms, talismans, scrys," he says, showing me the crystal hanging around his neck. "That's how I'll find the others later. Until then, you don't have to worry—Cemmy and Chase are very good at looking out for themselves." There's an edge to his voice that reeks of history.

"You don't like them," I say, and it isn't a question.

"I have my reasons not to like them."

"Even though they came to rescue you?" Twice in one day, no less; surely that should have bought them a little grace, perhaps an ounce of appreciation?

"It's what they think I'm owed." Ezzo's tone sharpens to a blade. "I notice no one's come to rescue *you*."

He sure has a way of getting under my skin, prying when I least expect it.

"You know what, I think I'm done talking now." I turn to stare at the wall. I don't need him to see just how hard those words have hit me, or how I've slowly been waking up to that reality all on my own. It's been hours since I bid goodbye to my mother; longer still since Akari and I left the Academy and agreed to meet at one of her usual haunts. She should have gotten worried bells ago, and even if she got distracted, Killen's threat from before we left the castle should have ensured that someone would realize I'm gone.

*So then, why haven't they found me?* The thought is a cancer, spreading through every one of my cells, tissues, and bones. Akari would have spoken to the class master, who would have alerted my parents, who would have asked the future for help in bringing me home. Likewise, Killen had threatened to tell Professor Lyons, who would have done that same thing from the Academy, which would have yielded the same result. So either they haven't raised the alarm yet or—

*The future isn't playing ball.* I shiver, the prospect chilling me from head to toe. Is it possible that the damage I wrought on my magic extends to those who see around me? Or am I just being overly paranoid, assuming that they *can't* find me, when they've simply not yet been asked to look? I mean, maybe Akari decided to do the searching herself instead of getting others involved? Or maybe Killen changed his mind about going to Professor Lyons—though I can't imagine why given the way I left things . . . wouldn't he have wanted to pay me back for that hurt? And for the love of all three Gods, is it too much to ask to contemplate the mess I made quietly, without this idiot Sapphire howling like a sullen ghost?

"Are the creepy wails really necessary?" I round on him with a vengeance, itching for a fight to distract from the questions I can't control.

"I was about to ask you the same thing," Ezzo says, slowly climbing to his feet. "But I think it's coming from over there." Inch by inch, he starts edging us towards the source, slow as the seasons and silent as a cunning fox. The wails stay faint at first, hopeless, broken, though as we delve deeper into the belly of the house, they intensify in grief and force.

"Didn't you ask the future to send us somewhere we wouldn't be found?" he hisses, keeping his voice low.

"Yes, I—" No, actually; what I chose to ask was: where will we not be found by the trackers? Which, in hindsight, wasn't the best form of that question—it was *too* specific, left us vulnerable to other dangers. But the bigger mistake I made was continuing to treat my magic like absolutely nothing's changed. I'm still following the old rules when the future's playing an entirely new game.

"For your information, I asked it to keep us away from the trackers—and that is most definitely *not* a tracker." The voice sounds far too young, for starters, far too timid and afraid. "Can you see what color Shade it is?"

"I'm trying," Ezzo says, eyes frosted white behind the veil of his gift. "But the trail they're leaving . . . it's not like anything I've ever seen. If I didn't know any better, I'd say it was an echo. Like the kind a typic leaves."

"That's impossible." A typic in the shadows isn't an option that makes the list. They can't phase, for one thing, nor can they survive the shadows long enough to fill a house with wails; they'd shatter instantly. Unlike Hues, they lack the magic to protect themselves with an In-Between, because they're not an in-between, and their blood is anathema to the Gray. Their presence would, quite literally, destabilize the realm.

"I know it's impossible." Ezzo tenses as the voice pulls closer still. "But that's what I see."

"Well, then look *again*," I urge, right before a stir from beyond the doorway makes that urging obsolete.

"By my colors, is that a—"

"Child," I finish for him, the word exhaling like a sharp stitch. "It's just a child."

Though as the girl steps into the room proper, I realize there's no *just* about it. I'd guess she's five or six years old—if a day— dressed in grimy, threadbare rags, and thin to the point of emaciation. A child of the slums, most likely, born and raised on the streets. But it's not the tragedy of her life that turns the air in my lungs to acid—it's her face, the blood crying crimson tracks along her cheeks. This girl is cracked china, a porcelain doll splintering under the weight of too much heat. And there's a wrongness about her, a festering rot that's eating right through her skin, leaving it raw and blistered. Leaving the shadows in her wake as wilted as a starving leaf.

"Can you help me?" Up close, her voice is a fraying wire, feeble and weak. "I want to go home."

"Look at her eyes, Raya." Ezzo's whisper is riddled with fear. "Have you ever seen anything like it?"

"No, I haven't." And the sight sends my hand clambering for his.

A Shade's magic presents as a spiked rim around the iris.

A rogue's magic burns black every chalky white inch.

A Hue's magic is invisible.

Whereas this girl's eyes look as though the magic is slowly breaking them from within, a spitting blaze glowing red between the fractures.

"I don't feel very good." She reaches out for us, her fingers cracking piece by piece. "Please, will you help me? Can I go home now, *please?*"

Without rhyme or warning, the magic holding her together turns that last plea into a scream, rending her cracks wider—her pain shriller—until with one final, malicious growl, the shadows rush in and shatter her to bits, leaving nothing behind but a grotesque memory and a jagged red heap.

*Holy mother of shit.* The cry that escapes me is a choked heave, it's ragged breaths, and stinging eyes, and dry retching. There's a storm building between my temples, bile rising in my throat, shock ringing in my ears. And I'm shaking, and I'm shaking, and I can't seem to make the shaking stop. I knew the shadows had the power to shatter; I've read the texts and I've learned the theory. But to watch it happen right in front of me . . . to see a person—flesh and blood and sinew—reduced to nothing but a pile of glass . . . it sickens me from soul to spleen. Though it isn't my knees that give way beneath me, or my hiccupping sobs that turn to a strangled wheeze. It's Ezzo's.

He drops like a ship casting anchor, the cuffs pulling me down with him.

"Gods, will you be careful—?" The moment I catch sight of his expression, the reprimand dies on my tongue. Where I'm shaking, he's vibrating like a plucked string, his cheeks wet with horror, his breaths sputtering like a dying fish.

"Ezzo?" I may have just watched a girl shatter, but he looks as though he lived it. His eyes are wild, haunted, his pupils blown as wide as the sea, staring at some distant memory that has him in an iron grip.

*Colors help me, he's falling apart.*

And I can't afford for him to do that. Not while we're still in the Gray, where he's in danger of shattering the same way she did. Cuffed together as we are, I can't take the risk that the shadows won't view us as one. So instead of railing at him to get up and snap out of it, I gentle, taking his trembling face in my hands.

"Hey—you're okay, okay?" I tell him, softly, like I believe the words leaving my mouth. "Whoever she was, she's gone now. We're safe. You're safe. Everything's okay." I keep repeating that refrain until slowly—so agonizingly slowly—he begins to respond to my touch, the frantic rise and fall of his chest calming.

"Raya?" My name escapes him in a waking rush, the clouds finally clearing from his expression. But even as he pulls the room back to focus and stabilizes his shield with a grunt, the pain in him remains grim and potent, as though he's still trapped in a nightmare that refuses to dull.

"It's okay—you're safe," I say again. Only for him to jerk beneath me like a scandalized buck.

"Erm . . . what are you—?" As Ezzo glances between us, I suddenly realize why he's so taken aback. When he fell, the cuffs ensured we'd fall together, and I landed smack bang on top of him with my knees hugging his hips on either side. Then I made it worse by leaning in closer, so close that I can practically feel his breath and taste his magic. Hells, another inch and we'd be kissing.

"Right—sorry." I lurch back as though electrocuted. "I'm sorry, but you were—"

"No, it's fine. My fault." Ezzo hurries to disentangle our limbs. "Seeing that just hit . . . it was just a shock."

I don't think he's lying, exactly, though I do get the sense that it's also not the whole truth, like there's another reason he felt that girl's death so deeply. But since now doesn't seem like the best time to press the subject, I pull us back to our feet and ask, "Any idea what kind of Hue that was?"

"That wasn't a Hue, Raya, it can't have been," he says, certain to a stubborn fault.

"Well, it wasn't a Shade, if that's what you're suggesting." My conviction is equally staunch. "Shades don't shatter."

"And Hues don't manifest the ability to phase until they're older. That girl was far too young to have come into her magic. And even if she wasn't, Hues don't wander around bleeding from the eyes before they shatter. We just . . . shatter." The hitch in his voice reeks of experience. Which—given his age—he's probably had ample time to gain.

"Okay, so then what does that leave?"

"You know what it leaves—you just don't want to believe it."

"*Want* has nothing to do with it." I'm refusing to believe it because it has no basis in fact. "If she was a typic, then how was there any magic in her eyes at all? Better yet—how was she walking? Or talking? Or begging us for help? Shouldn't the shadows have shattered her immediately?"

"Yes, they should have," Ezzo concedes, taking a step towards the room she came from. "So why didn't they?" He takes another, then another after that, tracing the trail of blood the girl left through the house. "And how did she get here in the first place? Typics can't phase."

*Yes, thank you, captain obvious, that's what I've been trying to tell you.*

"Maybe a Hue helped her across," I say, since no Shade in their right mind would ever dream of doing it. Not when the Gray is increasingly becoming our sanctuary—the one place that remains untouched by the clergy and the Church.

"Gods, is there anything you Shades *won't* blame us for?" Ezzo's tongue clicks against his teeth. "Think that accusation through to the end, Raya; why would a Hue want to phase a typic into the Gray? If the shadows destabilize, we die the same way you do."

"Yeah, well, maybe there's a Hue out there holding a grudge."

"Maybe they should be."

"And maybe they—" My contempt cuts off abruptly as we reach the scene of the crime, a room that glistens from wall to wall with a mosaic of splintered glass. "Is that—?"

"Far more than one typic." Ezzo's horror is a creature I can see, and smell, and touch, the shake in his voice a mirror to the quiver in mine. "I'd say this looks more like dozens." Each having shattered neatly into their own pile, a sea of reds, greens, blues, and yellows that thread a rainbow through the inky dark.

*The seven colors.* If Shades don't shatter, then why is this floor littered with every one of ours? And if typics can't phase, then how did so many end up here, in a room that stinks of death and perverted power? Where did they even come from?

"The missing typics." The answer to that last question hits me all at once.

"What missing typics?"

"The ones that have been disappearing across the city." Ezzo's spectacular lack of notice continues to astound. I was barely out of the Academy five minutes when I happened across the flyers; how could he have spent days in Sarotuza without spotting them? How is a Hue this oblivious still alive? "Maybe if you drank less, you'd pay a bit more attention."

"Excuse me?" Ezzo reels back as though I'd slapped him.

"Tell me I'm wrong," I say, meeting the indignity in his eyes. *Tell me you didn't go straight from your execution to the tavern. Tell me you weren't drinking yourself into an early grave when I found you.*

"You don't know the first thing about me, Raya," he spits, his rage simmering to a threatening boil. "So please, save us both the trouble of pretending you do."

"I know you gave up." As much as I shouldn't keep goading him, the flush staining his cheeks is making my anger bold. I've been wanting to rail at him since the moment he fed my magic to his Gold, and if he can so blithely strip me of color without consequence—without showing any regard for how much pain it would cause—then why should I care if I hurt his delicate little feelings? "I know your gift could have kept you safe if you'd bothered to use it; I know that you had the chance to escape Sarotuza, and instead, you allowed yourself to get caught—again. That you didn't even try to fight one passive Indigo girl."

"Shut up." The coward snaps his head away, unwilling to face the truth.

"Wow, is that the best you can do? How very cutting, Ezzo. I'm so impressed by your—"

"Raya, *shut up*. There's someone coming." In an instant, his hand is pressed to my mouth, his body crushing me against the wall. And though I don't immediately hear the same threat that he did, only a few seconds pass before a sickening crunch of glass validates his assertion, accompanied by two sets of footsteps and a trading of clipped remarks.

"How long did this one last?" The first voice is deep and melodic in tenor. A man's voice, without question, as cold as it is proud.

"Close to a bell and a half." Whereas the second one is timid, a woman who sounds frightened and desperate to avoid his ire. "A vast improvement on the previous tribute."

"Not nearly improved enough. Go get me another." His reprimand sends a physical tremor racing through the house, as though his irritation can infect the shadows. "And not some starving whelp of a street urchin this time, I want an older, healthier child."

I shiver as he confirms the worst of our suspicions. That yes, the shattered girl was a typic, and yes, they deliberately phased her into the Gray to do . . . Gods, I don't even know what.

*Let's go take a look,* I mouth at Ezzo, pointing towards the room they're inside.

*Absolutely not.* He shakes his head, eyes widening as if to add: *are you out of your fucking mind?* But since he made the oh-so-smart decision to cuff our wrists together, when I push off the wall, his choices narrow down to: follow me or fight. And if we fight, we'll definitely get discovered.

"Is that wise, Adriel?" The woman asks as we edge towards them. "A healthy child will be missed."

"I don't want excuses, Alara, I want another typic. If I was able to catch us a Red and an Orange in one day, then you should be able to wrangle a couple of children." Once again, his anger seems to rip through the shadows, delivering an admonishment I can feel.

"You're right, I'm sorry. I'll find you a better tribute." Alara is mousy, short, and obedient, but that's as much as I can glean before she dashes off in search of his prize. Him, I can't quite see yet, so I take another creeping step forward and will him to turn around. *Come on, Adriel, come this way. Come into the—shit!* My whole body freezes as a shard of typic cracks beneath my heel, echoing like thunder in the stillness of the empty house.

"Don't move." Ezzo's arm instantly snakes around me, keeping me from bolting with an urgency that's whisper tight.

An eternal second passes.

Two whole lifetimes.

Three.

Then, just as I'm about to lose my grip on my air—when I'm all but convinced that Adriel has grown wise to the intruders eavesdropping on his crimes—his attention drifts in the other direction and with a flourish of robes, he disappears into the night.

But not before I'm able to get a nice, good look at his face.

At the Divine Meridian's face, I should say.

Since he and Adriel are the same man.

# CHAPTER 16

# RAYA

I was twelve years old when I first heard of the Divine Meridian. When anyone first heard of him, to be honest, since before then, the Church's hold on Sarotuza was ironclad. It was their teachings the faithful followed. Their sacraments. Their hateful lies. Until one day, a cleric from their own ranks broke very, very bad.

He claimed to be the voice of the Gods.

He claimed to have the power to put an end to the magical scourge.

Though at first, nobody believed him. They had no reason to; he was just a disgraced minister who hadn't even reached the rank of Aralagio yet, an angry zealot wearing silver robes and drawing pictures of the sun. So instead of aiming big, he started small. He proselytized in the poorest parts of the city, targeting those the clergy had neglected and winning them over with the promise of shelter, food, and wine. It took years for his sigil to work its way out of the slums, but once it did, hundreds of sacred stars suddenly began to appear around Sarotuza. On walls, on shopfronts, on pamphlets that preached his message and bore his likeness, saint-like portraits that always depicted him with a kind smile and a gold-lit crown. A cult, the Church had called his congregation, even as it continued to turn a blind eye.

Right up until the day it couldn't anymore, when he commandeered one of their own houses.

There was no more ignoring him after that.

Then once he started bleeding Shades, the Council took notice, too; they set every guild to the task of tracking the Meridian down.

That was six months and ten dead Shades ago, and still, no one has been able to get within striking distance of that man.

Until today.

It takes a long minute for the blood to stop pounding in my ears, for my breaths to slow their gasp and my heart to find a steady rhythm.

"You can let go of me now." The moment I realize Ezzo's arm is still wrapped around my waist, I push away from him, cursing the iron that's keeping us connected, how it's constantly finding new ways to force him into my space. "They're gone."

"Any idea who *they* were?" The heat of his body—of the In-Between he's casting—instantly disappears. "Because not a word of that made any sense to me."

"Yes, actually." Even if I can't quite believe it. "That was the Divine Meridian. Head of the fringe group that broke with the Church."

"Wait—the man leading the Shade-killing cult is a *Shade*?" Ezzo's brows disappear into his hairline. "And you didn't think to mention that?"

"I didn't think to mention it because he's *not* a Shade." The idea is downright ludicrous. "The Divine Meridian is obviously a—" *Typic*, I almost say, before the truth of the matter catches up to me.

The Divine Meridian can't be a typic.

We just witnessed, first-hand, what the shadows do to typics, and even then, the protracted display we saw should have been impossible. That girl should have shattered the second she was phased into the Gray, not a bell and a half later, and no amount of cryptic ramblings about street urchins and tributes can change that. We're right back to: this doesn't make any sense.

"Hue is far more likely than Shade," I say instead, recalibrating my thinking. "It would explain his vendetta against the Council and the Church."

"But it wouldn't explain why he'd risk drawing so much attention to himself." Ezzo's tone is dismissive. "When your whole life is illegal, that's not something you do."

"Maybe it's not something *you* do." I reject his lack of imagination. "But you have to admit it's smart, hiding in plain sight." Hells, by sheer virtue of aligning himself with the Gods, the Meridian ensured that everyone would leap to the same conclusion I did, assume that *typic* is the only thing he could be. "You know what— why are we even arguing about this? Just use your gift." I kick myself for getting sucked into this inane discussion.

"Fine, I will." Ezzo blinks into the magic, though the heat pinking his ears suggests that he, too, forgot that was an option. Clearly, the shock of discovery is making us both a bit dim.

"Well?" I prompt when the whites of his eyes begin to clear. "Is he a Hue or a Shade?"

"Neither." The word is an exhale, a breath laden with disbelief.

"What do you mean, *neither?*" How in the name of all three Gods is *neither* even an option here?

"I mean, the woman he was with was a Hue; I could see her trail clear as day. Emerald, perfectly solid, exactly the kind of signature I expect. But his was more like . . . an absence. Not like he's masking his presence—I wouldn't have seen anything if that were the case—but more like the shadows are ending around him. Like he's swallowing them up."

"Okay . . . so then what does that mean?"

"I don't know." Ezzo drags a hand through his hair, sounding every bit as confused as I feel.

"How could you *not* know?"

"Because being a Hue doesn't come with instructions, Raya." He throws both arms up in the air, almost jerking me off my feet. "We don't live the same charmed life as you do, okay? We don't go to a fancy academy or learn to cast from a who's who of professors or a sprawling archive of books. My own mother couldn't teach me the ins and out of my power because your Council has spent four hundred years suppressing any and all information about our gifts. So, I'm sorry if you don't like my answer, but it's the only fucking answer I can give." His anger is hot and righteous, a flame that kindles both my embarrassment and my cheeks. I've never spared a thought for how his kind learn to use their magics; only for how their existence might one day come to threaten me, my magic, if their numbers weren't kept in check.

"You're right, I'm sorry," I say, and it isn't a lie. "But the woman with him—the Hue—you said her trail was visible?"

"Yeah." He deflates like a pricked balloon, as though a fleeting flare of temper was all he had in him. "Why?"

Because I'm starting to understand why the future sent me to find him at the Golden Stag tavern, and why it helped us escape together, and why it's choosing to only answer my questions when they somehow involve him. Because—judging by the conversation we just overheard—the appalling horror that played out in this house is about to cycle and repeat. And I'm pretty sure the future wants us to stop that from happening.

\*

Convincing Ezzo to hunt the Hue with me proves easy. Perhaps if he hadn't just watched a child die in the most grotesque way possible, his answer would have been different—perhaps then he would have decided to put an end to this misguided alliance and drag me back to his friends. Or perhaps I would have beaten him to the punch and dragged him to mine, got Akari to help keep him quiet while we sold the trackers a more flattering version of the day's events. A version where I didn't get myself caught and shackled. Where the iron around my wrist was a strategy not an embarrassing fail. Though right at this moment, it's just an inconvenient problem, a reason my hand keeps grazing Ezzo's over and over again. I would really—*really*—like to be rid of this cuff already.

Around us, the Gray has dimmed with the darkness, the shadows ringing with the midnight bell. Gods, I've been missing from the Academy for almost twelve hours, long enough that someone should have reported my absence by now—if not Killen, then Akari. Someone should have come looking.

"Are you sure we're going the right way?" I snap at Ezzo, pushing that thought down quick. The only thing I can control, in this moment, is my ability to shape the story the trackers will eventually hear, and that means having something useful to tell them, not letting Alara slip into the night and disappear.

"For the eighth time—yes, I'm sure." Ezzo rolls his eyes. Which only serves to prove that he can't actually be sure, because they're not clouded white with his gift.

"How do you know that if you're not checking?"

"Well, for starters, I *am* checking; I can blink in and out of the magic pretty quickly." He bristles, tongue clicking against his teeth. "And besides, Alara's only a few streets ahead of us; when she leaves the Gray, I'll see it."

"Okay, but *how* will you see it?" This time, my question is equal parts sullen and sincere. "I mean—what exactly would you see when she phases? What does it look like when you blink . . . in there?"

"Do you really care?" Ezzo asks, staring at me as though I've grown an extra head.

"Care? No. I'm just curious." I shrug. "But we can keep walking in silence if you prefer." With nothing to distract us from the gentle stir of the shadows and the forced proximity of the cuffs, the way his In-Between shudders a little every time it brushes up against my side. "Or I could keep incessantly asking if you're sure . . ."

His answering sigh is bone deep. "It's not the easiest thing to explain—the Gray sort of gets . . . lighter, I guess you could say. Like paint that's been watered down. Hazy is probably a better way to describe it—everything gets a little hazy, including all the buildings, and the landmarks, and the ground. Then on top of that, you have the trails."

"And those are different to echoes, right?" I feel like I remember him saying something to that effect, though at the time, my attention was fixed firmly on the wails screaming through the Meridian's house.

"Yeah, they're much less fleeting. It's more like . . . glowing lengths of string, but the strings are made of light, and they sort of hover at eye level, and they're the same color as the Shades who left them behind. So basically, I'm blinking into a hazier version of the Gray that's filled with a bunch of these colored lights, and sometimes there's lots of them, and sometimes there isn't, and they're all intersecting with each other and branching off in different directions, kind of like a giant web. Except the fresher trails are brighter and more solid than the older ones, and they also end abruptly whenever their owners phase in or out of the Gray, so it's not always as simple as following an unbroken line. And the strangest part is that I can see further than you'd expect, almost like I'm looking at a map—but only up to a certain point, it's not endless."

"Well, that sounds . . . confusing." As much as I can picture the scene he's describing, I can't quite wrap my head around how he'd go about deciphering the mess. There are hundreds of Shades in Sarotuza, and they're constantly shimmering, and wisping, and phasing between realms. If he's having to sort through them all to find one light trail, then where the hells does he even start?

"It was, at first," Ezzo admits. "And humbling. And overwhelming. And downright terrifying, if I'm honest, knowing just how many full-blooded Shades are in my general vicinity at any given time. But I got better at it with practice, same way everyone else does."

"Not everyone." The words escape before I can stop them, echoing my shame through the night.

"So that was true—what you said about failing?" Ezzo's voice softens around the ask.

"Trust me, I wish it was a lie." I wish I could have practiced my way to the right questions instead of having to gamble my future on a forbidden one. "But you were right about me: I'm not a great seer."

"Be great at something else, then," he says, like it's as simple as that.

"That's not how it works, Ezzo, I'm an Indigo; my choices are to see better or lose my magic. Those are the rules."

"Then forget about the rules for a second." He turns to face me with his whole body, so that he's walking backwards in front of me instead of at my side. "What would you want to do if the Council didn't get a say?"

"Erm . . . I've . . . never really thought about it."

"So then, don't think about it," he urges. "Just pick the first thing that comes to your mind."

"Okay, well . . . this might be silly, but I've always loved reading the Council's news blasts," I tell him, keeping my eyes fixed firmly on the ground. "Did you used to get them back in Isitar, too? The weekly papers they put out?"

"Oh yes, I'm familiar with the Council's news blasts." A wry edge creeps into his voice. "Though I can't say I approve of their content."

No, I don't imagine he does. They don't tend to be that Hue-friendly.

"Well, content aside, I've always thought it would be fun to write those pieces, or to research them, maybe—or even just to lay the pages out."

"Huh."

Every part of me reddens as Ezzo gruffs out a laugh.

"What? Why is that funny?" The blood in my cheeks begins to burn like wildfire. I should have known better than to tell a half breed anything—let alone something so fanciful and private. I should have never opened my mouth.

"It's not funny—it's just kind of ironic," he says, and I'm surprised to find that there's not one hint of mocking to his smile. "You're an Indigo Shade who can quite literally see the future, but you'd rather spend your life reporting on the past."

Oh.

Right.

That is kind of ironic.

"And I suppose you'd pick something better?" It takes everything I have not to drop the wounded pretense and smile back. When he's not lecturing me on all the ways Shades are evil, Ezzo's actually quite easy to talk to.

"I mean, 'better' is a pretty subjective term when it comes to day-dreaming, but I would probably run some kind of art class." It's the very last thing I expect him to say, and he says it so quietly that it almost feels as though he didn't intend to say it, either, like he's admitting to a dark past.

"So you—you're an artist?" Perhaps the reason that strikes me as so implausible is because I've never had to think of Hues as anything other than an illegal act. But Ezzo does have that look about him, I guess. The fine, pretty features; the distant, piercing eyes; the mussed, slightly too long hair that lends him a romantic charm. I can imagine him swanning around an art studio, his clothes stained with paint and his hands creating beauty with a brush. I think that life would suit him.

"What, *me?* Gods, no—there's not an artistic bone in my body." He immediately dispels that notion to dust. "I just miss being surrounded by it, is all. By the joy of creation."

"Then why did you leave it behind?" Even as I ask the question, I realize the answer might lay with my kind. "Did the trackers drive you out of Isitar?"

"No, it wasn't the trackers." The change in him is both instant and abrupt. In the space between heartbeats, his face hardens, the warmth in him chilling to ice. Gone is the spark of humor and the willingness to while away the walk with idle chit-chat. He's back to being the surly Hue again, his eyes blinking white as a way of announcing that this conversation is done.

And so, the silence stretches between us, growing heavy and loaded as we continue to trail Alara through the shadows. We've long since crossed out of Meridian territory, though the streets she's taking aren't telling me anything other than that she's headed towards the slums. It's only when Ezzo finally blinks out of his mood that I get a sense for what destination she has in mind, since the square we're in plays host to Sarotuza's biggest market.

The paupers' market, we call it in the snobbier parts of town, a sprawling bazaar when it's open—though at this time of night, it looks more like the carcass of a giant whale, all bones, no blubber, a maze of densely packed stalls that have been shrewdly stripped of their merchandise.

"This is where her trail ends," Ezzo says, cool and casual, as though he's not been ignoring me for the best part of half an hour.

"Okay, so then now what?" I shake my wrist at him. "While you were busy brooding, did you figure out how we're going to phase after her?" If I weren't so busy brooding myself, I might have thought to ask him that earlier, since this is one hurdle that no amount of discussion can overcome.

"Relax, I'm not an idiot." Ezzo's nonchalance fast turns smug. "I had Cemmy give me the key."

"You—"

*Unbelievable.* His admission robs me of breath. This whole time—this whole baffling conversation and the sulky silence that came after—my freedom has literally been on his person, mocking me from within arm's reach. He must think *I'm* the idiot for not realizing that.

"You are such an ass."

"Never said I wasn't."

No, he didn't. He just assumed the role of *pleasant* for a brief moment in time.

"Now, do you want to keep insulting me, or do you want to get out of these cuffs?" he asks.

"I'm actually quite capable of doing both."

"How very impressive of you." Ezzo turns to show me his back. "The key's in my pocket."

"And you want me to . ... what? Watch you get it?"

"No, I need *you* to get it," he says, in a tone which strongly implies that I should already know why.

"Because you're some kind of pervert? Get it yourself!"

"Raya, I *can't.*" I'm beginning to recognize the different tenors of Ezzo's sighs. "I'm not a Bronze and the key's not endowed with magic, that's why I had to ask Cemmy to uncuff you from the pipe." He swipes his foot through the nearest stall in demonstration, a reminder that he doesn't control his physicality like I do. The key would sink right through his fingers.

*Colors help me, how is this my life?*

"Left or right pocket?" I ask, since I have no intention of groping him more than once.

"Left, and don't worry, being a Hue's not contagious."

*Well, thank the shadows for that.* There is absolutely no non-awkward way to reach into his pants. No way to ignore the solid feel or the shape of him, or how his breath catches in his throat and shivers down his spine. The fates sure are getting creative in their endeavors to turn this foolishness into love. Telling me to kiss him in the tavern, shackling us together at the house, forcing us closer and closer—and now this? What's next? A single room at an inn with only one bed?

"What exactly would you have done if I'd said no?" I ask once I've snatched my hand back, trying to dispel the uncomfortably charged silence.

"It honestly didn't occur to me." Ezzo shrugs as I unlock my prison. "Why wouldn't you have agreed to get the key if it meant removing the cuffs?"

And all at once, it hits me. The sudden and monumental shift in power.

I'm finally free of the iron. Free of him and the disgrace that would come from allowing a half breed to tether me to his arm. I could shimmer him to the trackers if I wanted, and none of his incriminating stories would stick now that I'm the one in charge.

"If the Hue phases again, you'll never find her without my gift," Ezzo says, guessing at the nefarious thoughts I'm weighing up. *And following her was your idea*, the steel in his expression seems to add. Though I do also see a shred of doubt in him, a tiny flash of fear in the tightening around his eyes. Maybe he's decided he doesn't want to die today, after all. Maybe he's regretting the choice to let me hold the cards.

*He makes worse decisions than I do.* With a muttered curse, I reach for his cuff.

"We find Alara, we figure out what she's doing, then we're done. We pretend this"—I point between us—"never happened. Understand?"

He gets to live, I get to impress the Council, the future gets to stop the Meridian from killing another child. Everybody wins.

"Nothing would make me happier," Ezzo clips in reply, then together, we blink back into the physical realm.

The world explodes into sound and color, the darkness changing in texture as we swap the smokey ink of the Gray for the warm flicker of coal-burning lamps.

"Can you see her?" I whisper, scanning the near-empty market.

"Not yet, but she can't have gone far. Let's try back there." He motions towards the row of workshops that sits behind the stands. "If she's after a typic, then that's where they'll be."

Right, of course. Because there are always a few vendors who work late into the night, and work equals craftsmen and craftsmen equal apprentices. Older children, usually, the kind the Meridian asked Alara to abduct.

"There—by the blacksmith's hut." The moment we round the corner, I catch a glimpse of her silver robe and her mousy brown hair, making straight for a boy who's fetching water for his master's tank. He's older than the girl we watched shatter, stronger-looking by a decent margin and quite clearly better nourished, exactly per the Meridian's instructions.

"Okay, good." Ezzo pitches his voice low. "Then you distract Alara while I scare the boy away."

"What—no. That is not what we agreed."

"What do you mean *not what we agreed*? We agreed to stop her."

"*Stop* and *follow* are not the same thing, Ezzo. If we want to know what the Meridian is up to, then we have to let Alara take him."

"Let Alara take him?" he parrots, mouth gaping as though I've lost my marbles. "That is a *child*, Raya. He can't be more than fourteen!"

"And that girl couldn't have been more than six." I refuse to let his outrage shame me. "Every pile of glass in that house was a child, Ezzo—and poor children, at that, street kids people are quick to forget." I certainly forgot about them quickly enough; after a few short seconds spent reading their names on all those "missing" flyers, I put the thought right out of my mind, went to go annoy my rich mother. "If we run Alara off now, we'd only be sending her in search of the next. So yes, we have to let her take him. That's how we find out what the Meridian is doing—and how we stop him from doing it again." My logic is callous; I know that—but it's also sound and Ezzo is smart enough to follow it through to the same conclusion. He drags in a mouthful of air, then another, and another, mulling over whatever objections are still urging him to argue, discounting them one by one until there's no other option left.

"Gods, you Shades really are something," he mutters, even as he relents.

"Hey, that's a Hue doing the abducting, so you can put that sanctimony away. Will she use her gift to do it, do you think?"

"No, our gifts only work in the Gray—and she's an Emerald, anyway, so hers is a protective gift, not an offensive one, good for projecting her In-Betweens around others but not for much else. My guess is she'll use a charm—there, watch her hands," Ezzo says, right as Alara slips something into the boy's pocket.

*Well, I'll be damned.* A dazed look instantly clouds his face. "A compulsion charm. How did you know?"

"That's what I would have done."

It's quite the admission after the scolding he just gave me.

"Spoken like a true criminal."

"We are what you Shades make of us. Now, come on, I don't want to lose them."

We move as quietly as we can, keeping a healthy distance so as not to alert Alara to our presence. Once she's steered the boy out of the market, she sticks to narrow lanes and twisting alleys, leading us back towards the part of Sarotuza into which the Meridian has sunk his talons. But not to his church or to the halfway house—her destination proves to be far more mundane. A laundry hall. Where the sour smell of the city gives way to the pungent stink of lye and citrus water stewing in massive pails.

"What the hells is she looking for here?"

"No idea." An identical question is written into every line of Ezzo's face. "But if we follow them in there, she'll notice; we should phase back into the Gray, track their echoes."

With a nod, I blink into the shadows after him. Laundry halls are a physical endeavor, powered by sweat, soap, and dozens of typics who spend their days scrubbing away life's stains.

"Shit. Can you see her?" Amid all the pails and the workers, I instantly lose sight of our prey. "Where did she go?"

"Over there." Ezzo points to a pair of fireflies flickering through the haze. Though how he can tell one echo from another is anybody's guess.

"Are you sure it's them?"

"Pretty sure," he says, expecting me to take that answer on faith. It's only when I grumble at him to *say more* that he grudgingly adds, "The flickering makes it look as though all the echoes are moving, but most of them are actually not, that's just a slight migration. Whereas those two keep jumping larger distances between flickers— that's how you tell."

"You can really see that from here?" I ask, still struggling to make the distinction.

"I've had a lot of practice, remember?" His irritation blunts an inch. "This isn't all that different to watching trails."

Which makes the more interesting question: *why did he stop watching them?* Because someone this good at paying attention doesn't just slip up one day and get caught, let alone twice in the same week.

Something happened to him.

And I don't mean the story he told me about his parents— something more recent has made him lose the will to see. Maybe even the same something that turned him cold when my questions skirted too near.

I follow him through the laundry hall and down a narrow set of stairs, towards a dimly lit cellar that screams of danger and mal intent. Why else would Alara be leading a child into the darkest depths of this building? Why else would the door be made of iron and require three separate locks and a chain?

"We stay in the Gray until we know what's in there—agreed?" Ezzo asks, though he's asking in name only.

"Agreed." But this is one command I have no intention of fighting, because with each step we take, the dread in my bones is deepening, the churn in my stomach gathering in bile and strength. I already know what the Meridians do in the shadows: they shatter children and murder Shades. Whatever we're about to find in this cellar won't be good.

*Colors help me . . .*

The scene that greets us lives up to every one of my fears and worse. A double-width surgeon's table dominates the center of the room, with two sets of restraints set at intervals along the metal, made to hold a person by the neck, wrists, and ankles, like some kind of medieval torture. All manner of ominous tools hang off rusted hooks along the wall: needles, knives, tourniquets, lengths of rubber tubing and bottles filled to the brim with a liquid that's viscous and cloyed.

Blood.

Even stripped of color, the sight is enough to sicken, as is the fear emanating from the frantic echo flickering inside the cage in the corner. That makes four echoes total—Alara, the typic, the prisoner, and an unknown.

"We need to get in there." I scan the room for some crevice to hide in, desperate to blink back into the physical realm and see exactly what horrors are about to befall the boy we allowed Alara to kidnap.

"Over there." Ezzo motions towards the recessed gap beneath the stairs. "But if they spot us, don't think, just phase. We can't help anyone if we're dead."

*Well, isn't that cheerful?* I squeeze into the tight space after him, so close that we end up hip to hip and chest to shoulder, his breath hot against my neck in a way that feels downright lewd. Though the second we blink out of the shadows, all thoughts of our compromising position are gone, replaced by a jolt of the utmost revulsion.

The stench is overwhelming, not just lye and lemon, but blood and decay. Blasphemy and hubris.

"You've done me proud, Alara, this tribute will serve us well." The Meridian's voice immediately snaps me to attention, setting my nerves on edge. "Get him ready. I'll fetch the Shade."

"Let's get a better look. *Carefully.*" Ezzo's whisper is accompanied by a tiny shifting of weight, just enough of a lean to allow us a glimpse at the table.

The boy—still under the influence of Alara's charm—has already lain down without complaint, his eyes staring up vacantly as she restrains him, then steps away to fetch a wicked-looking needle. Once she returns, he doesn't stay listless for long.

With ruthless efficiency, she drives the needle into the crook of his elbow, eliciting a scream that rattles me to the bone.

"*Don't.*" Ezzo clamps an arm around my waist and a hand to my mouth, keeping me locked against him. Silent. Unable to interfere as Alara stabs the pain deeper and ties it off with a length of hemp. Clearly, she's done this before—though I can't even begin to imagine to what end. At least not until the Meridian drags a squirming girl out from the cage in the corner.

Unlike the boy, the Shade doesn't come quietly. From where we're stood, I can't get a good look at her, but I can see the struggle she puts up every inch of the way, kicking and bucking as he wrangles her onto the table, and railing against each snapping of iron as the restraints rob her of the fight in her legs, then her arms, then finally, her neck, leaving her entirely at his mercy. It's only once the Meridian is satisfied that all she can do is muffle obscenities into her gag that he moves aside and affords me a look at her face—and when he does, it takes every ounce of strength I have to not bite right through the meat of Ezzo's hand.

Because that's not just any Shade the Meridian has gone and shackled to the table; it's an Orange with dark, angular eyes and sharply cut black hair.

It's Akari.

# CHAPTER 17

# EZZO

I should have never allowed Alara to abduct the boy. Regardless of Raya's logic, I knew it was a bad idea; I felt the wrongness of it in my bones. But then I remembered the room full of shattered typics—all those piles of glass the Meridian condemned to a filthy floor—and I couldn't not do *something*. For the first time since Eve died, I felt the need to watch.

And it felt better than drinking.

It's always felt better than drinking, if I'm honest; it's why I used to spend so much time hiding inside my gift. An obsession, Eve often called it, though not the kind she discouraged unless I allowed myself to get too lost. She understood what the others didn't: that I don't watch because I'm scared, but because I'm guilty—that even a decade later, I'm still trying to atone.

When I watch, I'm useful.

When I watch, I can prevent the Council from inflicting more needless hurt—or in this case, the Divine Meridian.

*That's how we stop him from doing it again.* Heartless though it was, Raya did make a good point—and she made it sound convincing. How she did that, I don't know—I don't know why I chose to stick with her at all, what possessed me to cuff myself to a Shade, and go Hue hunting with a Shade, and make small talk with a Shade who looks at me like I'm a piece of meat to be fed to the dogs.

But I did.

Because something about her—and I don't mean the fact that she's pretty; it's not a physical thing, it's more like a . . . I can't even explain what—tugged at me in a way that felt important, like she was keeping a secret I desperately needed to learn.

So instead of leaving her to the trackers, I allowed her to drag me into this infernal plot.

I let her talk me into using a child as bait.

And now that child is being tortured in a cellar and I have no earthly clue how we're going to free him without getting ourselves caught. Already, his screams have forced me to clamp an arm around Raya's horror, but it's the moment she catches sight of the Shade strapped to the Meridian's table that her fear changes to abject shock, the kind that tells me I'll no longer be able to keep her panic under control.

*Shit.*

I phase us into the Gray before she can betray our presence, so that when she breaks free of my grip and spills her curses, they'll dissipate harmlessly into the void.

"Raya, don't—" I try to calm her, to stop her doing something reckless that'll land the both of us in that cage in the corner.

"Get off me, Ezzo, we have to go back!"

My only saving grace is that she's too incensed to initiate the blink on her own, to remember she has that power.

"Raya—"

"I said get off me, you filthy half breed! That's my friend in there! I'm *going back*!"

Ah. The force of her reaction suddenly makes sense. If it was Novi on that table, I'd be fighting me the exact same way.

"Not without a plan, you're not." I pin her to the wall with a sobering effort, keeping a firm grip on her shoulders as I demand that she look at me head-on. "If you want to save your friend, we need a plan."

"My plan is to kill them." Raya's eyes are wild, frantic, stray locks of russet framing her stern resolve. "Whether you help me or not."

"I am *trying* to help you. But you have to let me—"

"There's no time, Ezzo. Akari could already be—" *Dead.* The very thought strips the strength from her voice. And suddenly, Raya's not breathing anymore, she's gasping, her nails clawing into my skin as she struggles to keep herself whole.

"Hey—*hey*, listen to me." I tilt her face up by the chin and temper my words. "They're not going to kill her right away, okay? They could have done that in the cage if they wanted." And you don't shackle a person so tightly just to turn around and slit their throat. "You saw the tools they had in there, Raya; it's all bloodletting equipment, not designed to kill a Shade fast, but to bleed them out slow. That gives us a few minutes to think this through."

Though *why* I'm helping her do that is an entirely different question. Saving one Shade was madness enough, wasn't it? What am I even doing, conspiring to save two? I should be using the fact that she's distracted as a means to put an end to this disastrous detour, to go find the others and forget whatever evil the Divine Meridian is brewing.

*Except there's a child on that table.* It's Eve's voice chiding me from beyond the grave. A child *I* endangered and a girl for whom Raya would revolt. I remember what that kind of devotion feels like. How, to defend it, I'd have worked with any monster in the world—Shade, Hue, Council or Church. I wouldn't have discriminated across blood color, and I don't have it in me to inflict the pain I've been living with this past year on another soul, no matter how much I'm supposed to hate her.

And I don't hate her, I realize. I should but I don't. Maybe I've used up all my hate on Cemmy, or maybe I just find myself more intrigued by Raya than I am annoyed. A little impressed, even, given how much trouble she's managed to court, and how, in every instance, her first impulse has been to fight, not run; to scheme, not surrender; to hurl insults like she didn't care if they would hurt her cause. It's not every day that an acolyte breaks with the Council's edicts in an effort to prove their worth, and no normal Shade would ever work with a Hue no matter what a vision showed them or how dire that future looked. There's something else driving her, and despite my better judgement, I want to know what. Which is why—instead of abandoning her at her lowest—I allow the fledgling plan in my head to form.

"The Meridian is our biggest problem," I say, conscious of how every part of Raya is still shaking. "Since we don't know what he is yet, we don't know what he's capable of in the Gray, so you'll have to be the one who phases him out of there. I'll stay to take care of Alara and free your friend."

"No, absolutely not." The thunder in her refusal is pure steel. "I'm not leaving her."

"Raya, if he can shimmer, I won't last three seconds against him, and while I'm willing to help you, I'm not willing to die for you—or for her—so it's this, or nothing." I deliberately turn my words cold. She needs to know that a bitter pill is the only kind I'm offering and that her choice is to swallow it or not. And though that message takes a few seconds to fully register—to cut through the fog of worst-case scenarios her mind has surely decided to concoct—when it finally does, Raya bats me away angrily and pushes off the wall.

"I swear to all three Gods, Ezzo, if you're lying to me—"

"What would be the point in lying when I could have already gone?" This time, my words are sincere, and Raya believes them because she wants to believe them—because she needs to believe them—and because they ring true. She may not understand why I'm choosing to help her, but she will accept my help. When it's someone you love strapped to a madman's table, you'll do whatever it takes.

By the time we phase back into the physical realm, both the Shade and the typic are screaming. Though where her cries speak of fear and helplessness, his are of an entirely different sort.

Pain.

Potent and acute.

*By my colors . . . what did they do?* While we were sequestered in the Gray, a giant needle was shoved into the Shade's arm, as well, connecting her to the boy via a curled length of tubing. I think they're—oh Gods, they're draining her blood into him, and it's causing his skin to sear black and blister, writhing him with indescribable pain. Of all the sick tortures I'd imagined, this one didn't even make the list, a cruelty so bizarre it borders on insane.

*What in the world are these zealots trying to achieve?* Beside me, Raya pales to snow, her whole body tensing with the need to act, now, and to do it recklessly, forget the plan she'd just agreed to follow.

*On three,* I mouth, keeping a lid on her urgency until we're in position and ready to go. *One . . . two . . . three.*

With a purposefully obnoxious war cry, Raya charges at the Meridian and tackles him into the Gray at a run. Once they meet the shadows, she'll get in a good hit, if she's able, and then quickly shimmer away in the hopes that he'll shimmer after her, that he won't allow a Shade to abscond with the knowledge of his secret haunt. Hopefully, Raya is faster than he is, or else she'll probably end up right back here, lying prone on his table with a needle buried in her arm. But that's the risk she agreed to take so that I can get her friend—Akari—to safety.

The moment they're gone, I spring out from beneath the stairs, speeding straight towards Alara, who spots me a split second too late. We collide with a grunt and a sharp exhaling of air, my momentum propelling us into the iron cage in the corner, where she won't be able to phase. Without that ability, she's at the mercy of my height and weight, struggling to hold her own in a fight she didn't see coming. A fight she cannot win without magical aid.

"Oh no, you don't." I remember her taste for pre-spelled charms in time to stop her reaching for one herself, keeping her pinned down while I lay claim to the crystals and render her docile with a flash of Red. All the while, the screams coming from the table continue to echo around the cellar in panicked waves, the typic's pain growing in anguish, Akari's fear rising in pitch.

"Hold on." I lock the cage behind me before rushing to her side. "I'm going to get you both out of here. Just hold on."

Her protests immediately intensify beneath the gag. For while her eyes might be wide with terror, they're also clear and they're focused, and there's no mistaking the fact that she's recognized me for the

Hue I am. I recognize her, too, come to think of it. The bobbed, black hair, and the sharp-cut features, and the hidden fold to her eyelids. She was the one standing next to Raya during my execution, but unlike her friend, when it came time to enact my sentence, she didn't look away.

She wanted to watch me die in that court chamber.

She's a scared, hungry tiger and I'm about to snap open her chains.

"You can trust me, okay? I'm with Raya." The name appears to calm and confuse her in equal measure, as though she understands my words, but not this turn of events. "Now, I'm really sorry, but this might hurt," I say as I grab the base of the needle protruding from her flesh. It's a crude, cruel thing, and judging by the burgeoning flush of bruises, it took more than one clean stab for the point to pierce the vein. And though I tease it out as gently and quickly as I dare, Akari still bucks on the table, her hands clenching and unclenching, her muffled moans sharpening to a wail.

"Done, it's done." I toss the bloodied needle to the floor and take stock of her restraints. The iron has left a series of bitter burns along her skin, blistering it the way her blood blistered the typic's—albeit to a lesser extent.

*A problem for later.* Since I didn't find a key on Alara, I start searching the walls for something I could use as a pick.

"Sparing the Shade will only delay the inevitable," she seethes from inside her cage. "You cannot stop the will of the divine. He will cleanse the world of magic."

Oh, good, she's not just a fanatic, she's a fanatic who doesn't seem to realize that the rapture she's preaching would affect her, as well, that she's as tied to her color as the rest of us. Or hells, maybe she does realize it and that's actually part of the appeal. It's not uncommon for a Hue to grow self-loathing.

"Once these are off, I'll take you to Raya," I tell Akari, ridding her mouth of the gag.

"What did you do to her?" Her voice is weak and stripped raw from the yelling, but the fire in her question is all hate.

"I didn't *do* anything to her—and before you ask, she's fine." I hope. For both our sakes. "Her job was to lure the Meridian away, mine is to get you out of here, so please, don't try to kill me when I'm done," I say, getting to work on the cuffs. Cemmy's always been better at picking locks than I am, but I do okay when it comes to jail breaks, even if my skills are rusty. Knowing the theory is half the battle—the rest is muscle memory, luck, and a little patience. It only takes me a few seconds to release Akari's legs.

"Raya will explain everything properly," I add as I move onto the next fetter. "But until then, she said to tell you that she fucked up and asked an open question. She said you'd know what that means. Do you?"

"Yes, I know what it means," Akari growls, though there's no hiding the sudden storm in her expression, the flash of shock and the spark of anger, the stab of hurt that causes her pupils to dilate. "Will you hurry up?"

"I'm going as fast as I can." With a few more twists, her arms go free, then the last remaining shackle is the iron around her neck. The moment that springs open, she scrambles off the table with imprudent haste.

"Whoa—easy." The blood loss immediately buckles her knees, forcing me to lurch forward and catch her.

"Don't touch me, half breed." She shoves me away despite her inability to balance.

"No wonder you and Raya are friends, you have the same bedside manner," I mutter, turning my attention to the boy, instead. "Just try not to fall and hit your head for a minute. I'd rather not have to carry you out of here."

"Then stop wasting time on the typic and let's go," she barks, damn near stunning me silent.

"You can't be serious." I fix her a look that's pure judgement. "We're not leaving him."

"Why not? He's a typic."

"No, he's a *child*." Gods, what is wrong with these Shades? "And he was captured, same as you, and tortured, *worse* than you, so try to muster up a shred of compassion," I grit, though even as I clamber to pick open his shackles, I find myself wondering if it's already too late. Yes, the boy has finally quieted his screaming, but the transfusion has left him sobbing with misery, his body riddled with weeping blisters and oozing welts.

"Here, take these." I fish a handful of Green crystals from Alara's stash as the boy slowly staggers to his feet. Healing charms are rarely as powerful as a bespoke spell or a tonic—they're made to treat smaller ailments, not burns inflicted by a Shade—but it's better than nothing, especially since even the charms cost more than a blacksmith's apprentice would make. "Now, run."

Despite the pain of his injuries, the boy doesn't need telling twice.

"Great, he's gone, so take me to Raya."

I can't decide if I should be impressed by Akari's single-minded persistence or enraged.

"You know, you're really in no position to be making demands here." She's lost too much color, for one thing, and there's enough iron in this cellar to keep it from regenerating itself. "But since I made a promise to Raya, are you going to let me help you or not?" I almost wish that she would double down on her disgust and say *not*, that way, I could absolve myself of this responsibility and disappear into the night like I should have done earlier, when first given the chance to slip away. Because technically, I've already honored my promise; I've freed Akari and spared Raya the loss of a friend. So perhaps now's the time to stop playing with fire, acknowledge that she's a Shade and I'm a Hue and that our paths were never destined to converge. Find a different way to feel useful.

"Why did Raya want you to tell me about the open question?" Instead, Akari asks me the one thing Raya was certain she'd ask—before allowing me to lend her help.

"She said breaking her magic is the only reason you'd accept for why she's working with me."

And on that, it seems Raya was right. Because with a huff and a creative string of obscenities, Akari finally lets me drape her arm around my shoulders and phase us into the Gray.

# CHAPTER 18

# RAYA

Akari has never not been there for me—not once in the thirteen years we've known each other. Through every success, every failure, every fight with my parents and every subsequent despair, through my break-up with Killen, and the Council's threat to bind my magic, and the night I stupidly snuck into the seeing tower to ask an open question. She's always known exactly when I'd need her. To the point that *I* should have known something was wrong when I disappeared and she didn't come looking. I should have realized that something terrible had also befallen her.

Maybe if I had, she wouldn't have ended up strapped to the Meridian's table.

Maybe if I had, then her life wouldn't be hanging by a fraying thread and this embarrassment of a plan.

And as far as plans go, this one truly is bad. Tackle the Divine Meridian—the man whose color Ezzo's gift hasn't been able to identify—into the Gray and then hope that I can shimmer away faster than he can follow. Hope that Ezzo will keep his word to free Akari. Hope that all three of us live long enough for her to try and kill me herself.

Which she'll absolutely want to do; I made sure of that when I asked Ezzo to tell her about my broken magic—and I had to do that to ensure that she'd actually accept his help, understand how I came to align myself with the very Hue we left the Academy to apprehend.

*Better she kills me than the Meridian does.* The thought fuels me as I speed across the cellar and throw my arms around his waist, blinking us both into the shadows with a dramatic war cry. Because if Akari can kill me, it means that she's alive. It means that I am, too. That neither of us wound up dying at the hand of a zealot.

He's still mid-grunt when the air around us strips of color, which—just as I'd hoped—grants me the element of surprise. The moment I see Gray, I give him one good shove then shimmer off in the opposite direction.

*Please be slower than I am. Please be slower than I am. Please be slower than I am.* The first few seconds are an agony of paranoia. They're nervous glances over my shoulder and phantom claws tearing at my skin. They're a questioning of every ripple in the shadows. Though as the cellar gives way to the laundry hall gives way to the street, my heart slowly begins to calm its pounding. I can still sense the Meridian behind me, hear the rustle of his robes as he scrambles to give chase. But if he's not caught up to me yet, then the plan is working; I'm both avoiding capture and drawing him away, giving Ezzo time to save Akari.

I'm almost to the edge of Meridian territory when my feet suddenly grow heavy, as though I'm no longer shimmering through smoke but crawling through sand. No—wait; it's not my feet, it's the shadows. They're getting denser, somehow. Closing in around me.

*What in the hells—?* I don't jerk to a stop so much as I sublime to it, like a fly caught in amber and slowly entombed in bark.

"You can't outrun your betters, full-blood." The Meridian's voice is everywhere and nowhere all at once. In my head, and behind me, and assaulting my sanity from every side. "You are but a shade of the darkness whereas I am the absence of light." In the space between blinks, he's appeared before me, stepping out of the ether in a way that defies the laws governing our kind. Not like he's becoming one with the shadows, but like he's bending them, displacing them, swallowing them up. Using them to suffocate and restrain me.

*How will I get away from him?* I beg the future, groping, straining, clambering for the magic in my blood. But it seems whatever's affecting the shadows is affecting my power, as well. For the first time in my life, I can't reach it. And I don't just mean I can't get it to answer, but I can't feel it at all. Almost as if my color has already been bound.

"Tell me, what will you do when the well you draw from fills with poison?" the Meridian asks, appraising me the way one would a bug. "How will you survive when the power you've been leeching disappears from the Gray?"

Up close, he's even more intimidating than he looked from afar. Piercing blue eyes—devoid of the tells of magic; stern, hooded features; a smile that could rot meat. His ashy hair hangs down past his ears in a messy tangle, the waves falling like spent matches against the chalky white of his skin, pale as a deadly cliff. And yet, every part of him exudes charisma. He makes me *want* to watch him, even in the silence between threats.

"I don't know what you're talking about." It takes a staggering amount of effort to form the words. "You're the one leeching power." He's quite literally strapping Shades to a table and bleeding the color from their veins.

"I am setting the shadows free!" he roars, the rage twisting his expression into a livid mask. "I'm the only one who can live in harmony with the darkness, the last remaining void among a rainbow of thieves." His assertion doesn't make a lick of sense, though I don't expect that he'll explain it, nor do I intend to stick around and ask. Whatever his beliefs, we're never going to agree on his actions, and there's no point trying to reason with a madness this pronounced. What I need to do is figure a way out of here, before he grows tired of lecturing his prey.

*Phase, Raya. You need to phase.* In the Gray, the Meridian is a dangerous anomaly, but in the real world, he's just a man. There are no shadows for him to manipulate there, no darkness to do his bidding or magic to inflame his ire.

*Come on, come on, come on.* With his power deadening my color, blinking between worlds becomes as grueling as running through a wall of brick—yet I'm sure I can do it. When I commune with the future, I have to engage my magic, whereas phasing is more akin to a fluid changing of states. It's not casting, it's thinking your body across realms, either towards the pull of shadows or against it. And right now, every ounce of strength I have is begging the shadows to let me go.

*Let me go, let me go, let me go.* The pressure surrounding me increases, the weight of smoke and ink crushing the marrow from my bones. *Please, you have to let me go.* When finally they do, it feels as though my flesh is ripping, like the strain of victory might rear up and shatter me whole.

But it doesn't.

I return to the real world with a growl and a crisp rending of air, to a nausea so intense it doubles me over.

*Damn it, Raya, you don't have time for this. Run. Now.* I force my feet to start moving, to find the nearest shelter, the nearest alley, the nearest crowd, any place that could hide me should the Meridian choose to chase me across realms. It's only once I'm several streets removed, breathless and drenched in sweat, that I begin to suspect he didn't bother.

Clearly, he's decided that one lone Shade is unlikely to upset his plans.

And to be perfectly honest, I can't say I blame him.

Because what I watched him do was so impossible—so contrary to color theory—that I wouldn't believe my story, either. Without proof, all the Council will see is a desperate Indigo trying to save face with a lie.

*Akari's your proof.* The thought jolts me back to attention. What if Ezzo hasn't freed her from the cellar yet? What if Alara got the better of him? What if by the time we pulled our plan together, Akari was already dead? *What if, what if, what if . . .* my mind is suddenly awash with dread.

It was my fault that she was there to begin with.

My poor decision that kick-started this chain of events.

If she dies, it'll be because I was so busy thinking about myself—about my future, my problems, my broken magic—that I sent her off to sell her skills *alone* in some sleazy tavern, just so I could get the answers I wanted without her learning of my mistake. And I did that despite knowing full well how dangerous Sarotuza has become for Shades, that she wouldn't be safe out there on her own.

*Show me where I'll find her.*

It takes all of my courage to ask the future that question. So long as she's still with Ezzo, I'm confident it'll answer, but *what* it might show me is another question altogether, a whole different testing of fate. Though as it turns out, my fears have been concentrated in the entirely wrong place, on Akari's death instead of Ezzo's.

*Oh, crap.* The vision that greets me is almost too predictable. A relief, yes, but also a disaster I should have seen coming from several hundred miles away.

*Crap, crap, crap.* I immediately start running towards the inn the future is flashing in my head. Saving Akari from the Divine Meridian was one thing, now I have to go save Ezzo from the wrath of my best friend.

# CHAPTER 19

# EZZO

In hindsight, the mistake I made was trusting a Shade.

Again.

With Akari weak from the blood loss and barely able to stand, we didn't stray far from the laundry hall—or from the plan I'd made with Raya. *Just go to the nearest inn. That way, if the future won't show me where you are, I'll know where to look,* she'd said, right before we phased back into the cellar.

So that's exactly what I did.

I led us to the inn at the top of the street, a middling but clean establishment where I traded one of Alara's charms for a room and a couple of hot meals—both of which I gave Akari. Hells, I even offered to play lookout if she wanted to phase into the shadows and regain her strength.

Which she did.

Much faster than I expected.

And the moment she shed the effects of the iron, her patience for sharing space with a half breed dropped from "barely there" to "no longer exists".

*Where's Raya?* When she first barked that question at me, I told her the same thing I did in the cellar: Raya's job was to distract the Meridian and she'll double back to find us the second she gives him the slip. But as the minutes ticked by, that answer stopped placating Akari's anger and her questions began to grow teeth.

*Why is it taking so long?*

*When will she get here?*

*What if the future's refusing to show her the inn?*

That's when—in my exasperation—I made my second mistake of the day: I told her the future seems plenty happy to send Raya visions when they somehow involve me.

It was the wrong thing to say.

And it's the reason I find myself pinned to the wall by an angry flash of Orange magic, an invisible noose tightening around my neck.

"Akari—*stop*, I—I told you where she is." My protest is a feeble gasping of air, stifled by color and cut through with fear. Of all the ways I could have died during this rescue, this is by far the dumbest, but it's also the most likely to succeed. Because there is no fighting Akari's power; if I can't talk her out of strangling me, death is where this tantrum leads.

"Stop lying to me! If that was true, she'd already be here!"

Black spots start dancing at the edge of my vision, my lungs screaming—no, begging—for reprieve.

"Did you hurt her, huh? Is she dead?" Akari only intensifies her grip. "Damn it, half breed, tell me what you did!"

"I didn't—I'm—she's not—"

"Kiri—no!" The door suddenly bursts open, a very alive Raya barreling her way in. "Let him go!"

*Yes, please, let me go.* I never thought I'd be happy to see a Shade, nor that the relief I'd feel at seeing her would extend beyond her ability to save my skin.

"No. Not until he stops lying about what he—" Akari trails off abruptly, her mind slowly catching up to who she's seeing. "Oh my Gods, Ray!" In an instant, she's crossed the room to pull Raya into a tight hug, though her hold on the magic doesn't give an inch. "I thought he killed you."

"No such luck, I'm afraid," Raya says. "But you do have to stop killing him."

"Why? He's a Hue. Isn't this what we—?"

"It's a long story." Raya's quick to cut her off. "Just please, let him go."

"Fine."

As the noose finally slackens, I gasp and fall to my knees.

"But I suggest you talk fast."

*

"Of all the stupid, reckless, self-destructive things you could do." Akari paces her anger up and down the tiny room, though—thankfully—it's no longer directed solely at me. "You promised me you wouldn't do this, Ray. You promised me you wouldn't ask an open question."

"I know, Kiri, I—"

"No, uh-uh, you don't get to Kiri me right now. How the hells did you even manage it?" Her hands rake bruising tracks through her hair from scalp to tip. "Saleen's spell should have stopped you doing anything that irresponsible for days."

"Killen." Raya's reply is another unfamiliar name. "I asked him to accelerate off the compulsion."

"I'm sorry—*Killen?*" At that, Akari only grows more irate. "Your ex-boyfriend who hates you, Killen? That's who you chose to tell?"

From what I can gather, it sounds as though Akari went to great lengths to stop Raya from risking her magic, only for Raya to go to even greater lengths to do it anyway, and that between them, they managed to involve half the school.

"No, I didn't *tell* Killen, exactly." Raya's eyes stay glued to her feet. "He sort of just . . . guessed when he caught me looking up fate-touched magic in the archives the next day."

"Oh, well, in that case, it's definitely not a problem." Akari throws both arms up in frustration. "I'm sure he didn't go straight to Professor Lyons the second we left!"

"Erm . . . is that really the most important thing?" I ask, cutting into their inane argument. Because given what we watched the Meridian do, *to her,* only an hour ago, their standing at the Academy should be skirting the bottom of the list.

"No, you're right." Akari rounds on me with a vengeance. "The most important thing is why she's working with a *half breed.*"

"We prefer Hues, if you don't mind." I bristle. *Or, you know, just about anything else.*

"I do mind, actually—since just getting caught in this room with you would be enough to end our futures."

"Hey, I've been offering to leave since the last bell," I remind her. But every time I tried, a flash of Orange would pin me to the chair, or seal the door shut, or take another bite of my air, and she can shimmer where I can't so there was absolutely no point in phasing.

"But that's what I've been trying to tell you, Kiri," Raya says, stepping between us like a shield. "Our future is already at risk—that's what the open vision showed me."

"You have no idea what that vision showed you!" Akari's temper is growing thin. "You said it yourself, Ray: it was too abstract and it didn't make any sense. It isn't possible."

"Except it is possible," Raya insists. "Ezzo lived through something similar last year. Go ahead, ask him."

I'm pretty sure I'd die of shock if she did.

"I don't need to ask the half breed anything!"

Yup, there it is.

"If there was a threat to all magic, someone—your parents, for example, or . . . I don't know, the entire seers' guild—would have seen it!"

"Unless they didn't," Raya tells her, the words laden with plea. "I think the open question allowed me to see a future they can't. And I know how crazy that sounds, okay? But what if the guild has accidentally shut out our ability to see this kind of risk?"

"Colors help me, you're as bad as he is," Akari mutters, shooting me a scathing look. "We would have *felt* the effects of a Gray-wide catastrophe. Seeing isn't the only way to see."

"No, you wouldn't have, actually." The way she's railing at Raya—like she's right and we're a couple of stupid kids—irks me enough to wade back in. Raya just saved her life, for fuck's sake. She took on a man of unknown power without blinking; she could have *died* doing it—hells, I was starting to worry she *had* died, and not just because of what that would have meant for me. In distracting the Divine

Meridian, Raya did something braver than most passive Shades ever will—the very least Akari could do is shut up for a second and listen. "The power drain started in Isitar, and for months, the effects were localized," I say, spelling the point clear. "They didn't reach you because we stopped the shadows from collapsing. You'd have only felt something if we'd allowed the Church to win."

"Well, isn't that convenient? You have zero proof and we're supposed to just believe you."

What is impossible, on the other hand, is arguing with someone who refuses to hear.

"What you believe doesn't change what happened." I sigh, lacing my voice with indifference. "And after what the Meridian did to you and that typic, I think we can all agree that something *is* happening here."

"Come on, Kiri, you saw what he's doing with the blood," Raya adds, chipping away at her friend's resolve bit by bit. "You were there, on that awful table, and I know it scared you just as much as it scared me."

Judging by the violent shiver that rakes Akari, I'd venture it scared her more than she's willing to admit. That she'd prefer to keep masking the nightmare with fury, bury the fear.

"But that's the part that makes even less sense than the rest of it." With a long exhale, the fight in her finally yields. "Doesn't he realize the typics have already tried messing with our blood in every conceivable way? Eating it, drinking it, transfusing it . . . none of it works. You can't assume a Shade's color."

On that, she is right; this is hardly the first time someone's had this bright idea. The typics have spent their entire history trying to get at our magics; it was one of their favorite pastimes for hundreds of years. The only reason it doesn't happen anymore is because it always, *always* fails—and there's so much literature attesting to that fact that they simply resolved to hate us, instead, chose to align themselves with religion. So the Meridian is either laughably oblivious, or after something else.

"What if it's not about assuming your color . . ." I come at the problem a different way. "What Raya and I saw wasn't a typic using magic, it was a typic in the Gray—and then after she'd shattered, the Meridian said, 'how long did this one last?', like keeping her there was the point."

"And the room of shards we found suggests he's done this before," Raya adds, catching up to my thinking. "To a whole bunch of typics—probably at least as many as the kids that have gone missing."

"That's far more than the Shades he's killed." Akari's arms cross with a challenge. "There were dozens of missing kids on those flyers, but so far, he's only bled about ten Shades."

*Ten Shades?* That number is so much higher than I expected. How has the Council turned a blind eye to so many deaths? Why are they just standing idly by while the Meridian gives the typics exactly what they've always craved: public displays of violence against magic?

"He could be spreading the blood around . . . transfusing multiple typics from one Shade?" I counter Akari's objection. Which would make the girl we saw the last in a long line of tests, a casualty of trial and error.

"That would explain all those bottles he had in the cellar." Raya takes my suggestion and runs with it. "If he was bleeding them slowly, he could have used them as a source for days. Weeks, even."

"Okay, but for what reason?" Another stark chill shudders Akari. "Why would he want to phase typics into the Gray? They can't exist there. They'd be destabilizing the shadows, at best."

At worst, they'd collapse them entirely.

"So maybe he wants the Gray gone." I shrug, because who the hell knows what drives the whims of a zealot. Once they've stooped low enough to start killing, what difference does it really make?

"But . . . see, I don't think he does." It's now come Raya's turn to pace. "The way he talked about the shadows—the way he *controlled* them—it was almost as if he felt . . . entitled to the Gray. Like it was made for him, specifically. Not for Shades."

"Except he is a Shade." Akari offers up yet another wrong conclusion I'm forced to correct.

"Actually, we're not quite sure what he is. My gift, it—I've never seen anything like him."

"And he called himself something different, too," Raya's quick to jump in and say. "A *void* is the word he used. The last remaining void."

"Which isn't a thing." Akari groans as she drops down to the bed. "All that tells us is that a delusional man is delusional and that *he* is bad at working his gift."

"Come on, Kiri, that's not fair." Raya's beginning to sound as exasperated as I feel. "Did you notice anything strange about him? When he grabbed you, I mean?" She approaches the subject gingerly—delicately—and given the way Akari's cheeks pink with the question, I get a good sense for why that is.

Since the moment Raya got here, Akari has been steering this conversation away from herself—away from the series of events that led her to the Meridian's table—and if I had to guess, I'd chalk it down to shame. She is an Orange Shade, after all. Strength magic. Second in its formidability only to Red.

Yet we found her in a cage.

Then, to add insult to injury, she was rescued by a half breed.

As far as embarrassments go, this one has to sting.

"No, I didn't." She lies back to stare at the ceiling. "He looked like every other typic in that tavern. No fancy robes, no sacred sun sigil, and he must have been wearing a glamour since I didn't recognize his face. He asked me about my magic, then my prices, then the next thing I knew, I was following him to that cellar. I didn't want to, but I did, even though I never saw him cast a spell."

"He must have slipped you a compulsion charm," I say, seeing how the method's a perfect fit. "His Hue did the same thing to the typic."

"Do I look like an idiot?" Akari's shame fast turns mean. "I would have noticed if he tried to slip me something."

No, I very much doubt she would have; people rarely ever notice the dance of thieves.

"Show me how you were standing," I tell her, reaching for one of Alara's crystals.

"Excuse me?"

"Just . . . pitch me your magic, exactly like you did him." I make to help her back to her feet.

"No, half breed, I don't think I will." She bats me away, and that split second of movement is all I need.

"Fine, you don't have to pitch me—it's already done. Check your pocket." I take immense satisfaction in watching her face flare a deeper shade of beet.

"How in the—?"

"If he's a practiced hand, that's how easy it would have been." Hells, I'm not even that good at it—picking pockets has always been more Cemmy's thing. In comparison, my technique is downright sloppy.

"Gods, of course you'd be a thief."

"Your kind never left me much of a choice." I meet her derision with a scowl. In fact, they have a whole guild dedicated to making sure no Hue is ever safe enough to hold an honest job. There was a brief time, a few years ago, where Eve and I did try to go straight, work instead of steal. We became messengers for Isitar's elite, used the Gray as a means of outpacing their regular couriers. And it was fun, while it lasted—a way to make some coin and get one over on the typics. But as with everything in our lives, the fun only lasted until it didn't. The moment our superior delivery skills started drawing attention, we stopped playing with fire and went back to thieving.

"That's because *your* kind is a threat." Akari hurls the charge at me. "You take power from the Gray."

"No, we *don't*." Nor do I have it in me to rehash this argument for the second time today.

"But the Meridian thinks *we* do," Raya mutters, less to us than to herself.

"What?" both Akari and I say.

"The Divine Meridian—he said something else before I could get away. He said: *what will you do when the well you draw from fills with poison? How will you survive when the power you've been leeching disappears from the Gray?*"

"So . . . what do you think it means?" I ask, trying to make sense of the words. Stealing from the Gray has long since been a charge levied at Hues but never at Shades. The story is always that we take while they balance, that they live in harmony with the shadows while we drain.

"I don't know, but it has to be related to what he's doing, right?" Raya worries at her bottom lip. "If he's bleeding Shades and phasing typics, then he must think that it will somehow . . . stop the leeching? Or protect the shadows, maybe? What do you think?" She aims the question my way. "Is this the same thing you encountered last year?"

"No, that man wanted to expand the Gray into the physical realm, kill every typic."

"Okay, so then maybe this one wants to do the opposite, kill every Shade."

"Well, I, for one, am just about done with these hypotheticals." Akari's patience finally gives. "I say we do what we should have done an hour ago—hand the half breed over to the Council and focus on what's important: fixing your magic."

My entire body tenses, even though I should have seen that declaration coming from a whole continent away. They're both Shades, after all—and not rogues, either, but Academy bred. The Council's lies are far too entrenched.

"We can't hand him in, Kiri."

Which is why I find myself surprised that Raya objects.

"The future, it . . . it seems to want him here, for some reason. We might still need his gift."

Less surprised that it's for an entirely self-serving end, and not because I've earned my freedom by saving her ungrateful Orange friend.

*She is never going to believe you deserve freedom.* For the first time since Eve shattered, I feel my sense of self-preservation kick in. No matter what I do or what I say, Raya is never going to see me as anything other than an illegal half Shade. That's just who she is, and who I am, and it's not a reality either of us can change, regardless of what the future wants or how deeply the mystery of the Meridian has worked its way into my veins. How it kept me here far longer than it should have.

"Forget about his gift, Raya." Akari continues to talk about me like I'm not standing three feet away. "He's already dead, don't you see that?"

I mean, I certainly will be if I don't hurry up and make my escape—especially with the way she's casually advocating for my murder. So, while the two of them are lost to their bickering, I do what I should have done in the first place: I fish out a couple of Alara's charms—an Orange to distract them while I flee the room and a Red that'll compel them not to give chase—and toss them into their midst.

This ill-advised alliance is officially over.

# CHAPTER 20

# EZZO

The urge to find a tavern and drink myself into oblivion is almost overwhelming. For a brief second there, I'd felt useful again; I had a trail to follow and a puzzle to distract me from the pain. But now, I don't really know what to do anymore. On the one hand, I want to keep tugging at this tangled thread, see what answers I can unravel. On the other, I want to leave Sarotuza to the monster it created, let the Divine Meridian continue killing Shades. It's nothing less than they deserve, and the shadows, well . . . it doesn't seem fair for their fate to once again fall to me. I've already done my part, haven't I? Given all I had to give?

*That's not how it works, Ez.* Eve's voice wraps my fingers around my scry, the ghost of her patience making the decision for me. *Where are they?* The cynical part of me says they're long gone, that when I ran off with a Shade they decided that two saves was enough contrition, they didn't need to stick around for number three. But down deep, I think I knew that they'd still be here, that my scry would lead me to another abandoned house, where they'd decided to hole up while they waited to see if I would require that third rescue. That whether I want them to or not, they're trying to make amends.

"We were just starting to get worried." Cemmy welcomes me back with only the barest amount of grief. "I see you dumped the Shade?"

"Turns out you were right, she was a bad idea." The moment those words leave my mouth, I sag against the wall, consumed by the crushing weight of the day. Of the last few days, actually. From capture, to court chamber, to cellar. Chase might have healed the injuries to my body, but there's some damage that no amount of Green magic can fix—like a fundamental break in spirit. Why else would I have been so happy to let the trackers catch me again? Why else would I have risked my freedom for a drink or willingly shackled myself to Raya?

"You look terrible, Ez," Cemmy says, low and quiet. "When was the last time you ate?"

Honestly? I can't remember. But the second she says it my stomach growls with a hollow ache.

"Too long ago."

"Then come on, we've got plenty of food to spare." She leads me into the front room, where she and Chase have turned an old trunk into a makeshift table, laden with a modest spread. A loaf of bread, a heel of cheese, a cup of caramelized nuts and a handful of stale pastries—all things Cemmy can steal without drawing attention, even in the real world, though she tends to do her stealing in the Gray, where no merchant could race after her should her sticky fingers accidentally reveal their bent. A perk of the physicality of her gift.

*Speaking of gifts* . . . Before I fold down to the dusty floor, I phase into the shadows for a moment and blink into mine, quickly scanning the area for trails.

"All clear?" Cemmy doesn't so much as blink when I reappear. She's used to me popping in and out of existence without warning, though there is a tiny hint of a smile playing at her lips.

"For now." I do my best to ignore it. I didn't check the coast for them, I did it for me; I'm not ready for another cell yet.

"How'd it go with the Shade?" Chase asks, adding to the table a wrap of butter and some cured meat. "She give you anything useful?"

Gods, how to even begin answering that question.

"It's a long story."

"We have time, Ez." Cemmy motions for me to tuck in. "If you want to tell it."

So, I do tell it, if only to purge the wealth of questions and contradictions from my head, share the madness with other people.

"A void?" Cemmy asks once I'm done with the telling, turning the word on her tongue. "I've never heard that term before—at least not in relation to Shades."

"Me neither." Chase drums a restless tattoo against the trunk. "Could the Indigo have misheard him, maybe? Or misunderstood?"

"It's possible," I say, since I wasn't there with her. "But I saw his trail for myself and it was definitely . . . different. Less like a trail and more like a dearth in the shadows—an absence—but one I could feel."

"Okay, so then what do you want to do next?" Cemmy asks, arms wrapping around her knees.

"What do you mean?"

"I mean, we're not leaving Sarotuza until we know you're safe so . . . do you want to stay, do you want to go? Tell us what you need."

"I can't go yet." That realization dawns on me unbidden, like a midnight sun. Hells, I'm not altogether sure that I *could* go, even if I did want to, that the future would actually *allow* me to leave. *It seems to want him here.* If Raya was right about that assertion, then the fates would only conspire to lead me straight back to the city, because while changing the future is possible, fighting it is an exercise in futility. Mom taught me that. But it was her death that taught me never to ignore my suspicions, no matter how absurd they might feel, to keep my eyes open, always, and rely on the strength of my gift. "For some reason, the Council is blind to what the Meridian is doing to these typics; I can't go without first finding out why that is, and why he's doing it."

"Then that's what we'll do," Cemmy says, as though I'd meant that *I* as a *we.*

"No, that's—Just because I'm choosing to stay doesn't mean the two of you have to get involved."

"We're already involved, Ezzo." Chase's voice is resigned. "I saw the same future the Indigo did, remember? And it was all our colors in that vision, so if you're going to stay, we may as well stay with you, get to the bottom of it together."

"Any idea where we should start?" Cemmy asks before I can disagree, almost as if to stop me doing it.

"None whatsoever." So instead, I concede. "I only got this far because the future was guiding Raya."

"Then maybe it's time to ask a different Shade for help." Cemmy trades a meaningful look with Chase. "The Red did say we could reach out again if we needed to—and she knew an awful lot about a whole bunch of illegal things, so maybe she'll know something about this."

"I'm sorry—the Red?" That's about the last thing I expected Cemmy to say. "What Red? Since when do you know a Red?"

"Since the day we had to rescue you from an impenetrable castle." Her head shakes with the question. "How else do you think we learned about the portals, Ez? Or managed to subdue an entire court? Did you really think we did that by ourselves?"

"I—" Didn't think about it at all, to be honest, though now that she's said it, it feels downright obvious. Of course they'd have needed help breaking into the Academy; until this morning, none of us even knew portals existed, never mind how to find or use one, and we've certainly never gone up against a room full of Shades—few Hues ever attempt that and live to tell the tale. "Gods, where did you even find a sympathetic Red?"

"That's also a long story," Cemmy says, climbing back to her feet. "We can catch you up once I've set the meeting."

*

The meeting, as it happens, is to take place in a very normal-looking house, on a very normal-looking street, at the very heart of the one part of Sarotuza that's dangerously low in iron. The color district, Cemmy called it, which feels like the last place three Hues should ever be—especially in the Gray, where our eyes are a death sentence and we can't disappear among the typics.

"You didn't want to go anywhere a little less . . . Shade-friendly?" I ask, blinking out of my gift. The number of trails in our vicinity is a rainbow sea, stormy and shark-infested, a shipwreck waiting to happen. "We're pretty exposed here."

"I didn't pick the place, Ez, she did." Cemmy strides up to the door with a confidence I don't feel.

"*She* being the Red that got you into the Academy?"

"That's the one." Cemmy's knock is a rhythmic pattern they must have pre-agreed. Four raps of her knuckles followed by two more, then another three. "And while it may not have been my first choice, she said it would be safer for us to make the approach in the Gray."

*Yeah, I'm sure she did.* The blood starts pounding in my ears. It's the perfect trap, after all, allowing the trackers to catch us here; it would prove, beyond a shadow of a doubt, that there's illicit color flowing through our veins.

"Don't worry—if she wanted to set us up, she would have done it at your execution." Chase's attempt at comfort isn't quite as reassuring as he thinks. "It wouldn't make sense for her to do it *after* she helped us escape."

"I still don't understand why a Red is helping us at all," I mutter, just in time for the door to swing open and that Red to say, "Because you really seem to need it." She's nothing like what I expect. She's young, for starters—eighteen or nineteen, at best—with skin as dark as mine and a thick braid that snakes down past her hip. But the most surprising thing about her is the eyes. Not their deep brown color, but the black spiked rim. This girl's not a rogue, she's a Council Shade. "And I prefer Saleen to 'the Red', if you don't mind," she continues. "Referring to a Shade by their color is a bit reductive."

"Erm . . ." *Saleen?* That name rings a bell for some reason I can't quite place. "Sorry, I—"

"Relax, I'm just messing with you." Saleen winks, beckoning us inside. "He looks better, by the way," she says to Chase. "I guess that means you found the Green?"

"Right where you said she'd be—I appreciate the tip."

"Anytime. Oh, and we can phase back now if you want to drop your In-Betweens. The neighbors get a little twitchy when they see an unfamiliar face in the physical realm—we've had some problems lately with the Church trying to sneak iron into the district—but come in the Gray and they don't so much as blink."

"Then why not meet somewhere else?" I ask once the world has bloomed into color, draping the rooms in a soft palette of creams and yellows that warm like a flame.

"Because Cemmy's message said you need information and this is where the illegal books live."

*The illegal books?* I feel as though I've walked into a strangely lucid dream, where a Red in what has the feel of a family home is disclosing crimes and harboring Hues as though that's an entirely normal thing.

"Judging by the look on your face, I'm going to go ahead and guess that you're not completely up to speed, so let me give you the highlights," Saleen says, ushering us through to the living room to sit. "Once upon a time, my parents were trackers—still are, actually, but before you freak out, they're no longer playing for the Council's team. Because ten years ago, during a raid, they came across a library filled with all manner of seditious materials and discovered that the Council lies, a lot. About Shades, about Hues, about our history, about our magics, about anything and everything, really. They've been working to sabotage the guild ever since." She makes it sound so simple—so easy—as though countering a lifetime's worth of hate only takes a moment of clarity and the right reading.

"So, you're telling me they found some books and then they up and switched sides, just like that?"

"Ez, don't—" Cemmy starts, only for Saleen to wave her off with an indifferent flick of her wrist.

"It's okay; I don't blame him for not trusting me." She shrugs, then to me, she says, "Though I wouldn't say there was any *just* about it. It was more like . . . the lie that broke the camel's back after years of questioning. But the point is, they kept the books, and they kept digging, and then once I was old enough to *understand the gravity of the situation*"—she lowers her voice in a way that, I assume, is supposed to mimic her father—"they brought me into the fold, as well. Though strictly speaking, I'm not meant to get involved. My parents want me to keep my nose clean while I'm still at the Academy."

"Wait—you're still at the Academy?" The more Saleen says, the less I understand. "Why? If you all hate the Council so much, why stay instead of going rogue?"

"Because going rogue changes nothing." She absently picks at the tip of her braid. "It would only rob my parents of the access they already have as trackers and any opportunity to help. And besides, it's kind of hard to get stuff done when you're constantly being hunted. I imagine you know a little something about that."

Yeah, I guess we do.

"So instead, you . . . what? Go around saving Hues from their executions?"

"Actually, you're the first." Saleen manages to sound both guilty and pleased in the same breath. "Most of what we do is preventative—getting Hues out of the city instead of caught—since, ninety percent of the time, they're flat-out killed before they reach a cell, either by the trackers or by the Gray. If they do make it to the prison, freeing them is way too complicated to be an option; the best we can do is try to ease their stay there, slip them a few healing charms while they're being interrogated or a numbing tonic to take the edge off on trial day. But since my parents are off on assignment, there was nothing they could do for you, and that didn't sit right with me, so I tried to break in myself. That's where I ran into your friends, and well, you probably know the rest."

Most of it, yes—though Saleen's side of the story lends the impossible escape they staged a whole new shape. It can't have been easy, choosing to align themselves with a Shade, having to hope that she'd make good on her promise to get them in and out safely in lieu of leading them to their deaths. And yet they did it anyway.

"Thank you," I say, since it's somehow easier to thank her than it is them.

"You're welcome, Ezzo. Now, maybe the three of you can tell me why you're still here?" Saleen looks between us. "Don't get me wrong, I'm happy to share whatever information you might need, but wouldn't you be better off with some more Red and a safe route out of Sarotuza?"

"Probably," Chase agrees, leaning forward in his chair. "And I'll happily take the Red if you're offering, but first, have you ever heard of a type of Shade or a type of magic called a void?"

"Can't say that I have." Saleen shakes her head. "But I've also never gone looking, so we might well find something in my parents' collection. Follow me, they keep it in the study," she says, springing back to her feet.

"Your parents keep a collection of illegal books in their study?" I ask as she leads us through the house. "That seems . . ." *Reckless. Unwise. Downright dangerous.* "Bold of them."

"I mean, it would be—if the whole room wasn't protected by a pretty powerful glamour." She flashes me her teeth. "And besides, if you've got trackers rifling through your stuff, then you're already made. At least this way, we could get the books out if we got the sense that they were coming. Here we go." With one hand, she flicks on a set of hex lights and with the other, she brings down the spell, rippling the modest study back to its true form.

"Whoa." In the blink of an eye, the room fills with oak and leather, deep stacks of floor-to-ceiling shelves materializing to cover every inch of wall space. "There's got to be a thousand books in here."

"Fifteen hundred, give or take." Saleen's pride could eclipse the moon. "All originals, from before the Council started altering records."

"That's a lot of texts, Saleen." Cemmy, on the other hand, looks flat-out dismayed. "Unless you know where to start, this could take days."

"These should help with that." Saleen grabs a jar of purple crystals off the desk. "Indigo magic is tricky, but if you ask it simple questions like: *in which book will we find the term 'void'*, it should work," she says.

And since the future seems rather invested in my endeavors of late, there's a good chance it will.

# CHAPTER 21

# RAYA

Akari and Ezzo were never going to mix; I should have realized that the second I forced them together. That Akari wouldn't allow me to keep working with a Hue, and that Ezzo wouldn't stand idly by while the two of us discussed his fate, that he'd find a way to escape this room and the Council's clutches. Again. He has, after all, spent his entire life ducking Shades.

*Good for him.* A small part of me is glad he's gone. Because despite what he is, and the pain his Gold put me through—the pain he *let* his Gold put me through—it feels as though he's earned the right to see another day. And no, I never thought I'd say that, but I also never thought a Hue would risk his life for a Shade. Ezzo didn't have to stop me getting caught in the Meridian's cellar. He didn't have to help me save Akari. And he sure as hell didn't have to stick around while she regained her strength.

But he did.

He kept his promise.

Which is making it damn near impossible to root for his death.

*There's a difference between not rooting for his death and hoping he'll get away.* The guilt coils inside me like a snake. I shouldn't be swayed to a Hue's side so godsdamned easily. I shouldn't be worried about where he's going, or what he's doing, or who he's doing it with. And I should definitely not be so affected by the look I saw on his face.

He was surprised when I told Akari we shouldn't hand him in.

Pleasantly surprised, I'd venture, until I went and ruined it by implying I only cared about his gift.

After that, his expression didn't fill with ice or anger the way it should have, it filled with something far, far more gutting: disappointment, like I had just lived up to all of his worst expectations, like he had finally caught a glimpse of the true me.

*And he didn't like her.*

I doubt I'll ever forget the sheer weight of that realization. So if the future still thinks we're destined to fall in love, well . . . it might want to get its fated paths checked.

*Or maybe it should go reveal itself to a better Indigo.* I never was much good at interpreting my visions, and this one seems to be going the same way as all the rest. So maybe I didn't actually see what I thought I saw. Maybe I inferred the wrong meaning from the future's abstract offering, or misinterpreted the haze of feelings, colors, and tastes. Or hells, maybe it was all an elaborate trick, a red herring designed to coax me into showing Ezzo some grace, so that he could help me learn about the Divine Meridian—or perhaps so that I would help him. I honestly don't know what to believe anymore. The only thing I know for sure is that Ezzo's gone and that has to be for the best. For everyone.

"I told you he couldn't be trusted." Akari tosses the spent charms onto the bed. "Do you see that now, Raya? Do you see what he is?"

"Forget about him, Kiri—he can be the trackers' problem," I say. They're more equipped to deal with his kind than we are anyway, and I want Ezzo to stop cannibalizing all the space in my head. "Let's just focus on the Meridian, okay? If we can find out what he meant by he's a *void* or why he's phasing typics into the Gray, then that should buy us plenty of favor with the guilds."

"You're right, we should forget the half breed." Akari nods, dropping down to his vacant chair. "As for the Meridian, well . . . could you ask the future where we should start looking? Or is that completely off the table now that you're, you know—?" She doesn't use the term fate-touched but I can see it written into every line of her face. I can see her hurt there, too, feel it in the way she can't seem to hold my eye without quickly glancing away, in how tightly her shoulders are wound and the way her voice has filed to a blunt edge. She's grateful for the rescue, yes, but that doesn't mean I'm off the hook for going behind her back to break Saleen's spell. Which is why—even though I fear it's futile—I reach for the power in my blood and say, "I can try." Regardless of the fact that Ezzo has been at the heart of every vision the future has granted me all day.

*Where will we learn more about the Divine Meridian?*

Since I don't truly believe it'll answer, I'm completely unprepared for the sudden assault of sights, sounds, and pain, for the fates to awaken a memory so ugly and vivid it sends me crashing to my knees. And while it isn't me Chase is draining in the vision, I still remember the way it felt to have his magic rip the color out through my skin. It's the kind of torture I wouldn't wish on anyone. Not even a selfish viper like Saleen.

"Ray? Raya? *Ray!*"

By the time Akari snaps me out of the vision, I'm shaking—or rather, she's shaking me back to the present, her hurt entirely replaced by panic, the worry in her expression cut deep.

"By my colors, Ray, what happened? Are you okay? Was that a vision?"

"Yeah, I—" A violent one. And not the kind of future she'll want to hear. "Akari, did you—you didn't tell Saleen we were leaving the castle, did you?"

"What? *No.* Of course I didn't tell Saleen." She reels back as though offended. "When would I have even had time? You were with me from the moment we decided to leave."

While that's technically true, I did spend a few minutes arguing with Killen, and scrys do exist—so does shimmering.

"I'm not asking because I'm mad, Kiri—it's just, if you didn't tell her, then can you think of any reason why she might have done the same thing?"

"Gone after the half breeds? No. Never. You know how she feels about tracking." Akari's words turn bitter, since that was the cause of most of their fights before they split, the way Saleen kept shaming her for wanting to pursue a job that made sense to everyone except Saleen.

"Then might she have come looking for you, do you think?" I ask, gentle as I can manage. "If she noticed you missing?"

"What are you getting at, Raya?" Though not gentle enough, it seems. "What does Saleen have to do with your vision? What the hells did you see?"

"I saw her," I say, trying to keep my voice level. "And she's in trouble, Kiri. I think she's been caught by the Hues. Their Gold, he—I saw her getting drained."

"No. That's not possible." Akari's head shakes and shakes and shakes. "The Sapphire only left here a few minutes ago, there's no way he's had time to find them and then find her and then overpower a Red." She forgets, for a moment, that I see the future not the present, and that Ezzo's gift could have put them straight onto Saleen's trail. "And didn't you ask the future about the Divine Meridian, anyway? Why would the vision show you Saleen?"

Because the future seems to be playing by its own rules today, answering questions with whatever vision it deems relevant, even if that relevance isn't immediately clear. And because, where one of these Hues goes, the other two follow, and I just gave the fates the perfect opportunity to steer my path back to Ezzo, like it's been doing all fucking day.

"Fate-touched magic is unpredictable, remember?" I sidestep that unhelpful observation. "The important thing is that it's not been wrong since I asked the open question." Every one of my visions has come to some manner of fruition, even if there are parts of them that I'm actively refusing to believe.

"Well then . . . shit, did you see where they'll be?" Akari runs both hands through her hair, hard, as though she can claw the truth away.

"No, but I could probably find them." I guess the future just wants to hear the right question from me.

"Then please, Ray, I know you don't like her—hells, *I* don't particularly like her right now—but Saleen's important." The fear in Akari's voice almost breaks me, the idea that she'd think, even for a second, that I wouldn't help her just because I don't like Saleen. So as much as I don't want to give the future the satisfaction, doing it for her means I cast the question quick.

*Where will I find him?*

When it comes to Ezzo, I don't have to be specific for the fates to reward me with all the detail I need. And just like that, there's no more talk of leaving the Hues to the trackers. Now that Akari's learned Saleen's in danger, the only thing on her mind is the looming Gold threat, and while, yes, her fear scares me, what scares me more is that, deep down, I'm relieved. Not that Saleen's in danger, but that we've found a reason to go after them—to go after *him*.

I'm relieved because I *want* to go after Ezzo.

And I don't have the faintest clue what that means.

\*

*It just means you want to thank him.* As we follow the future's directions, that conviction solidifies in certainty and strength. I want to apologize to him, is all, to not let *we might still need his gift* be the last memory he has of me. I want him to know I'm grateful—that Shades can be grateful. That we're not all the selfish monsters his kind was conditioned to see.

Around us, the world has smudged to ash and cinder, the shadows wisping to vapor as we shimmer like two Shades on a spree.

"Are you sure we're going the right way?" The closer we come to the street in my vision, the more uncomfortable Akari seems.

"I'm sure," I say, though I share her unease. The color district is the last place I'd ever expect to find three Hues—let alone three Hues holding a captive Saleen. And yet, that's exactly where my vision leads, to a two-story house that clearly belongs to a family of healthy means. Not rich, like my parents, but comfortable. The kind of house where a couple of well-regarded guild members might live. "Why? What's wrong?"

"Nothing, it's just . . . this is her house, Ray." Akari's words don't strike me as *nothing*.

"Who—Saleen's?" Because as far as coincidences go, this one feels pretty fucking big.

"Yeah." Akari's face is as pale as porcelain, her worry beading sweat along her upper lip. "I don't understand, her parents aren't due back from their hunt for another week, so why leave the Academy to come here?"

The better question might be: why would Chase choose to top up his Red in the most Shade-rich part of the city, where they're more likely to be seen? Has Ezzo's lack of self-preservation finally spread to all three?

"I don't know, Kiri, but they're definitely inside—I can feel it." And as we scale the porch one careful step at a time, I start to hear it, too, the sounds of a Shade who's desperately trying to keep her pain locked up within, to not show the Gold draining her an ounce of weakness.

A feat at which she's slowly failing.

*Oh Gods.* I'm suddenly back in that abandoned house, chained to a pipe while *my* color is being stripped, begging Chase to stop, and to show mercy, and to go rot in every one of the nine hells.

Akari has no such memories pinning her in place. The second Saleen betrays a scream, she dispenses with caution, wisping through the door with a frantic call for her ex.

"Sal?" She charges through to the living room at full pelt. Without a plan. Without my help. Without so much as checking to see if she'll be facing one Hue or a Gold and both his friends. "Saleen! Where are you—? Get away from her, you filthy—"

Time slows to a crawl as Saleen's surprise meets Akari's rage. As Akari makes to unleash a violent spell in Chase's direction and Saleen is forced to raise her own hand in his defense, her yell of "Ari, *don't*" ringing not with a plea, but with the command to obey. She compels Akari to cease casting.

*What in the—?* And everything about the scene is wrong, from how at home Chase looks in this house to the irritation flitting across Saleen's face. That's when I realize that she isn't tied up or being held down, she's sitting—willingly—on the floor opposite Chase, even though he was very clearly draining her magic; I can tell that much from the pain still wincing her expression and the swiftness with which her spell breaks.

*So then, why compel Akari and not him?*

The moment she regains the ability, Akari asks a similar question herself. "What the hells is going on, Sal? Why did you—? Why is the half breed here?"

"The *Hue* is here because I invited him," Saleen says, her voice drawn with fatigue.

"You *invited* him?" Akari's eyes bug out of their sockets as, with Chase's help, Saleen climbs to her feet. "Why would you do that? And how can you let him touch you right now? He's a—he was *stealing* your color!"

"It's not stealing if I agreed to give it away, Ari, and would you please stop yelling? My head is pounding from the drain."

"I'm sorry, you *agreed* to that?" I gape at Saleen—and glare at Chase until he has the good sense to look embarrassed. "But we heard you from the porch; you were in pain."

"Yeah, well, it's never the most enjoyable experience," she mutters, in a way that strongly suggests this exchanging of power wasn't her first.

*Because it wasn't.* All at once, Ezzo's unlikely escape from the court chamber starts to make sense. The sheer amount of magic Chase would have needed to glamour an entire room full of Shades was always more than could have reasonably come from one Red, never mind one Gold. But add another Red into the mix—specifically, the most promising Red the Academy has seen in years—and suddenly, the deed becomes far more conceivable.

Saleen must have helped them get in and out of the castle.

And ludicrous as that might seem, I believe it from Saleen; the Shade who's made it plenty clear how she feels about the Council's justice, who's made public her disdain for the trackers—despite her parents' occupations—and who was in that hall when she'd usually have spurned such a summons, perfectly placed to indulge her lust for rebellion.

"The glamour at the execution, that was you. Your power," I say, and it isn't a question.

"Huh. You worked that out faster than I expected." Saleen shrugs, entirely devoid of shame. Then to Chase, she says, "You should blink back and join the others, this may take a minute."

A little more than a minute, I'd venture, judging by the storm brewing in Akari's veins.

"Colors help me, Sal—are you *insane*?" she hisses the moment he's phased. "Helping a half breed escape is treason. The Council could kill you for that!"

"They kill Hues for absolutely nothing, so why should I be any different?" The bitterness in Saleen's reply is bewildering. She's outspoken, yes, but I've never heard her express any kind of opinion about Hues before, let alone show them sympathy. Then again, most of our interactions have been colored by her dislike of me—"she's like a dog with separation anxiety"—and my anger towards the way she ended things with Akari—"what kind of coward leaves a fucking note? After three years!". I have no earthly idea what goes on in that self-important head of hers, though even in my wildest dreams, I wouldn't have imagined this.

"What are you two doing out of the castle, anyway?" Saleen asks, dropping down to the couch before she loses her feet. "How did you even know I was here?"

"No. Uh-uh. You don't get to change the subject," Akari spits. "What are you playing at, Sal, harboring a half breed? Giving him your color?"

"You know what, fine, you want to do this, we'll do this. But for the love of all three Gods, Akari, would you please stop yelling and come sit? I'm not going to explain while you're both glowering over me." Saleen crosses her arms in challenge until, with a huff, Akari rolls her eyes and folds down next to her, leaving me to take the armchair.

"This had better be good," she grumbles, staring daggers at her ex.

"That's really going to depend on your definition." Saleen nervously tugs at her braid, steeling herself with a breath before starting. "You're already well aware that I have no love for the Council, and I know that's never sat right with you given what my parents do, but the truth is, they have no love for the Council, either. For the past decade, they've been working against the guild from the inside."

"What do you mean, *working against the guild*?" Akari repeats the words like they're of another language. "You told me they were out on a hunt this week, how is that working against anything?"

"They can get more done from the inside," Saleen says it simply. "Warn rogues, hide evidence, help steer their colleagues away from suspected Hues. It's a tricky balance, but they've done a lot of good over the years."

"So, you consider saving half breeds a good thing, now?"

"Hues, Ari," Saleen corrects with a sigh. "And they're not what you think. The Council's been lying about their kind for centuries. We have the books to prove it."

"To prove what, exactly? That all three of you have lost your minds?"

"No . . . to prove that four hundred years ago, a Hue was born with the power to steal magic from the Gray. Just a single Hue, Ari—an exceedingly rare dilution of Yellow. But the Church found that Amber and they used his power to try and collapse the shadows. Came pretty close to it, by all accounts, which freaked the elders out enough to eradicate the rest. They've been feeding us lies ever since."

"You can't actually believe that." Akari scrubs a hand over her face. "I mean, come on, Sal, how would the Council even orchestrate such a conspiracy?"

"By disseminating misinformation," Saleen answers the question as though it was asked of her in good faith. "By burning records and having them altered. We have a whole library in this house of the true texts—and even if they didn't believe the books, my parents saw the truth for themselves last year, when they were called to Isitar to help track another Amber. But by the time they got there, someone had already put an end to the threat—just in time, too, though it sure wasn't the Council," she says, inadvertently confirming Ezzo's tale.

*I was there when we stopped the Amber.*

Somehow, he and his friends managed to succeed where the trackers failed.

"Okay, but if anything, doesn't that prove the opposite?" Akari's voice turns imploring. "That Hues *are* dangerous?"

"I can see why it might seem that way, but just . . . think about it for a second. Forget everything we've been taught and think about it logically," Saleen says. "If the Council has purged all the Hues—if instead of the thousands that had existed for centuries, there are only a handful left—then how could they still be destabilizing the Gray? How could the same thing that happened four hundred years ago have happened again last year? Doesn't that feel more like deliberate malice to you than some quirk of fate?"

Her point hits me square in the chest. A handful of Hues shouldn't affect the Gray the same way thousands do; if they did, the shadows would constantly be in dire straits.

*Which is exactly what Ezzo said.* My gut squirms with the realization. When he first told me this story, I dismissed it as a self-serving tale, yet here I am, considering its merits now that it's coming from another Shade. Hells, now that it's coming from Saleen, even Akari's resolve is beginning to wane.

"Let's say I believe you." The pitch of her voice tells me that's still a pretty big *let's*. "If the Council really are lying and your parents really are working against them, then why are you so outspoken? Why draw so much attention to yourself?"

"Because I wanted them to stop wanting me, Ari," Saleen says, falling back against the cushions. "I'm a promising Red with two tracker parents; the guild's been courting me for years—they *expect* me to join them and *no* isn't a word they like to hear. But I'm not like my parents; I can't compartmentalize my conscience and I won't go hunting Hues in the hopes that maybe I can help a few escape. I don't want that life, and my parents don't want it for me, so we decided that I should play the problem child for a bit, ruffle some feathers until the guild decided I was more trouble than they needed."

"Saving a Hue from execution is hardly ruffling some feathers, Sal." Akari's head shakes with disbelief.

"I know, I wasn't actually supposed to do that. My parents are going to kill me when they find out."

She's assuming the Council won't find out first, that their investigation won't connect the dots between the Gold wielding stolen magic and the rebellious Red in their midst.

"So, this is something you've known for a while, huh?" Akari asks, glancing up at Saleen through her lashes. "The whole time we were together?"

"Not the whole time, no." Saleen worries at her bottom lip. "I only got read in a couple of years ago, when I was old enough to keep the secret."

That's right around the time the two of them started fighting, when Saleen's views on the Council shortened the fuse on her temper and turned her barbs mean.

"And you didn't think to tell me?"

"It wouldn't have been fair to, Ari." Saleen's words are as sad as they are convinced. "It would have put you in an impossible position and you were so intent on being a tracker that I didn't—I couldn't—trust what you'd do, whether you'd choose to hand me in."

"You thought I would hand you in?" Akari reels back as though she'd slapped her. "Seriously?"

"No, I—yes, maybe. I don't know." A frustrated rush of air deflates Saleen. "That's the point, Akari, I couldn't take the risk."

"Is that why you broke things off, too? Because you didn't trust me?"

I suddenly feel as though I'm trespassing on something private, something weeks—if not months—in the making that isn't meant for me.

"Trust had nothing to do with it, I just couldn't lie to you anymore." Saleen aims that truth at the rug. "It hurt too much, okay? Being with you. Knowing that come graduation, I'd have to watch the person I love most turn into a mindless killer."

"Then it's a good thing you had a whole castle of girls to cry it out with." Akari lurches to her feet, her anger rippling through the shadows like spilled ink.

"They didn't mean anything, Ari." Saleen springs up after her. "I just figured it would be easier if I gave you a reason to hate me."

"Well, it wasn't *easier*." Akari bats her away. "It actually made things so much worse."

"Then I'm sorry." Saleen's voice is as soft as I've ever heard it. "It was stupid of me to lie, and it was stupid of me not to tell you, and if I could go back and do it over, I would. All of it, including the girls. If you believe anything, then believe that."

As much as I'm glad Akari's finally getting some answers—not to mention the apology she was so desperately owed—there's still a bigger problem at hand and this conversation has veered way too deep into the personal.

"Look, I hate to interrupt but"—*I honestly think you've both forgotten I'm here*—"you have three Hues in your house right now, Saleen, and the Council isn't going to upend four centuries' worth of thinking on nothing but their word—or yours, for that matter—so can we maybe focus on that for a second?"

"Gods, there's nothing to focus on, Raya." It's comforting to know that while some things change, Saleen's disdain for me remains as solid as a rock. "They came to raid the library and get a top-up of magic, that's it. I'm not looking to pick a fight with the trackers or reform the Council all on my own. I'm just trying to keep them alive until they leave Sarotuza. So, unless *you're* planning to turn me in, there's nothing for us to do."

"Except that's what I'm trying to tell you," I say, meeting her tone for tone. "I don't think they can leave Sarotuza. Not yet, anyhow, the future won't let them." I feel that truth in my gut and the marrow in my bones.

When they escaped from the castle, the fates sent me after Ezzo.

When we escaped from the tavern, they kept us tied together and led us to Akari in the laundry hall.

Then when Ezzo escaped me and Akari, they wasted no time in steering the five of us to Saleen's door.

So while the future can be changed, this particular path seems inordinately stubborn—and if fighting it won't get us anywhere, then maybe we should be embracing it instead—while we can still avert the parts of the vision I can't allow to happen—try to understand the task it's setting us before we collide over and over and over again.

"Raya's right, I don't think it will." It's Ezzo's voice that jumps to my defense, resigned as it is unexpected. "That's why we came here, to try and figure out what it wants."

The sight of him is like an iron fist to the jaw, a sudden blow I'm entirely unprepared for. When I told myself I wanted to thank him, I didn't imagine that this mess of revelations would be the circumstance involved, or that Chase and Cemmy would be standing on either side of him. I don't even know what I imagined, to be honest, but I guess I was hoping that his expression would be a touch more . . . warm. Not that it has much cause to be.

"Wait—did you just call her Raya?" Saleen seems more surprised by that than by their sudden appearance in the living room. They must have left the library and phased while we were still arguing. "Do you two . . . know each other?" she asks. "How? When?"

"It's a long story," we both say at the same time, but since today is shaping up to be the day for those, between us, we do tell it, taking it in turns to fill in the gaps until all six of us are fully looped into the fold—albeit reluctantly and with no love lost between Hues and Shades.

"So, you didn't find anything useful in the books?" Saleen asks once we're done with the telling. "Nothing about voids?"

"Not even a mention." Cemmy sighs. "And we used over a dozen charms to ask every question we could think of, so either we're doing it wrong, or the future sent us here for a different reason."

This reunion, would be my guess. It couldn't have Ezzo and me separated for long.

"I still don't understand why it would want *us* to do this." Chase paces his agitation across the room. "As far as the trackers are concerned, we're as much of a threat to the Gray as the Divine Meridian. Anything we do would be tainted by that mindset."

"If this is really about the Meridian, then I think it's more of a need than a want." Cemmy's reply is reluctant, as though it physically pains her to say the words. "You believe that he's somehow connected to the deaths you saw in your vision, yes?" She aims that ask at me.

"Yes."

"And the trackers haven't been able to infiltrate his church because it's warded?"

Also yes. "The entire block around it is impenetrable to Shades."

"Then there's your answer. We can—"

"Beat the wards," Chase finishes for her, scrubbing a hand hard through his hair.

"Exactly. This isn't something their kind can do on their own."

*Right, of course.* The future's meddling suddenly makes sense. It's impossible to ward against Hues—there's not enough magic in their blood to trigger the spell—so they can go where we can't.

"Then help us." I try to catch Ezzo's eye, since in this, he seems to be my staunchest ally, the Hue that convinced the rest of the palette to continue the search. "If there's a reason for what he's doing, there must be a record of it somewhere. In some kind of office, maybe, or in whatever private sanctum he keeps in that church. Help us find it."

"Why? So your attack dog can turn us in when we're done?" His bite is every bit as harsh as I deserve. The last time I talked him into helping, it ended with Akari tightening an Orange noose around his throat, swiftly followed by me not making a particularly noble case for his freedom. Any goodwill we'd been building is gone now.

"No, so that the future will stop pushing us together," I say, as that would put an end to both my guilt and this bizarre attachment I've inexplicably formed. "It's got us doing all the same work, anyway, so wouldn't it be easier to just . . . find the answer so we can be rid of each other already?"

"Will *she* agree to that?" Ezzo cocks his head at Akari, the accusation in his eyes burning cold.

"Yes, she will," Saleen says, looking to Akari to confirm. "No one's turning anyone in, right?"

"Gods, yes, right," Akari mutters, though it's clear she's only doing it for Saleen, to prove that she'd never betray the Red's trust. But no matter the reason, the six of us are finally aligned on a course, so without any further bickering, we blink back into the physical realm and get to work.

CHAPTER 22

# EZZO

"How do we keep ending up in this position?" The Meridian's church looms large before us, a plain construction of magnolia brick and terracotta tile—so different to Isitar's holy houses in its appearance, yet equally effective in its capacity to incite hate.

"Hey, you're the one who decided to save the Shade." Cemmy looks about as happy as I feel, though it's Chase who boasts the deepest resentment of religion, which is entirely understandable given how it was the clergy who triggered his sister's power and threw her in an iron cage.

"Really starting to wonder if that was my decision," I grumble, less to her than to myself. The future has always been a nebulous concept—even my mother struggled to fully articulate the erratic whims of fate. How they're driven by us every bit as much as we're driven by them. How our choices all exist in the liminal space between destiny and free will.

"But I am sorry for dragging you both into this," I say, since now that we're stood on the cusp of even more danger, it feels important for them to know that I only ever meant to endanger my life, not theirs, that no matter how much anger I'm still harboring, I'd never willingly put another Hue in harm's way.

"Don't be sorry, Ez, just be more careful, okay?" Cemmy's shrug is both an acknowledgement of my apology and an attempt to hide how much it meant—though I've known her long enough to read the softening in her expression. "Now, come on, we have to go save these idiot zealots from themselves. Again." She turns her attention back to the task at hand. Since we still don't know exactly *what* the Divine Meridian is, we can't risk a confrontation, so we'll be making our approach in the physical realm, not the Gray, and waiting until he's deep in his sermon. Usually, that would mean an early morning, but unlike the Church's clerics, the Meridian prefers to regale his followers in the evening, so we spent the day at Saleen's, searching her parents' library for anything the future might have missed—or withheld—and snatching some scattered sleep, avoiding the three Shades we've found ourselves in bed with.

Or rather, I spent it avoiding Raya. Because I could tell, while she was recounting her part of the story, that she was treading around some fractured piece—but when I asked her about it a little later, she looked me straight in the eye and said that I was imagining things, that she owed me a thank you for saving Akari, and that was it, she'd already told me everything else.

*Except for why she was lying.*

There was no mistaking the edge to her voice and the guilty flush to her cheeks, the way her eyes wouldn't meet mine for more than a second, like she was afraid to look at me for some reason. Like in a house filled with full-bloods, I was the biggest threat.

We steal into the church among the masses, dressed in the same palette of heavy blacks they favor, our irises glamoured to match the pigment shimmering in theirs. Silver flecks in place of the gold that marks those who haven't broken with the sacraments, another brazen perversion the Meridian uses to mock those of traditional faith. The very fact that he was able to commandeer a church of this size is a true mark of the power he holds in Sarotuza, a feat I wouldn't have thought possible—but according to Saleen, his ascendency is the product of a calculated effort that preyed perfectly on the typics' wants and fears.

"He was a Church cleric originally, so he already knew all the tricks," she'd said. "Most of his rhetoric is the same as theirs: Gods good, magic bad, etcetera, etcetera. But while their dream is to rid the world of magic *and* the Gray, he only wants to rid it of magic. He seems to think that doing that will have some sort of transformative effect on the shadows, and he's promising the typics that it'll benefit them, as well. A lie, probably, but they believe it."

Which made the real question: why does *he* believe it? Why is a Shade or a void, or a Shade who thinks he's a void, waging a war on magic when the shadows *are* magic? Kill one and you kill the other.

"Maybe he doesn't realize that," Saleen had ventured. "If he grew up surrounded by faith, then who the hell knows how twisted things got in his head. He could even be making it all up as he goes along— that's certainly what the Council thought at first; they chalked him down to a crackpot the Church should deal with itself. By the time he actually started killing us, it was already too late, he had wards and an army of followers; he'd become too insulated."

Funny that, isn't it? How the Council is always creating problems through its inaction—or worse, through the actions it does take. The trackers have spent so long chasing scapegoats within their own ranks, they've forgotten that the true threat is coming from outside the Gray. They keep handing faith the win.

Once we snake our way into the nave, we stay at the rear of the congregation, hidden behind a towering effigy of the Gods where we won't be noticed when it comes time to phase. Though this church clearly belongs to the Meridian now, it still bears the marks of having first been loyal to a different master, the walls riddled with scars from where the old paintings were unceremoniously ripped down and replaced, usurped by the sacred star sigil.

"That's our cue," Cemmy says as the Meridian emerges from the annex behind the altar, eliciting a roaring wave of adulation, complete with fevered cries of "prophet" and "messiah" and "save us". These typics don't just worship this man, they adore him, with their whole hearts and entire chests, entirely oblivious to the fact that they're devoted to a fictional tale.

*Truly the consummate con artist.* The moment he begins his sermon, we blink into the Gray as one, not lingering to hear the falsehoods and the vitriol in his address. Our time in his sanctum will conclude when he does, so we don't have a single second to waste, we're already hinging far too much on the hope that he hides his secrets in an obvious place.

Crossing the nave once we're ensconced in the shadows is easy, but the door to the annex presents a hurdle we should have—but didn't—think to expect, a solid barrier Cemmy's physicality won't allow her to wisp through.

"Go without me." Since opening the door in the Gray would open it in the real world, too, she instantly decides against taking that risk. "I'll stay and watch the echoes, scry when it's time for you to leave."

"Are you sure?" Where I expect Chase to argue, he merely asks if she's certain and gives her hand a squeeze. Whatever these two have spent the past year doing, it's only strengthened the bond they forged in Isitar, the first time we were forced into a fight against a zealot and the Church. And Gods, I resent it. I don't mean to, but I do. Because his betrayal cost Eve her life, yet Cemmy chose to forgive him—to love him—anyway, and I can't forgive her for that. I can't forgive either of them. Then again, that's not what they're asking me to do right now, and working together is like slipping on an old glove that still fits.

One by one, Chase and I wisp through every door in the adjoining passageway, looking for a room that might reveal the Meridian's true aim.

"I'm not seeing anything, are you?" I ask after finding nothing but a bedroom, a water closet, and a small kitchenette. This must be where the Aralagio in residence used to live—back before they were summarily expelled.

"Maybe . . ." Chase points to a stretch of wall that seems newer than the rest, almost as if it's been recently plastered over. "What better place to hide his secrets than a room that can only be accessed from the Gray?" he says, flitting through to the other side.

And he's right.

For it's both the perfect ruse and the Divine Meridian's lair.

"By my colors, it's like a scribe exploded in here." The sight that greets us robs me of breath. It's not so much that the room's untidy—quite the opposite, in fact, everything inside feels deliberately arranged, a sparse smattering of furniture that serves a purpose in lieu of decorating the space. No, it's the way the Meridian has covered the walls with his musings that raises the hairs on my neck, the scribbles that extend floor to ceiling, all in the same tiny, meticulous text.

"More like a madman," Chase mutters, staring wide-eyed at the chilling tapestry. "You take the right side, I'll take the left? Look for . . . anything that feels relevant, I guess."

"I don't suppose you've stolen any magic that could help us?"

"Sorry." He shakes his head. "And I didn't think to take any Indigo charms from Saleen. Probably should have, to be honest—but I wasn't expecting . . . this."

"The old-fashioned way it is," I say, since I didn't think to take any either. Then once we've phased back into the physical realm, I make a beeline for the most distinctive part of the Meridian's mosaic, the giant family tree he's inked along the wall behind his desk.

*By Gods, the man did not skimp on the research.* This tree spans at least two dozen generations, stretching back to long before the Council began purging the world of illegal Shades.

"Well, this can't be a coincidence . . ." I hone in on a branch towards the very bottom edge, where the name Lars Vancent Denata has been circled in angry red. "That's the elder who presided over my trial." An Orange, according to these notations, which also happen to include the word *liar* in big hulking letters.

"You think he's keeping tabs on those in power?" Chase asks, crossing the room to examine my find with interest.

"Could be." Though it strikes me as more deliberate than that— more specific. "Or maybe he's . . . tracing blood lines, or . . . documenting magics," I say, since every name is accompanied by a color, with Council Shades denoted one way and rogues another, those who married typics another way still. The real curiosity, however, sits right beneath Councilman Denata, where a branch has been furiously crossed out and severed, with no reason given for the disavowment—of his only son, it looks like, though the lack of siblings could be due to the fact that his wife has been marked as dead. A sad story, yes, but not indicative of anything, and hardly worthy of this level of rage.

*Why are you so special?* There are six other brutally severed branches on this tree, one every four or five generations, all of which bear the disturbing note: terminated at birth. *Illegitimate children, maybe?* Though that seems a monstrous way to deal with those—even for families back then—not to mention that there are plenty more bastards signified elsewhere, and none of them appear to have met such a gruesome end.

*What the hells is he tracking here?* The more I lose myself in the details, the deeper the mystery gets, and it only grows more bewildering when I happen across his accomplice.

"Here's Alara." I point the Emerald out to Chase. Alara Francis Hayes, her name is, and her lineage tells exactly the story I expect: two dead parents and no offspring to speak of, the standard Hue fare. Though one leaf over is where the story takes its curious turn. There's a brother inked in beside her but not stemming from the same chain. Adopted into the family, unrelated by blood but her brother just the same.

Adriel Lars Denata.

"Adriel is the Divine Meridian's name," I say. It's what Alara called him back at the halfway house—I remember it all too well. "This must be his family tree. He's tracking his own heritage." Which somehow includes a sitting councilman.

*Well, that definitely can't be a coincidence* . . . It's much too far-fetched to think that the two Denatas are unrelated—especially when Adriel made such a point of branding the councilman a liar and crossing out his son. The only explanation that makes sense is that the Divine Meridian was born to Councilman Lars Denata and then— for some reason—transplanted elsewhere. And recorded in a wholly unique manner. Underlined, embellished, and described with—not a color—but a single word: void.

"But if he was born to two full-blooded parents, then why is he different?" I ask, fingers drumming against my leg. "Why does he affect the shadows in such an impossible way?"

"No idea." Chase is clearly wondering that same thing himself. "Maybe we'll find the answer somewhere among the rest."

"Maybe." We continue scouring the walls for an explanation that would shed light on what a void is—and what he's doing—though it quickly becomes apparent that the bulk of these ramblings are incoherent. Petty grievances, frivolous observations, trifling squabbles with the Church. It's as if Adriel's committed every errant thought in his head to the plaster, in a completely random order that defies logic or sense.

"Hey, I think I have something here." After a few minutes of solid searching, Chase calls me over to a particularly feverish stretch of scrawl. "Take a look at this."

*The fools don't understand the old language. They butcher it. They defile it. They don't even realize their mistake. They think the typics "destabilize" the Gray but that's a gross mistranslation of the effect they have on the shadows. The true meaning is "poison". Their blood is a poison that corrupts the well. May it poison them all into their graves.*

"That's more or less what he told Raya," I say. But ascertaining the hows or whys of that poisoning is a whole different game. There's just so much penned across these walls, so many accusations, and annotations, and random thoughts that meander, and trail off, and pick up randomly elsewhere, all of which paint a picture of a man who absolutely detests Shades. A man with a clear vendetta.

*I am the last and so the shadows welcome me home. That's what their Council is so afraid of—they've always feared this power for they don't understand it and they can't harness what is ours alone.*

*The voids.*

*The rare occurrences.*

*The children they seek to destroy.*

*Okay, now we're talking.* The rant begins to pull into focus the pattern of severed branches from before—even if I do have to hunt down its continuation on the opposite wall.

*We are superior to them, to their feeble colors—my Gods, what a disgusting term, too pretty for their crimes.*

*They thought they could kill us all.*

*They thought they could kill me—left me for dead while they continued to pillage my birthright for magic. But I exist beyond their magic and I will deprive them just as they deprived me—and oh how the shadows will rejoice! They will prove that I'm their savior, not the abomination he left to rot.*

*Just you wait, father, you will pay for the sins you committed.*

*You will pay a hundred thousand times in blood.*

*But . . . how?* I curse his lack of specificity. *What exactly do you intend to do to the councilman? And what were these sins he committed? Damn it, why do madmen always speak in riddles and splintered thoughts?*

"Ezzo—you need to see this." Chase beckons me towards his next discovery, a list that tracks—with all the unnerving detail I wished for—the experiments Adriel's been running in the Gray.

*The blood must be fresh and from a living donor; bottling negates the effects. Longevity does appear to correlate to volume but doesn't vary with color, nor is it impacted by the donor Shade's skill or age.*

   *1 pint: 17 minutes*

   *2 pints: 24 minutes*

   *3 pints: 38 minutes*

   *4 pints: 51 minutes*

   *5 pints: 66 minutes*

   *6 pints: 79 minutes*

   *7 pints: 87 minutes*

   *8 pints: 93 minutes*

"The human body holds around ten—so why stop at eight?" Chase's disgust is evident even as he asks the question.

"I don't think it was by choice," I say, pointing him to the adjacent excerpt.

*Another day, another dead whelp of a disappointment. These street urchins are too weak to accept the full measure of a Shade—or perhaps they're too young or too sickly. We need a better caliber of tribute.*

"It explains why he sent Alara to fetch him an older child—he must think that's the key to transfusing them with the rest." A nauseating prospect given how much pain Akari's blood caused the boy from the onset. How much more does he think a typic's body can take?

"But for what reason?" Chase asks, running his hand along the damning text. "Why does he need to drain an entire Shade into one typic? Wouldn't it make better sense to spread the blood around? Send a whole group of them into the Gray?"

"Not according to this." I finally find the crux of Adriel's plan.

*Seven is the important number. Seven Shades, seven colors, seven tributes. A one-for-one trade. Enough poison to wither the magic from the well.*

"So, he really is mad, then?" Chase stares at the words as though they might suddenly up and change. "He really doesn't realize that doing that would kill the shadows, as well?"

"I guess not." Hells, based on some of his other assertions, he believes the exact opposite—that the shadows will *rejoice* at this turn of events, that he's flat-out saving them. "I don't suppose you've found anything else on him? On voids, I mean? Their power?" I ask, since all I've been able to discern is that they're rare and possibly killed as infants.

"Nothing yet." Chase's sigh is a frustrated breath. And though we keep combing the walls for that answer, we're still none the wiser when our scrys warm with the warning that Adriel's sermon is fast approaching its end.

"We should go before he gets here," I say, since the last thing either of us wants is to run into him in the Gray. "Maybe Raya managed to coax the future into helping back in Saleen's library."

"Tell me you remember what she is, Ezzo." Chase grabs hold of my arm before we phase. "How dangerous she could be."

"Yes, thank you, I'm fully aware." I break out of his grip. "Do I have to remind you that Saleen is the same thing?"

"Saleen is *not* the same thing—and you thinking that is what has us worried."

*Us* not *me*. I don't miss the fact that, clearly, he and Cemmy have been talking.

"Saleen has had years to unlearn the hate the Academy teaches—and parents who've helped her unlearn it. Raya hasn't, and don't even get me started on Akari. They might be swept up in the mystery of it all right now, but they are not on our side, and they never will be. So whatever bond you think you have going—"

"Gods, there is no bond, okay?" I tell him. There's only a guilty truth and some stunningly bad decisions. "None of this has even been about Raya, not really." Except for a few sparks of curiosity that ignited along the way. "It's just that I've—I've thought about her less today," I say, and by *her*, we both know that I mean Eve. "It helps to have something different to focus on. To feel like I'm . . . part of something again, like the future sees me as part of something." As *worthy* of being part of something. "And whether we like it or not, we've stumbled into something big." Something important.

"You're right, we have, and I'm not saying that we should leave, or that we could even do this without them." Chase's expression thaws as we make our way back to the nave. "Just . . . don't forget what they're capable of, okay? What *Raya* is capable of. Because when this is all over, she's going to remember that Hues and Shades don't mix."

# CHAPTER 23

# RAYA

"I'm sorry, but . . . you actually expect us to believe that the Divine Meridian is Councilman Denata's son?" I don't mean to turn Ezzo's claim into a question, but the charge is so laughably ludicrous that I can't keep my voice from rising in pitch.

"What you believe doesn't matter. What matters is that *he* believes it," Ezzo says, leaning back in his chair. The tavern we reconvened in is a packed but private affair, closer to the Meridian's church than Saleen's house, but far enough away that the streets are only lined with a tolerable amount of iron. As safe a place as we could find for such a treasonous conversation, where the bustle of the crowd keeps our voices drowned beneath the boisterous din.

"Then clearly, he's even madder than we thought." Akari throws both arms up in the air. "Since Councilman Denata doesn't have a son."

"How sure are you about that?" Cemmy asks, though not in a combative way; it feels as though she's really asking.

"A hundred percent. His wife *was* pregnant back when they were first married, but it was a stillbirth and she took her own life a few weeks later. You can ask anyone; the story's been public for years."

"She's right," I say. Because she is. "He's been pretty open about it."

"People lie," Chase reminds us, glancing up from his drink. "Especially when it comes to their sins."

"They don't usually lie about having kids, though," Akari tells him. "I mean, what would be the point? There's either a baby or there isn't."

"Or there's a baby *until* there isn't." Saleen's eyes turn thoughtful. "While you were gone, I did find something in my parents' library. Not about voids—I think that's why the charms didn't work—but about how a small number of Shade-born children don't immediately register a specialization. Apparently, it can take up to an hour for their affinity to settle, especially if their parents married across color and are both equally powerful."

"Okay . . . but how is that relevant if they *do* ultimately register a specialization?" I ask. "Doesn't that just make them regular Shades?"

"I was getting to the relevant part, Raya," Saleen says, fixing me with a glare. "The book I found it in was an old medical guide, for the midwives that perform the test, and there was a note at the end of the passage that said if the child continues not to show an affinity, they should immediately contact the Council. I assumed it was because that would make the kid a Hue—your colors don't show up on the test, right?"

"No, they don't," Ezzo confirms.

"Right—which is why the note struck me as odd, because most Shades know if they fell into bed with a typic and they don't tend to get their illegal kids tested, so what if this was about something else? What if this is how they identify voids?"

"But wouldn't that mean that voids are just a spontaneously occurring thing?" That idea feels like a stretch. "Is that even possible?"

"New Hues spontaneously occur from time to time." Chase, on the other hand, seems to be considering it. "Or at least, they did before the Council started killing us off. That's one of the factors that led to the purges—they were afraid of the new magics that could be born."

"As fascinating as this thought experiment is, what does it have to do with Councilman Denata's non-existent baby?" Akari is no more in the mood for hypotheticals today than she was yesterday. She's here because Saleen is—because, right now, the prospect of getting her back is stronger than the need to hand the Hues into the court—but everything from the rod-straight tense of her spine to the rigid set of her jaw tells me that she's still struggling to accept any of this. I don't know why I'm not, to be honest, other than the fact that the Council's rules for magic have never worked in my favor and I'm only a month shy of them binding my color, so maybe I was primed to believe where she's not. In her case, the system is working precisely the way it's meant to.

"Don't worry, I'm getting to that, too." Her rebuke from Saleen is much gentler than mine was. "Ezzo said that he'd—the Meridian—Adriel—whatever we're calling him—moved his name to a different place on the family tree, so what if that's because the councilman knows about this rare type of spontaneous power and disowned him or something?"

"Left for dead, is what he wrote on the wall," Ezzo tells her. "But we didn't find any other details."

"And a lot of the details you did find aren't true," Akari reminds him. "Like the thing he said about us mistranslating the old language? That's pure fiction."

"Actually, that part's accurate," Cemmy says, as though she knows some secret we don't. "We have a friend who speaks the old language. We scried her a message and she confirmed it."

"I'm sorry—you have a friend who speaks the old language? The *shadows'* language?" Akari's eyes narrow down to danger. "Just like that?"

"Hues befriend other Hues." Cemmy shrugs, taking a sip from her glass. "Is that really such a surprise?"

"Colors help me, how many of you are there?"

"More than the Council would like." This time, the snipe comes from Chase. "But since it's our gifts that got you this information, maybe try complaining a little less."

It's only the hand Saleen puts to Akari's arm that keeps her from lunging at him across the table and sending this mismatched assembly of colors up in flames.

"Look, let's say, for a minute, that it is true." I'm quick to cut in and steer us off the ledge. "Let's say that Adriel's seven typics will poison the magic instead of destabilizing the Gray—and that he believes he can survive that—why does he want to do it? What does he gain?"

"An entire world, I'm guessing," Ezzo says. And maybe I'm imagining it, but it feels as though he's been doing his utmost not to look at me since they returned, even more so than back at the house—which I didn't think was possible. "There might not be a better reason; his goal could very well just be . . . vengeance. He used to be a cleric, right?" But he has no problem looking at Saleen.

"Grew up in the seminary and everything," she tells him. "He was one of their orphanage-to-altar stories."

"Well, then imagine that you're a forbidden type of power—so rare that no one even knows you exist—and you're growing up in a Church orphanage, hearing the absolute worst rhetoric about Shades, only to discover that not only are your own parents Shades, but your father—the man who rejected your power—is the Shade responsible for hunting those with illegal magics. That could easily inspire this level of hate."

As much as I'm loath to admit it, Ezzo's logic is solid. It's a little twisted, sure, but it's also exactly the brand of fanaticism this kind of upbringing might beget—and it would explain why he decided to form his own religion, a version of the Gods where he could keep the bits he wanted and leave the rest.

"If you're right, then his next step will be to prove that he can transfuse that much blood into a typic." I shudder as I realize how close Akari came to facilitating that end. "He'll probably go out looking for another—" A flash of blond hair banishes the remainder of that thought from my head.

"Erm . . . Ray?" Akari gives my shoulder a gentle shake. "Are you okay?"

No, I'm not, actually. In fact, I feel as though my organs have just escaped my flesh. Because standing not ten feet from us is the girl from my vision, the one I solicited all those months ago because I needed an excuse to kill my relationship with Killen dead. Her eyes were closed in that vision, so I didn't notice her irises, couldn't see the distinct lack of a spiked rim. *A typic? That girl was a typic?* It's a truth I never thought to entertain, and yet, here she is, weaving through the crowd like a blushing maid. *No . . . more like a courtesan,* judging by the flirt of her smile and the cut of her dress.

*Killen was going to cheat on me with a courtesan?* The sudden rush of insecurity almost knocks me off my chair. If we'd stayed together, is this really where our path would have led? To Killen stealing out of the castle to pay for sex—breaking my trust and several laws in the process?

"Raya?" This time, it's Ezzo's voice that fills with concern. "What's wrong? Did you see something?"

"Yeah, I—" *In a manner of speaking.* Though what I see next is infinitely worse. Because if spotting the girl was a gut punch, then watching the Shade now striding into the tavern is a spear through the chest, an inevitability unfolding right in front of me.

"Shit, Raya, isn't that your ex?" Saleen spots him a split second after I do. "What the hells is he doing here?"

"I don't know," I say, though I don't think it's a coincidence. It can't be a coincidence, can it? That this particular vision is fulfilling itself now, with me as its captive audience?

"He did see us leave the Academy," Akari replies in my stead. "Maybe he got worried when we didn't come back? Decided to look for us himself?"

*Instead of what he said he'd do?* I swear, nothing about Killen makes sense. He was definitely mad enough to go to Professor Lyons; he's been mad since the day I called us quits.

*So then, why didn't he?*

The answer is as obvious as it is soul-wrenching.

He still loves me.

I lied to him, and used him for magic, and he still couldn't bring himself to hurt me the way I've hurt him, not even after what I said to him at the archives, when I took the heart I already broke and shattered it to smithereens.

"But *how* did he find you?" Saleen asks, sinking low in her seat. "We only picked this place a couple of hours ago."

At which point, the future will have marked that decision as made, available for seeing.

"His roommate's an Indigo." I curse my own inability to predict. "He's found me this way before." I used to think it was charming, back when we were still a *we*. It used to be romantic as opposed to a death sentence for this table of six.

"Then let's phase and run." Ezzo's not avoiding my eyes anymore, he's urging me to flee. "He can't find you if you're not here."

"No, but he'll only keep looking." That's something else I used to love about Killen: when he put his mind to a task, he'd pursue it relentlessly. If he's here, then it means his worry was bigger than his anger, and if he's worried, then he won't stop until he knows I'm safe.

*Oh my Gods.* And suddenly, I get it. Not just the solution, but my mistake. How, once again, I asked the entirely wrong question, then misinterpreted the answer in the worst possible way. That is what Raya Wryvern, of the venerated Wryvern Indigos, has always done best.

"I have an idea—but, Saleen, I need your help," I say, getting up from the table.

"Okay . . . and are you planning to fill me in?" she asks as I carve a path towards the blond in the revealing dress, her brow furrowing in question.

"No, I just need you to trust me and do as I say; it'll take too long to explain." And I'm not sure I could explain it even if I tried to, all I know is that I've seen the exact way this scene has to play.

*Do Killen and I have a future?* I honestly thought I'd worded that question properly, that the fates would understand that I was asking about our relationship and not the part we'd end up playing in their game. But if the past few days have taught me anything, it's that there's no point straying from the path they set, especially when it turns out to be this premeditated. Killen came here to save me, and now it's my turn to save him, because while I can afford to throw away my future, he can't, and I won't be the reason he gets tangled up in this web. I've done enough damage to him already.

"Glamour our eyes, quickly. His too," I command before we reach the courtesan, since most typics in her line of work wouldn't dream of offering their services to a Shade.

"You need something, honey?" She looks me up and down with suspicion, as though trying to decide if I'm summoning the nerve to solicit her or rail against her trade.

"Yes, I—erm . . ." *Just do it, Raya. There's no use fighting fate.* "Do you see that guy over there? With the green eyes and the sandy hair?"

"Hard to miss, that one," the courtesan says. "Why? You going to tell me to stay away?"

"No, I—" *Want the opposite, actually.* "I'd like to hire you to keep him company."

"Raya, what—?"

I silence Saleen with a sharp elbow to the ribs, though I do hurry to add, "No sex, just . . . kissing, some conversation. He'll want to pretend that you two used to date—go with it; it's part of the game. Tell him you're sorry and that you want to get back together, then when your hour's up, send him on his way. Can you do that?"

"That depends." If the courtesan is surprised by my ask, she hides it well. "Can you pay?"

The stack of coins I drop into her palm confirms I can. "He'll call you Raya, that's important, okay?"

"Don't worry, honey, I'll take good care of your friend."

The second she slinks off in his direction, I beat Saleen to the protest and say, "Compel him to believe she's me."

"Holy fucking shadows, Raya, are you insane?" Her eyes bug open with rage. "I am *not* compelling Killen to court a hooker!"

"Please, Saleen, you have to trust me." She can't hate me more in this moment than I hate myself. "This has already happened—it's *supposed* to happen—and it's the only way to save the three of them." I point towards the Hues she deliberately disobeyed her parents to protect.

"You had better have the world's greatest explanation for this," Saleen mutters, but with a flick of her fingers, the spell takes effect, plunging Killen into a Red haze.

"Believe me, I do," I tell her, no matter how unlikely it is or how far-fetched. When you're an Indigo, you're always peripherally aware of the future's twisted threads, how they move and shape us even as we move and shape them. But this is the first time I've ever truly felt them move and shape *me*, seen the hand guiding my footsteps. Or in this case, the self-fulfilling prophecy I just committed to fate.

*Gods, please let me be right about this.* As the courtesan approaches Killen, I force myself to watch the horror for which I paid, to watch Killen's face relax as he spots "me" and the tension in his shoulders bleed away. Because what he's seeing isn't a buxom blond stranger, nor does he hear the courtesan's true voice when she whispers my lies in his ear, and he believes them not only because he's spelled to believe them, but because he *wants* to believe them, as well. I just broke his heart for a second time and he doesn't even know it yet.

*It'll be worth it when he's back in the castle and safe.* Away from me, and the Hues, and the Divine Meridian's murderous intent. Though that doesn't make it any easier to watch him recreate the betrayal I saw in my head.

When the future first sent me this vision, I experienced Killen's feelings, not the wrongness now flooding my veins. The future didn't let me taste the guilt in my stomach, or the regret in my throat, or the self-loathing that's ripping me tooth from nail. It showed me only the parts that would lead us both here. To now. To today. To the betrayal I was destined to inflict on *him*.

And if nothing else, that is one horror I deserve to see.

CHAPTER 24

# RAYA

It hurt more than I thought it would, watching Killen kiss another girl. Not because he was cheating, or because the future planned it, or even because I paid a courtesan to do the kissing. It hurt because watching him kiss her made me remember all those times he'd kissed me. How, despite the fact that I wasn't in love with him, the friendship that held us together was real.

And now he'll never forgive me—not once he finds out what I did. I'll never forgive me.

"Raya—are you listening to me?" A snap of Akari's fingers jerks me out of my guilt.

"Sorry—what?"

"I said: have you ever known a vision to manifest this way?" she repeats. "To self-fulfil?"

Right, yes. I was mid-explanation when a peal of the courtesan's laughter pulled my attention away, drew it to the fact that she and Killen were leaving the tavern.

"Erm . . . no, but I have heard of it happening." *They are allowed to leave.* I try to shake off the nausea and focus on what's important. *Leaving doesn't mean she'll do anything you didn't ask for.* Or at least, I don't think she will. That's not how courtesans work, is it? They don't offer up extras just because they like who they're dallying with?

"Damn it—*Ray*!" This time, Akari's reproach includes a none too gentle poke to the ribs.

"Sorry—sorry." I dig my nails into my thighs and force my attention to stop wandering. "It's an incredibly rare type of prophecy. Only ever seen in relation to a very specific kind of fated path, called a fundamental."

"A fundamental path? You're sure?" Ezzo immediately understands what that means, the potential ramifications.

"I'm not sure about anything," I tell him. Not the vision, not my actions, not our future—never mind something as monumental as this. "But I don't know what else to think."

"And is either of you going to explain what *fundamental path* means?" Saleen leans forward in her chair, her displeasure drumming angrily against the table. "Or are the rest of us supposed to just *guess*?"

"Sorry, it's . . ." How to even begin describing such a nebulous concept? Let alone to the livid Red I dragged into my scheme. "Think of the future as a tapestry—an intricate image made up of millions and millions of threads." I decide to start at the very beginning, with the same analogy Professor Lyons teaches every class of Indigos on their first day. "Individual futures—or threads—aren't set in stone, they're altered by the choices we make. But there are certain futures that are integral to the big picture, and we call those fated paths, because they're less amenable to change. It doesn't mean they *can't* change, just that the future will endeavor to maintain them wherever possible, because if they do veer too far from the big picture, then it'll affect all the other threads—though usually, the tapestry can survive that. Fate . . . destiny . . . whatever you want to call it, is pretty adaptable; free will couldn't exist if it wasn't. But there are some rare circumstances in which a fated path becomes fundamental to the big picture. Stray from it, and one by one, every thread unravels until there's no big picture left, just a cataclysm. I suppose that's why my original vision was filled with so much death." Including my death, their deaths, and the death of the Gray.

"So, you're saying we have no choice anymore?" If Cemmy grips her glass any tighter, it's going to shatter in her hand. "We're just stuck doing the future's bidding?"

"Yes and no," Ezzo cuts in on my behalf. "She's saying the future will continue to nudge us along this path until we get to the end, but that it can't decide what we do when we get there, whether we live or die, succeed or fail." He sums up our predicament perfectly. We can choose to keep fighting the future—and each other—but we'd likely still find ourselves in exactly the same place. With a front-row view of the catastrophe I saw in my head.

"Then why us?" There's an exhaustion to Chase's ask, a hopelessness that reaches down to the marrow. "Why are we responsible for saving the Gray?"

"Probably for the same reason it was us last year." Ezzo shrugs. "The future needs our gifts."

Their very *scarce* gifts, I realize, because thanks to the Council—thanks to all of us full-bloods—there's hardly any of them left. We've been systematically purging their magics for centuries, and then we went and closed off the mechanism by which our seers could have predicted this type of event. In trying to do good, we turned what might have otherwise been a regular path into a fundamental thread.

Though all that does is bring us right back to the Divine Meridian.

We need to stop him—that much, my visions have made clear—preferably before he drags another Shade into his cellar. But the truth is, we don't yet have enough information to do that, and even if—by some miracle—we do manage to puzzle out his plan and save the future, nothing I ever do is going to change the past, excuse the fact that I allowed Killen to get caught in the crossfire.

*Allowed? You practically served him up to the fates on a platter.* The shame in my stomach begins to prick. Because the truth is, I didn't have to self-fulfil that prophecy; I could have made a different choice—any different choice. Forced the future down a less offensive track.

But I didn't.

I went along with its machinations without so much as thinking the word *no*.

I let Killen leave this tavern with a courtesan.

"I have to go after them." That reality lurches me to my feet. Paying her to distract Killen was one thing, but I should have demanded that they stay here, where I could keep an eye on any unintended consequences. Because what if the compulsion spell breaks? What if she grows wise to the fact he's a Shade or he wakes up to the fact she's a courtesan? What if their excursion leads them somewhere rich in iron and full of hate?

"Go after who, Ray?" Akari startles at my sudden urgency. "We don't know where Adriel's going to strike next, remember? That's the whole problem."

"No, not Adriel—Killen," I say. "I have to go after Killen."

"Erm . . . but . . . wouldn't that kind of defeat the purpose of what you did in the first place?" Her head cocks with the question. "If he, you know, sees that she isn't you?"

"No, that's not—I'm not going to do anything," I tell her. Or rather, I'm not going to *undo* it. "It's just . . . letting them leave was a bad idea; I need to make sure he's safe. And look, none of you have to come, okay?" I hurry to add before she can protest. "You should all go back to Saleen's, see if anything Adriel said leads to something new in the books. I'll catch up."

"Uh-uh." Akari crosses her arms and worries at her bottom lip. "That's not a good idea. What if something happens and we need to find you?"

"Then I'll . . . take . . . Ezzo with me." I volunteer him for the task without thinking. "He can track you; you can scry him—if you don't mind coming, I mean?" I turn to give him the option, all too aware that, once again, I reduced him to the usefulness of his gift.

"It's fine," he says, less to me than to Cemmy and Chase. "If we're going to split up, doing it like this does make sense."

"Great, then let's go." I practically wrench him from the table, steering us out of the tavern before the others can muster up another reason to object—which Chase very much looks about to.

"Raya, would you please slow down?" Ezzo sighs as I barrel us into the street. "They can't have gone far. We'll find them."

And he's right; we do find them. It only takes a few minutes of searching to stumble across the courtesan's melodic laugh and her cascade of golden waves.

"There—in the park." She and Killen are sat beneath the canopy of a weeping willow, cuddled together in a way that stings far worse than watching them kiss. It's like looking back at an old memory, of a boy who's happy and a girl who's pretending to be, a Blue who deserved better then and deserves better now. *So much fucking better than this.*

"Come on, let's phase. We can keep an eye on them from the Gray." Ezzo blinks me away by the elbow, lending the scene around us a wholly different feel. The air strips of sound and color, the trees blooming to smokey charcoal, the water in the stone fountain darkening to glossy black ink. This late in the night, there aren't that many others here, only a few scattered echoes passing through the park like phantoms, so even if Ezzo wasn't as well versed as he is at tracking flickers, we'd still be in no danger of losing them.

"He's important to you, isn't he?" he asks, voice kinder than it's been all evening.

"He was." I sink down to the grass and wrap my arms around my knees, keeping my eyes fixed firmly on the sky, the wildflowers, the path that snakes between privets; on anything other than Killen.

"And he wanted to be again?" Ezzo guesses at the reason that led him to the tavern, why he left the Academy to come searching for me.

"Yeah."

"But that's not what you want?"

"Not because he did anything wrong." It feels important for me to say that, for him to know that Killen did nothing that would warrant . . . *this.* "He just thought we would be forever and I didn't—even though I wish I did." As if on cue, Killen's echo shifts closer to the courtesan's, their lights encircling each other playfully until I grow violently ill.

"We don't always get forever, Raya." There's a sadness to Ezzo's words that speaks of experience, to a loss he's had to endure because of *us* probably. Because for a Hue, even tomorrow isn't guaranteed. "If you didn't love him, then you did the right thing."

I assume he's talking about the break-up rather than this horror I'm now inflicting.

"I owe you an apology, Ezzo." Since I can't tell Killen I'm sorry, I placate my conscience by apologizing to him.

"For?"

My kind. My contempt. My beliefs. Lying to get out of the Academy for the sole purpose of handing him in.

"All the really crappy things I've said to you these past two days." As far as apologies go, this one feels wildly deficient, but it's the only way I can bring myself to begin.

"I can deal with a few insults, Raya." Ezzo bristles, as though he'd hoped I'd say something else. "What I want to know is what happens *after* we stop the Meridian." He turns to look at me head-on, spelling his distrust clear. "How sorry are you going to be when you no longer *need my gift?*" Those words sound even harsher coming from him than they did me.

"Enough to lie to the Council," I say—and I mean it. "I have no intention of telling them about you or Cemmy or Chase." For while I can't call off the trackers' search for them or change four centuries' worth of deceit, I can control what I do.

I can stop perpetuating this vicious cycle.

Win back his goodwill.

"Then your apology is accepted," Ezzo says, shooting me a small smile.

He doesn't do that a lot, I realize—and even when he does, the action feels mechanical, a smile in name only that never seems to reach his eyes. Which is a shame because Ezzo's face is truly lovely when he smiles. It's lovely when he doesn't, too, if I'm honest, but there's something about the way his lips crook and his angles soften that makes it impossible not to smile back. In fact, sitting here, engulfed in the glittering darkness, I finally understand what the future thinks I'll one day see in him, how easy it would be to forget the rules now that I've learned they're based on a lie. Because somewhere between escaping the Golden Stag tavern and forcing him to follow my ex to this park, my certainty has shifted—or at least, my feelings have, the conviction that I could never, *ever*, fall for an illegal half. I mean, hells, we've only known each other a short while and already, I can see exactly how necessity might slowly breed closeness—might gradually turn into love. I'm no longer even sure I should be fighting it.

*You've already self-fulfilled one prophecy, so why not just give the future what it wants?* Why keep pushing and pushing against it when I could just lean over and kiss Ezzo right now, find out if every part of my vision is fundamental.

*So then do it, Raya. Stop beating around the fucking bush.* I'm vaguely aware that I've started staring, tracing the line of Ezzo's jaw, and the curve of his mouth, and the way his lashes graze the top of his cheeks like dandelions. He's so different to Killen, more delicate than he is rugged, but every bit as beautiful. If not for the fact he's a Hue, that would have been the very first thing I noticed about him.

"Erm . . . Raya, is everything alright?"

His question slams me out of that strange fantasy.

"Yes—uh, fine. Everything's fine. I was just—" About to make another baffling choice. Gods, what was I even thinking? Am I so desperate to justify what I did to Killen that I would simply roll over and cede the fates control? "I may have . . . overreacted," I say in an effort to distract from the gawking. "Killen's clearly not in any danger here; we don't have to stay and watch."

"Are you sure?" Ezzo asks, stealing another glance at the echoes. "Because staying's not a problem."

"No, let's go." Now that I've said it, I realize it's true. I've already exacted this cruelty on Killen; if I stayed, I wouldn't be doing it for him, I'd be doing it for me—to alleviate my guilt, not his heartbreak—and that's not something I deserve.

I deserve to live with the shame of this decision.

And helping the others figure out how to stop Adriel is the best way for me to atone.

\*

Unfortunately, that's proving to be damn near impossible. By the time Ezzo and I returned to Saleen's house, the others were already sequestered in the library, scouring her parents' collection for anything we might have missed. But several hours of searching and an empty jar of charms later, all we've managed to find is the dawn, and one by one—page by page—our hope is beginning to wear thin.

These books may hold a ton of secrets, but they don't contain the answers we need. There's nothing about bleeding Shades, nothing about phasing typics, no ritual involving the seven colors or the full measure of a Shade. Hells, there's not even a single mention of the word *tribute*, so either Adriel *is* making it all up as he goes along or he's got access to a more extensive library than we do.

"So . . . is anyone else planning to admit that this is getting us nowhere?" Akari's supply of patience is the first to wane. "Or are we going to just keep pretending?"

"I hate to say it, but she's right." Cemmy sighs, adding another useless tome to the pile. "We've been at this all night. Maybe it's time to take a break, get some sleep, come at the problem with fresh eyes in the morning."

Except it already is the morning—there are tendrils of light threading needles through the darkness rippling outside the window—and the longer this takes, the longer Adriel has to commit another senseless murder.

"No, we can't stop—the future's counting on us to do this," I say. Which doesn't feel at all fair when everyone in this room is exhausted, and fed up, and getting real tired of making no progress.

"Then why isn't it helping?" Chase cracks his neck, lending voice to the question that's been plaguing me, as well—since fate-touched or not, I assumed the fates would be more forthcoming now that I've joined them on the same page.

"I don't know," I admit, because I don't understand it, either. I mean, I'm here with Ezzo, aren't I? Playing by the rules of their new game? So then, why didn't they answer a single question I asked when he and I first joined the others? How much more compliance do they really expect to get?

"When was the last time you asked, Ray?" Akari drums her frustration along Saleen's leg. It's hard not to notice how close those two have gotten these past few bells, how they're both sat against the wall with their sides pressed together—not unlike the way Cemmy is pressed up next to Chase. It makes me miss the days when I shared that kind of closeness with Killen. It makes me wonder who Ezzo's thinking about when he stares intently into the distance to avoid looking at them.

"Erm . . . three or four hours ago, maybe?" I guess. I gave up on being ignored somewhere around question twelve.

"Well, then can you maybe try asking again?" she suggests, grasping at another straw. "I know the future doesn't like repeat questions, but if it's not actually been responding, then couldn't it just be a matter of timing? Waiting for all the necessary decisions to be made first?"

"It's worth a try," I say, since yeah, she's right: asking a question too early is ultimately as ineffective as asking it too late—even if I'm not entirely sure what decisions Adriel won't have already made.

*How will we stop him?* I close my eyes and imbue the words with every ounce of my desperation, praying that the color in my blood will finally live up to its name. And I suppose it's a good thing we have Akari here to do my thinking, because just like that, the future relents, rewarding our tenacity with a vision that snaps my head back and sends me crashing into the desk.

A church, grand in stature, the grandest in Sarotuza. A body, shrouded in twilight, hanging from a cross of iron pitched above the gate. Crimson threats written across the flagstones. Guilt and horror. Fear and regret. The taste of violence and the smell of death. The sense that I should have prevented this from happening, but I didn't, and I couldn't, and I have to do exactly what the vision says next: I have to let them take me.

"Take you where, Ray?" Akari's shaking me back to the library, where five pairs of eyes are now anxiously trained on my face. "Who are they? Where are they taking you? What did you see?"

A future so awful I must have said it out loud, spoken it into the present.

"Adriel, he . . . he's killed another Shade." And my very bones are shaking with the brutality he inflicted—with the *futility* of knowing I'm destined to find the body, not spare it from its fate.

"Another Shade? How—when?" Akari's asking the wrong questions, because there's no use dwelling on the hows and whens when they're already beyond change. The only thing that matters now is getting me to that church.

"We need to go." I'm on my feet and in the Gray before they can stop me, shimmering despite the fact that only Saleen and Akari can follow me with the same haste.

*Ezzo will track my trail.* I don't agonize over leaving them; there's no point when I'm the one the future needs to trigger the next set of events. Around me, the shadows blur to dread and ring with sorrow, as though, they, too, have glimpsed the tragedy awaiting me at the vision's end. *Too late, too late, too late*, they seem to whisper, though it's actually Akari calling after me through the haze, begging me to slow down, to talk to her, to tell her what I saw in more than just a ragged exhale of panicked air.

But I can't.

Because something deep in my soul—in my color—wants to ensure that I reach this Shade before the trackers learn of his death. I have to be the first to reach him.

The typics' screams don't assault me until I arrive at the towering cathedral and phase out of the Gray, emerging at the heart of a paved basilica that's ringed with enough iron to rob me of breath.

*Suck it up, Raya.* I force myself to forget the weakness, forget the nausea, forget the pain, to focus only on the body dangling lifelessly from the gate, left for the pious to discover as they arrive to begin their early morning worship. He's been stripped of his shirt, draped in a ceremonial silver robe, with a deep hood covering his face and the sacred sun sigil branded across his sternum, shining bright above the message that's been crudely carved into his stomach and echoed in blood on the ground beneath his legs.

*You will all pay.*

The bile in my throat is acid, the sickness entirely divorced from all the iron in the square. It seems Adriel is finally ready to declare his war in earnest, which likely means that this latest test has been successful—and that it was the reason the future couldn't answer my questions right away; it had to wait for him to prove the theory, to impose on a typic the full measure of a Shade.

*Of this Shade.* A chill joins the churn in my gut, my feet moving me closer step by agonizing step. Whoever he was, he deserves better than a sacrificial hanging. He deserves dignity, not a spectacle, to escape the scrutiny of this unholy place.

"Raya—*don't.*" Akari's arms clamp around my shoulders. "We have to go before the trackers arrive, understand? They can't know we were here."

Except they have to know, the future said so.

And they will know because I refuse to leave.

"Then go, Kiri," I growl, breaking out of her grip. "But I'm not going anywhere until I see who that is." Until I get to the bottom of this feeling that it's my fault he ended up on the Meridian's table, that I'm the reason he's been bled dry of his color and hung up like a spit pig.

It's his hands I recognize first, the long fingers and the quick-bitten nails, a habit he picked up in childhood when his father left and the weight of his mother's expectations became his burden to bear.

*No.*

How many times did those hands wrap around my waist? How many times did I let them run through my hair, or dance across my ribs, or dip under my shirt and explore my body until we were both left gasping for breath?

*No, it can't be.* With trembling fingers, I reach for the hood hiding his face. *It can't be him; it just can't. There's no way this can be—*

Killen.

The scream that rips from me is a broken, feral thing. It's disbelief, and it's denial, and it's a guilty conscience; it's every frayed emotion the future predicted I'd feel, a pain so raw and primal it guts me worse than the iron.

*No—I won't let you be dead.* I attack the ropes pinning Killen to the metal. Not Killen's body, *Killen,* because I won't accept that he's dead when I saw him only last night, at the park. When he was *alive* last night, at the park, not cold to the touch and ghostly pale. When him being there in the first place was entirely my fault.

He left the Academy to find *me*.

Then he left the tavern after *I* paid a girl to trick him into thinking he had.

And then to make matters worse, I didn't stay. I talked myself out of staying and ensuring that once she'd left him to his own devices, he got back to the castle safe.

Gods, forget cruel, how could I have been so stupid?

How could I not have seen exactly where that choice would end?

"Raya, *stop*. He's gone." Even as I fight the knots keeping him captive, Akari's fighting me, her efforts tinged with horror and her voice heavy with tears. "There's nothing we can do for him anymore. He's gone." That word exudes finality, like hammering a nail into a coffin and burying it six foot deep. "Now, please—we have to go." She steals a glance at the crowd converging on the cathedral, the growing number of typics observing this macabre performance in lieu of their morning prayers. When they whisper to their companions, it's irritation I hear in their scandal, not outrage or grief. They don't care that a Shade is *gone*, they care that a Shade saw fit to exist, that even in death he's sullying their church, somehow, disrupting their fragile peace.

*Vultures, all of them.* Not for the first time, I wish I'd been born with an active power, so that I could hurt them the way their hate has hurt me, use it to cut Killen down from view.

"I'm not leaving him like this, Akari—so either help me, or leave." I don't mean to take my anger out on her, but there's just so damn much of it, ready and eager to turn inward and rend me limb from limb. Killen was right to call me a coward. He was right about my propensity for bad decisions, and he was right about me. He was right about everything.

"I can try." Akari sends a labored flex of Orange at the ropes, though thanks to all the iron, it takes several more before they finally fray enough to give.

"Thank you," I say as—breathing hard—she helps me ease him down from the gate, ignoring the way the square around us ripples with the arrival of more Shades.

"Ari—Raya—what the hells is going on? Is that a—*oh Gods*." It's Saleen's shock I hear first, followed by Ezzo's gasp and Cemmy's revulsion, Chase's distaste for the irate wave of jeers that tears through the crowd. They're not used to seeing us phase so brazenly around their house of worship, and they don't much like to watch a group of us blink between worlds en masse. It makes them feel inferior.

"Get Akari out of here, Saleen! Get them all out of here!" I yell for her to spare them the capture the future has in store for me, to get them to safety while she still can. But for the second time tonight, I'm too late, because with a faint pop and a rustle of air, we're suddenly surrounded by trackers on every side.

"Go—now!" What happens next is a tangled mess of spells, curses, and charms. It's surprised screams and growled obscenities, iron-damped magic and crystal-borne power. It's clutching Killen in my arms until the dust settles to reveal that we're not the only casualties of fate's meddling.

*Ezzo.*

He's on his knees across the square, lip split and nose bloodied, driven to surrender by a swell of magic and kept from running by two hulking Reds.

He doesn't say anything as we're phased away.

He doesn't look at me.

He doesn't protest.

Though his hand does brush mine for the briefest of seconds, as if to remind me that we're still allied. That's when I understand the gift he's buying me with his silence. If Ezzo doesn't acknowledge me, then I can claim that we're not together. I can claim that I was just at the wrong place at the wrong time, a spectator to the violence while he's the cause, the evil Sapphire acting on the Divine Meridian's behalf. But no matter how hard I work to catch his eye and tell him that I won't do it—that I won't be responsible for the death of another Shade, however diluted their color—Ezzo only heeds me long enough to give an almost imperceptible sigh. *There's no point in them killing us both,* it seems to say, and it makes me want to slip my shackles and shake him until he understands that *I* did this, not him. The future showed me *my* capture, not his, and he shouldn't have to pay for *my* willingness to follow that instruction blind, without taking a single second to think.

Except that truth won't save him.

He's an illegal Hue who'll be executed regardless; the only question now is whether I'll also be standing trial.

*Was this your plan, huh?* I ask the future. *Is this what you wanted? For both of us to end up in cuffs?*

But of course, the future can't answer that question, and even if it did, I imagine it would simply confirm what I already know in my heart: that the only thing it wants is its own survival—and that I truly am a coward down to the last. Because when the trackers lead us off in opposite directions, I don't make a single plea for them to spare Ezzo's life.

# CHAPTER 25

# EZZO

This time, I *really* didn't mean to get caught. I was only in that square because of Raya, and it was clear, from the second we got there, that it was already too late; the Shade was already gone. And not some random Shade, either, but Raya's ex, Killen—I recognized him from the park and the prophecy she'd self-fulfilled. He was the Shade we'd both left with the courtesan, though never in my wildest dreams did I think that decision would condemn him to such a gruesome death. Drained, branded, carved bloody, and left to hang on the Church's doorstep. A fate I wouldn't wish on anyone, not even an Academy Shade.

Though that didn't make lingering in the square any less dangerous, surrounded as we were by faithful eyes. Then when the trackers blinked into that basilica a minute later, I knew our time there was well and truly spent.

Raya was too far out of my reach to help.

But Cemmy and Chase weren't.

What happened next happened quickly, though in the moment, it felt as though I was watching the world through molasses, glimpsing the violence in fractured fits and bursts. I saw the spells flying, the typics running, the Council's justice closing in around us like a trawler's net. And then—right as I was about to try my luck in the shadows—I saw the mirth of a tracker who had Chase firmly within aim.

And just like that, I was back in the theatre house in Isitar, watching a flash of magic build to murder in a Green's hand. To my murder—until

Eve threw herself in front of the spell and saved my life. She died so that I wouldn't, and now, here I was, in a position to make that same decision, to step in front of the spell hurtling at Chase and spare Cemmy that same heartbreak.

I didn't have to do it; I could have easily just phased and ran, taken from her the same thing she took from me. But that's not who Eve would've wanted me to be and it's not who I wanted to become. Because deep down, I knew Cemmy didn't deserve that. She didn't deserve to lose her happiness to the trackers and spend the next year drinking herself stupid in some filthy tavern. And so my best instinct took over and I stepped in to spare her that pain, only to find that it wasn't a deadly Green spell this time, it was an excruciating Orange.

I lost sight of what happened next—there was too much magic screaming through my blood—but when the spells finally stopped flying, Raya and I were the only two the trackers had successfully trapped. And while they very much wanted to put an end to me immediately, our capture had the distinct misfortune of causing a spectacle, which prompted the lead tracker to stay my execution with a growl. *Not here*, he'd said—now that they had an audience, they had to at least pretend they meant to give me a trial. Or hells, maybe they just wanted the option of questioning both me and Raya, to see if our stories aligned, use me against her. And *that* was preventable.

My fate was sealed at birth, but she could still talk her way out of this, continue walking her fundamental path. So I said nothing to the trackers, and when Raya caught my eye, I shook my head ever so slightly and made it clear that there was no point in us both dying. And I swear, I didn't mean it as a test of loyalty—I really didn't—I *wanted* her to look away so she'd survive.

So then, why does the fact that she stayed silent suddenly feel like a betrayal?

Why is the last thing I hear before they separate us an echo of Chase's warning whispering through my mind: *remember what she is.*

# CHAPTER 26

# RAYA

The trackers don't take me to the prison, they take me to the Academy, to a holding room in the basement where they leave me for hours on end. One bell passes, then two bells, then three, four, five, eight, ten. And still no one comes for me, nor does the castle thrill with a summons to the court chamber, so if they're planning to execute Ezzo, they've either done it behind closed doors or they haven't done it yet.

*They won't kill him until they've questioned you.* I spend the silence clinging to that hope with each breath, too afraid to reach for my magic and learn the true answer. *They're going to want to compare your stories. They may not give him another trial but they'll want to find out what he knows first.*

It would be easy to believe that—if not for the fact that no one's come to ask what *I* know all day.

*That doesn't mean they won't.* It's that single thought that stops me from crumbling while I wait and wait and wait, while I pace my tiny box from corner to corner in an effort to keep the guilt at bay. *They could come for you at any minute, so you have to be prepared. They are going to come for you, Raya, probably just as soon as they've finished dealing with Adriel's last—*

*No.* I refuse to let my mind go there; I block out the memory entirely, because if I don't, then all they'll find when they get here is a broken, blubbering mess, and I can't allow myself to show weakness. I can't allow myself to think about Killen, or Ezzo, or whether the others managed to get away safe. Because the future *chose* to lead me here and it still needs me to save the fundamental thread. Which means I have to be ready. No matter how long they plan to let me stew in this fucking basement.

By the time the trackers are sent to fetch me, dusk has already come and gone and the shadows have dimmed at the edge, the castle filling with the warm glow of a thousand hex lights. And though my captors don't tell me where we're going, it quickly becomes apparent that we're heading to the court chamber; then once I'm led inside, I finally understand why it took so long for this interrogation to be arranged.

The entire tribunal has been called.

All seven Council elders, here, for me—despite the fact that a Shade was just brutally murdered in their city and that Adriel has threatened to make us all pay.

But it's not their stern expressions or their willingness to convene that prickles the hairs on my neck, it's who else they thought to involve in these proceedings, the two Indigos stood beside the judges' bench, exchanging heated words with Councilman Denata.

My parents.

The very sight of them pales me ashen.

I should have known they'd be here to witness my downfall—or to try and stop it, maybe, depending on how much they've been told. When you're the daughter of the two most celebrated seers in the city, there's no way for your crimes to go unnoticed. The second the trackers connected me to Ezzo, they'd have been summarily informed.

*And summarily enraged.* As the trackers shackle me to the dock, my father's face bruises to match his color.

"Have you lost your minds? Uncuff my daughter at once!" He wastes no time before voicing his indignation, though his tone suggests that he's less worried about *me* than about how it looks for me to be dragged into this room in chains.

"Your daughter was caught with a half breed and a dead classmate in her arms, Bastian," Denata barks in reply. "She will not be released until we ascertain if she played a role in his murder."

*A role in his murder?* As much as I should have seen that accusation coming, it still hits me right in the gut. *I would never hurt Killen,* I want to scream at them, except I can't because it's a damn lie. Because I did hurt Killen, over and over again; and I did play a role in his murder, just not in the way the councilman expects.

"That is an absurd accusation, Lars." But my mother doesn't know that and so she jumps to my defense. "The Divine Meridian killed that boy; any idiot could see that. Raya was merely out there in search of a friend. The half breed is who you should be questioning—he's clearly working with that zealot."

"Nothing is clear, Minerva, that's why we're here: to establish how Raya found herself in such terrible company at that church."

Every eye in the room snaps to me in anticipation, hungry to hear this good reason I must have for consorting with an illegal Shade.

"I—" And I know what I'm supposed to do now. I'm supposed to deny, deny, deny, then apologize, confirm the tale my mother already thought to prepare. *I was merely out there in search of a friend.* I should tell them I'm sorry for leaving the Academy, for not returning when I was supposed to, for not ceding the business of tracking to the trackers and beating them to the dead Blue.

For being a consummate disappointment.

But the second I'm faced with the councilman's scrutiny, an anger ignites inside my veins. Because why am I the one chained to this dock when he's the reason there's a murderous zealot out there in the first place? When it's his own son doing the killing?

"I know who the Divine Meridian is." The words escape before I can stop them, before I can talk myself out of saying them aloud. "His name is Adriel, Councilman, does that sound familiar?" I watch to see his reaction. It's a gamble—and a pretty big one at that. Even if Denata did disown his son, that was over thirty years ago, and Adriel is not such an uncommon name that he'd necessarily connect the dots.

"Excuse me?" But the way his face pales tells me he does, that everything we've uncovered is true.

"He also has an impossible power," I say, lacing my voice with steel. "I saw it for myself, Councilman—I heard him talk about it. He calls himself a void and I'm pretty sure you know what that means. I'm actually pretty sure you're his—"

"Lars, it's plain to see that Raya is extremely upset," my mother cuts in abruptly, as if to save me from my lack of sense. "You've been holding her all day; she's tired and grieving, and I think we can agree that there is no need to keep blaming her for this tragic—"

"The Divine Meridian is your son, isn't he?" I continue speaking over her. "That's why his name is Adriel Lars Denata."

"What nonsense is this?" The councilman booms, even as he chalks whiter. "I have no son."

"But you did have one, didn't you? A child born without color?"

"Raya—stop this at once," my mother hisses, glaring at me with pleading eyes.

But I can't stop it. Or perhaps I simply don't want to. Not now that I'm certain I'm right.

"Did you intend for him to end up with the Church or was that just an accident?" So, despite her protests, I keep right on pushing. "Because he believes you left him for dead, Councilman, and all these years, he's been holding a grudge. You made him hate Shades so much he started killing us. He wants to poison our magic, did you know that? Was abandoning him the reason your wife took her own—"

"Enough!" A flash of Orange rips the air from my lungs. "I will not stand for this brazen slander, Miss Wryvern. To spread such lies in my own chamber—"

"Councilman, my daughter doesn't know what she's saying." My father sweeps between us, his tone sharpening to jagged glass. "Raya—tell him you don't know what you're saying. Apologize for this folly right now!"

I mean . . . it's probably a little late for that.

For while I could take the words back, I can't make Denata unhear them; he'll never forget that I've seen the truth he's kept buried this whole time; he'll always consider me a threat. And getting caught with Ezzo—in a place I shouldn't have been to begin with—has given him all the excuse he needs to remove that threat from his life.

In choosing to expose him, I also chose to doom me.

Though I can't, and I won't, and I downright refuse to regret dragging his lies into the light. Maybe when I'm gone, my parents will be angry enough to ask their own questions. Maybe when the magic's dying, the rest of the elders will remember the accusations I levelled at the man in charge. Maybe this is the part I'm supposed to play in stopping the Divine Meridian.

"Silence!" Denata roars, quieting the scandalized mutters coming from the Shades at his sides. "Given the appalling lack of respect Miss Wryvern has shown this tribunal, it is my recommendation that she be taken to the cells for further interrogation, and if it is found that she has conspired with the half breed, she will be returned to this chamber to answer for her crimes."

I'm fairly certain that "if" will become a firm condemnation soon enough—that, come morning, I'll have magically confessed to a whole slew of wrongdoings he'll then use to bury me at trial.

"All in favor, say aye."

"Aye." The echo of agreement that follows is as swift as it is damning.

"Lars, please—don't do this!" My mother's voice turns shrill as the guards wrench me from the dock by the arms.

"She is our daughter, Lars," my father adds, outraged. "You cannot treat her like a common criminal!"

Except he can.

And he will.

And he does.

And no amount of blustering will change that.

My death warrant has already been signed.

# CHAPTER 27

# RAYA

It's not until I'm led from the court chamber that I start to feel the full weight of what I've done; the futility of railing against the council-man and the finality of that act, the sentence that'll soon be enacted. *She will be returned to this chamber to answer for her crimes.* My breaths begin to grow sharp and short and labored. What the hells was I thinking, picking that kind of fight? Have I really learned nothing from Ezzo? How the truth makes zero difference when those in charge have a vested interest in propagating the lie? How they'll always choose to protect their own power?

The journey to the Council's prison passes in a blur of realization, fear, and doubt, a rush of moments I only register in fragments. It's swirling shadows and the echo of my parents' increasingly incensed shouts, empty corridors and a portal that deposits us back in Sarotuza. It's an explosion of color as we leave the Gray, that's soon replaced by a maze of moldy brick that's filthy and stark. It's an iron cuff around my wrist and a swell of nausea as I'm shoved—none too gently—into a ferrite-laced cell at the very end of a long line, far enough from the guards' station for the metal to affect me but not sicken them. This is where they put the traitors, I'd venture; the rogues, the Hues, the Shades who recklessly accuse an elder of having a secret son.

It's also where they've put Ezzo.

*He's still alive.* There are so many emotions warring inside me, that I barely even notice the surge of relief that sings through my blood, nor can I decipher the storm brewing in his expression, why he seems less than happy to see me. *Does he think I betrayed him?* As I wade into the cell proper, he tracks my steps with a hard-set jaw and a wary eye, as though wondering if this is some kind of trick or a novel new method of interrogation.

But it's not a trick, and once the guard leaves us to fester in silence, I lose grip of the last shred of strength that's been keeping me up. *What in the nine hells have I done?* I fall to my knees, the tears coming freely now that he and I are alone in the dark. After a full day of fighting to suppress it, Killen's death hits me with a vengeance, the part I played in it and the way he looked with his blood drained and his skin carved, how I'll never get to tell him I'm sorry. How instead of learning from my mistakes, I keep making them over, choosing the wrong battles and letting everyone down. How after all the truths Ezzo's shown me, I wasn't even brave enough to stand up and own our alliance.

And for a long second, the air around me stays absolutely still, my sobs bouncing off the walls like thunder, splintered and snubbed. Until, in the space of a blink, Ezzo's arms are around me, his voice low and gentle as he attempts to soothe the pain raging inside my heart.

"I'm sorry about Killen," he says, guessing at the worst of my guilt. "I'm sorry we couldn't stop Adriel from doing what he did."

*What about what I did?* There's not enough contrition in the world to excuse the way I treated him, the way I used his love as ammo and sent him out to wander the streets with a courtesan.

"You couldn't know this would happen, Raya," Ezzo whispers into my hair, as though reading my mind. "This isn't—"

"Please don't say it isn't my fault," I tell him. Because it very much *is* my fault—and no amount of empty platitudes will change that. I could have left that tavern with him myself, not paid another girl to do the lying. I could have ensured that he returned to the castle safely, not made an excuse to spare me having to wait and watch. I could have told the future where to stick its twisted prophecy.

"Do you want to talk about it?" Ezzo asks instead, shuffling us over to sit against the wall. And though I want to say no—to keep this worst part of me locked away—I find myself telling him everything, a full recounting of my history with Killen and every callous decision I made, including the ones that eventually led to his murder. And Ezzo just listens to the full story without judgement, his arm staying locked around my shoulders no matter how awful my confessions get, even when they make me sound like a monster.

"You can say it, you know, that I'm a horrible person. That I . . . I deserve this."

"No one deserves this, Raya. No one," he says, turning to look at me head-on. "And I know it doesn't feel that way right now, but this pain will get better with time. It won't disappear entirely, but you will get better at carrying it."

"Did you get better at it?" I think I finally understand the reason he'd all but given up when we met.

"I didn't want to get better at it. I haven't wanted much of anything this past year, to be honest, other than to drink until I could forget, drown out the past." Ezzo's admission is its own weight.

"Is that why you let yourself get caught?" I ask, the question little more than a breath.

"The first couple of times, yes," he says, equally quiet. "I guess I figured if I was careless enough, the trackers would make the hard decision for me, save me doing it myself." He confirms what I'd long since begun to suspect. "But when we were in that square, I wasn't thinking about dying, I just saw a chance to help the others get away. And you were supposed to get away, too, Raya." His eyes sharpen back to the cell. "They had no reason to think you were working with me, so why didn't they let you go?"

"Turns out, I'm not smart enough to save my own neck." I sigh, hugging my knees to my chest.

"What do you mean?"

"I mean, when they put me in front of the tribunal—in front of Councilman Denata—I decided to ask him about what you saw in the Meridian's church."

"You asked him about Adriel?" It's hard to tell if Ezzo's appalled or impressed.

"Among . . . other accusations."

"And?" Though at the very least, he's certainly entertained. "What did he say?"

"He denied it, of course, but he also sent me here, so I'm taking it as a yes." I shrug, trying to relay the next part lightly, like it isn't churning my insides with dread. "For 'further interrogation', apparently, but I'm betting that's just a pretense. He won't want me running my mouth again."

"Then so much for saving the fundamental thread." Ezzo's resigned huff is sadder than I expect. "Unless maybe you already saved it in the court chamber? Do you think your confrontation with the councilman could have been a trigger in some way? The catalyst the future needed to course-correct?"

That might make sense if not for the original vision it showed me, where the arm draped around my shoulders had graduated from comfort to something else.

"Maybe." I drop my head to the mold-bitten brick, trying to ignore the fact that the idea no longer strikes me as so far-fetched. "But I've never been a very good seer, Ezzo, and I'm fate-touched now, as well, so I wouldn't put too much stock in anything I say. I probably read the vision wrong." Otherwise, why would the future have forced me to lead Killen to his death? Surely that only brings Adriel *closer* to poisoning the shadows? Surely locking us up in here does, too, since there's not much we can do to stop him from behind bars, and the others aren't likely to succeed, either, if their efforts are distracted by the need to get us out. No, my being wrong is the more likely scenario—and far more true to life.

"Why do you keep saying fate-touched like it's a bad thing?" Ezzo's voice lilts with the question. "Didn't you say that's how every Indigo used to see?"

"Erm . . . yeah, we—" How is that his take-away from this? "We learned a better way to solicit visions, a way that avoids us getting punished by the fates."

"Punished, huh?" He raises a brow. "Is that your word or the guilds'?"

"The guilds' . . ." I still don't understand what he's getting at. "But being fate-touched can make you lose your magic altogether; wouldn't you call that a punishment?"

"I think my mom would have called it a gift."

*A gift?* I can't quite believe what I'm hearing. "You think it's a *gift* that I might lose my magic? Gods, don't tell me you're starting to side with Adriel."

"No, I'm not starting to side with Adriel." He rolls his eyes. "It's just . . . not all magics are created equal, Raya—some exact a heavier toll. My mom always described the future as her burden, something she had to see while everyone else got to enjoy the present, skate through life without constantly having to predict. She made it sound pretty exhausting, actually—hells, I just watch and that's exhausting enough for me. So if being fate-touched makes it possible for you to see even bigger and more imperative things—like fundamental paths and cataclysms—then yeah, maybe losing your magic is the future deciding that you've already done your bit, allowing you to live your life unencumbered."

"I—" Have never thought to look at it that way before; as a Wryvern, that's not really something I'm allowed to think. My magic—my lineage—has always defined me. It's who I am, who I've not become yet, and who people expect me to be. It's the only part of me my parents care about. "I guess that . . . could be nice?" I say, since it's not the worst fantasy to believe. "How come your mom taught you so much about this stuff, anyway? Fated paths and fundamental futures, I mean? It's hardly the stuff most Indigos care about."

"My mom wasn't most Indigos." His lips quirk with a smile. "She used to talk about them all the time, always insisted that she and my dad were fated."

I'm assuming she meant that in a romantic sense rather than a literal one, since their illicit coupling couldn't have been preordained.

*Unless it was . . .* That thought takes me by surprise—but if there's anything these past few days have taught me, it's not to underestimate fate. If, for whatever reason, it did decide to push a Hue and a Shade together, then it would have had to ensure that Hue had been born in the first place, which would have meant prompting a Shade to turn rogue and marry a typic, then teach her son how to survive long enough to fulfil his purpose and start the cycle again.

"But I'm sure that's a little hard to understand," Ezzo's quick to add, as if expecting me to minimize the idea. "Choosing to believe that the fates would orchestrate something so forbidden."

"Not as odd as you might think," I say, since minimizing it hasn't been working for a fair while. It was hard to understand when Akari and I first left the castle, and when the future led me to the Golden Stag tavern where Ezzo was drinking himself numb, and especially when he invited Chase to feast on the color in my blood. But three days and a whole bunch of revelations later, I'm starting to consider all manner of odd things. Like finally coming clean.

"Ezzo, there's—there's something I haven't told you," I say, since given where we are—what's about to befall us—keeping this secret feels kind of pointless.

"Well, now's as good a time as ever." Though his voice stays light, his body stiffens, bracing for whatever admission is to come. He knows I've been hiding something—he even asked me about it back at Saleen's, when I was still intent on being less forthcoming—he just doesn't know what that something is yet, and I have no earthly clue how he's likely to react.

*Gods, then spit it out already,* I will myself, doing a little bracing of my own. *At worst, he'll reject the very idea of you.* And mortifying as that would be, it isn't much of a problem, seeing how we're both slated to die.

"The original vision I had, after I asked the open question—it wasn't only about the Gray dying; it was also about . . . me and you," I say, slow and quiet. "Us."

"Us?" He repeats the word as though it belongs to another language, the tension in him snapping taut. "As in—?"

"Yeah." Since I can't bring myself to look at him, I drop my gaze to the ground, counting the cracks in the grimy concrete. *One, two, three, four, five* . . . I'll count them all if I have to, if it keeps this charged silence from sparking and setting my skin on fire. *Six, seven, eight, nine—*

"Raya." An entire age seems to pass before Ezzo speaks, before he says my name and forces me to meet his eyes. And perhaps he is open to that possibility, because what I see in them isn't pity, or embarrassment, or even disgust; it's more akin to indecision, and understanding, and want, I think—or rather, the want to want, to lean in closer and give the future the ending it demands.

*Do it.* I'm suddenly staring at him every bit as intently as I did in the park, aching to know what his kiss might be like, how it would feel to break a rule this fundamental. But the difference today is that Ezzo isn't oblivious; while I'm staring at him, he's staring right back, tracing the line of *my* jaw, and the curve of *my* mouth, and the way *my* lashes graze the top of my deepening blush, the way I'm slowly starting to tilt my head up and up in his direction, a mix of air and hope bubbling in my lungs, waiting, waiting, waiting for him to make the final choice I can't, to ask our very own version of an open question.

Except he doesn't.

And all at once, the desire I felt in him turns to panic and a self-loathing flush, a heart-wrenching torrent of pain.

"I'm sorry, Raya, I—I can't." Ezzo jerks away from me, leaving my nerves stinging with his absence. "It's not that I don't—that you're not—this just can't happen, okay? Not now, not ever. It wouldn't be fair—to either of us."

*Because he's still in love with someone else.* That answer is clear as day and hot as lightning, a truth I should have seen the second he told me the pain will get better with time—but that his hasn't. That we don't always get forever.

"What happened to her?" The question slips out unbidden—in curiosity, sure, though it's also an invitation for him to talk, if he'd like. If he needs to.

"She shattered." And I guess Ezzo does need to, since after a long moment, he whispers that awful truth into the dark. "She stepped in front of a Green spell meant for me and then I had to watch her lose her magic one splintering crack at a time, until the shadows shattered her to pieces. There was nothing I could do to stop it," he says, though the sentiment sounds oddly flat, as though he doesn't quite believe it. "Eve died, and I couldn't save her, and then I couldn't find the strength to follow her into the black."

*Colors help me.* His heartbreak far outweighs the rejection squirming in my gut. It's little wonder he lost his head when we watched Adriel's tribute shatter, and it certainly does explain the reckless disregard he's shown for his own life. The girl he loved died and ever since, he's been aching to join her. He's been living with her ghost this entire time.

"We were supposed to die together," Ezzo continues, lost to the telling now that he's begun. "We always knew that death would find us sooner rather than later—we'd already lived much longer than most Hues tend to last. Sometimes, we'd even plan for how it might happen; I know it sounds morbid, but it felt like we were keeping that possibility at bay by looking it in the eye. And when we did, we'd imagine it happening in some wildly spectacular fashion, the sort of death the bards would one day sing a song about. We called it dying like the stars."

If I didn't resent the fates before, then I sure as hell do now. It was cruel of them to feed me those words, to have me manipulate him with them, tarnish a cherished memory. Gods, I don't blame him for lurching away from me; he's still deep in mourning and yet, here I am, telling him the future wants me to be the new her.

"I'm so sorry, Ezzo," I say, and I don't just mean for the part *I* played in his misery, but for the part we all did, every last Shade from Isitar to Sarotuza. Because it breaks my heart that our hate took from him that love, that he's in pain and we're the ones who caused it. It breaks and it breaks and it breaks me.

Just like in my original vision.

CHAPTER 28

# EZZO

Shame surges through me, potent and strong. Not just for having told a Shade, of all people, about Eve, but for what that Shade saw in my future, for allowing myself to wonder whether I might one day want that.

Hells, for a brief second there, I did *want* that.

I wanted to lean in closer and prove the future right.

Until I didn't.

I can still feel the ghost of Raya at my side, taste how easy it would have been to do away with logic and jump head first into the unwise. To kiss a Shade. Regardless of how illegal or unlikely that idea was. And it really would have been easy; I mean, Gods, Raya's beautiful—that's what first drew my eyes to her in the court chamber during my trial—and even if she wasn't, she's brave, and stubborn, and endlessly surprising. Infuriating, too, but in a way that forces me to stay sharp. I could absolutely imagine kissing her, shutting out the guilt, and the memories, and convincing myself it's time. Because I've missed closeness. I've missed the thrill—the longing—of craving another's touch.

But if there was ever a combination more misguided than a Shade and a typic, it would be a Shade and a Hue. We would be hunted forever.

*Why are you still considering this?* I shake the errant thought from my mind.

Eve was my future.

She was my past, my present, my always.

And that doesn't change just because she's gone.

*So then, tell Raya that*, my conscience whispers, as if in challenge. It's the only fair thing to do—especially if the fates are promising her something I can't.

"Raya, I—"

"You don't have to explain, Ezzo, I get it, I really do." She makes a concerted effort to meet my eye. "And I'm not expecting anything, okay? I told you because I didn't want to lie anymore—but when it comes to the future, I'm very rarely right."

*Oh.*

The sudden pang of disappointment takes me by surprise.

"So you . . . don't think that's supposed to happen?" I force my shoulders to relax, closing a fraction of the space I'd put between us.

"I don't see how it could when we're stuck here." Raya does her own bit of reshuffling, inching further away from the iron bars, though there's no escaping the cuff on her wrist or the ferrite deposits laced into the walls and ground. "Unless you can think of some way out?"

"Not really, no." The guards may not have gotten around to beating me senseless yet, but they were smart enough to slap a cuff on me, too, and to take my lock picks, and I doubt Cemmy and Chase could pull off a miraculous save for a third time—even with Saleen and Akari's help. "What I'd give for a more active power right about now."

"Gods, wouldn't that be nice," Raya mutters, as though she's also wished for that more than once. "The funny thing is, I'm actually pretty powerful, for an Indigo—that's why I messed with that open question in the first place, because of all that useless, passive, family pow—" She cuts off abruptly, as though some bright idea has struck.

"A silver for the rest of that thought?" I prompt, hoping she'll catch me up.

"Erm . . . yeah—so . . . there might be one more thing I haven't told you." A slow blush creeps into her cheeks, like she's remembering where those words led last. "About who I am."

"About who you are," I parrot, entirely baffled. "Why? Did you give me like . . . a fake name?"

"No, Raya's my real name," she hedges. "It's just not my . . . full name. My full name is Raya Wryvern."

"Okay . . ." If there's a train of thought here, I'm still following the wrong track. "Am I supposed to know what that means?"

"Seriously?" She blinks at me for a long second before realizing what's keeping me stumped. "Right, Hue, sorry—why would you know that?" The red deepens to a darker flush. "My parents are Bastian and Minerva Wryvern," she offers in explanation. "The joint heads of the seers' guild."

Well . . . *huh.*

"So, you're the daughter of two guild masters?" I honestly don't know whether to be impressed or offended that she thought to hide that.

"And their presumed successor." Raya shrugs. "Or at least, I was, until it turned out I was terrible at seeing."

"Okay . . . and you're mentioning this now because . . ?"

"While you had me chained up didn't seem like the best time?" She interprets my question in a different way than I'd meant it. Though she is right, I suppose—back then wouldn't have been the best time; we absolutely would have used her as leverage—though I imagine she thought we'd go much further than that, try to extort her parents for coin, maybe, or even kill her as a *fuck you* to the Council. Back then, she had no reason to trust us.

"Yes—fair point. But what I was trying to say is: why is this relevant now?"

"Because it's going to get us out of this cell." Raya grins, so either she's seeing something I'm really—*really*—not, or she's getting addled by all the iron.

"I'm going to need a little more than that," I say, raising an eyebrow. "Like *how* it's going to get us out?"

"Well, after the stunt I pulled in the court chamber, the councilman wants me dead, right?" she starts, not giving me the chance to answer. "But he can't just kill me; he has to give my very important, very powerful parents a reason, or else they'll kick up too much of a fuss. He has to go through the motions on this, drag me back into that court chamber and declare that, under interrogation, I confessed to working with you and the Divine Meridian. The elders are real sticklers for that stuff."

"Yes, I remember." The memory is like an open flame to dry brush. How they paraded me in front of a room full of Shades to deliver their sham of a verdict, just so they could cling to their belief that they treated me fairly, when in truth, they were punishing me for the crime of being alive. "But I still don't understand how that gets us out of here."

"It gets us out if the guard is too afraid to let a Wryvern die on his watch," Raya clarifies. "For all he knows, I could be found innocent tomorrow, so if he thinks I'm, say . . . choking, or seizing, he'll have to open that door and come inside—then we could overpower him."

*Well, I'll be damned.* This time, I am impressed—though it's certainly not a foolproof plan. The guard could easily decide not to care, for instance, or he may be stronger than we realize, or one of the more dangerous colors. He might even bring a second Shade with him and then we'd stand absolutely no chance. But a flawed idea is better than no idea, and I've not been able to think of anything more inspired, so it's either this or die.

"You'd better make this convincing," I say, climbing to my feet.

"Don't worry, I've been known to trick a few class masters in my time." Raya flashes me her teeth. Then, with a theatrical flourish, she flops into position and starts coughing like she's actually dying.

"Help!" I call out the moment she's ready. "Please—you have to help her; you have to help her, *now.*" I rattle my cuff against the bars for good measure, though since the guard left us to rot at the forgotten end of the prison, it takes a solid few minutes before he hears me and ambles down.

"What is the meaning of this?" he growls, voice hard and face angry, his hand skirting his saber as if for luck.

"It's the Wryvern girl." I make sure to emphasize that name, in case he wasn't told about his guest of honor. Which—judging by the gurn of his jaw and the widening of his eyes—he wasn't. This is the first he's learning about the very important problem in his cell, and just as Raya predicted, he's at a loss for what to do next.

"Please! She can't breathe!" So I lay the rhetoric on thick, making it clear that it's act now or face her parents' wrath later, that it'll be on his head to explain why he stood by and did nothing while their daughter gasped for air on the ground.

"Get in the corner and stay there, half breed," he barks, drawing his saber from its sheath. "And don't even think about trying anything."

*I wouldn't dream of it* . . . I do as I'm bid, grateful that the words aren't accompanied by a binding compulsion. "But please, hurry!"

On the cell floor, Raya's coughs go silent and her body goes limp, adding a sense of urgency to my panic.

"Gods, *please!*"

The guard starts grappling with his keys, then the lock, then the nausea from the iron, his gaze bouncing between me and Raya until finally, the door swings open and he wades inside.

*Wait for it* . . . I make a show of clinging to my corner, slouching my shoulders to appear less threatening, less like I'm about to strike. *Don't move until he's completely distracted.*

It takes far longer than I'd like for the guard's suspicions to dampen and the point of his saber to lower down.

*Now!*

The second it does, both Raya and I move in sync. Me, to kick the saber out of his hand. Her, to lurch up and land a knee to his groin with enough force to make me wince and shudder.

*That's got to sting.* As he grunts and doubles over, I spring forward to wrap my arm around his neck and squeeze—hard, harder, hardest, until he succumbs to oblivion and slumps lifelessly to the concrete.

"Quick, get his keys—he won't be out long."

Raya nods and scrambles for the ring.

"We need to find the others," she says once the cuffs are gone from our wrists and the guard is the one languishing behind bars. "You track, I'll shimmer?"

"Sounds like a plan to me." Not a plan I ever thought I'd be willingly making with a Shade, but a lot has happened since the first time I was imprisoned here, a lot has changed.

I've changed.

Enough to hope that this will be my last encounter with the Council's justice.

Enough to hope that I'll never see the inside of another cell.

CHAPTER 29

# RAYA

By the time Ezzo and I break out of the Council's prison, Sarotuza is in the throes of a full-scale riot, the streets consumed with so much hate and anger it's downright palpable, even from inside the Gray.

"This can't be good," Ezzo mutters, directing me through the swarm of echoes from behind the veil of his gift.

"What do you think's happened?" I ask, since without phasing back into the physical realm, their dissent is impossible to hear.

"Given the number of Shades I'm seeing, I'd say Adriel happened." His eyes are darting back and forth with unnerving speed. "Looks like every tracker in Sarotuza is out here."

Which probably means we shouldn't be.

"And the others?"

"Back at Saleen's, all of them," he says. "I'm reading all four trails."

*Well, thank my colors for that; they're safe.* The relief breaks over me like a wave. *They're safe and they're still working together—and they haven't killed each other yet.* Which, after a full day, feels like a huge win. A sentiment Akari echoes—with a few added curses—when we reach the house and blink out into their midst.

"I thought for sure you were dead, Ray," she whispers, her arms wrapping tightly around my neck. "We wanted to come get you, but . . . we couldn't find a way in. How did you get out?"

"It's a long story," I tell her. "So, let's just say it's a good thing I have famous parents. Now catch us up on what we missed—why has the whole city erupted?"

"Because our divine friend, Adriel, set his followers loose." Saleen's sporting a nasty set of bruises, not unlike the ones decorating Cemmy and Chase, a mark of this morning's skirmish with the trackers. Only Akari seems to have left that confrontation unscathed. Perhaps she was being watched over by a guardian Red. "They started attacking Council and Church buildings a couple of hours ago."

"I don't understand—why are his followers suddenly attacking buildings?" I ask. "They've never done that before . . . what's changed?"

"We don't know, exactly, but we think it may be a diversion," Akari says.

"A diversion?" That doesn't make any sense. "A diversion from what?" Why would Adriel want to divert attention now that he's proven his theory? Isn't the spectacle of success the best way for him to instill fear?

"The fact that Killen was only the beginning." Akari's voice softens around his name, like she's afraid it might break me.

"He took another Shade?" It does break me; it fills my mouth with bile and my stomach with lead, shakes my legs with a violent grief. "Already?"

"No, this time he's taken typics." Akari steers me over to the couch to sit. "We think that's what kicked off the riots in the first place. He took a bunch of initiates from the junior seminary and then set fire to the place. Which, as you can probably imagine, didn't go over too great."

No, I don't imagine it did.

"Problem is, no one seems to know where he's stashed them, and so the faithful have taken to the streets. They're protesting, and they're searching, and they're rioting; I don't really think they know what they're doing, to be honest, other than trying to find their kids. But then Adriel's followers started attacking buildings, and it wasn't long before the faithful got a taste for that, as well, and that's how we ended up here."

"Then could it be a ruse instead of a diversion?" Ezzo asks, leaning against the armchair. "If Adriel's taken typics, then now he'd need Shades. What better way to get them than to draw them all into the city?"

It's not a bad theory—except for the parts that don't fit.

"No, those aren't the kind of Shades he likes." Saleen is thinking along the same lines as me. "When you start a riot, you get trackers, muscle, Shades sticking together or working in groups—he likes to prey on them when they're vulnerable. That's why he's mostly been targeting lone Shades and rogues."

Why he grabbed Akari while she was out trading and Killen while he was wandering the streets alone.

"She's right." Things must really be bad if I'm agreeing with Saleen. "Adriel's gotten this far by skirting the trackers, not courting them. If they're here, then I'd bet my magic he's not."

"Okay, so then where is he?" Cemmy asks the pertinent question, pacing the rug from end to end. "Where would he go to find seven non-threatening Shades and no trackers?"

"I mean, the Academy would be the obvious choice," I tell her. "But—" *No, no buts.* I swallow the protest as that idea begins to form. *The Academy. He's gone to the Academy.* Implausible as that might seem— impossible, even—I feel the truth of it in my bones. It's where I'd go if I was looking to have my pick of colors, especially this close to midnight, while the acolytes are sleeping, and in the midst of a riot that has the trackers off dealing with the very unrest he caused.

"But he can't be at the Academy," Akari finishes the protest for me. "It's the most secure building in Sarotuza."

"Yes, but . . . secure from *typics*," I say. Saleen proved that much when she helped two Hues get in and spring a third. "And in the event of a riot, all the seasoned Shades"—the portal keepers, the court guards, the class masters—"would actually be sent off to help. It's a castle full of sitting ducks right now." And the Council won't think to protect it because they don't realize that Adriel can access the Gray. The only man who does is both in deep denial about it and more interested in saving face.

"So, you think his plan is to . . . what? Break in, grab some acolytes, then bring them back into a city that's now full of angry Shades?"

Judging by the skeptical edge to Saleen's tone, it appears I've lost our brief alliance. "That feels way more dangerous than just grabbing them off the street."

Yes, it does. But that's not what I'm thinking.

"No . . . I think he's going to take the typics there," I tell her, even though it sounds insane. "He's obsessed with Councilman Denata, right? Well, that's where he commits his sins. I think the Academy is where he'll want to do the poisoning." Specifically, the court chamber, his father's domain. "I think he'll think it's poetic." To deprive us of magic in the magical institution he never got to attend.

"Except he can't take the typics there, Ray." Akari's shaking her head. "The Academy only exists in the shadows, remember, so he'd have to portal them in. And even if he did somehow manage to commandeer a portal, how would he keep them alive long enough to bleed the Shades? They'd shatter immediately."

All perfectly good questions.

Though now that this idea has taken root, the answers are quickly pulling into shape.

"He doesn't experience the shadows the same way we do, Kiri; he can bend them to his will, deaden their magic—our magics, as well. So, what if he *could* get into the Academy without a portal?" I say. "And what if he could create a safe space to hold the typics in while he's there? Or if he brings Alara with him, maybe she'll keep an In-Between around the initiates until he's done bleeding the Shades—that's what Emeralds do, isn't it?" I look to Ezzo. "They have the gift to project that spell?"

"I mean . . . yes, but—"

"But that's an awful lot of *ifs*, Raya." Saleen seems to have contracted Cemmy's incessant need to pace. "And don't you think we would have heard if he'd infiltrated the castle? There are half a dozen portals servicing the Academy, surely somebody would have reached one of them by now, crossed back to report the threat?"

"Unless they couldn't." I shrug, hazarding another guess. "A portal is just a permanent spell, right? It's magic. Adriel could have disrupted it along with everything else, made sure no one could interrupt him. Just think about it for a second—" I hurry to add before Saleen can object. "First, he very publicly abducts the most high-profile children he can get—he's never done that before, he's always taken street kids—and even if he wanted a better caliber of tribute, there are so many safer options than *Church initiates*. Then he sets a seminary on fire and has his followers start a riot? Why? That's not going to help him do the poisoning—unless you were right and it's just to distract from his actual destination: a castle everyone thinks is impenetrable because no one believes he can phase. In the middle of the night, too, when the portals are basically closed anyway—so even if Shades do stop crossing back and forth, it'll be hours before anyone finds that strange."

The silence that greets my declaration is thick.

"Okay, so then let's check the portals," Chase finally suggests. "Wouldn't that be the easiest way to figure out if Raya's right about Adriel?" Though it sounds less like he believes me than he simply wants to put this idea to bed.

"Easy isn't the word I'd use, no." Saleen withers me a glare. "The Academy interchange is always guarded—and with the faithful on a rampage, it'll be damn near impossible to lure those Shades away. We're not going to get anywhere near a portal."

"Then isn't talking ourselves in circles about this pointless?" Cemmy asks. "Even if Adriel is in the Academy, if we can't reach the portals—or if he's disabled them—then there's nothing we can do to help."

"Unless he didn't know to disable the private ones," I say. And there's a good chance he didn't, since most people don't even realize they're there.

"Erm . . . what do you mean by private ones?" Saleen's surprise illustrates that fact well. "There are private portals? Since when?"

"Since the Council started conducting all of its sensitive business in the castle," I say. "They're only for elders and the heads of guild."

"Which could have come in handy except—no offence, Ray—but your parents are the last two Shades in Sarotuza who'd ever willingly let three Hues into their house, let alone allow them to use their secret portals." Akari points out the glaring flaw in my plan. "They don't even let *you* use their secret portals."

Nor am I ever likely to earn that privilege now that they've watched me leave the court chamber in chains.

"I still have to try, Kiri," I tell her. And, more than anything else, that's what convinces her to relent. Because she knows, without a shadow of a doubt, that I would never involve them in this unless I truly believed that it was life or death.

Persuading the others is easier once she's on board, since the Hues don't have any better ideas and Saleen has no intention of letting Akari accompany me alone. It's kind of sweet, actually, even if I've not quite forgiven her for all the needless pain her secrets caused. Though I guess I'm not really one to talk, in that regard, nor can I claim the moral high ground. I kept my own share of secrets these past few days. Hells, I've still not told Akari the most damning of the gory details.

*If she can forgive Saleen, then she'll forgive you.* I'm fully aware that it won't be that simple, that nothing will be simple if the future gets its way. Right now, we're all being held together by necessity, but come morning—if we're still alive—the true consequences of this alliance will emerge, and none of us can predict what they'll be.

*You've got to survive this first.* The moment my parents' house slips into view, my organs fist into a tight ball. The lights are on in their towers, which means they're home from the guild but still at work, sifting through the fickle threads of fate.

*Maybe they'll be happy to see you* . . . the hopeful side of me wants to see them, too, to show them I'm okay, that I've escaped the Council's corrupt brand of justice. But the other side—the cynical side that watched my father rail against my shame instead of for my freedom—would rather jump off a cliff than see them both again. When forced to make the choice, I turn towards my mother's study.

"Just give me a minute with her first, okay?" I tell the others, then with a steel of my shoulders, I wisp through the door.

"Mother?"

It takes her a long second to clear the future from her eyes, to double take and realize that I'm really here.

"Raya!" She lurches up from the sea of cushions lining the tower floor. "By my colors, did the tribunal let you go?" She pulls me into a brief and rigid hug. "The fates wouldn't give me a clear vision of your trial, but I knew the elders would see sense eventually. Your father and I were just *livid* at the councilman—though you didn't exactly do yourself any favors. What were you thinking with all that nonsense about a son? That was cruel and disrespectful, Raya. Why would you risk your standing with the guild in such a way?"

"I—"

"No matter—"

*. . . Guess that was more of a rhetorical question.*

"—what's important is that they've released you, quickly and quietly, without making too big of a fuss. That's good. That means we can still salvage your reputation."

Her priorities cut me deeper than I expect, sending a blunt ache shooting through my ribcage. Just a few bells ago, she watched her daughter get hauled off for interrogation, accused of working with a Hue and murdering a Shade. But instead of haunting that court chamber like a vengeful ghost—instead of protesting the councilman's decision with every fiber of her being—here she is, worrying about the scandal.

"They didn't release me." I break the news with a sigh. "I escaped."

"Escaped?" Her face puckers in horror. "Why would you go and do a foolish thing like that? This will only make the matter harder to resolve!"

"It wasn't going to get resolved, Mother." My throat begins to tighten, the cruel sting of salt pulsing beneath my lids. "The councilman was never going to set me free after I learned about his son, don't you get that?"

"Get what, Raya? That you're convinced Lars has a son that doesn't exist? That if you continue down this path you'll destroy your future for good?"

"I am trying to save the future!" The words explode out of me like a storm. "I asked an open question and it showed me my death, and your death, and the death of the Gray, and I've been trying to stop that from happening ever since, and if you would just listen to me for one minute so that I could explai—"

"You asked an *open question?*" Her incredulity fast hardens to rage, her voice sharpening to a deadly spear. "How could you be so stupid, Raya? How could you throw away everything your father and I have—"

"Sorry, Ray, time's up." Akari doesn't wisp into the study gently, she bursts in with an overblown flair. "Hi, Mrs Wryvern, I hope we're not interrupting, but we've got a future to save and we need your portal."

My mother's jaw practically detaches as Akari's joined by Saleen and three illegal Hues whose eyes give them away. In the shadows but sporting no spiked rim? That's proof of a crime right there. Now she knows exactly what kind of treason I've been brewing.

"Raya, what have you *done?*"

"Everything the future asked of me." I force my head up and my spine straight, shaking off the bite of her disappointment. "Now, if you don't mind, we have to go stop a cataclysm that you and your entire guild couldn't see."

"You will do no such—"

"*Quiet.*" Saleen silences her with a flash of Red, clearing the way for me to issue a command of my own.

"If you love me at all—if you've ever cared about me as your daughter rather than your legacy—then you'll pass along this message," I say, ignoring the indignity paling her to chalk. "Tell the elders that the Divine Meridian means to poison our magics. Tell them that he's a void and that he's holding the Church initiates in the castle. Then tell them that I've seen what he means to do because I'm fate-touched now and walking a fundamental path. And if they have a problem with any of that, tell them to take it up with Councilman Denata, since he's the one the Meridian is pissed at. Can you do that?"

Another flick of Saleen's power compels my mother to answer, though the *yes* she grits through her teeth is reluctant and hard won. *And noncommittal.* I'm perfectly aware that the way I built my question could lead to more than one outcome, that I left her a way to weasel out of following through.

*If you love me.* I have no earthly idea if I'd meant it as a test or if—as always—my phrasing is just bad.

*I guess you'll find out.* There are so many unknowns in this moment that I don't see the point in putting it right. We don't even know if *I'm* right yet, for starters, or if the elders are sitting on enough knowledge to understand my message—it's possible that too much truth has been lost to the whims of time. Though if I'm being honest, the real reason I don't want to stay and fix it is that I can't stand to look at her anymore—to feel the way she's looking at me, the way she will look at me if I *force* her to take my side.

I need to get the hells out of this tower. Immediately. This second. Right the fuck now. Because I'd much rather portal into a castle and face a madman than watch my mother grapple with the choice of legacy over love. Isn't that how Adriel became so twisted in the first place? Because a man with color decided not to live with the shame of having a child he thought had none?

So instead of fixing my question, I lead us towards the door to her portal and ignore the throbbing pain in my heart. When Ezzo brushes his hand against mine in offer, I take it.

CHAPTER 30

# RAYA

The moment the portal spits us out in the Academy, my leap of logic is confirmed. I instantly sense the change in the shadows, the oppressive nature of a power that's stifling the magic in the air and sapping it of color.

"Do you feel that?" I ask the others, scanning the entry hall for hostile eyes. It's not the same hall the public portals lead to, it's much less extravagant and smaller in size, a sparsely decorated rotunda that hosts a ring of doors labelled only by shade and rank. The private offices of the elders and guild masters, I'd venture, where they conduct their business when they're called to convene.

"Yeah, I feel it." Akari looks to Saleen who also nods in reply. "It's like my magic is . . . heavier, somehow. Sticky."

Sticky seems a good word for it, as if someone's gone and added a thickening agent to my blood. Not quite the overwhelming deadness I'd felt in Adriel's presence, but I can only assume that is soon to come, that we're not yet in range of his full power.

"What about you?" Though my hand was only briefly clasped in Ezzo's, he's still stood close behind me, almost as close as Chase is standing to Cemmy and Akari is to Saleen. "Is it affecting your gifts?"

"Doesn't seem to be affecting mine." Cemmy leans against the wall in demonstration, her physicality remaining very much intact. "Could be we're less sensitive to the effects—though I wouldn't bank on it lasting. Ez—can you see where Adriel is holed up?"

"I can try." Ezzo blinks into his gift. "But . . . it's kind of a mess of trails in here, to be honest; I'm not usually surrounded by so many Shades at once." His eyes are clouded white and narrowed with the effort, trying to make sense of the picture to which the rest of us are blind. "Okay, so . . . you were right, Raya, he did bring Alara with him, and she's on the east side of the castle, moving up towards the fourth floor."

"That would be the dorms," Akari says. "So maybe she's gone to fetch the acolytes for him? They would be in bed at this hour."

"That could explain why the freshest trails seem to be moving from there towards . . . what looks like the court where they held my trial." Ezzo also validates my theory that Adriel would be drawn to his father's chamber. "Only three of them so far—a Yellow, an Indigo, and a Violet, so if he's after the seven colors, she's still missing a bunch."

"And are the typics with her, too?" I ask, since he's not yet mentioned them.

"No, I can't see the typics—but I also can't see into that room at all, it's like the trails around it just . . . stop. Like there's a void in the shadows."

"Then that's got to be where he is, right? In the court chamber?"

"I mean, I would have thought that, except . . . I'm actually seeing his absence of trail towards the top of the castle—but in a really odd place, as though he's standing *on* the tower instead of in it. And there's an Orange trail there, too, so either someone's about to jump, or they're—"

"About to get pushed," I finish that sentence for him, though I don't think that's just any *someone*, I think it's his father.

"He's going to kill the councilman—we need to split up." I snap to a decision the moment I realize what Adriel means to do. "Saleen—take Ezzo, Cemmy, and Chase and see if you can free those acolytes; Akari and I will go after Denata." Not that he deserves our help, but he's currently the only one who knows a damn thing about voids. If he dies, we may never learn how to stop his son.

"No, absolutely not." Saleen steps between us. "Splitting up is a horrible—"

"Yes, of course it's a horrible idea, Saleen, but we can't be in two places at once."

"She's right, Sal," Akari says, putting a hand to Saleen's arm. "They need a Shade and Raya needs an active power; this is the safest way to do it." The look that passes between them is a silent battle, a war of attrition Akari eventually wins. As much as Saleen may hate the idea, she's smart enough to recognize that we're right, that unless my mother chooses to relay my message—and that's a feeble hope, if that—we're on our own here, there'll be no cavalry coming.

"Be safe, Raya." Ezzo's whisper is low and quiet, a tiny exhaling of air as he brushes past me.

*You too.* There's no time for me to breathe a reply, no time to lament the fact that this may be the last I ever see of him. Now that we've reached the end of our fundamental path, the future can't guide our steps anymore; it's already done its part, led us to the critical thread in the tapestry. What happens next is solely up to us.

"So . . . just in case we die and I don't get another chance to say this: I'm sorry for giving you such a hard time about the open question, Ray. And the Hue." Akari, however, has never been one for holding her words back—even while we're mid-crisis and shimmering towards danger.

"Eh, I would have done the same in your shoes." I shrug. "I'm sorry for always being such a stick about Saleen."

"Eh, I would have done the same in your shoes." Akari parrots the sentiment, because—let's face it—neither of us would have put our money on Saleen being the linchpin that would keep this strange little group from collapse. Though I guess I should have known that she's the *only* one who could have convinced Akari to risk the future she's been working towards. Because while I was never in love with Killen, Akari's never *not* been in love with Saleen. I'm not surprised their paths led back to each other.

*And yours led to a Hue.* It's amazing, isn't it? How fast things can change? How one truth can unravel a whole history of lies? Just a few days ago, I genuinely believed that Ezzo's kind was a blight, that it was righteous to hunt them—to kill them—even when they were barely surviving. Maybe if I had asked the right questions, I would have seen the lie sooner, stopped believing everything the Council fed me as fact. Then again, I never was much good at doing that, and I'd always been too afraid of disappointing my parents to break with the guild's sanctioned method of asking.

Councilman Denata was afraid, too—of a fucking baby.

All because he was born with a power the Council didn't like.

And now, here we are, thirty years later, and that fear's about to cost us our lives.

*If it hasn't cost him his already.* The closer we get to the seeing tower, the slower the shadows appear to stir, thickening to quicksand until we lose the ability to shimmer altogether and start having to wade through the clotted dark.

"We'll never make it to the roof like this," Akari yells as we scale the stairs one grueling step at a time. "How did they even get up there? It's not like there's a way to climb ou—" Her voice shocks to silence as we finally reach the room at the top of the tower, and the furious tempest raging inside. "By my colors, Ray—can you—? Are you seeing this?"

It would be impossible *not* to see it, not to notice how Adriel's reformed the tower's apex into a cyclone that devours the sky. He's not merely bending the shadows anymore, he's perverting them, mushrooming the roof to form a jagged ledge over which he can suspend his father.

*Oh Gods—what was I thinking? We can't fight this kind of power.* My realization comes too little too late, a split second after he's whirled towards us and deadened the magic in our blood. A split second after that, we're both sucked into the swirling night.

# CHAPTER 31

# EZZO

If you had asked me a week ago, I would have said to hell with the magic. To hell with the typics, to hell with the Shades, to hell with anything I couldn't find in a tavern. I didn't want to care anymore. Not about my life, not about their lives, not about the Gray. Yet, here I am, a week later, racing to save all three.

In the Academy, no less.

The one place no Hue should ever be.

This is Raya's world, not mine. It's where—until just a few days ago—she lived, and learned, and loved, where she grew to doubt her magic so deeply that she risked it on a forbidden question.

It's hard not to see fate's hand in that.

It's hard not to see it in the way we keep finding ourselves at the heart of these impossible tasks.

*The future doesn't think they're impossible.* Hells, it seems to think I have a future with Raya, which does suggest that we might make it out of this alive. *That's not what it suggests, and you know it.* I mean, sure, Raya's vision means it might be a possibility—but that's all the future is: a possibility. A hundred thousand of them, in fact. Ask a slightly different question, get a slightly different answer. Make a slightly different decision, kick destiny onto a different track. Being on a fundamental path doesn't change that. The future may have nudged and nudged and nudged us in order to try and stop its own demise, but now that we're here, it's powerless, and there's absolutely no guarantee that the choice to split up was right.

We might not survive it.

Even if we succeed, we might not survive it.

Raya might not survive it.

It wasn't until I watched her shimmer away that I realized how much I've come to worry about her. That all the *be safes* and casual touches might add up to more than just friendly like. That, despite what I told her in the cell, I might actually want the possibility the future's offering—but that the very thought is also riddling me with doubt. Because it's not been long enough, has it, since Eve died? How long even is long enough? How do you suddenly reallocate the space in your heart?

And Gods, how do you do it with a Shade?

"Any change?" Saleen's voice snaps me back to what's important: Adriel, the castle, the room full of acolytes and initiates we're somehow supposed to save.

*Right, yes.* I force myself to focus, to replace the thought of Raya with the trails of light flickering behind my eyes. "Not much. Looks like Alara's got a Green with her now, but they're still by the dorms—and I'm still getting nothing from inside the chamber." Which means we still don't know exactly what we'll find when we get in there, whether the typics are alive or dead or how Alara is keeping so many of them under control.

"Then it's a good thing we're almost there—just around the next corner," Saleen says, though even without her direction, I'd venture we'd have recognized the right door.

"Holy fuck." Cemmy's curse is an echo to my own, her hand pitching out to grip Chase's. The entire corridor ahead of us is engulfed in a dense and heavy fog, as though the shadows around the court are congealing.

"Is it me or do they look a little . . . angry to you?" I finally understand what Akari meant by the Gray feeling sticky. Not because casting my In-Between has become harder—if anything, it's actually grown easier, like the shadows are too distracted to bite at my spell—but because the weight of my magic suddenly feels different, like it's thickened in depth and coarsened in texture, hooked razor-sharp talons beneath my skin.

"Oh, they're definitely angry." Saleen takes a hesitant step forward, shuddering as the darkness parts to allow her through. "But not at us, I don't think—it feels more like they're . . . angry at the room. Stay close, okay? I'll shimmer us out if there's trouble."

Though as it turns out, trouble is too weak a word.

*What in the name of all three Gods . . .* The sight that greets us is enough to rip the air from my throat. Gone is the court from my execution, with its gallery, and the judges' bench, and the dock. It's as if the entire chamber has remade itself for Adriel's purpose, the shadows reshaping to form a ring of vertical tables, each pair designed to hold an acolyte and an initiate while the needles in their arms do their work.

"How is this possible?" Cemmy's gasp is almost lost to the muffled chorus of fear and pain. We've seen the shadows manipulated before—cajoled into ignoring her physicality or even spurred to attack, on occasion, when their existence was threatened by a different zealot with a different goal.

But not on this scale.

Not to the point where their original shape was lost.

"I don't know," I say, though the Academy is an anomaly, I suppose, a castle made entirely of magic that has no counterpart in the real world. Maybe that's why these shadows are so ripe for manipulation, because there's no physical structure out there anchoring them to their form.

"If Alara's not here, then how are the typics not shattering?" Chase's question, however, is answered the moment we step through the door.

*Whoa.* The shift in pressure is immediate, like walking into a cave or diving too deep into the ocean.

"Erm, so . . . did your In-Betweens also just vanish?" I ask, trying furiously to reignite the spell. As much as casting it has grown as natural as breathing, I can always feel the magic when it's active, sense the Gray searching for any cracks it can exploit. Whereas now, I feel nothing. Not my shield. Not my gift. Not the shadows.

"Yeah, mine's gone, too." Chase is hopping back and forth across the threshold, as if testing to see where the deadening stops.

"And mine—but weirdly not my physicality," Cemmy says, running her hand along the nearest wall. "Give it a try real quick for me, Ez? I want to see something."

*Well, I'll be damned.* I let out a long whistle as the stone refuses to yield beneath my touch. "Looks like you called it right, Cem—I'm physical now." A first for me in the Gray. I've always wisped through everything.

"Then I'd guess that's also how Adriel solved his typic problem." She loops the logic back around. "He's quite literally created a void where the normal rules don't apply."

"So then how do we un-create it?" Saleen's voice is shaking with disgust. She wasn't there when Raya and I found Akari strapped to his table; this is the first time she's actually witnessing the horror. And this is only the tip of the iceberg, there's still over half a rainbow to go—though Alara sure didn't waste any time bleeding the first half. All three of the acolytes she's already fetched are screaming into their gags, their fear as pained as it is potent. But it's the initiates I truly feel for, the kids dressed in Church vestments writhing in agony as they blister from the Shades' blood.

"I don't think we can un-create it." My stomach sinks as I realize that Adriel's typic problem just became ours to solve. "Not until we figure out how to get these kids to a portal." Because no void means no protection; the shadows will rush back and shatter them whole.

"We can use our In-Betweens," Chase says, like it's blatantly obvious. "That's what we assumed Alara was doing, isn't it? No reason we can't do it, instead."

No, I suppose there's not. I mean, none of us is an Emerald, so we can't project our shields the way she can; we'd have to keep the kids in direct contact—but since there's three of us and seven of them, that's not exactly unmanageable.

"Let's just stop the transfusions first." I relegate those thoughts to later and quickly formulate the now. "Saleen and I can get that one over there—" I point to the acolyte on the far side of the tables, a boy of fourteen, if a day, who looks as though he's teetering on the edge of unconsciousness from the blood loss, the typic beside him crying a crimson river. "You two can take the others."

But we never make it to them.

Hells, we've barely even started running when all four of us are seized by the overwhelming and absolute need to stop.

"You shouldn't have come here."

Though I can't turn my body to look at her, I recognize the seething edge to Alara's voice.

"Damn it, what happened to being in a void?" Saleen grits through the compulsion. And it clearly is a *compulsion*—there's no other explanation for why my legs are suddenly refusing to move—even though that should be impossible.

"Oh, you are." Alara's satisfaction turns cloying as she steps into view, two dazed acolytes trailing behind her. "But a void only deadens the inertia which allows your magics to work, the act of casting; it doesn't affect pre-spelled charms. That's why we need the typics, to put an end to all magic for good." She says it so carelessly—so *gleefully*—as though that wouldn't also put an end to her.

"Alara, please—you don't want that. Adriel is lying to you. He's just using you to get back at his father."

It's the wrong thing to say.

"That man is *not* his father," she growls, her face hardening to stone. "He's a coward who wanted his son dead but was too weak to do the killing; he left him to rot on the Church's doorstep so that the clerics would do it for him, murder Adriel when they found out about his power. But they didn't find out—just like they didn't find out about mine. They didn't look at us too closely in the orphanage, but *I* saw him, *I* felt the power in him, and *I* kept him safe. *I* am his family—not that Orange waste of bones."

"Then why isn't he trying to keep *you* safe?" I ask, coming at her from a different angle. "If he loves you as much as you love him, then why would he poison the Gray? Why would he take away your gift?"

"Of course you wouldn't understand—you still call it a *gift*." With another charm, Alara compels her acolytes to pick a table and gets to work. "Our *gifts* are such a perversion that even the shadows want them gone. Why else do you think they try to shatter us?" The air fills with a fresh chorus of pain as she begins the nasty business of shoving needles into arms. "Once we're free of them, we'll no longer have to rely on an In-Between. The shadows will welcome us home."

So that's the lie Adriel's been feeding her, then, the way he's chosen to twist the dogma.

"That's not true, Alara—it's just not true," I say, though I fear I'm arguing with a lost cause. "We can't live without magic. If you do this, you'll die. We all will—the Gray, too. Tell her, Chase—tell her what happens when you take magic from a Hue—"

"Enough!" Alara doesn't want to hear it; she'd much rather shut me up with an Orange crystal and a magical noose.

"Let him go!" Cemmy yells, but another crystal silences her, as well, and the torrent of expletives Chase begins to spew.

"And why should I do that?" Alara only tightens her grip on my air. "If we're all going to die anyway, then what difference does it make if he chokes to death? Or if your full-blooded friend here dies a little early?"

I'm granted a modicum of relief as she turns her attention to Saleen.

"You wouldn't happen to be a Red, would you?" She fishes out a Violet crystal and asks the magic to check. "Oh, good. I was avoiding your prickly kind until last; you'll save me a trip upstairs."

"What—? *No.*" The blood preemptively leaves Saleen. "No, you can't, *please!*" Her feet start moving of their own accord, propelling her towards one of the two remaining tables. "Please, I'm not a Red. *I'm not a Red.* Cemmy—Chase—help me!"

But she is a Red, and so she knows, better than anyone, that compulsion is the hardest spell to break, that while we remain in Adriel's void, Alara's crystals will ensure that all we can do is watch, helplessly, as a needle is shoved mercilessly into her flesh. As her life begins to drain into a screaming initiate.

And more than anything else, it's the satisfaction grinning Alara from ear to ear that tells me there'll be no changing her mind or Saleen's fate.

She believes Adriel's truth. Unerringly. With her whole entire chest.

She's going to destroy the Gray for it.

There really is nothing more intractable than faith.

# CHAPTER 32

# RAYA

Adriel doesn't subdue us with magic, it's the shadows he uses to suspend us high above the ruined tower, Akari pinned beside me, our colors deadened to hollow silence.

"Like old friends, we meet again, full-bloods," he says, though there's nothing friendly about the silk in his voice or the chill in his smile, the way he's appraising us like a pair of pinioned butterflies, as if he'd like to rip our wings off one by one. "But I'm afraid that this time, there's nowhere for you to run—isn't that right, Father?" That word is curdled milk on his tongue. "Why don't you tell our guests what'll happen if they try?"

A groan of agony escapes the councilman as his own shadowy bonds splay his arms out wide, bowing his body to the point of collapse.

"I know what he did to you, Adriel," I say in a bid to talk him down. "I know that he threw you away and that the pain of it drove your mother to suicide."

"Ah, so you're familiar with our history." Adriel seems entirely unfazed by my knowledge of his past. "How the great Lars Denata was so ashamed to learn he'd sired a void that he gave away the child his wife so desperately wanted. For what a colossal embarrassment it would have been for him had the Council found out, how it would have derailed his lofty ambitions. Would you like to tell them why, Father? I'm sure they'd love to know the reason they'll be losing their magic."

"You are an abomination," Denata spits through the pain, his precarious position doing nothing to dull the hate in his eyes. "I was merciful, considering what you are. The edicts demanded I kill you the second you failed to register a color. But I didn't. I gave you a chance."

"You gave me to a Church that despised my power more than you did!" Adriel growls. "You hoped that they would do the killing for you, but instead, they taught me exactly how to claim my birthright. If only you knew the depth of the records they keep, Father, how much information the Church has squirreled away in its archives. So maybe I should be thanking you, after all." With a curl of his fingers, Adriel lowers the councilman so that they're nose to nose and fear to anger. "I might have never learned to use my power if you hadn't placed me with them. I might have never learned just how afraid your Council is of voids."

"That's because you're a threat." Denata's face puckers as his bonds give another savagely hard tug. It's almost impressive, actually, how even trapped and tortured, he sticks so adamantly to the party line. "You don't belong in the Gray."

"You'd like to believe that, wouldn't you?" Around us, the shadows start swirling faster, roaring louder, as if responding to Adriel's fury in kind. "You'd like to believe that you're superior on account of your magic, when the truth is, all magic is the result of the Gray being stripped into its constituent parts. Perverted. It's your kind that's the real threat, Father; magic is the cancer that needs to be stamped out."

Well, now, he sounds exactly like Denata did at Ezzo's trial, when he declared the same to be true of Hues.

"And what about Alara, huh?" Akari's voice is a drop of ink bleeding through the dark. "She won't survive the loss of her magic. If you do this, it will also kill her."

"And I will mourn her death," Adriel says, though the sentiment sounds cold and matter of fact. "She's the reason I survived the orphanage, and I must admit, I've grown rather fond of her. But she believes in my mission as staunchly as I do; I'm certain she'll understand."

Just not certain enough to have told her the full consequence of his plan.

"Except you're wrong about the shadows." As much as it's impossible to fight madness with logic, I still have to try. "They're made of magic, Adriel, they *are* magic. If you go through with the poisoning, the entire Gray will die. I saw a vision of it happening!"

"But of course you did, full-blood—a cancer always seeks to prevent its own demise." Adriel's head cocks with sympathy, as if speaking to a daft child. "You trust your magic because *his* Council taught you to trust it, so that you'd continue to propagate their lies. Isn't that right?" Another flexing of fingers turns Denata's groans to outright screams as his arms finally pop from their sockets with a sickening snap. "Forgive me, Father, my hand must have . . . *slipped.*"

The most unnerving thing about Adriel is how he seems to relish the violence, how his hand continues to *slip* until the councilman hangs as limp as a puppet whose strings were mercilessly cut.

"You are no son of mine," Denata manages to hiss around the agony, and I can suddenly see exactly where Adriel got his vindictiveness from, his taste for cruelty. "You were a mistake then and you're a mistake now. Killing me won't change that."

"Oh, I have no intention of killing you here, like this; I just wanted you to see how powerful I'd become—ahead of your true purpose. You're going to serve as my final tribute." Adriel's delight is a snake slithering through tall grass. "Just imagine it, Father, your blood—your color—flowing through the veins of one of the Church's children, poisoning the rainbow you can't envision living without."

When faced with the full scope of his son's depravity, Denata stuns to silence, his eyes darting between me and Akari as though we could somehow help him escape Adriel's wrath. But we're every bit as trapped as he is, and with our magics deadened, there's nothing we can do to stop his raving zealot of a son. Hells, Adriel is so thoroughly unconcerned by the threat we pose him that when he disappears them both into the castle, he doesn't even bid the shadows to end our lives.

"Ray—watch out!" With his power gone, the storm raging around us quiets back to a windless night, sending us crashing down to the ruined tower.

*Oof.* We hit the stone with enough force to rend the air from my lungs, to vibrate the marrow in my bones and knock the world off its axis.

"Are you okay?" I ask Akari, blinking through the shock of survival.

"Argh, I think so." With a groan, she braces and sits back up. "And I can feel my magic again. Can you feel yours?"

"Yeah, I can." The warmth of it is unmistakable, and the second it sears through my veins, I ask the question that's been itching at the edge of my mind, just waiting for me to break free of Adriel's suppression.

*How will we stop him?*

It's the same question I asked the future back in Saleen's library, the one that led me to Killen's body, and the Council's prison, and the confessions I made to Ezzo in the dark. To the chain of events that saw us return to this castle. And while I don't know if the fates will answer it a second time—or if they can even offer me something new now that we've reached the cataclysm at the end of our path—Adriel didn't betray a single weakness and I'm all out of ideas. I need to try.

**You must show her his true plan**. It's Alara's face the fates choose to flash me, along with a page from a book I've long since relegated to the past. *A curiosity of fate-touched visions is that they can be projected from mind to mind.* I'm not entirely sure why they're reminding me of the least relevant of Fernay's ramblings, but I suppose I should just be grateful they're desperate enough to answer.

"Erm . . . Ray? Are you still with me?" Akari waves me out of the vision. "Did you hit your head or are you casting right now? You look a little zoned out."

"I was casting," I say, though where to even begin trying to explain what the future showed me in reply, that I'm supposed to convince Alara of something she's never going to believe about her brother.

· 260 ·

If she's as zealous as he is, then telling her the truth won't achieve much; she'll simply brush it off as a lie, like Adriel did when I told him about the shadows. Her entire life, he's been the only one she's had to confide in, and the faith they've concocted together has been her reality for a long time. Unless he's the one doing the telling, words aren't going to be enough.

She needs to see it.

In full taste and color.

With all the necessary conviction attached.

*So, exactly what the fates just told you.* All at once, Fernay's ramblings feel far less redundant. If there's a way for fate-touched visions to be projected, then I do have a shot at convincing Alara. The only question the future didn't answer is how.

*Then figure it out.* If there was ever a time for me to trust my instincts—to trust my power—it's now. Because I'm still a Wryvern, godsdamn it. No matter how much I suck at the guilds' chosen method for seeing, I still have that legacy flowing through my blood. Maybe I'm just built differently to my parents.

"Kiri, I need your help," I say, moving to stand right in front of her, so close that we're almost touching.

"Okay . . . you want to clue me in here?"

"Just try to keep an open mind for a second—like, literally an open mind." I lean our heads together and close my eyes, willing my magic to pass between us, to take the calamity the fates showed me and show it to her.

*Come on, please work.* I'm doing everything Chase did when he set his color to stealing mine—holding physical contact, concentrating, taking deep breaths in and out—and while his gift is hardly the ideal model to follow, when it comes to exchanging power, it's the only model I have. *Come on, just work already, just let this one tiny thing go right.*

The moment Akari gasps and grips my arms for purchase, I know that finally, it has.

"Holy shadows, Ray, what in the nine hells was that?" she asks once the vision's over.

"I'll explain later. All that matters is that it worked, Kiri." And that she happens to be the exact shade of magic I need to make it work past this tower.

Akari's the Orange Shade from my vision—not Councilman Denata as I first thought.

She can take my power and amplify its might.

Together, we can make Alara see.

# CHAPTER 33

# EZZO

Drop by drop, Saleen's blood is agonizing a typic, his screams rising in volume even as hers begin to fail. And hers aren't the only ones—around the chamber, more and more of the acolytes are inching towards death, their bodies shaking with the blood loss and growing clammy with sweat. If we don't do something soon, we'll lose every single one of them, all seven colors—or rather, all six, since there's still one terrified initiate for whom Alara hasn't yet fetched a mate. One conspicuously empty table.

*What is she waiting for?* Around the typics, the poisoned shadows are slowly starting to wilt, their smoke darkening to an ash that's pocked and brittle, as though the very fabric of the Gray is disintegrating. If there was ever a time to complete the rainbow, this feels like it would be it. *So why is Alara still here, then?* I trace her movements as she stalks between pairs, adjusting the tourniquets and needles where necessary. Why does she seem wholly uninterested in abducting the last kid?

*A great question for later.* I strain against the compulsion pinning my feet in place, searching for a crack, a weakness, some way to break free of the crystal's spell. Pre-made charms have a relatively short lifespan, and she's using it to immobilize me, Cemmy, and Chase, so the magic must be close to reaching its limit. I just need to apply the right pressure, find a critical spot against which to—

The vision hits me mid-struggle, entirely unsolicited and unexplained.

Or at least, I think it's a vision; it's playing out exactly how my mom always described the pictures she saw in her head. One second, I'm in the court chamber, watching a group of acolytes bleed steadily into their graves, then the next, it feels as though I'm in another place altogether, watching the very end of their story—of our story—and the Gray's.

*This is Raya's vision.* I instantly recognize the cataclysm she's been warning about since we met. Except this time, I see every part of it. The death, the love, the heartbreak, the pain, the absolute certainty that our paths were always destined to collide over and over again, to bring us here, to this moment, where our choices would decide the fate of an entire realm.

"Did you just see that?" Cemmy's shock makes it plenty clear that I'm not the only one who received the future's sending. In fact, judging by the sea of wide eyes and stunned expressions, I'd venture everyone in the court chamber did; the acolytes, the initiates, and—if I'm not reading her hesitation wrong—Alara, as well.

"That's the future your brother wants," I call out, seizing the opportunity to shake her faith. "It's what we've been trying to tell you, Alara; Hues can't survive without magic—we die without it—and Adriel knows that. He knows that if he poisons the shadows, you'll die, and he's doing it anyway. He's sacrificing you every bit as much as he is them."

"Shut up!" she roars, but there's a hint of a quiver to her voice now, a tiny fracture of an invitation.

"He's using you, Alara." I push the advantage. "You're a means to an end for him, disposable labor. Adriel put you at risk each time he sent you out to fetch him tributes and he's put you at risk today, left you to do the dirty work—the *dangerous* work—while he's off catching up with the councilman."

"I said, *shut up.*" Word by word, my truths are beginning to flame her cheeks red. "My brother—"

"Hates all magic, Alara." So I don't shut up; I keep right on pushing. "That means *your* magic, too, the magic running through *your* veins. Do you really think he'll make an exception once the shadows have been cleansed?" I ask, throwing in another wedge. "He thinks you're a mistake, Alara, don't you see that? He thinks all Hues are a mistake. He's counting on the poison to kill you for him. He doesn't even care about you enough to admit that himself."

"Shut your filthy mouth!" All at once, she's careening towards me, a knife clasped between her fingers and her eyes sizzling with rage. "My brother would never lie to me! He loves me!" The force of our collision breaks what's left of the charm's spell.

"Alara, don't—" As we both crash down to the marble, I barely just avoid the tip of her blade. "Cemmy, Chase—go!" I yell, because while I didn't mean to bait myself into a knife fight, a distraction is still a distraction and if she's fighting me then she can't be stopping them. "Go help Saleen!" A sharp sting grazes my ribcage as Alara angers at that idea.

*Oh no, you don't.* With a hiss, I buck out of harm's way, my hand jerking out to catch the charm she tries to throw in their direction.

"Alara, please—Adriel's not worth your loyalty," I grit as the resulting flash sends us rolling arm over head, the knife trapped precariously between us. "He's not worth your life!"

But in the end, that's ultimately what he costs her.

I don't see the exact moment she loses control of the blade, I hear it, her pained surprise and the soft squelch, the sickening gut of flesh parting around metal.

*No, no, no, no, no.* I'm quick to shove away from her, though there's nothing to be done about the wooden hilt protruding from her chest, the shock creeping across her expression.

"Well, isn't this unfortunate."

Before I can so much as think to press my hands to the wetness blooming her robe red, the shadows harden around me, the oppressive nature of the void intensifying as Adriel suddenly appears in the chamber, the councilman hanging limp behind him.

*But no Raya or Akari.* I don't get the chance to dwell on what that might mean.

"I'm afraid I can't allow you to do that." Adriel's first port of call is to send Chase and Cemmy flying back from Saleen, landing them in a tangled heap behind the tables.

*Shit, the needle. They haven't taken out the needle.* Cemmy had only gotten as far as loosening the tourniquet—which Adriel immediately refastens with a flick of his wrist.

"Help me, Adriel." Alara's plea is ragged but optimistic, brimming with a hope that swiftly wavers as he sweeps past where she's lying. "Please, I need a Green. You can shimmer me to a Green."

"I could." He briefly turns to appraise her, his face filling with pity and regret. "But that would only prolong your suffering and that's not something I want. You were a good sister, Alara—a loyal sister, brave. If not for what you are, we could have remade this world together, but your color makes that impossible. I can only pray that you'll take comfort in knowing your sacrifice helped usher in the new age."

"My color—?" Her understanding dawns gradually, grudgingly, as though she can't quite fathom the betrayal. "Adriel, please—we're *family.*"

But the only family he's interested in is his father, the final tribute he means to drain.

"Do you believe me now?" As he binds the councilman to the last table, I drop my voice to a whisper and rekindle my efforts to make his sister see sense. "He lied to you, Alara—this entire time, he knew that you would die here today. But you don't have to die here—you don't have to die for him. *We* can take you to a Green, *we* can get you out of the castle, all you have to do is tell us how to stop him; he must have a weakness." And having spent her whole life by his side, she must know what it is. "Your brother's not a prophet, Alara, and what he's doing isn't going to free the shadows, it's going to destroy the Gray—I know you saw the same vision that I did, I know you felt the truth of it—so please, help us. Don't let him do to you what the councilman did to him; don't let him throw you away."

It's those last six words that break her, I can tell by the way her chin starts to tremble and her eyes fill with pain. Not the physical kind—like from the knife wound bleeding her chest—but the kind that comes with having your heart broken by someone you trust and respect. By being betrayed by your own brother.

"Color," she finally rasps, betraying his trust in return. "The presence of it is anathema to his power, that's why he deadens it in others. If you attack him with my charms, it'll buy you a few seconds."

*Seconds.* I'm still grappling with that grim reality when she grabs the front of my shirt with surprising strength.

"When he's gone, the shadows won't wait; they'll come for the typics."

"That's okay, they're protected," I tell her, working through the problem in my head. "The initiates all have some color in them now." The fresh screams coming from Denata's table are proof of that, proof that Adriel wasted no time before sticking a needle in his dear old father—and according to the list we found in his sanctum, even a little blood should be enough to shield them for a few minutes. "We'll be able to get them to a portal."

"No, you don't understand." Alara's breaths are growing heavy, her words barely audible above the din. "With seven colors bleeding, the poison will spread through the shadows fast. Any magic that touches it will wither."

*But isn't it already withering?* I steal a glance over at the initiates, at how the air around them continues to crack and pucker like dried ink. *How is that different from—?*

*Oh.*

It takes me a long moment to understand what she means.

If that's what the poison can do now, in a void, then I shudder to think what it'll do when it's not being suppressed, especially in a castle made entirely of magic, with no physical counterpart to phase to outside the Gray. If we allow the poison to spread, there might not be an Academy left. And if it dies, we die with it, Hue, typic, and Shade.

*Shit.* Our original plan isn't going to work if that's the case. The three of us won't be able to maintain physical contact with all seven initiates. Not immediately, anyhow. Not while we're also juggling the needles, and the acolytes, and the panic, and . . . everything else.

"Then use your gift, Alara," I beg, since she's not limited in that same way. "You're an Emerald—you can project your In-Betweens, keep the kids safe."

"I don't have any Green charms." Her reply is as knowing as it is labored. Because I have no magic with which to heal her and she's lost too much blood to sustain such a spell. Hells, half this chamber's lost too much blood and the other is fast approaching that point as well. No matter how hard we try or how quickly we work, lives are going to be lost here.

Though I can think of one way to minimize the death.

Even if the cost is monstrous.

"Are you truly willing to help us, no matter what it takes?" I look Alara dead in the eye, imploring her to absolve me of this sin.

"Yes." There's now a crimson veil staining her teeth.

"Then I know what to do." With a bitter sigh, I search out Cemmy and Chase, grateful for the language that allows me to sign out the plan to them unheard, unnoticed by Adriel who remains preoccupied with his father. And while they don't like my idea any more than I do, we're officially out of time and options, and we still don't know if the cavalry is coming or what has become of Akari or Raya. We don't have the luxury of a plan that's perfect.

*"On three,"* I sign, swallowing down the dread. *"One . . . two . . . three!"*

I toss a fistful of Alara's charms in Adriel's direction, watching the spells detonate in a color-rich mist. He snarls in surprise, the explosion slackening his grip on the shadows just a bit, just enough to allow us to move more freely.

"Now!"

We all charge at once—Chase towards Alara, Cemmy towards Saleen, me towards the man who styled himself as the Divine Meridian, the knife I pulled from Alara's chest ready to deliver him a kinder end than he means to inflict. And though it strikes me that by doing this, we'll be propagating a cycle that's been repeating itself for centuries—turning on another because of how much, or how little, magic they bleed—I don't see any other way to save the shadows. Whether I like it or not, fate has conspired to rob us of good choices, so today, a bad one is going to have to win.

# CHAPTER 34

# RAYA

By the time we make it to the court chamber, every last hell has broken loose.

*What in the—?* The scene that greets us is so gruesome and chaotic, I hardly know where to look. The Shades bleeding, the typics screaming, the shadows around them curling like a bolt of hot silk, and at the heart of it all, a storm of color and a roar of outrage. Ezzo, charging into the midst of the churning rainbow, a knife clasped in his hand and a zealot almost within his reach.

"We need to help him!" I urge Akari forward, only to find that she's already sped off in the opposite direction, towards where Cemmy is struggling to wrestle a needle out of—*oh Gods, Saleen*. I don't know how she ended up on one of Adriel's tables, but judging by the way her head is lolling and her skin has paled, she's been there long enough to have lost a lot of blood.

*Akari's got her—go help Ezzo.* I start running, though I'm barely to the ring of tables when a crash of thunder ripples across the court, Adriel's power rearing up in retaliation. *No, no, no, no.* A whip and a crack later, Ezzo's flying through the air, a strangled mix of pain and surprise ripping from his throat. When his body slams down to the blackened marble, he doesn't get back up.

*Son of a—*

I don't think, I just move, rushing towards the knife that slipped from between his fingers.

"Forget the knife, Raya. Adriel's weakness is color!" Chase yells from across the room, where he's hunched, inexplicably, over what appears to be a dead Alara. "You need to hit him with charms!"

But I don't have any charms; the only color I have is running through my blood—and even if Adriel's void wasn't suppressing it, I don't have an active power.

*Though you do have a renowned legacy.* The idea that strikes me is so simple, so reckless, that I don't doubt, for a second, that it could work. I am Raya Wryvern, after all, the daughter of an esteemed line of undiluted Indigo—the most powerful Indigo the Academy's seen in years—and this wouldn't require me to ask a single question. There's literally no way for me to get it wrong.

*Unless I lose my mettle.* The main problem with this idea is that it has a cost, the potential to end deadly. *Yeah, well, so does not doing it.* I refuse to allow myself any more time for thought.

I can't think about *me* right now.

I can't think about Saleen, or about Akari, or about how Ezzo's still slumped lifelessly against the wall, about how desperately I want to go and check if he's still breathing.

I have to think about the shadows.

Because the future's shown me where this story ends if we don't stop Adriel, and what's the point of seeing the future if you can't change it, and if you can change it, then was it ever the future at all?

Except for the fact it was.

Except for the fact that thousands will die if I don't find the strength to pick up the knife, slice my palm open, and make one last-ditch attempt at destroying the void.

"Adriel, I'm—I don't have any charms or a weapon, I just want to talk." I approach him slowly, deliberately, counting on his hubris to mask the danger a single Shade can pose, the cut hidden beneath the hem of my sleeve.

"You should save your breath, full-blood, savor your last few minutes on earth," he says, though once he sees that my hands are, indeed, empty, his curiosity piques and his guard lowers. "Or perhaps you still believe you can change my mind? Convince me to spare your kind?"

"Can I?" I take another step towards him, letting him lead the conversation wherever he wants.

"No, though I applaud the effort. You and your friends have certainly proven to be more of a hindrance than I first thought. A truly valiant showing."

"Then will you at least let us go?" Another step, then another, closing the gap between us until the deadening buzz of his power silences everything but the race of my pulse. "It would be nice to say goodbye to our families."

"Ah, I'm afraid that won't be possible," he says, voice dripping with feigned remorse.

"Oh, okay." One final step brings me close enough to drop the ruse. "Well, in that case, *this is for Killen*—" I spring before he can see it coming, thrusting my palm upward so that the blood will get into his eyes, mouth, and nose.

The effects are as devastating as they are immediate. Until now, the color in this room has been mostly contained in acolytes, initiates, needles, and tubes, kept at a sterile distance. Whereas now, it's on him—in him—and when presented with such a rich supply of Indigo, the void in his veins can't help but do exactly what it was born to do.

Consume color.

Just as I'd hoped.

*Though maybe not quite so violently.* The second I make contact, I realize that there'll be no letting go, that I couldn't, even if I tried to—that Adriel can't either, no matter how hard or desperately he fights to claw me off. His power is stronger than both of us, and it's tugging, and wrenching, and sucking the color right out of my bones—right out of my marrow. Until my pain is his pain and our screams are the only sound left in the world. Until the room dims and the shadows quiet and I go from feeling everything to feeling nothing at all.

# CHAPTER 35

# EZZO

The space between life and death is quiet. It's free from the screams, and the pain, and the crushing weight of responsibility; it's free from the grief that's been eating at me every day.

I am no place and everywhere all at once, walking hand in hand with Eve through a vista that never changes, never darkens, never fades, a sky painted at twilight. Just as it should be.

"Not anymore." Her voice is warm and musical, even as it fills with regret.

"Always, Vee," I say, adamant. "It's you and me, remember?" Until we die like the stars in a glorious blaze. Together. Always together. That last part isn't up for debate.

"The world had other plans for us, Ez," she whispers into the silence, and that's when I realize that she's as blurred as the scenery around us, that I can no longer see her as clearly as I used to, I can only remember—but at the same time, I can't actually remember the exact shade of her eyes, or the exact shape of her smile, or the exact pitch of her laughter.

"Well, then I don't want to live in that world." I cling to her memory the way a drowning man would a raft, like it might somehow sharpen her edges. "I don't want to live without you." And this might be the very first time I've admitted it out loud. All year, I've been racing towards this moment, searching for it, hoping for it, dousing the ache for it with drink.

So then why, now that I'm here, does it suddenly lack the feel of truth?

"I think you may have found yourself again, Ez," Eve says, as though reading my mind. "You always did need a purpose—watching out for us, it wasn't just what you did, it was part of who you are. A part you forgot, for a little while, but it never went away. All you needed was to get your hope back."

"I don't want hope, Vee—I want *you*."

"I'm right here." She places a hand to my heart, and despite the blur of her features, her touch is real and solid, a comfort and a surprise. "The shadows can't shatter love, Ezzo, no matter how hard they try. Nothing can ever change it. Nothing and *no one*. And being happy again won't change it, either; our story will always remain ours." She's fading faster now, waning, disappearing before my eyes.

But I don't want her to go.

I want us to stay in this in-between forever, frozen in time.

Except I also want to go back to the court chamber; I want to help Cemmy and Chase make it out of that room alive.

I want to live to see Novi again, and Lyria, and Magdalena.

And more than anything else, I want to ensure that Raya survives the night.

*Raya*. Gods, just thinking her name ties my stomach in knots. I saw the vision the future sent her—I don't know how I saw it, but I did; I felt the inevitability in it—the need, the longing—and now all I feel is guilt. Because how can I be here, with Eve, and even think about another girl? How can I ever allow myself to replace her?

"Don't question the good things when they come, Ez." Eve's ghost merely smiles the dazzling smile that I remember. "The only future I want for you is the best. I want you to live because you can and because you deserve to—and I want you to love because you deserve that, as well. Even if you choose to love a

Shade," she says. Then with a force I'm not expecting, she pitches me back into the Gray.

\*

The ringing in my ears is deafening, the pain in my head blinding, and the chaos raging around me a disorienting rattle to the brain.

*Colors help me, what did I miss?* The court chamber is alight with activity, though the tenor of the fear inside it has changed. There's still screaming but also screamed instructions, a frantic scrum of bodies, cries of relief, along with Shades in various states of consciousness, freed from their tables and stumbling like newborn deer. I see Akari, holding up a trembling Saleen; Cemmy, working to rid a sobbing initiate of his needle; Chase, on one knee in the center of the chamber, his jaw set with concentration and his arms braced wide against the air, a terrified group of kids gathered behind him.

*He's casting.* That realization dawns a split second before it's joined by the rush of *whys* bubbling up in my veins.

The void is gone.

*Oh, shit.* All at once, I grow wise to the hungry storm of shadows, no longer cracked and wilting, but livid, and vengeful, and biting furiously at my shield. *At Chase's shield.* I quickly shake off the last of the fuzziness and take over the cast, relieving him of the burden of having to keep me from shattering, as well.

*He's really doing it, though.* Projecting his In-Between like an Emerald, using the stolen power he drained.

From Alara.

I shudder as that reality pummels me with its full weight.

*You'll have to take her color.* I don't know why I'm so surprised when I'm the one who told him to do it in the first place, begged him to do it, in fact, even as his answering signs turned sharper and a disbelieving anger soured his face. *You know I can't do that—it'll kill her,* he'd clipped. But thanks to me, Alara was dying anyway, and since the choice was between doing the unthinkable or letting the unthinkable happen, it was no longer a question of *if*, but *when*, and Alara's last act in this world was to help us stop her brother from destroying the Gray.

She let Chase take her color.

Just as she told me Adriel's weakness, how to throw him off-balance so that I could rip the knife from her heart and stick it through his. A void is still a man, after all—when you stab him, he bleeds. Dies.

*Except you didn't get that far.* That much I remember clear as day, getting close but not close enough—so if Adriel's gone, he must have been bested by someone else. Though if Chase was busy draining Alara and Cemmy's job was to save Saleen, then who—?

*Raya. Where the fuck is Raya?* I'm instantly on my feet. If Akari's here, then she must be, too, the Orange would have never left her behind, not unless she was—

*Oh Gods.* I finally spot her at the very back of the court, sprawled beside Adriel in a way that feels irrevocable, her chest still and silent with the absence of breath.

*No. Absolutely not.*

All I can think as I spring to action is that I cannot go through this again.

Not like this.

Not today.

Not when our story was only just getting started.

*You don't get to die, you hear me? I'm not letting it end.* I blink into my gift, searching out a Green from among the mayhem. There's still a whole rainbow of Shades in this room—and what looks like a dozen more racing towards it, which is another problem, sure, though it is the kind I'm able to prevent.

"Get the initiates out of here!" I yell for Chase and Cemmy to begin making their escape, to take Akari and Saleen with them. They might yet require their magics if they run into those Shades on the way, Shades who'll see two illegal Hues and nothing else, who won't understand the crucial part they're currently playing in keeping the shadows from sickening with Adriel's plague, who won't care about the senseless death of a few typics.

"But, Ez—"

*No, no buts.* "You have to go *now*, Cemmy." I try to impress on her that this is need, not recklessness, an effort to save their lives, not throw mine away. "I'll be right behind you." *With Raya.* That's all the time I can spare arguing while she's still slumped lifelessly on the other side of this chamber. I also have to go *now*. I have to get her a Green.

"Hey you—come with me!" I practically snatch the shell-shocked acolyte off his feet, half dragging him across the marble. He's a slightly older Shade—sixteen or seventeen, maybe—and burly enough for the blood loss not to have left him uselessly dazed, especially now that the shadows are replenishing his color. "Heal her," I bark, though in reply, he merely shakes and shakes and shakes, his cheeks wet and his skin ruddy. "*Hey.*" I snap my fingers in front of his face. "She's one of you, understand? A Shade. And she's the only reason you made it off that table, so pull yourself together and *fix it.*" My gruff method of asking finally sets his fear straight.

*Please don't be dead, please don't be dead, please don't be dead.* As the Green loses himself to the healing, I try to make sense of how Raya ended up here, with only a cut to her palm but not breathing, lying next to what remains of the Divine Meridian. She wasn't even in the room when I endeavored to attack him; I don't think she had any charms on her and there's no sign of a weapon, and she's an Indigo so it's not as if she could have hit him with a spell. Hells, I don't even know if there is a spell that would wither a body like this, as though it's been collapsed from the inside and then seared, wilted to ashes.

None of this is adding up.

Though for once, I don't need it to.

I just need the Green's magic to work.

And when, at long last, it does, I'm the one who stops breathing, and when her eyes flutter open, the rest of the court disappears. I barely notice the Green scramble away from us or the way the chamber is slowly beginning to fill; all I see is her, and me, and this kernel of possibility, what we might one day become now that the life's returned to her cheeks.

"Did it work?" she croaks, trying to blink herself back to the present. "Adriel—did I—? Is the void gone?"

"It's gone." With a soft hand, I pull her up to sit. "You stopped him. I don't know how you did it, but Adriel's dead," I say. And then I do the very last thing I ever thought I'd do again—the very last thing I ever thought I'd *want* to do again, let alone so badly that every part of me aches—I lean my face into hers and I kiss her. It's a tentative kiss at first, little more than a chaste brushing of lips. And it isn't enough. The sudden hunger it ignites is insatiable, a spark kindling to a full-on blaze, burning brighter, raging hotter, dousing only when, all at once, Raya stiffens and pulls away.

"Gods—sorry, I shouldn't have done that." I should have asked permission before assuming she felt the same.

"No, that's not—" The hesitation in her eyes is a bucket of cold water. It's jumping into a freezing ocean when you don't know how to swim. "I'm not her, Ezzo." Raya's voice is quiet, the charge in it gutting deep. "I'm not Eve."

No, she's not.

Nor do I want her to be.

Because I'm not looking to replace Eve—what we had can't be *replaced*, it can only be remembered, and holding onto it too tightly almost cost me my friends. So no, Raya's not a replacement, she's a chance to start again. A chance at something completely unexpected—completely misguided—but as a Hue, my life has never been without risk. And this is the first risk, in a long time, that actually feels worth taking.

"I know exactly who you are, Raya Wryvern," I say, tilting her head up by the chin. "That's why I kissed you, and if it's okay with you, I'd really"—*really*—"like to do it again." Because it doesn't much matter that we're still at the Academy or that the room around us is now flooded with Shades. Right at this moment, all that matters is her name on my tongue, and my hands in her hair, and the way she shudders when my fingers graze her skin.

Because it feels *good*.

And I'm done questioning the good things.

# CHAPTER 36

# RAYA

I've never thought of the future as having a sense of humor, but mine is certainly getting a few laughs off of me. First, it gets me into a cell, then, it gets me out of it, only to conspire to lead me straight back in. It doesn't need me anymore, I guess, not now that Adriel's gone and the fundamental thread is safe.

*So, you did do one thing right.* I shiver, but not because of the chill in the air. I can still remember the sheer depth of his power, how it felt to feed my color to the void in the hopes that it would poison him faster than it drained me. Hardly the way my parents hoped I'd fulfil my legacy, but hey, at least all that Wryvern power was finally good for something. It ensured that the shadows will live to see another day—though I doubt you could say the same for me and Ezzo. Because this time, there'll be no scheming our way out of here.

The guards have separated us, for one thing, stuck us in adjacent cells instead of together, with cuffs chaining us to the floor and enough extra iron to keep me too nauseous to try much of anything. They also know exactly who I am now and that I'm here *despite* that, so there goes our other trick. The Indigo responsible for the *false vision* that gripped the castle, they're calling me. The architect of a smear campaign against the councilman who tragically lost his life bringing the Divine Meridian to heel. How he did that with a needle in his arm and all of his joints ripped out of their sockets is a question no one has thought to ask yet, nor do I expect them to ask it, given how badly they need us to play the villain. Hells, I'm not even surprised by the speed with which they chose to ignore the accounts coming from the rescued acolytes. That is what they've been doing for hundreds of years, isn't it? Rewriting history to suit their needs, regardless of the cost or consequence?

Which is why it makes no difference that we saved the Gray, or the Church initiates, or even a rainbow of their own kids; what the trackers saw when they breached the court chamber was a dead councilman and an Indigo kissing a half breed. A previously condemned half breed, for that matter, so there could have been no pretending that I didn't know who he is.

Not that I would have even tried that.

Because without him, and Chase, and Cemmy, today would have ended with far more than one dead councilman—and he only died because the injuries his son inflicted left him too weak to survive the bleeding. Today, three Hues willingly risked their freedom to put an end to the zealot we created with our fear; they've earned my loyalty in a way the Council never did. And besides, if the elders were scared of the truth before, they're now scared of the truth and me. They don't know the part Akari played in amplifying my vision—and they've long since forgotten the quirks of fate-touched magic—so as far as they're concerned, they have an Indigo on their hands with a rogue ability. And it's no secret what they do to rogues.

"Do you think the others are okay?" I whisper the question through the bars, a worry meant only for Ezzo and me.

"They're not here," he breathes in reply. "So that's what I'm hoping it means."

Hope. Right. I fight the urge to succumb to my anger and scream: *hope for what?* That they were able to get out of the Academy? Escape the city in one piece? That Akari and Saleen will get to spend the rest of their lives on the run now? That come morning, the Council will decide to kill us both quick?

"It's not fair," I say, since I trust Ezzo not to judge. "We did everything right"—*everything the future asked of us*—"and the Council's just going to bury it. Nothing's going to change."

"Maybe not overnight, but I do think change is coming." He shifts his weight to look at me head-on. "I don't think it's a coincidence that two separate zealots, in two separate cities, on two separate sides of the continent have come within an inch of destroying the Gray in two years," Ezzo says, his eyes shining like beacons in the dark. "I think their lies are what got us here and I think it's going to keep happening until the Council can't bury the truth anymore; one way or another, it *will* force itself out. There's a reckoning coming for them, Raya, I can feel it. And as much as I'd love to be there to see it, too, I can live with being the Hue that lit the final match."

*Yeah, well, I can't.* Ezzo's words only serve to intensify the wrongness churning in my gut.

Because I don't want to be the match, I want to be the flame.

I want to be there when the Council is made to answer for its crimes.

But more than anything else, I want to live to finish what we started.

I want the future to make good on the life it promised us.

"I don't want to die, Ezzo." That's the true fear festering in my heart. Death looked different in the court chamber; it looked like a worthy choice when I didn't have time to think about how big or final it was, how absolutely binding. Whereas now, all I have is time to think about it. Borrowed, limited, fast-ending time.

"I don't, either." Ezzo's hand grazes mine through the bars.

"Then I suggest you both do exactly as I tell you." The frosty voice springs us apart.

A voice I know.

A voice I dread.

A voice I never expected to hear again.

"*Mother?*" I shuffle as close to the door as my chains allow. But even in the dim light of the prison, there's no mistaking the face staring back at me, the pinched cheeks, and the sharp chin, and the disapproving tilt to the brow. Though today, there's worry in that face, too, along with regret and something else I can't quite put my finger on, something that warms my insides. "How are you—? What are you doing here?"

"Changing my daughter's future," she says, placing a series of blue charms along the iron.

"But . . . why?" I gape at the crystals as they start accelerating the metal to rust. It makes no sense for her to act against the Council now that my connection to Ezzo has been made public. If anything, she should be renouncing me twice as hard, protecting the Wryvern name.

"Because I won't stand by and watch an Indigo punished for following the future's path—especially when she saw something the rest of us didn't." Her answer goes a long way to explaining what swayed her mind.

"You heard about my vision," I say as the door to my cell breaks apart.

"I was made aware of it, yes."

"And you believed it?"

"I don't believe you deserve to die." Coming from my mother, the evasion is as good as telling me she's proud. "No matter how much I might disagree with your . . . choices." Her nose scrunches with distaste as she turns to appraise Ezzo.

"I won't leave without him," I say, before she can think to ask. "He saved my life."

"Yes, I was made aware of that, too." She sighs, but the minute my cuffs snap open, she begins to rust his cell with a second set of charms.

"Made aware by who?"

"Your Orange friend has always been convincing. I'm glad that, going forward, you'll have her on your side."

*Going forward.* I'm suddenly hit by the truth she hasn't yet said out loud. My mother has no intention of leaving the guild over this; she's not planning to try and prove my innocence or expose the Council's lies—freeing us is the full extent of her rebellion.

"Does Father know you're doing this?" So I ask her the one question I probably shouldn't ask.

"Your father is a difficult man, Raya," she says, the pitch of her voice growing sad. "I hope that one day, you'll forgive me for not telling him."

*Right.* This truth cuts me even deeper than the last. She didn't trust my father's reaction enough to share her plan with him. She couldn't be sure that, if she did, he'd choose me over the Council.

The rest of our escape passes in a swift and silent rush. My mother doesn't volunteer how she broke into the prison, but both guards have a decidedly dazed look about them when the three of us steal past, as though they're lost to a glamour.

"I don't suggest you linger in the city," she says once we're safely out on the street. "It's likely they'll think to check your cells before sunrise."

Yes, I imagine they might. We have made a bit of a habit of evading their clutches.

"Mother, I—" Can't seem to get the rest of that sentence out. Because I honestly don't know what to say to her in this moment. I don't know how to thank her, or absolve her, or how I'm supposed to say goodbye—for what could be forever.

"Be free, Raya." She pulls me into a hug that says everything I can't. "Be as great as I've already seen you are." And while those words don't make our parting any easier, they do leave it tasting sweet rather than bitter or sour.

For the first time in my life, I don't doubt that my mother loves me.

For the first time in my life, I'm sure that she wanted a daughter more than an heir to the Wryvern line.

# CHAPTER 37

# EZZO

Escaping execution three times in as many days is more luck than a Hue should have. Then again, most Hues don't survive a trip to the Academy, or get sprung from prison by a guild master, or offer a Shade their hand. It's safe to say that the future knocked me onto a wholly unexpected path.

Raya's mother doesn't prolong their goodbye, nor does she acknowledge my presence any more than she has to, other than to issue me a stern bid to treat her daughter right.

"Are you okay?" When she finally phases away, Raya's face is awash with too many emotions to count. Love, grief, gratitude, doubt, longing and pain and an uncertainty at what's to come. For all that's happened this past week, my life won't actually change much; I'm still a Hue, still illegal, still perpetually on the run—but that's been true forever so it's hardly an adjustment. But for her, today marks the end of everything she's ever known and loved: her home, her family, her chance to become a seer—that's all lost to her now. She's no longer the same Raya Wryvern.

"Let's just go find the others," she says in lieu of answering my question. "I really need to see that they're alright." And judging by the welcome we receive when I trail them to a secluded alley a few streets over, that feeling is mutual.

"Holy shadows—your giant stick of a mother did it." The moment we blink out into their midst, Akari sweeps Raya into her arms.

"Turns out, you're pretty convincing," she says, then our next few minutes are lost to the story of our latest brush with justice and their unlikely escape from the castle.

"Once the void lifted, the portals were back in action." Every line of Chase is still drawn with exhaustion, the stolen magic he'd wielded having exacted a heavy toll. "Which was lucky since I couldn't have held that In-Between much longer."

Just long enough to get the initiates back to Sarotuza and stop the riots from burning too hot—though the violence raging through the city is far from over. From where we're stood, we can still hear the anger and smell the smoke, taste the tension lingering in the air like a grudge. And once those kids recount their torture, the Church's ire is only likely to get worse. I'd be surprised if they allow Adriel's followers to continue preaching their blasphemies; for once, they even have a common enemy with the Council.

"I still can't believe you went to my *mother*," Raya says when Akari reaches that part of the telling, her head shaking and her pupils wide.

"I mean, it worked, didn't it?" Akari shrugs, leaning back against the alley wall. "And besides, it's not like you two left us much of a choice. There was no way we were getting you out on our own—it's kind of a miracle we managed to get out ourselves, to be honest, but seven screaming typics stumbling around the Academy inter-change did prove quite the distraction." She grins with her whole body. Whatever my views on Akari, she's taking her transition from aspiring tracker to exile much better than I would have thought. Seeing Saleen on that table has clearly shed new light on her priorities.

"So anyway, once we realized you'd been caught, we had to get creative," Akari says, speeding the story along. "And your mother did send in the cavalry like you asked her to, so I figured it was worth a shot. But don't worry, I had Sal there with me, just in case she couldn't be convinced."

"What's one more illegal spell, right?" It's actually Saleen who looks a bit overwhelmed by the turn the night took—even now that she's regained most of her color. She's the one who still has to explain this mess to her parents, and given their position as trackers, they'll either be forced to double down on the lie and start hunting their own daughter, or join her in going rogue. Her decision to help me has come at a pretty massive cost. For all three of them.

*Cemmy and Chase took some big risks, too.* As Raya thanks her friends for what they did for us, I realize it's high time I do a little thanking of my own.

"Forget it, Ez—" But since Cemmy's no better at forgiving herself than I am, she immediately makes to cut me off.

"No, please, I—I need to get this out," I tell her, forcing myself to go on. "I've not been fair to you this past week"—*this past year*—"and I'm sorry for that. I'm sorry for being so angry that I blamed you for something that wasn't your fault—or my fault, or Chase's fault." I nod an acknowledgement at him, as well. "Eve's death didn't just happen to me; it was a terrible thing that happened to all of us." And if the last few days have taught me anything, it's how easy it is to put everyone you care about at risk with a single choice. "So I guess what I'm trying to say is: we're even, okay? I don't want to be angry at you anymore, and if the two of you are planning to go back to Isitar, then I think that maybe I'd like to join." The words aren't as hard to say as I expected—they actually come as more of a relief.

"We'd like that, Ez." Cemmy seems equally relieved to hear them, and happy—though that doesn't stop her arms from crossing or her eyes from narrowing to a playful glare. "But only on one condition."

*Oh good, we're already back at conditions.* "Which is . . . ?"

"You have to be the one to tell Novi about the Shade."

# CHAPTER 38

# RAYA

I'm going to miss Sarotuza. I'm going to miss the Academy; I'm going to miss the house; hells, I'm even going to miss my parents.

My life. I'm going to miss my life.

Or perhaps I'm just afraid of the absolute way in which it's about to change.

For the past nineteen years, all I've cared about is becoming a seer, proving that I was as good as the Indigos who came before me, and worthy of the Wryvern name. But now, that future is firmly off the table. I'm condemned, a blood-traitor, every bit as illegal as the three Hues I'm currently following through the Gray. And Gods, I don't even know if my magic still works; I've been too afraid to reach for it since I put an end to Adriel, too afraid to find out if the fates are done with me forever. Because while I could see myself wanting that one day—being free of the burden of having to predict—I'm not ready to lose my ability to cast yet. I want to be able to use my power. I want to protect my friends with it, and make my mother proud with it, and learn how to wield it in my own way. I want to show the Council that being fate-touched is a decision not every Indigo comes to regret.

"I'm sorry for how things turned out, Raya." Ezzo reaches for my hand as we leave the city proper, slowing us out of earshot of the others.

"Well, I'm not," I say, and it's true because there was no other *how* for things to turn. The moment I asked my open question, I knocked my life into a different orbit, became something the guild was never going to accept. "I don't belong here anymore."

"Yeah, but . . . that doesn't mean you have to tie yourself to a bunch of Hues." The sincerity in his eyes is soft and solemn. "You don't have to come to Isitar with us—you, and Saleen, and Akari could do this on your own. And I'd understand, if that's what you wanted. You don't owe me anything here, you don't have to choose the hardest version of this life for me."

"Then it's a good job I'm choosing it for *me*," I say, pulling him to a gentle stop. "And before you ask: no, I'm not doing it because a vision told me to. I'm doing it because I like you, Ezzo." There's something I never thought I'd say to a Hue. "I like who I am with you." A bolder Shade, braver, more compassionate and self-assured. "So, if you're not too freaked out by this whole . . . 'she's a full-blood' thing, then I'd really like to see where this goes."

And I'm perfectly aware that it won't be easy, that one stolen kiss in a room full of trackers doesn't guarantee a love story. But for now, I'm choosing to follow the pull in my gut, and the butterflies in my stomach, and the warmth I feel when Ezzo smiles and the hesitation in him dims. And hells, maybe our part in fate's tapestry is now complete, maybe the only thing we have to look forward to is an ordinary life, and a mundane death, and a fling that dissipates at the first gust of a strong wind. All I know for sure is that here, today, this feels like the right path for me. *He* feels like the right path for me—and I think the future just happens to concur. Because when I ask it when I'll kiss Ezzo again, it answers.

# Acknowledgements

Another year, another book. Somehow, they never get easier to write—even though the village around me just keeps getting bigger and better.

I have to start by thanking Andrea Morrison at Writers House. We worked together for five years and I honestly can't thank you enough for everything we achieved during that time. And that thank you extends to Alessandra Birch and Cecilia de la Campa, who continue to work to ensure the *Until We Shatter* books pop up in as many places as possible.

Next, I need to thank Rachel Neely and the team at Mushens Entertainment for being my next chapter on this journey. Thank you for picking up the baton and running with it. I can't wait to see what the future holds for us and the new books we're cooking.

As always, I must thank my editor, Molly Powell at Hodderscape, who is the reason my books make any sense at all. I originally told you there wouldn't be a book 2 in this world, but you let me change my mind (as you always do) and then you helped me pull together yet another magic system absolutely nobody asked for. I'm so proud of the books we create together.

To my wider Hodderscape team: Kate Keehan, Laura Bartholomew, Sophie Judge, Marina Dominguez-Salgado, Priya Das, and Jo Dickinson—thank you for making everything work behind the scenes and getting these books to all the places they need to be. And thank you to Alyssa Ollivier-Tabukashvili and Sharona Selby for ensuring they arrive there in grammatically correct fashion.

A huge thank you also goes out to Jeff Langevin (illustration) and Natalie Chen (design) who looked at the piece of art that was the cover for *Until We Shatter* and said: hold my beer, we can outdo perfection.

To my friends and family: by now you know who you are and why my sanity needs you. If you're in my DMs, then this thank you is for you.

To all the booksellers and book creators who've supported me throughout this journey: your support truly means the world. I couldn't do this without you and I'm so lucky to have you in my corner.

And to every reader who's stuck with me through all four books, or just discovered me with this one: I appreciate every last one of you and I really hope to see you again for the next one.

# About the Author

Kate Dylan is a video editor by day, science fiction and fantasy author by night. Her love for creating new worlds is fuelled by a steady diet of coffee, books, and Marvel movies, and when she's not telling stories, you can find her haunting London cafes like an over-caffeinated ghost.